Mail Order Bride Box Set

Sun River Brides

9 Mail Order Brides
Story Collection

Karla Gracey

Dedication

I dedicate this book to my mother, as she was the one who kept urging me to write, and without her enthusiasm I would never of written and published my books.

Contents

A Bride for Carlton
Book 1

Chapter One

Myra Gilbert sat in the nursery alone while her charges took their music lesson with Master Julian. She cherished these rare moments of solitude. So much of her life was taken up with caring for twelve year old Margaret and fourteen year old Carolynn. They were lovely girls, but boisterous and rarely sat still for a moment. But they would have no need of her soon enough and she wondered if she would ever find a position that was so amenable when the time came.

It had been the tragically early death of her dear Papa that had left her alone and with little to support herself with. Thankfully, as the daughter of the local Schoolmaster she had enjoyed the privilege of a good education, and so becoming a governess had seemed a most logical step. Now, after eight years with the Fitzherbert's she could feel her role had changed. She had no desire to remain with the family as simply a chaperone, though she had so loved teaching the girls. But there was little more she could impart to them now. They were young ladies; she had taught them to read and write, to draw, and they were good and kind. They would make excellent marriages, if only they could learn to curb their excessive exuberance for life.

She sighed heavily. She had once been just like her charges, dreaming of her future husband and children. She too had longed to be swept off her feet by a handsome young man who had eyes only for her – yet her chance had never come, and now she was destined for spinsterhood and a life as a governess. She wished she didn't mind, but she had yet to reconcile herself to her fate. She still hoped, against all the odds, that there was love and a family in her future. But as each year passed, that hope became less and less strong. It was now but a mere flicker in her heart. But she enjoyed her work, and that was a consolation to her, and her girls had won her heart and her devotion.

A newspaper sat on the table to her side, and she picked it up - surprised to find that it wasn't the usual Daily Bugle – but the Matrimonial Times. She could only presume that there must have been some mistake with the delivery that morning, the Fitzherbert's would have no need of such a publication after all. Intrigued, she flicked through the pages, amused by the pleas of lonely farmers, ranchers, miners and their like. So many of them sounded so very like her after all; lonely and feeling that time had passed them by. She could feel the pain in so many of the words, and her heart went out to them. But though she so desperately longed for a family of her own she could not understand how any woman could ever bring herself to respond to such advertisements; heading off to who knew where to live with men they knew little to nothing about. No, she prayed she would find a man using more traditional means, though she was beginning to think it unlikely. She was fast heading towards the spinsterhood she so dreaded; at twenty-seven she was often passed over at social events for the younger and wealthier young women of her acquaintance.

She was about to put the newspaper down and go in search of her novel, when she caught sight of an advertisement that seemed completely unusual, though she only had this morning's perusal of the publication to judge. She read it once, then again, and again:

A Gentleman of Montana, wishes to enter into a correspondence with a view to matrimony; she must be gentle, kind and full of courage. A liberal education, and love of theatre and music would be highly prized, and to be a fine cook and care for hearth and home would be preferred. The subscriber is a man of modest means, with land of his own and believes that he has qualities that such a woman would appreciate. Address in Sincerity E.T.C., Box 483, Matrimonial Times

So many of the advertisements that she had skimmed over had been almost gushing in their sentimentality, yet this one was not. It gave no clue as to the character or habits of the man who had submitted it in the hope of attracting a wife. It seemed almost cold, unfeeling. She was sure that it would have been unlikely to catch the eye of many women, who seemed to want romance more than the things that would truly last. Not that she thought marriage should be a mercenary act, but a good home and friendship would stand a couple in far better stead than hearts and flowers she was sure. Yet, for some reason the words resonated within her, and she felt a brief flutter of excitement deep in her belly.

Hardly believing that she was doing so, with her curiosity getting the better of her, she began to pen a letter to the mysterious man who had put himself unwittingly into her line of sight. She scribbled hastily, barely heeding a word she wrote, and then sealed her missive in an envelope and addressed it carefully. She tucked it into her reticule and rushed out of the house to the postal office. She barely dared to catch a breath, barely took a moment to think until she walked back outside and realized what she had done. What if he replied? Even worse, what if he did not?

* * * * *

Carlton Green stared at the stark black and white print of his advertisement. It shocked him to see how foolish it seemed to be doing such a thing, now he saw it nestled within the pages of this ridiculous newspaper. Whatever had he been thinking, to advertise for a wife in such a way? He could see nothing in it that could interest a young woman worth having; in fact he thought it made him sound pompous and unlikeable indeed. He seemed to expect much of a wife and yet was offering her nothing in return. He had slaved over the words for days, had thought he had chosen so carefully, and yet now they looked dull and expectant. Exasperated, he threw the newspaper into the fire certain he would have no replies, and got on with his chores. There was time enough for him to find a wife – but the sowing would not get done on its own.

He held enough land to eke out a comfortable living, but it was hard. He worked from sun up to sun down, no matter the weather. He grew oats and some wheat on his one hundred and sixty acres, granted to him now in perpetuity thanks to the Homestead Act. He often wondered how he had stayed the course required to be granted the deeds to his lands. But despite some very difficult times, terrible harvests and having to work himself to the bone he had done so. Many had failed, their steadings had been left abandoned as disease and the sheer enormity of the task had become clear to those with less hardy natures than his own. He had lost many friends to the cemetery, and even more back to the lives they had left behind thinking that the opportunities here in Montana would be better. He missed them, and life out here miles from the nearest town could be all too quiet. It was time to settle down and make this land a home, and so his search for a wife had begun. He needed somebody to share in his good fortune, to care for and to protect, and to fill his life with joy and laughter.

He was still here, and he was not just surviving – he had begun to truly thrive - and it was now time to settle down and make Montana a home as well as an adventurous enterprise. Stepping outside into the warm sunshine, he gazed proudly at his neatly furrowed fields, and the large yard that would make a wonderful playground for young children. The paddock held horses and ponies that needed to be ridden, and the peace and quiet ached to be rent with the sound of fun and family. Then he turned and looked behind him at the ramshackle cabin he had laid his head down in for the past five years, and laughed. His dreams may seem achievable when he looked at everything else he had – but he could hardly expect any woman to wish to live there. The sod cabin was just a room; it had no windows and the chimney belched smoke so badly he had to put out the fire over night to ensure he didn't choke in his sleep.

He vowed to head into Sun River to speak with Ardloe Reed once the spring sowing was done. The carpenter had built many of his neighbors some sturdy looking homes in recent months, and it was time he did the same. He could have no illusions that any young woman seeing how he currently lived – without having been entirely enamored of him - would be right on the next train out of Great Falls or Billings before he could stop her. He chuckled wryly as he thought of some Eastern city girl hitching up her skirts and making a run for it, it seemed most unlikely but it amused him nonetheless.

He shrugged his oilskin jacket on as he crossed the yard. The air in the barn was cold no matter the time of year, and he was glad of the hardwearing coat and his second best hat to keep the worst of the chill breezes from tearing through to his skin. He blew on his fingers to warm them before lifting a sack of seed. He'd check it over and then get going. He had three more fields to sow with wheat today, and a further four with oats tomorrow. Half his fields needed to see the run of the plough still too. He whistled as he began to stack the sacks of seed onto the cart, enjoying the brief respite from the cold that he got from being in the spring sunshine. He hitched Marlin, his broad-backed and sturdy cart horse into the shafts and with a click, and a swift flick of the whip to the reliable animal's flanks, the two of them set off to the high fields.

Carlton loved the land he had chosen with all his heart. He had been lucky enough to take his pick. There had been so few homesteaders coming out this far when he first arrived, but he didn't doubt that more would come, especially if the rumors turned out to be true that the Government wanted to extend the scope of the Homesteading Act. The land was fertile, both crops and livestock seemed to thrive here if you worked hard enough. Men who were hungry for success and weren't afraid to work for it could do very well here.

But his was a lonely life. Many of his contemporaries, those brave few that had come out here to try and make new lives, had brought wives and children with them or at the least sent for them once they had gotten settled. The transition could be harsh, and many families had not managed to secure the deeds to their lands. He was proud he now had his securely stored in the vaults of the Great Falls bank - and that he had done so alone. But he longed for companionship now the lands were in good heart and he could afford to hire some help. At least that was a task that would be easy to fulfill. There were always men looking for work at the Saloon in Sun River, and even as far away as Great Falls and Billings. Eager young souls arrived on the train every day.

Carlton longed for sons, to bring up and to show what life could be like if you worked hard and earned your rewards; to work alongside him on the farm to create a family empire and so in his loneliness had placed that advertisement. He couldn't help but regret having done so now as he thought about how cold he had sounded against the other Matrimonials he had spied on the page near his own. Maybe that was to be expected. Maybe Fate had taken a stand as he had penned his own words, to ensure he would remain alone.

After all, he wasn't entirely sure that he should ever be a husband or father given his checkered history. He had made such a mess of it all the first time around, had caused such pain that it hardly bore thinking of. But that was the past, and he prayed every day that his loneliness here in Montana could make up for his past digressions, that his commitment to the earth would somehow redeem him. That he would one day deserve the happiness so long denied him.

Chapter Two

Once the ploughing and sowing was finally complete Carlton managed to make a trip into town. It felt good to have a little bit of energy left at the end of the day to go and relax with friends. "Just the fella I needed to see," Carlton called across the street as he spied Ardloe staggering out of the Saloon. The old man wasn't much of a drinker, but when the weather was cold his arthritis played him up and made him limp a little. One or two whiskeys and it became almost dangerous for the old coot to be out anywhere alone. Carlton had helped him up off the ground on more than one occasion as carriages and buggies came at him too fast and knocked him off his shaky limbs.

"Whatever it is can't it wait 'til the mornin'?" the crusty carpenter grumbled.

"I won't be in town in the morning my friend, but I am here now. I'm in need of a new house."

"Sure y'are. Ev'yone in town's in need, so they keep on tellin' me anyhow."

"Can you do it Ardloe, or should I ask that young fella from down the valley?" Carlton knew full well that threatening to bring in the competition would rile him up, and he was right.

"Sure I can do it, no need to bring in that slipshod fool. Thinks he can build a house, can't even build a henhouse!" Carlton chuckled and Ardloe looked at him with the dawning comprehension that he had just been hustled. "Green, you have a mighty nasty sense of humor. But, I'll build ya a nice house. When d'ya want it done by?"

"Soon as you can. You just let me know what you need and I will make sure it is all ready for and waiting for you."

"I'll send ya a list," the old man said grudgingly. "Now, may I go home to my wife and some liniment for these aches and pains?" Carlton patted him on the back, and watched as he limped slowly across the street towards a smart little clapboard home. It was typical of all Ardloe's work; neat, precise and downright sturdy. They truly were built to last. "Oh, Postmaster was looking for you earlier. Something about a letter from Boston?" the old man said over his shoulder as he went inside.

Carlton swiveled on his heel, as the door slammed shut - stunned. The newspaper's offices were in Boston, but surely it would just be a letter telling him that they were sorry but his advertisement had yielded no responses and they needed his box for another subscriber? Yet his heart gave a little leap, hope refusing to die. It would be so much easier if it would. He tipped his hat at his friend and headed inside to see what he might find.

When things weren't too busy at the farm Carlton came into town no more than once a week to have a few drinks, and maybe play some cards with his neighbors, but mostly he was just too tired to do much more. During early spring and round the harvest he rarely even made it to church. He knew that if there was mail for farmers like himself it was often left behind the bar at the Saloon so he tried not to leave it too long to drop by. The arrangement made for an easier system; no long and drawn out deliveries for the Postmaster, and no need to get into town during office hours for men who worked all the hours God was good enough to send them. Just knowing that Tom would hold his correspondence until he dropped by was a huge help.

8

"Green, I got some mail for you," Tom said as he served him a mug of ale. Carlton slipped his money over the counter and waited as the lanky Saloon owner brought him the letter. The envelope felt heavy and substantial in his hand. His bright and ambitious friend grinned at him, a knowing look in his eyes. Tom had come out here when there were only the trappers and miners brave enough to take the trip. He'd brought good looking girls and good beer and whiskey at cheap prices. His success had been assured from the off. But, he could be too observant sometimes – though he was also highly discrete.

"Thanks, is the back room taken?" Carlton asked, wanting a little privacy to open the letter. He didn't want his friends to think him soft, if he showed his disappointment – and he certainly didn't wish for the teasing that might follow if any of them found out what he had done. He knew that Tom wouldn't tell a soul, but the same could not be said of some of the other faces in the bar.

"Empty for about half an hour, but the Women's Suffrage meeting will be starting then, so best to get yourself out of their way," Tom said rolling his eyes. Carlton winked at him companionably, but unlike so many men Carlton strongly agreed that women should have the vote. They worked as hard out here as any man, harder than many – and bringing up children was no easy task either. They deserved a say in how the Government was run, it affected their lives as much as any man's after all. Secretly he considered them to be far wiser than his own sex too – he had never yet known a woman who had gotten herself into the sorts of scrapes he did on a regular basis.

He walked through into the large reception room, and ripped open the envelope. Inside was a letter on flimsy paper, with the address of the newspaper stamped across it. He flicked his eye over it, and saw much as he had expected to see, that his box was now required by another and that unfortunately they could no longer keep it open for him. It had been three months and he was a realist – if he was going to receive a response he supposed he would have done so by now. But a second envelope was also included. He looked back at the last line of the letter he had only barely read, and saw that they had included the single response he had received, and that they wished him much luck with it.

He felt his chest constrict with fear as he wondered what kind of woman could possibly have responded to him. She would either have to be desperate, or downright unpleasant, he was sure of that. But as he took a deep breath and opened up the thick parchment envelope and took out the soft and creamy paper inside, he tried to gulp down his anxieties. Maybe she would be perfect, maybe it was a sign that there truly was only one woman for every man after all?

Dear Gentleman of Montana,

Please forgive my being so bold as to reply to your advertisement. I was not brought up to do such a thing, but I find myself alone and without guidance as to what may be proper in such a situation as this.

I am sure you have probably received many responses; your advertisement struck me as the only one I read which could truly have been said to be honest. Though, I want you to know I do not regularly peruse such a tome. I am still not even sure how it was in the house, but I was intrigued and simply could not help myself from writing to you. I don't know what came over me.

I am governess to two young women who are nearly old enough to come out and find husbands and lives of their own. My Papa died when I was just seventeen, my Mama just after I was born. Papa was a Schoolmaster, and he insisted I have as good an education as the boys he taught. He believed a day would come when women would finally achieve the place in Society that they deserved –not as simply ornaments. But, you do not wish to hear of my Papa's politics, I am sure.

I have always longed for a family of my own, though I am past the age of expecting to be able to command exclamations of undying love. Nor do I crave romance. But I would love to have my own home, and a husband who might permit me to teach in a local school so I can continue to use my education to prosper other young women – and if there is no provision for them in Montana, to maybe set up a school for girls myself.

I have no dowry but myself. I am hardworking and used to hardship. I am told by my charges and their wonderful parents, my employers, that I am kind and good as your advertisement requested, but I couldn't possibly be so immodest as to say so myself.

I have read about Montana in the newspapers, of course, and I understand it is a place of great beauty. I should very much love to see it with my own eyes. At present I travel only through my storybooks and the wonderful travelers' tales that get printed in the newspapers here in Boston. I do love music and theatre, and I forever have my nose in a book. I can cook, though it has been some time since I needed to – but I did keep house for my Papa from a very young age. I like to think that household management skills are amongst those that you never forget.

I fear this has been a terribly garbled account of myself, and probably barely even scratches the surface. Should you wish to know any more I would be much inclined to answer any questions you may have. Please, do write to me and tell me of your life in Montana, and maybe even a little about why you would like a wife – your advertisement was very hazy on the details after all!

Yours in Sincerest Hope

Myra Gilbert

Carlton stared at the elegant script that had clearly been written hurriedly as the page was covered in ink splatters and crossings out. He couldn't take the smile from his face, this woman most certainly had a sense of humor, and she was eager and keen. He could sense the urgency of her response; it was as if she had simply written the entire letter without taking a breath. Quickly he downed his ale and rushed through the Saloon and into the street where he had left Canton, his horse. Unhitching him quickly he raced back to the farm to pen his response.

* * * * *

Myra stared at the envelope sat on the silver salver by her plate at breakfast. She rarely received much correspondence, but it was not that which had so perturbed her. It was the sender's address, so neatly penned in a simple and unadorned script that had taken her breath away. It had come from Montana. It had come from him. And his name was Carlton Green. She rolled the name around in her mind, foolishly even trying it out for size, Myra Green sounded quite respectable and fine.

As the girls clattered in to the room and took their seats she shook her head to rid herself of such foolish notions, and scolded them tenderly. "Alice, Grace must you always behave like hoydens? I am sure that both your Mama and myself have taught you better."

"Apologies Miss Gilbert," they chorused, grinning madly. Myra chuckled.

"I can always get my revenge, that is where the two of you can be so foolish," she reminded them. "I think Latin immediately after breakfast, and maybe mathematics to follow."

"You wouldn't, not on such a glorious day," Alice said aghast. "Surely today should be about biology; capturing frogspawn and learning about nature?" Both girls were bright as a button. If they were boys they would both be preparing to enter the university. Myra thought it terribly unfair that such enquiring minds would be lost within marriage, and so soon.

"You are right, I would not," she reassured them both. "But, we shall not be going to the park, but to the zoological gardens. I hear they have some wonderful new animals for us to learn about." She was rewarded with squeals of delight. "Now, eat up and then you shall need to get your coats and hats so we can enjoy as much of the day there as possible."

She watched them carefully as they ate; giving gentle nudges to remind them of etiquette they were forgetting and ensuring that they remembered to leave just a little on their plates. She insisted that they rise gracefully from their places and walk elegantly up to their rooms. She knew that they would race up the stairs however much she tried to exhort otherwise, but every little bit of ladylike comportment she could insist upon she would.

As the peace descended around her once more she looked back at her letter. She simply couldn't wait until they returned from their excursion to know what Mr. Carlton Green wished to say to her. She clutched it to her heart and prayed his words would be kindly. Carefully she slit the envelope with the ivory handled knife laid out on the salver for her. She carefully extracted the paper, and laid the envelope back down neatly. Taking a deep breath, she began to read the scruffy script. It was a little difficult to make out at times, but it pleased her nonetheless.

Dear Miss Gilbert,

I cannot tell you how delighted I was to receive your letter. I shudder to make you blush, but it seemed that you must have written it in a hurry? I wonder if writing to me was something that made you perhaps a little nervous, as writing to you now is for me. I must confess I have screwed up many sheets of paper and fed my fire well to get even this far.

I enjoyed hearing of your work; you seem very enamored of it. I think it is good to be passionate about what one does. It must run in your blood, what with your Papa being a School Master. I am passionate about my land. I work hard because it inspires me to do so. I am a farmer, and I grow mainly oats and wheat, though I do have some vegetable crops too. The soil is good here, fertile and rich.

I do not mind your talk of politics, though I understand it is often considered rude in polite society. I too think it important, that anyone who has the ability to do so should be able to learn. I must confess to you that I am a secret supporter of the suffrage movement too – though I ask you to kindly keep it to yourself, my compatriots out here aren't all so amenable to the thought! Isn't it strange how writing makes it so much easier to impart confidences?

You wished to hear more about me, and Montana. There is little to know about me – I have little time to be anything other than a busy farmer. But as it may have been clear from my advertisement, I do love music and I especially love intellectual discourse. I should be glad to continue a correspondence with someone as clearly well informed as yourself, and hope that by doing so I will learn much.

Montana however is a different story. It is vast, and the terrain can be rugged in parts. The mountains are more than majestic – they make you feel small, so humble and yet closer to God somehow. My farm is situated in the most glorious of valleys and the views all around are breathtaking. The blues never seemed so blue back East, the greens dull and tired in comparison. Everything seems brighter, fresher and clearer out here.

I am building a house, or rather my friend Ardloe is building me a house. For too long I have lived in a shack not truly fit for habitation of neither man nor beast. He showed me a drawing of what he thinks it will look like once he is done. It will be very fine. There shall be four large bedrooms, a smart parlor, a vast kitchen and even an indoor outhouse! Should we decide that we might suit I should be most grateful of your assistance in furnishing it and making of it a real home – I hope you do not think me too presumptuous in such a request?

As to your possible occupation should you wish to join me here, there is a school in Great Falls, and one in Billings too – for boys only as far as I am aware. Sun River is much smaller, but people are content to travel for an education. I am sure that the townsfolk would be more than happy for you to set up a local school – though I must warn you that there are many here who would disapprove of educating women. However the local Women's Suffrage group I am sure would assist you, and I would be more than happy to give you my support in doing so.

I feel I may be rushing things terribly, but do you think you might consider me? I am not perfect and I can assure you that living here will not be easy, but I have the most wonderful feeling that we just might suit.

I look forward eagerly to your response, and pray you will not be scared off by my ardor.

Yours Most Sincerely

Carlton Green

P.S. May I please call you Myra? It is such a lovely name!

Myra hugged the letter to her breast, after pressing it gently to her lips. He had not been put off by her ridiculously hasty response. In fact, it seemed to her that her impetuousness was exactly the thing that appealed to him about her, and it would appear that he had a similar streak inside him too. She longed to be able to send a reply immediately, but the girls were now stood in the doorway looking smart and presentable in their coats, hats and gloves and so she tucked the letter safely into her reticule and stood up to join them. "Are you both ready?" she asked smiling at them both, her heart light with joy and hope. They nodded eagerly. "Then let us go and see the animals."

Chapter Three

Despite how much work he had to undertake, Carlton seemed to find more and more reasons as to why he must go in to town after he received Myra's first letter. He tried to tell himself that it truly was because he needed to speak with Ardloe about plans for the house, or to arrange the deliveries of seed he needed, and the materials for the house of course. But, he knew in his heart that it was because he kept praying there would be another letter from her waiting for him at the Saloon. It seemed to be taking an age to hear from her.

But on a crisp spring morning, just as he had finally sown the seeds in the last of his fields, her next missive appeared. Her beautiful sloping script brought a surge of pleasure to his heart, and relief as he had begun to wonder if he had somehow managed to put her off.

Dear Mr Green, Carlton

Why of course you must call me Myra, and I shall gladly call you Carlton if I may. It would be too peculiar to be talking of marriage with someone who could only ever bring themselves to be so formal and polite. I am so glad that you think we may suit. I am not perfect either and would never expect a husband to be so. We are all human and have our little foibles after all.

Your description of Montana makes me long to visit there. I have never been outside of the city before, but I am sure that I would suit a country life. I have never felt at home here, it is too busy and crowded, though it is wonderful to have the concert halls, theatres and museums to visit. I think I long for open spaces. I take the girls to the park every single day – whatever the weather. They often grumble terribly if it is cold or wet!

Oh, and I would be so happy to teach a small local school. The children could gain so much more from it than having to travel long distances to learn – and of course I would hope that their parents could see the benefits of them being so close too, that they would have more time to study or to help out at home if they did not have to go so far to school. I am so glad that you would support me in such an endeavor. I truly could not give it up I don't think.

You must be doing very well indeed to be planning such a house – with an indoor outhouse of all things! You will be telling me next that you intend to have electricity installed throughout too! I am sure your current home is not the hovel you cite, but if it truly is then I am glad that there will be something a little more comfortable. I am not sure that I could manage to live in a sod built shack. I have been living in a very fine town house here in Boston, though of course only in the servant's quarters, but it would be quite a change otherwise.

I am not afraid of hardship though, merely a little apprehensive about the unknown. Maybe you could come and visit me, so we could see if we would suit? It would put my mind at rest to know that should we wed that I could at least rely upon my husband to care for me and help my adjustment. I can arrange for you to stay at Young's Hotel, it is quite fine and has a good reputation and is only a couple of blocks from my home. We could maybe attend the theatre and undertake some excursions?

Though of course, I am being ever so presumptuous, as you

are probably very busy at this time of year and would have no time to just take off for a period of weeks just to put my mind at ease. I would understand if it were not possible. I suppose I could even come to Montana, but that would mean I would have to leave my position and it would be hard to find such a good one should we decide we do not like one another in the flesh.

I am sorry, dear Carlton, I am blathering on about nothing of consequence and must be boring you. I shall stop now before I embarrass myself further. I do look forward to your next letter, and I pray we will meet in person very soon.

Yours hopefully

Myra

Carlton's heart had taken a little leap as he read her witty response to his request to use her Christian name, but had lurched into his boots as she spoke of foibles. He wondered if she would ever be able to accept his. He had done so well to keep them from his mind, to build a life once more without his failings being known. But, if they were to marry, surely it would be better to be honest, to be truthful with her of his past?

But he wasn't sure he could be. What if she turned away from him, and no longer wished to even correspond with him? It had been such a short acquaintance, but he already treasured her words more than anything. He simply could not, would not, imagine a life without her. But that meant he would have to ensure that everything about his history remained hidden from view forever. Was that even possible? He knew all too well that bad news always travelled – and just because it hadn't caught up with him yet did not mean that it wouldn't some day.

He longed to do just as she asked, to join her in Boston, to see the sights. He was in the perfect position to. All of his sowing was done. He could afford to hire someone to oversee the farm while he was gone, while there was little that had to be completed. It would be the ideal time to do so. Yet, there was a gnawing in his belly that told him that no good could ever come of this. He had left the East for a new start, in a place where nobody knew him. Returning to the world that had so broken him would be the hardest thing he had ever done – yet he could not expect her to come to him. It would not be right for a woman to cross the country alone, heaven alone knew the dangers that she would have to face.

No, if he wanted Myra to become his wife then he would have to go to her. He would have to hope that he had reformed himself sufficiently that nobody would ever recognize him as the man who had left all those years before – that nobody would tell her his secrets, at least not before he had been able to gauge if she would ever forgive him should she know it all.

* * * * *

Myra had become a fidget. She only prayed that her employers had not noticed it. She was on edge constantly, waiting for another letter to come from Carlton. She hoped he would not think her too forward for virtually demanding that he come here to meet with her. She couldn't remember ever having been so forceful about anything in her life. Yet, there had been so little in her life that she had wanted so badly. She knew it was foolish, and she knew that she knew so very little about him – yet still she knew she loved him. She simply couldn't bear the idea of living her life without him now, and though that was terribly exciting it was also frightening too.

Myra's life had been a lonely one, and to combat the losses she had turned to her books. Suddenly they were no solace to her as every night she was assailed with dreams of becoming Carlton's wife. Of making his lovely new house into a comfortable and loving home for him and their children. She was barely managing to maintain discipline over the girls, as she became less and less connected to her life here. Her lack of care would soon be noticed, and then she would be out on the streets without a character, and if Carlton did not make her his bride that would be disastrous.

She bit at her nails, as she re-read his last letter. His words were warm and friendly. He had seemed even jovial. She pored over every syllable, trying to find a reason not to trust him, not to give her heart to him and she found none. He seemed good and kind, generous and clever – everything she had ever longed for in a husband. She had never known just how much she longed to be free of her current life until now. Just a few short months ago she had believed herself to be content and now she longed for the mountains and clear skies he spoke of with such affection.

Her reverie was broken by a knock on her door. "Miss Gilbert?" Annie, the chamber maid, called. "There is a young gentleman caller for you Miss," she said as Myra opened the door.

"A gentleman caller? But I am expecting no-one," she said puzzled. The only person who ever called for her was Mrs Cartwright, the Minister's wife. They took tea together on Myra's day off.

"He is ever so handsome Miss," Annie said with a grin. "I'd be ever so happy if he came a callin' for me!"

"Get back to work Annie, less of that nonsense," Myra scolded gently. She quickly smoothed her hair back and secured it with a couple of extra pins in the practical bun she always wore. There was only one person she could think of who might come calling on her without having announced a visit beforehand; only one person in her life who seemed so impetuous. But it couldn't be him? Carlton would have had to have left the very morning he received her last letter to have gotten here this quickly.

Her heart full of hope though, she ran down the stairs, curious as to who had come to ask for her, nervous that it may be just who she believed it to be. Whoever it was had clearly upset Mr Graham, the butler, as he had come to the front door. She stifled a giggle as she saw his stern face.

"Miss Gilbert, please ensure that your friends know to call for you at the servants entrance in future please."

"Of course, I do hope you haven't left him on the doorstep though?" she asked looking around and seeing no sign of a caller.

"Of course not. I had him sent to the rear parlor. He did not give me a card so I cannot tell you who he might be."

"Thank you Mr Graham, I shall see what he wants and send him on his way."

"That would be best," he said haughtily as he turned sharply and stalked off down the corridor towards the library. Myra could hold it in no longer, and she laughed out loud. He truly could be such a pompous prig.

She hurried to the little parlor that the staff used to read or unwind in quiet moments of the day. There were few of them, and so it was rarely used. She hesitated before she opened the door to enter. She truly did wonder who would be on the other side of it though she knew the only way to find out would be to enter. She took a deep breath, trying to calm the jumble of butterflies that seemed to have overtaken her entire torso, and turned the handle.

A tall, broad shouldered man stood at the mantle. He wore a black Stetson and boots, and a smartly tailored suit. The combination was strangely incongruous – and yet it suited him well. His obviously muscular body filled out the grey cotton and silk blend beautifully; his slim hips and flat stomach letting the fabric glide in the most flattering way. Whoever he was, he was quite the physical specimen. Her heart began to flutter, sure that her dreams had come true – that Carlton was here, in Boston, for her!

She coughed politely to alert him to her presence, he turned. She was struck dumb by the greenest eyes she had ever seen. Mesmerized she could hardly catch her breath. "Miss Gilbert? Myra Gilbert?" he asked her tentatively. She nodded, her throat suddenly so dry she feared she wouldn't get even the most simple of words out. "I am so sorry for the intrusion, but once you said you wished for me to visit, I simply couldn't bear to waste any time. I was on the first train out of Great Falls, and so here I am."

"Indeed, "she managed to croak as he took her hands in his and searched her face eagerly. She moistened her lips and swallowed a few times. "How was your journey?" she asked foolishly. He grinned at her.

"It was very enjoyable, just knowing I was on my way to meet you made it fly by. But I can see my presence has disconcerted you. Would you like me to leave? I can go to the hotel and give you time to process things should you wish?" Myra was touched by his consideration. But now he was here she didn't want to let him out of her sight. He was such a picture to gaze upon after all, with his chiseled jaw and smiling eyes.

"No, let me get us some tea and we can sit down and talk," she said hurriedly, as she backed out of the tiny room slowly.

She shut the door on him reluctantly, and walked a few steps towards the kitchen. Suddenly she found herself gasping for breath. She stopped, and leant against the wall, pressing her forehead to the cool plaster. He was simply too perfect. Whatever would he see in a woman like her? She was too plain, too dull, and too ordinary for any man who looked that good to ever consider. "Stop that," she commanded herself as she tried to pull herself together. "You are as good as any woman, and better than many. Any man would be lucky to call you his wife." She didn't believe her words, but she tried to imagine them the way her Papa had always said them, and knew he had believed every word.

"Cook, could you possibly prepare me afternoon tea for two please?"

"Annie said you have a visitor. Do you need me to come and act as chaperone?" the portly woman asked with a teasing smile.

"I think I am old enough to take care of my virtue Cook, but I am grateful for the offer," Myra responded cheekily.

"Is he truly as handsome as she said?"

"That would depend upon your definition of handsome I suppose," Myra said thoughtfully. "If you think a city boy with a fancy moustache and slicked back hair to be handsome then you would be sadly disappointed, but if your tastes run to a rangy cowboy, all muscle, with wicked green eyes, rumpled hair and a lopsided smile then he might be for you!"

"Sounds like you are smitten already. However did you meet him?" Cook bustled around as she asked questions, putting together a tray worthy of royalty. She laid out cakes and scones, sandwiches and a large silver teapot.

"I didn't. I have never seen him before today," Myra said honestly, trying to dodge the personal question. Cook had already spotted that she liked him and found him attractive. She would have to be very careful not to give anything away until she knew where she stood with the devilishly handsome man awaiting her in the parlor. "Now, if I may I shall go and find out what he has come to see me about," she said as she picked up the tray and made her way back to the man she prayed above all else would become her husband, and soon.

Chapter Four

Carlton was grateful for the moment of respite. Seeing Myra in the flesh had surpassed all of his wildest imaginings. She had a trim figure, and the biggest blue eyes that he had ever seen. The neat blonde hair looked as though it would be long and curling, if the wisps around her cheeks were anything to go by, but he couldn't be entirely sure until he had the pleasure of unpinning it and letting it fall down her slender back in waves. Yet, she seemed to have no idea of her physical impact upon men. He had known beautiful women before, they tended to walk into a room with the confidence that they can have whatever they desire-Myra did not have that arrogance. She seemed almost timid in fact.

He took the opportunity to gather his thoughts, and to try and calm the purely physical reaction that had occurred as he had taken her hands. It had felt as if a bolt of lightning had shot through him, setting every part of him on high alert. He wanted her; that was without doubt. He thought he had seen a flicker of desire in her eyes too – he prayed he wasn't just deceiving himself, seeing what he longed to see. He hadn't expected to find love, much less passion when he had advertised for a wife. At best he had hoped for companionship. So, to find a woman he was clearly so attracted to physically was more than he could ever have imagined.

His breath caught once more as she re-entered the room. "Here, let me help you with that," he offered taking the tray from her hands. She smiled at him nervously. "I won't bite Myra, I promise."

"That is good to know," she said bravely. "It would be ever so difficult to explain after all." He grinned. That was good, the feisty woman from the letters was in there, he had just taken her by surprise. "Now, how do you take your tea?"

"Hot and black," he said and chuckled as she looked at him in surprise.

"No milk, no sugar?"

"I ran out one day, drank it anyhow and never really worried about it since," he admitted. "I don't often have a lot of time, and it just makes things a bit easier. I am sorry I turned up out of the blue, I should have written to say I was coming."

"Please don't apologize, it was a wonderful shock. I should have guessed – our correspondence has been impulsive on both sides from the start." She smiled and handed him an elegant china cup. Her entire face lit up as she did so, revealing cute dimples that he just longed to kiss.

"So, will it be convenient for me to stay for a few days so we might see if we suit?" he asked boldly.

"It would. Something is clearly working in our favor, as the girls are currently away with their parents in Europe and so my duties are much reduced. I have all the time in the world to show you Boston," she said eagerly.

"That is fortuitous indeed," he agreed. "But, I came from a little place not far from here. I know Boston quite well, and so I already have us tickets for the opera this evening. I do hope you like Mozart?"

"I do indeed, I so wanted to attend the performances of Don Giovanni – but the tickets were prohibitively expensive," she said, her little rosebud mouth open in shock. Unable to resist, he reached out and gently pushed her chin up to close it. He stroked her cheek. It was soft, and yielding. She shuddered gently at his touch, then pulled away hastily. "I could not possibly let you spend such an amount on me."

"I didn't. I spent it on myself – I would just like you to accompany me." He took her chin in his hand once more and held her head so he could stare deeply into her eyes. "You won't leave me to the mercy of all the Boston socialites alone?" he begged. She shook her head out of his grasp and laughed nervously.

"Of course I wouldn't. But are you truly sure?"

"Myra, I have just travelled across the country to see you. I intend to spend as much time with you as I possibly can for that was the very purpose of my visit. If I can add in some theatre, a few museums and the opera whilst doing so I shall consider this trip perfection."

* * * * *

Myra had never blushed quite so furiously in her life. She had been glad to hurry him off to the hotel so she could bathe and dress for the evening's entertainment, simply because she had been sure that she would soon go up in flames - her face had felt so hot. His compliments had seemed genuine enough, yet she couldn't quite bring herself to believe him. She saw her image in the mirror every day, she was no socialite beauty. She was a simple woman, with simple tastes. But, Carlton was not simple. He was intelligent, funny and too good looking for her to trust herself.

She had already fallen for him in his letters; to meet him in the flesh had been overwhelming. She did not know if she would be able to survive the rejection that would be sure to come as he got to know her and decided that he wanted someone younger, prettier, less determined to be independent. She would be unable to temper that in herself. Her work was important to her, and she truly believed that women deserved more than they settled for in life. Few men were able to accept that, let alone encourage it in their wives.

She looked at the gowns in her closet. She owned three: her cornflower blue, for Sunday best; her grey cotton for in the school room; and her cream velvet for outings during the day. None of them was suitable for a night at the Opera. She sighed and sank onto her bed. There was no time to have one made, no time to even purchase something from one of the department stores as they would all now be closed for the day. She held up her blue gown against her, and looked at herself in the mirror. It would have to do.

"Miss Gilbert, Miss Gilbert, there's a package for you," Annie yelled excitedly as she burst into the room without knocking. Myra tried to look at her sternly, but Annie's eyes were alight with pleasure and she simply couldn't bring herself to chastise the girl. "Your young man just delivered it personally," she said in a conspiratorial whisper.

"I don't have a young man Annie."

"Whatever you say Miss Gilbert, but where I come from if a fella takes you out for the evening and buys you a new dress, that means your courtin'."

"Well, if you put it that way – but do I need to ask how you know that this is a new dress?" Myra asked shaking the large oblong box at her.

"No Ma'am, he told me so. Said it would look lovely with your eyes, and would you consider wearing your hair down."

"Well, he is certainly impertinent," Myra chuckled. "And you should know better than to encourage such behavior."

"Oh Miss, he's ever so handsome and he seems to really like you a lot. Why not give yourself the chance?" Annie asked wisely as Myra opened the package. Inside was an elegant evening gown, in a deep blue with tiny seed pearly sewn all over the bodice and a swirling skirt that would swish and whisper with every step she took. "Oh my!"

"Oh my indeed Annie. Well, it would appear he has good taste."

"Try it on Miss, I can make any adjustments you need while you bathe."

Myra slipped out of her clothes and with Annie's help she stepped into the silk gown. It felt soft and cool against her skin, the cut accentuating her curves. She felt like a fairytale princess off to the ball to meet her Prince Charming. Annie began to dart around her, tucking and pinning swiftly. When she had finished the fit was perfect, and Myra almost broke down in tears. She barely looked like herself at all. "Miss Gilbert don't cry, you're beautiful," Annie said, her voice full of wonder.

"That is why I am crying, I never knew!"

"Tush, of course you did. Lovely lady like you. Only difference is a posh dress. Don't you be so silly. Now, get out of that carefully so as not to prick yourself and I'll run up the alterations sharpish."

Annie disappeared with the sumptuous gown as Myra sank into her warm bath. She played distractedly with the rose petals floating on the surface, and wondered if she was dreaming. Things like this simply did not happen to women like her. She was a dowdy spinster, and yet here she was being swept off her feet by a handsome stranger, showering her with gifts. It was delightful, but it wasn't real life and she needed to get to know the real Carlton Green – not just this chivalrous and romantic one. She couldn't make a decision to make her life with him based on his generosity alone.

When the time came, Myra could hardly believe it was her as she gazed upon her reflection. Annie had pinned her hair carefully so that curls escaped in a gentle froth from behind her ears, her blonde locks streaming down her back in a silken tangle. Annie had even shown her how to apply some simple makeup to enhance her eyelashes and make her eyes look enormous, and a little rouge on her cheeks and lips. The blue gown now fit her perfectly, and she looked just as beautiful as any of the women of quality she had ever seen. "Now, don't cry Miss, or you'll ruin it," Annie warned her as a tear had begun to threaten to appear. Annie wiped it carefully away.

"Thank you Annie. I don't know what to say."

"Don't say a thing Miss Gilbert, just go and have fun."

"Annie, call me Myra – I'm certainly no better than you in any way."

"Yes ma'am, you are. You're an educated lady, and I am a common maid. But, I will gladly call you Myra."

"Education is something I was lucky to receive because of who my Papa was – not because I am in any way your superior Annie. Don't ever let anyone tell you they are better than you because you are 'just' a maid. You work hard, and have many skills – but even without them you have just as much right to be on this earth as anyone else." Annie grinned at her.

"Careful the bosses don't hear you teaching the girls things like that!" she warned.

"I should hope they already know that I have."

Chapter Five

The evening at the Opera had been magical. Myra had looked more perfect than Carlton could ever have imagined she would, and he had fallen head over heels in love with her as they discussed the quality of the production in the interval over a glass of wine. Myra was intelligent, sensitive and funny. He had enjoyed being with her more than he could ever have believed possible. Outings to the Zoological Gardens, museums and the theatre since had only convinced him that at last he had found the woman he would spend the rest of his life with.

He had begun to breathe just a little more easily with each outing they had undertaken where he had not bumped into anyone he had known before. It had been confusing, to be so excited and eager to see Myra, and yet to have his fears of discovery lurking in the back of his mind every time they were out. Today was the last day he could afford to spend here in Boston, and he had to admit he would be glad to not have to appear relaxed and carefree whilst constantly looking over his shoulder.

But, it also meant that today was the day that he and Myra would have to make a decision. He knew what he wanted that decision to be – but he was not sure if Myra felt the same way. Oh she was polite, and always seemed to be interested in his opinions. She laughed at his jokes and teased him more and more. But, it seemed that there was something in her that was holding her back too. He was sure her secret could be nothing like his own – but he was sure there was something. But, feeling optimistic he had planned this final outing down to the exact contents of the picnic basket he now carried on his arm.

"Would this be a spot you may consider?"Myra asked pointing to a spot under the shade of an old oak tree. He shook his head.

"I told you. I know exactly where I wish to take you," he said mysteriously.

"But we have almost run out of park!"

"Not at all. Though I am surprised that someone as curious as yourself has never found this place."

Myra gave him a wry smile and tucked her arm more tightly through his. He liked that she always wanted to walk arm in arm. He felt proud to be the one escorting her, and so the fact that she seemed to be proud to be with him made him happy.

He continued to tease her as they approached a wooden door tucked into the park wall. "See I told you we would run out of park," she scolded him.

"Nonsense," he said as he moved to open the door. She gasped as he stood back to let her enter in front of him. Before them was a beautiful garden, in the English style with formal box-hedging and blousy floral borders. It was a riot of color, and in the center was an elegant bandstand. He could hear the strains of a string quartet and smiled. He had wanted to ensure that everything was perfect, and the sweet romantic music just made it all the way he had planned for.

Myra's face was a picture of delight. He couldn't help but smile at how clever he had been to give her such a surprise. "However did you know of this place?" she asked.

"My Father proposed to my Mother here. I guess I wanted to uphold a little family tradition," he admitted as he put the picnic basket down on the steps of the bandstand, and knelt down upon one knee. "Dear

Myra, will you marry me and return to Montana and make me the happiest man alive?"

"We shall need to marry here in Boston, or in Great Falls though, there is no church or chapel in Sun River yet, though I doubt it will be long before we build one," he said suddenly. She simply smiled at him and pulled him onto his feet, and standing on tip toe reached up to kiss him. He pulled her close to him, cradling her lithe body against his own and lost himself in her lips. He had so longed to claim them as his own, but had always held back. Now, here she was kissing him, setting him alight with passion, her eyes blazing with joy. Carlton had never felt so happy in his entire life.

* * * * *

Myra could hardly contain her happiness. She longed to shout it out to the entire world - that she was to marry this kind, generous and wonderfully handsome man. She had to stop herself from doing just that with every person they met in the Park as they made their way back home. Her eye kept being drawn back to the perfectly cut Sapphire on her ring finger, fiddling with it nervously as she got used to the weight of it on her hand. Carlton would just pat her hand gently where it lay on his arm, as if to reassure himself that she had said yes and was indeed wearing his ring.

"Be careful, you shall rub it away to nothing," Carlton teased her.

"I simply cannot believe that this has happened to me," she admitted.

"To us. I am so glad that you said yes, my love." The little endearment touched her more than she could ever have explained and she ducked her head into his chest to hide her blush. He kissed her on the crown, and smiled at her happily.

Couples and families smiled at them, as if sensing their news. Myra basked in the glow of their good feeling. Then as suddenly as everything had become perfect, it felt as if a cloud had covered the sun and doused them in the cold and harsh reality of life. Myra was not sure what had happened, nor if it was her fault – but Carlton suddenly went stiff, and unresponsive. "Carlton, are you quite well?"

31

"Of course," he replied tersely, his words and tone clipped and distant. All of a sudden she was confronted with a man she simply did not know. She longed to ask what had happened to make him so aloof – but she did not dare. His face, usually so open and full of laughter, was like a closed book. She looked around them, trying to see if there was a clue, anything at all that could tell her why the man she loved had become a complete stranger to her – and as she followed his gaze she saw an elderly gentleman, playing with a young boy. He could not have been more than ten years old, and they were playing with a wonderful sail boat on the lake. "Carlton, do you know them?" she asked tentatively. Carlton just kept staring.

"Carlton, please talk to me! Whatever is the matter? Who are they to you? Why do you look so stern?"

"Myra stop fussing. It is not important. I shall escort you home immediately. Please, do not ever speak of this again." Myra nodded, unwillingly. Clearly something about the pair had unsettled Carlton, but she could not force him to confide in her. She would be patient, would let him come to her when he was ready. She prayed that he would be one day. She did not want there to be secrets between them, especially not now. But she had the worst feeling that this was something that could drive a wedge between them that may never heal.

"I shall come by at ten o'clock in the morning," he said briskly. "My train leaves at eleven. Should you wish to accompany me immediately, or would you like to wait and serve out your notice?"

"I should like to come with you, but I must wait and at least say my goodbyes to the girls. It will give you time to have the banns read so we can wed as soon as I arrive," she said gently. He nodded, bent his head and gave her a chaste peck on the cheek.

"Until the morning then."

"But, what of supper tonight? Cook has prepared your favorite-roast beef?" she asked, feeling tears of confusion and unhappiness pricking at the back of her eyes.

"Please make my apologies. I have something I must attend to after all."

With that he marched down the steps and then swiftly down the street and out of sight. Myra stared after him. How could the most wonderful thing to ever happen to her have soured so fast? Overwhelmed and unsure if he even wanted to marry her now, she sank to the floor and sobbed.

Chapter Six

Carlton stormed past the elderly butler and into the impressive hallway. He was not going to leave without some answers. He knew he had made terrible mistakes, but he did not deserve this, to find out such a thing in such a way. "Havershall, you damned dog. Where are you? Come out and face me you coward?" he yelled up the stairs.

"Sir, Mr Havershall is not at home."

"He damn well is, I just saw him come in." Carlton growled. "Now, you can tell me where he is Galen, or I will break down every door in the place." The butler shuddered, but pointed to the library.

"Thank you. I'm sorry to scare you, none of this is your fault my old friend."

"Young Master Carlton, your Father is an old man – like I am. What he did, he did for a reason I'm sure."

"Why didn't you tell me? Why didn't Mother tell me?"

"How could we young Sir?" Carlton had to agree with that. How could an employee, a wife go against the head of the household. But this was too important to have kept silence – whatever it may have cost them. "I was in no position to do so, and well your Mother died four years ago. I thought he would have at least written to you and told you. I shouldn't say – but I think she died of a broken heart. She was never the same after you and Miss Abigail well…," he tailed off unsure what to say next.

"Mother is dead?"Carlton stared at the old butler dumbfounded. For a moment he had been about to give his Father the excuse that he hadn't known where he was to let him know – but he was sure that his dear Papa would have known exactly where he had been from the moment he left the house, tormented by grief all those years ago. The man never let anything get past him.

He burst into the library, and stared at the image he was greeted with. His Father was sat on the settle, the young boy curled up by his side reading a book. It brought back so many memories of having done the same thing with his Father as a child. There had been many such happy days, before he had been sent away to boarding school to be prepared to enter the family dynasty.

"Run along Benjy, I need to talk to this gentleman in private," his Father said warmly. The boy looked up at his Grandfather with eyes as green as Carlton's own. He obeyed unquestioningly, but his intrigue level had clearly been piqued as he gave the intruder into his world a thorough looking over as he walked past.

"You told me he was dead Father," he said nodding at the door the boy had left through.

"And you told me you would never return to Boston."

"There is a massive difference in expecting me to stay away from the scene of such heartbreak – and you never telling me I didn't need to be half as unhappy! He's my son Father, and you told me he was dead. You allowed me to think I had killed him – and Abigail."

"I did what I thought was best."

"By depriving us both of nine years together? In what twisted world does that make sense?"

"You drove your wife to her death. I would not take the risk that you would do the same to my grandson. I shall never let you do the same to him. He believes that you are dead. I intend him to never know anything different."

"So you still believe that Abigail took her own life because I mistreated her?"

"What other reason could she have had?"

"I don't know Father, but I am fed up of trying to work out why. I am also fed up of blaming myself. I treated Abigail well. She never loved me, never wanted to marry me – she did so to please her Father who didn't care one whit about her happiness, only that he create an alliance with you. Well I hope all the money you made together was worth knowing that a kind and gentle woman took her life to escape the life the pair of you created for her. I will not let you do the same to my son. You will not manipulate his life like you did mine, or his Mother's."

"You can do nothing," his Father sneered. "Look at you, you can't hope to win against my wealth, my contacts – not here in Boston."

"Well then, it is as well that I don't live in Boston isn't it. If it takes me the rest of my life, my boy will be coming home with me. I won't have him thinking that this," Carlton looked around the cavernous room disparagingly, "is everything there is to life."

"If you wish to lose, then so be it. You shall never take him from me."

Carlton turned and stormed out of the room. He should have known better than to try and bait the dragon in his own lair, but seeing them like that in the Park had been too much of a shock. His Father had told him that Abigail had taken not only her own life, but Benjamin's too. He had been utterly devastated, and had blamed himself for their loss. But he had thought about it all so hard and so long, for so many years up in his desolate isolation. He had probably been the only person to ever show Abigail even one iota of kindness. He hadn't loved her, not the way he did Myra, but that didn't mean he hadn't been tender towards her. Benjamin had been such a blessing – to them both. He had so prayed that their son would be enough to help her to find enough joy to stay with them. She had always been so melancholy, a pawn in the game of two powerful men who thought that people could be used for their own ends.

Well, he would avenge her death for them by ensuring that Benjamin had a better life – one full of love and joy. He would fight his Father with every penny he had, would even sell the farm if needs be – but he would not abandon his boy to the soul-less world in which his Father lived. But, he had just proposed marriage to Myra, and she knew nothing of his past. He couldn't expect her to marry him and then be saddled with a ten year old boy she hadn't known existed. He couldn't expect her to even want him after the way he had treated her this afternoon.

* * * * *

Whoever was knocking on the door was clearly determined to gain access, Myra thought as she listened anxiously to the heavy pounding. Nobody ever called at this hour, and the entire house had been readying themselves for bed. She clutched her dressing gown around her and made her way downstairs. She peeked out of the window on the landing and saw Carlton there. He looked distraught. She rushed down the final flight of stairs and beckoning to Cook and Annie to go back to bed she opened the door.

"Carlton, whatever is the matter? You have the entire house scared out of their wits?"

"Myra, I am so very sorry, but I must break off our engagement," he said hurriedly, tears flooding down his face.

"Now, don't be so silly. Come in. Nothing so bad can have happened in just a few hours that means we need to rethink our plans," she said pragmatically, though her insides were churning with fear. She simply couldn't bear the thought of losing him, not now she knew without doubt that she loved him with all her heart.

"I'm sorry, I can't tell you."

"Yes you can, and you will. That is what wives are for – to help you shoulder the burdens," she reminded him adamantly.

"You will never forgive me, you are better off without me, everyone is." Myra was stunned by the maudlin tone, and the defeatist language.

"This has something to do with the old man and the boy we saw in the park doesn't it? Now, I'm guessing he must be your son. Now, my brain can go on a little jaunt to try and workout what is going on here – or you can give me the quick version. I'd hate to end up with something completely wrong and I probably would as I have a very fertile imagination," she said with a gentle smile as she tenderly wiped away his tears, and kissed him on the mouth.

"You don't mind that I have a son?" he asked incredulously.

"Not in the least, why ever should I?"

"Because I didn't tell you about him, or that I was married before," he said as if it were the most obvious thing in the world.

"Carlton, I am not so naive as to think that at your age you have never had a relationship with a woman before me. What matters to me is our future, not your past."

"Yes, I was married. It was arranged by my father. Poor Abigail was so unhappy. She and I, well we weren't well suited and though I cared for her as best I could and she tried she just got more and more unhappy. I blamed myself. When Benjamin was born we both hoped things would get better, but she just got more unhappy than ever. She took her own life."

"Oh Carlton, that must have been so terrible for you to bear. I'll wager you blamed yourself and went off to lick your wounds in the wilds of some far off place, like Montana?" she said, very gently teasing him.

"I haven't told you the worst part. My Father told me Abigail had killed Benjamin too." Myra had nothing to say to such cruelty. She stared at him, then took his hands between her own.

"Then we need to make sure that your son is taken away from such a monster, and finds out that he has a Father who loves him and a stepmother who will too."

"I cannot ask that of you. It is too much."

"No it isn't. Now, my Father may be dead but he had some very influential friends. He taught most of Boston's legal profession. I am sure we can find someone who will be more than happy to help us to get your boy back."

"Myra Gilbert, I do not know what I ever did to deserve you, but I am so glad that I found you. You truly are a marvel, a treasure, the most wonderful creature I have ever known!"

"You are just a little punch-drunk right now my love, but thank you for the lovely compliments. Now, get back to the hotel and get a good night's rest. Then go to the station and amend your ticket so we can hire a lawyer before you go back to Montana, and I shall try and find somewhere where we can marry right away. I am not ever going to leave your side again."

Chapter Seven

Myra still did not know if Carlton loved her, but she knew she would do anything for him. His revelations of the night before had done nothing to change that. She prayed he would one day come to love her with all his heart, but she was more than happy to accept his pleasant companionship and obvious physical attraction towards her. She prayed that they would find a way to reunite father and son once more, maybe if she could do that for them it would be enough to make him love her too.

She hurried out of the house at first light, to visit with Reverend Cartwright. She was sure there must be some way that she and Carlton could be married today. The kindly man was more than happy to help her out, and agreed to read the banns in the morning service and marry them after evensong. It wasn't the dream wedding that every girl planned and hoped for, but she would be walking down the aisle with the man who held her heart and that was more than most could ever hope for.

She then rushed to Uncle Peter's chambers. He had been Papa's closest friend, and was now a Judge. If he didn't know what they could do next, then no man alive could help them. She had told Carlton to meet her there, and as she rounded the corner and saw him waiting for her, kicking nervously at the step her heart filled with love. She rushed towards him, and was overjoyed when he took her in his arms and bent his head down to kiss her passionately on the lips. "You are sure you want to help me with this?"

"Of course, and we shall be married after evensong, so I shall have to!" she quipped.

"I am so glad you did not turn away from me. I blamed myself for so long for Abigail's death, my son's death – but I shall never do so again. Shall place the blame where it truly lies – with my Father and hers."

"Good." She ushered him inside and they were shown into Uncle Peter's office. He stood up and hugged her warmly.

"How can I help you my dear?" he asked. She indicated that Carlton should tell his entire sorry tale.

Myra watched as Uncle Peter made notes, occasionally querying the points Carlton made. He listened so attentively, and she could see her fiancé begin to relax and feel at ease with him. When Carlton finished speaking he carefully reviewed the notes, then looked up at them. "Well, this should be relatively straightforward," he said. Myra and Carlton looked at one another, and heaved a sigh of relief. "Your Father has no rights to the boy if you are still alive and no charges have ever been pressed against you. The fact that Myra intends to marry you will stand you in good stead amongst a good three quarters of the legal profession in this city, and the other quarter are in the pockets of those men like your Father. If we can get this before the right judge, and quickly, I see no reason why you shouldn't be able to take your boy home with you immediately. The quicker we act, the less time your Father has to try and subvert us."

"Truly?" Carlton asked. "I can hardly believe it. I only found out he was alive yesterday, and he could be coming home with us tomorrow?"

"If I can manage it, maybe even today!" Peter said as he shook Carlton's hand. He hugged Myra close. "I'll be in touch."

They walked out of his chambers hand in hand, and made their way back to Young's Hotel where Carlton had been staying. They went into the restaurant and ordered a celebratory lunch, but both of them were too nervous to eat much of it. They knew there were still too many hurdles to climb before they truly had their happily ever after.

* * * * *

A note was delivered to them as they sat drinking their coffee. "Uncle Peter says we should be at the courthouse at half past two," Myra said reading the note carefully. The look of hope on her face was adorable, and Carlton leant over to kiss her gently. He checked his pocket watch, and seeing it was almost a quarter to two they got up and he helped her into her coat. The court house was not far, but the streets could be busy and this was too important to miss.

When they arrived there Peter was waiting with a young man by his side. Myra clearly recognized him, and Carlton was rocked by jealousy as he watched her embrace him affectionately. "Carlton, this is my Father's favorite pupil, Myles Clannon. Papa used to say he was a genius."

"I was never as clever as you Myra, if I'd ever had to stand and face you in a court I shouldn't stand a chance!" His flirtatious and over familiar tone grated on Carlton, and he longed to punch this new intruder rather than to take his advice – but he knew he had to accept the man's help. His boy needed a father who loved him – not a Grandfather who would use him eventually for his own gain.

"Are you ready? Peter told me all about your case. This really should be very simple and we should be able to serve your Father with the court's decision almost immediately." Carlton choked down his envy, and managed to smile at the man. He really was grateful for how kind everyone was being. But he couldn't help longing for his home, the peace and quiet. It would be wonderful when he, Myra and Benjamin could return there.

"I think so," he said cautiously, trying not to get his hopes up too high.

His father hadn't even bothered to come. His lawyers sat at their table looking puffed up and important, and so very arrogant that Carlton prayed Myra's faith in Myles Clannon was justified. The Judge was called, and when he saw Peter's smiling face enter the courtroom suddenly all his fears evaporated. Just thirty minutes later he and Myra walked out of the

42

courtroom, arm in arm, clutching the court's decision.

"Just because you have a piece of paper does not mean you take the boy from his home, from the people he loves!" his Father said looking flustered.

"That is exactly what it means Father. I know you thought that your money could buy you everything you want – but not this time I'm afraid. Now, where is the boy? Where is Benjamin?"

"I shall appeal!"

"And you shall have to do so in Montana, which is where we shall be. If you ever wish to see Benjamin again, I suggest you learn to live with this court's decision Father. I shall be happy for you to come and visit if you choose – but I shall never trust you with my boy. You will not make his life as unhappy as you made mine and Abigail's."

The old man crumpled in front of Carlton's eyes, but he could feel no pity for him. He looked up as he heard footsteps on the stairs. Benjamin was standing on the third step. "Is it true? You are my Father?"

"Yes Benjamin," Carlton said frankly. Myra squeezed his hand. He was so glad she was by his side.

"Why did they tell me you were dead?"

"My Father did what he thought was best, for you and for me. But he forgot one vital part of that – that it is best to ask people what they want and need before deciding for them." His Father winced, and in that moment Carlton was sure that he would never need anything more than that.

"Did you not want me?"

"I have always wanted you. I have grieved for nine long years thinking you were dead too. Had I known, I would never have left you."

"I must come and live with you now?" his little face was so earnest. Carlton nodded.

"If you want to. If you would rather stay here in Boston with your Grandfather then I would understand. I am a stranger after all."

"No, I want to come with you. I don't like living here. I love Grandfather, but I don't want to go to boarding school. You won't send me away will you?"

"No my dear boy, never."

Epilogue

The church was full. As Myra peeked through the doors she was amazed that so many people were here at such short notice. She almost cried as she saw Carlton standing at the altar with his handsome son by his side. The two were smiling at one another, Carlton's arm loosely about the lad's shoulders. It was almost as if they had never been parted. Annie quickly dabbed at her eyes and carefully placed her veil over her face. "You look lovely Myra," she said, her voice a little choked.

"Thank you."

The organ started up and she took Uncle Peter's arm and walked slowly down the aisle towards the man she loved. She proudly promised to love him and honor him, and couldn't keep the smile from her face as they walked back down the aisle as man and wife. "Well, I have to say life with you is never dull," she teased. Carlton kissed her tenderly.

"I truly hope it will be a little quieter once we get home!"

"Indeed, now will I be living in a sod cabin, or that lovely house you told me all about?"

"I have no idea – I suppose we will find out when we get there! But, wherever we end up, I want you to know just how much I love you

Mrs Green. You have changed my life, helped me get back my son, and you are more precious than anything else on earth."

"Except Benjamin, of course," she reminded him, but she could feel the blush on her cheeks and her heart fill with love at the truth in his words. "I love you too, and I am afraid you are stuck with us both forever now.

"I can't think of anything more wonderful," he admitted and kissed her again.

The train journey had been fun. Benjy had very much enjoyed learning all about how the engines worked from the drivers and firemen. Every evening at dinner he regaled them of his adventures, and insisted that when he was older he was going to work on the railways too. She had laughed as Carlton had smiled and told him that whatever he wanted to do was fine by her, though it was clear he wasn't sure how safe it would be. But, he had been more than happy to trust the kindly men with his son as Benjy had been determined to spend much of his days assisting them. Myra didn't complain, it had meant that she and Carlton had been able to spend some time alone, and they had enjoyed getting to know one another as man and wife. She certainly had no doubts now as to whether or not he loved her.

She had enjoyed the long train journey, she had never known how very different all the States were. They passed through green fields, red dust, desert, plains and mountains on their cross country adventure. But when they reached the borders of Montana she gasped out loud at just how beautiful it was. She could never have imagined anything quite so perfect, and it made her feel small to witness such majestic mountains. Their snow-capped peaks made it seem almost unreal, as if she had stepped into a picture book – but this was to be her home now.

She and Benjy had stood patiently waiting as Carlton arranged to borrow a neighbor's buggy so they could drive home in comfort. He had already warned them that they still had quite a way to go from the station in Great Falls. But, both were excited and eager to see more of their new home. Once their trunks were strapped firmly onto the backboard, they set off at a gentle trot. Myra marveled at the rock strewn river that guided them along their way. The track was a little rutted, and took them up into the foothills, then back down onto the valley floor.

"My farm is just up around the next bend," Carlton said excitedly. "I wonder what we shall be sleeping in tonight?"

"Well, I'd say Ardloe has been busy!" Myra said, relief in her voice as they rounded the bend. A smart clapboard dwelling now stood where his old sod cabin had once been.

"Is that our house?" Benjamin said, his eyes wide with wonder.

"I think it just might be?" Carlton said ruffling the lad's curls. "Do you like it Mrs Green?"

"It'll do," she said with a grin. "I just hope he remembered the indoor outhouse!"

"Oh, I told him you insisted on electricity too – we are going to be the fanciest farmers in the valley!"

"Why don't you go and explore Benjy," she said as the gig came to a stop. He raced off and only his foot thuds could be heard as he rushed onto the broad porch.

"So, what do you think of Montana, wife?"

"I think you were right about those beautiful mountains, and that the peace is so welcoming and wonderful. And you were right about this beautiful house. I truly do love it. Thank you husband, this is going to be such a wonderful place to bring up a family."

"It is perfect now," he admitted as he pulled her against him and kissed her. "It was always just a little bit lonely before, but I doubt that I will ever feel that way ever again."

The End

* * * * * *

A Bride for Mackenzie
Book 2

Chapter One

"Annie, I need my reticule. Do you know where I left it when we came in from the recital?" Carolynn yelled angrily. Annie sighed. The girl could be all elegance when she wanted, yet as soon as her parents were out of the house, out came the hoyden and made a perfectly turned out young woman appear more coarse than a common fishwife.

"Miss Carolynn, why not try retracing your steps?" Annie replied patiently. There was no point in trying to reason with her once she was in high dudgeon, even though apparently this was her job until a new governess could be found for the two girls. She was simply too tired, and had too much to get done to get involved in Miss Caro's petty concerns today. Mr and Mrs Hepworth had only just come into their money. Mr Hepworth had made a lot of money selling hardware to miners, and they liked to show it off in any way they could. But that meant a lot of useless trinkets and too much furniture and it was always down to Annie to make sure that the house looked as immaculate as possible. The sad thing was that they simply didn't understand that buying everything new, and at the highest possible price, did not convey the appearance they longed to portray. It just made their home cluttered and made for more cleaning for their poor overworked staff.

"But however can I do that? I cannot go to the theatre alone and just walk back now can I," the young woman added sarcastically. She was about to turn fifteen, and believed she was cleverer than anyone older or younger than herself. Annie was sure the phase would pass and the sweet girl she had once been would return, but it was proving hard to tolerate while she continued to have these tantrums over nothing. With a sigh she put down the silver coffee pot she had been polishing and tucked her cloth securely into her apron.

"Come now, you will surely find it faster than I Miss Carolynn," she added as she reluctantly bustled into the hallway to try and calm the young woman. "Ask Miss Margaret to help you to search. Your Mother and Father will not be best pleased if I haven't finished the silver in time for their supper party tonight after all."

Annie had prayed over and over since her dear friend, Myra

Gilbert, had left for Montana to become the bride of Carlton Green that a new governess would be found soon. Trying to keep up with the two girls and her chores was leaving her worn to the nub. She was sure she hadn't enjoyed a quiet moment in weeks. Though the girls could be kind, and very sweet at times, they interrupted her all the time and that meant she got the telling off from her employer that her usual tasks were either not done, or not up to her usual standard. Mrs Hepworth in particular simply didn't seem to understand that doing two jobs that both needed a person's fullest attention would mean that corners somewhere had to be cut.

She turned her back and went back into the dining room and the seemingly endless task ahead of her, praying that Miss Carolynn would stop bothering her over something so trivial when she had so much still to do. But sadly, the young woman followed her. "But Annie, it has my letter from Myra in it. I would have thought that you would be as eager as I to hear news of how she is faring in Montana," she said slyly as she appeared in the doorway. She was a dear thing, but lazy as a cat in the sunshine. Myra hadn't let her get away with it, and neither would Annie. She simply didn't have the time.

"I have my own letter Miss Carolynn, and I shall enjoy reading it when I have finished my work. I don't know how you ever intend to keep a husband young lady. You simply don't seem to understand that there is work to be done before you can play. Miss Myra would be heartbroken to think that all her lessons and her hard work had been so easily forgotten." Even Annie could hear the uncharacteristic exasperation in her voice, and Carolynn flushed with shame.

"You are right. She would extol the virtues of assisting you as much as we can, and to be self sufficient. But she isn't here is she?" Annie gave her a stern look. "Oh Annie, you can't blame me for at least trying to take advantage of the absence of a governess. Who knows what kind of dragon Papa will appoint next!"

"If he did employ someone a little stricter it would be for your own good."

"I know, I know. I am sorry, honestly. Is there anything we can do to help, dear Annie?" she said, moving towards the vast dining table, her doe eyes imploring Annie to forgive.

"Pick up a rag and polish everything you can see 'til it shines," Annie said with a smile, not expecting the girl to actually do an ounce of work, but it had been good of her to at least offer her assistance.

"Margaret? Come down. Annie needs a hand. Stop being such a lazy puss!" Carolynn called to her sister, leaving Annie open-mouthed. A younger, and quieter version of Caro appeared, book in hand. She put it down without a murmur of complaint, and both girls picked up their cloths and began to copy Annie's example. Annie smiled at them kindly.

The girls really weren't so bad, they just needed a little reminder every now and again of how to behave and to think of others every once in a while. Myra had told her just that as they had said their goodbyes, when the clever governess had been whisked off to the wilds of Montana by her handsome and dashing farmer. Annie couldn't help it, she had dreamed of something similar happening to her for weeks after their departure. But, she was just a chamber maid. Romance wasn't for the likes of her. She took her frustrations out on her work, and there was never a single bit of the house that wasn't spotlessly clean because of it.

The afternoon passed swiftly. The girls were excellent company, and they worked hard. When they stood back to admire their work all three young women put their hands on their hips and sighed contentedly. Annie chuckled. "Thank you," she said as they admired their gleaming work together.

"However do you do it, day in and day out Annie? I am quite fagged and we have done barely half the amount you did," Carolynn said in admiration.

"I'm used to it I suppose, and don't say 'fagged'! Your Mother would have the vapors if she heard you."

"What she doesn't know won't hurt her. And she would have the vapors if she heard you say such a thing of her too Annie! Now, may I please take Margaret and go in search of my reticule now?"

"Of course," Annie said with a grin.

"It is in your room, on your bed," Margaret said with an exasperated look. "You really are quite stupid sometimes." Carolynn looked at her, her brown eyes flashing in her sudden fury.

"You could have told me!"

"That wouldn't have been half as much fun. And, you didn't think to ask!"

"Get on with you, leave me to my work. I have a lot to do before tonight," Annie said ushering them out of the room. "Get up to your room, and stay there. I'll be up around six with the water for your baths; I shall be so glad when your Papa finishes getting the house fully plumbed and I can save my poor aching back! Remember your Mother will expect you both to be clean and presentable when the Montagues arrive."

"Yes Annie, of course Annie," they chorused as they raced up the grand staircase before she could scold them further.

Annie looked over the silverware. It was good. She wouldn't have to redo a single piece. Her day suddenly felt so much lighter, a task that usually took four hours had been completed in just two – she may even get to stop and rest for a few minutes before supper after all. Swiftly she fetched her brushes and the big tin of beeswax polish and began to sweep and dust the grand dining room, the drawing room and the library. She had already ensured that the grand hallway and the water closets were all sparkling before she had accompanied the girls to the recital at the Opera House. She hummed as she worked, a tune she had picked up whilst there. She had never been in a box before, and it had been a shock to her how luxurious it was in comparison to the gallery at the very top of the theatre that she occasionally managed to save enough to purchase a standing ticket for.

When she had completed her tasks she glanced at the large grandfather clock in the hallway, and was pleased to see it was only five o'clock. She still had an entire hour before she had to assist the girls to get ready, and her final task of the day was simply to lay the table. She would have a full forty minutes to herself if she was lucky. She moved with haste to the china cupboard. They would be using the Lenox chinaware this evening. It was brand new, and very delicate. She and Cook had been almost nervous as they had unpacked it and washed and dried it carefully before putting it away. She took each plate carefully between her fingers, placing it delicately on each setting. She wiped the crystal glasses carefully as she put each one in place, and gave each piece of cutlery a final polish as she laid it in place. Glancing over the table with her practiced eye, she wandered slowly round the table, nudging and tweaking until everything was perfect.

The clock chimed for the quarter hour, and Annie grinned. She had achieved perfection in record time. Praising herself she headed downstairs to the kitchen and her rocking chair by the fire. She would put her feet up, read the newspaper and her letter from Myra. It would be wonderful to know how she was doing, and if she was still as happy as she had been the day she set off on her big adventure. Annie hoped so. She had been a good friend, and she deserved a good life.

The kitchen was abuzz, Cook had hired in a couple of ladies from her church to help her. The three of them were up to their elbows in flour, pies, and vegetables. It felt wrong to sit and rest her weary bones while they rushed around, so Annie grabbed a newspaper from the rack and headed upstairs to her room. It wasn't much, but she did at least get to keep it all to herself. She looked around at the sparse furnishings, and was grateful she lived so simply. When you spent your life cleaning up after others – especially those with so many beautiful things that needed such special care, having nothing but a bed and a chest of drawers was restful.

She threw herself face down onto her mattress, and lay propped up on her elbows. She read Myra's letter first. It was short but she was clearly happy in Montana, and couldn't' seem to stop extolling the virtues of her handsome farmer. Annie felt a pang of jealousy as she read her words. It all seemed to happen so quickly, so simply. But she was sure that not every woman who set off into the West in search of love was so lucky. Annie missed her terribly, and she longed to have a husband and a home of her own. She was tired of always caring for everyone else but herself.

She put the letter down, and picked up the newspaper. Quickly she flicked through the pages to the Society section. She loved to read about all the gossip and scandal. She knew she shouldn't, but living vicariously through others was her only real pleasure in life. She was simply too tired by the time she finished her work each day to go out and be sociable, though it did mean that her nest egg of savings was growing safely and securely. She gasped as she read about her favorite actress being found in a hotel suite with a ridiculously wealthy banker, and about the opera singer who prided himself on being a family man being found in flagrante with one of the corps de ballet. To have such free time to make such foolish mistakes made her chuckle to herself. It was oddly reassuring to know that having wealth and fame did not necessarily make your life any happier – or make you even a jot wiser than those who served you.

She thumbed through the rest of the pages, wondering if anything else might catch her eye. She didn't much care for the news; it was too often full of tragedy and horror for her liking. But occasionally she would find a story that gave a little ray of hope and stoked her faith in the goodness of people. Sadly, there seemed to be little of such interest today, yet she stopped suddenly when she reached a page she had not seen in the Boston Globe before - a page of Matrimonial advertisements. She couldn't stop herself, her curiosity was piqued. She began to read, and was surprised at how many were actually from lonely women. She wouldn't have thought any woman would be so desperate as to degrade herself in such a way in front of the entire world.

The greater majority of the advertisements were from men though, and from all over the country, even some here in Boston. Clearly finding a bride in such a way was becoming so common place that people weren't just using it as a last resort. She wondered if any of them truly was as wonderful as their carefully chosen words made out - not one seemed to ring true to her. If they truly were such paragons, finding a wife should surely be no difficulty at all? But one simply worded advertisement made her stop and smile, a warm sense of connection settling over her in a way that felt like she was coming home.

A Gentleman of Montana, seeks a woman with a view to Matrimony. She should be polite and kind, and be able to make of his house a home. His needs are few, and his wealth not extraordinary, but there is enough to support us both and for us to consider a family some day. The subscriber is a man of simple tastes. All responses to Box 378, Boston Globe.

He sounded like her. She didn't need much in life. But, she did want a home and a family. Myra had been lucky, why couldn't she be as content with a match made in this way? Didn't she deserve to have something of her own? Hadn't she spent enough of her life alone? Surely she had more than made up for her mistakes by now and was due some kind of happiness? Maybe the gentleman might live near to Sun River and she would be able to visit with her friend? Eagerly, recklessly she penned a response and wondered if she had lost her wits as she rushed out of the house to mail it before she had to return to her duties, and the dull and uneventful life she knew she deserved.

Chapter Two

Dear Gentleman of Montana,

    Good day to you, I pray this finds you in good health. I do not know exactly what to say, so please forgive me if my words seem stilted or even rushed. I have never done anything so impetuous as to contact you in my entire life. I don't even know what possessed me to put pen to paper and write, but I just felt the strangest urge that I should regret it if I did not do so.

    I am a chambermaid, and I live and work in a big house in Boston for a lovely family. I have been working extra hard recently as a friend left to get married and she has not yet been replaced. I have some education, but not sufficient to be a governess to two young women who already outstrip me in their knowledge. Yet, I try my best to at least teach them useful skills and try to keep them to their studies in comportment and manners.

    I cannot say I enjoy being a maid, but I do get an immense sense of pleasure from seeing a job well done. I am a quiet sort, love reading when I have the time. But I am happiest when I am busy *and have plenty to keep me occupied. I should very much like to correspond with you, to get to know you with a view to seeing if we might suit. I should very much like to be mistress of a home I could make with a supportive partner, and to become a mother someday.*

Please tell me of yourself, I should love to hear of your home and what you do. Do you enjoy music and the theatre, or are you a homebody happy to curl up with a good book and a warm fire at the end of the day?

I look forward to your response, though I am sure you will receive many replies from women far more interesting than myself. I shall understand if I hear nothing further.

Yours most hopefully

Annie Cahill

Mack put the simple little letter down on the left hand side of his large oak desk. He looked at the towering pile on the right. It surprised him how so many of the women who had replied to his advertisement had not asked a single thing about him. Annie Cahill was the only one so far who had not only wanted to know more of his life, but had even asked after his wellbeing.

He could not explain it, even to himself, but something about her short missive made him feel comfortable and content. He was no fool; he knew that feeling passion for a woman one met through an advertisement in the newspaper was not ever going to be likely, but he did at least want to not feel revulsion towards the woman he wrote to, maybe considered bringing here, to Montana, to be his bride. As he looked over the other responses once more, looking for any hint of kindness, humility or even simple politeness he could find nothing. He threw them on the fire, and stared again at the plain spoken words of Annie Cahill. This quiet and unassuming woman intrigued him. She had told him little of herself, and he was sure it was not because there was little to know - but because she believed her life to be of little interest. That in itself put her head and shoulders above the vapid and vain women whose letters were now crisping and crackling up in the flames.

He leaned back in his chair, and ran his fingers through his hair. The ends curled as they reached his collar, reminding him he really needed to get a haircut. He rubbed his hands over his heavily stubbled cheeks; it had definitely been too long since he had visited the barbers. Mack looked out at the sheeting rain and decided that he would take a trip into Great Falls, he would get nothing done out on the land in weather such as this. It had been stormy for days and he was beginning to feel confined. His place was out on the land herding his cattle – but even he knew better than to do much more than check on them once or twice a day when thunder, lightning and wind raged outside. He couldn't afford to get sick and so he had learned to temper his naturally adventurous side – his sister called it recklessness and she was probably right.

"Mackenzie if you are going to be under my feet like this, you could at the very least clean up after yourself," Penelope's voice called down the stairs. Mack listened to her steps, the wooden floorboards creaking as she made her way towards the cozy little room he used as an office. "Anyone worth responding to today?" she asked him, her tone a little more kindly.

"Just the one." He handed over the letter. Penelope read it in silence, but a smile began to play around her lips as she did so.

"She sounds lovely – what little she has given away." She looked back at the address. "She's from Boston, and the governess at her place of work has just left - I wonder if she knows Myra Green," she mused. Mack looked at her confusion knotting his brow.

"Why ever should she know Mrs Green?"

"Because Mrs Green was once Miss Gilbert, and because she was a governess in Boston until very recently! Do you not ever listen to a word anyone tells you dear brother?"

"Not such things as that, no! I just knew Carlton looks like the cat that got the cream since he brought her home. It is good to see him happy. He works too hard, and has no help."

"Well he does now - and he's hired Ted Holkham and young Eric Graham. He should find things much easier now."

"And a pretty wife to keep his home and make him fat. Sounds like bliss," Mack joked, but he couldn't deny that a small part of him was more than a little jealous of his friend. He had gotten lucky.

"I know you'll never admit that you would miss me if I weren't here, but one day I shall be married and out of your hair, and then you will regret not having taken a wife," Penelope said poking her tongue out at him.

"I know, and that is why I agreed to let you put that blasted advertisement in the newspaper in the first place. Now, I have found one woman out of too many to count that I would consider writing to I thought you would be happy."

"I am, and I shall tell Callum that finally there may be hope that we can wed and I can leave you to your own devices!"

"I have told you a hundred times dear sister; do not put off your nuptials just for me. He is a good man, he won't wait forever – no matter how besotted he is with you right now. You're not getting any younger after all," he teased. "I shall be fine, can take care of myself you know."

"If I left you for even five minutes you would burn your supper and the house down." She patted him affectionately on the cheek.

"Well, maybe Miss Annie will be able to come and take care of me and you will be free to burn Callum's toast every morning instead of mine!"

"Ha, ha! What are you doing today? Please tell me you will be getting out from under my feet you pest?"

"You'd send me out in that?" he asked incredulously, a grin tweaking at the corners of his mouth. "Don't fret. I shall be out of your hair. I am going to take a little trip into Great Falls. I need to go to the bank and discuss my plans for the herd. I may even stay overnight, take in a show, go to the barbers and get a good shave and trim. I may even pop by the station to find out how much passage to Boston on the train would cost."

"That sounds hopeful, and after only one letter too," Penelope said smiling, but Mack could see her brain working. She knew him too well, knew that he had found something in this young woman's words that had touched him and made him curious.

His curiosity had done them both a lot of favors over the years. Without it they would not have made the move here, and would not have taken the chance to become ranchers. His curiosity about their neighbor, Callum Walters, had also paid off handsomely. The quiet man had kept himself to himself upon his arrival in Sun River, but the perfectly tended fields full of handsome and hardy horses and his immaculate fencing had intrigued Mack. He had to know who was capable of such precision – especially as he was out there doing it alone. The moment the reclusive horse breeder had met Penelope had changed everything for them all.

Yes, his curiosity was a good thing, and Annie Cahill made him curious and he longed to unravel the mystery that surrounded her. Why should a woman with a good position wish to leave it and take the chance on a stranger? Why did her plain and simple words make him feel as if he had known her for a lifetime? Why did he want to find out more about her? He let Penelope leave the room and began to pen a reply, there was so much he simply had to know and he had a feeling that just a correspondence spread over weeks and months as their missives crossed the entire breadth of the country wasn't going to be enough to unravel the mystery she posed to him quickly enough.

Chapter Three

The letter that sat on Annie's bed was much thicker than anything she had ever received before. She didn't often receive mail, and rarely on such fine paper. The envelope was creamy, and the parchment like paper was soft and silky under her fingertips. She opened it carefully, keen not to damage even the tiniest bit of such elegant stationery. She pulled out quite a short letter and a train ticket to Great Falls, Montana. She picked it up and looked it over. She was sure it must be some kind of prank, or mistake. She only knew one person in Montana, and Myra's handwriting was altogether neater and prettier. Then she remembered, she had answered that ridiculous advertisement. It had been weeks, and it truly had slipped her mind as she had been so very busy.

He had responded, and had sent a ticket for her to use to join him. If it weren't so preposterous she could have jumped for joy. Who sent a ticket to a woman he had barely corresponded with? She should be ashamed of herself for presuming it meant he intended marriage immediately too – for her heart had definitely leapt with excitement at the prospect – because a one way ticket could only mean one thing, surely?

Dear Miss Cahill,

Thank you for your response to my advertisement. I am in good health I am gratified to let you know. Your hasty and apparently uncharacteristic missive pleased me and left me with many questions I simply must have answered. But, I must first do you the courtesy of enquiring after your wellbeing and pray that this finds you in the very best of health.

Please forgive my presumption for including a ticket at this ridiculously early stage of our correspondence, but I understand you are acquainted with the wife of one of my closest friends, Carlton Green. Dear Myra has offered to have you come for a short visit, so that we may see if we might suit. I do hope you will not mind my having spoken to them before I asked you – but when my sister Penelope put two and two together from the information in your letter I couldn't contain my curiosity that there may be somebody acquainted to you living just across the valley!

Please, if it is possible for you to do such a thing, I ask you humbly to join us here in Sun River for a short visit. It is a truly wonderful corner of the world. There are craggy, snow-capped mountains surrounding us and the valley is rich and fertile. Should you wish to, I would love to be able to show you the beautiful features of my home – especially the waterfalls that give the nearby town of Great Falls its name – there are five, and all spectacular in their own way. Sun River is a tiny hamlet, with only a few basic shops and a Saloon, but it is growing fast and looks likely to blossom in time. There is a good community, and the local minister comes to visit us every Sunday for services if you wished to attend.

There are three of us that farm here. Carlton grows crops; my sister Penelope's fiancé, Callum Walters, breeds fine horses and I raise cattle. So, we ride on sturdy mounts, eat well-grown grains and vegetables and have plenty of good quality beef – reasons to visit a place if ever there were any I hope. But the true blessings of this place are the people who live here and work here. It is an industrious community, and people have little free time – but they care greatly about each other and are always willing to lend a hand if they can. I hope that you will like it, at least as much as Mrs Green seems to be doing. She is settling in and making friends well, I am sure you will be glad to know.

Now, I believe you wanted to know a little bit about me. I am a bit of a lone wolf by nature. I enjoy ranching because it means I get to spend so much time alone, in the wild. I grew up in New York, always felt it too claustrophobic. There seemed to be so few opportunities. I was expected to become a ship builder like my Father, yet I could not take to that life. I became a sailor for a short time, travelled the world but never saw more than the ports of anyplace I travelled too. Soon I felt just as stifled being aboard a tiny boat as I had trapped in the city.

So, I came home and found that in my absence my Father had sadly passed away. Mama and Penelope were living on the tiny amounts I managed to send home. Something had to change, and so when the newspapers started talking about land, for free if you could work it and make it pay I tried to convince them that this was our chance. Penelope was all for it, but Mama didn't want to leave her home and friends. I could understand that, and so I tried to find work in the city as a laborer. There is always work in the docks, and so I spent my days as a stevedore, my nights I am ashamed to say were spent in bars. I tried to drink away my unhappiness.

Eventually I could take it no more, and I said that I was coming here, to Montana, whether my family would accompany me or not. I truly believe that I might not be still here had I not done so. Penelope would have followed me anywhere, but Mama did not wish to leave still. However, my Aunt Gwen was glad to take her in as my Uncle Harold had passed away and she too was lonely. They are both now thriving. They do all manner of charity work around the tenements near the docks. So many people have so very little there and disease is rife. They do good work and are content.

I have not been back to New York in over seven years, but I should like to see Mama. Penelope hopes she will come to Montana for her wedding, but I am not so sure she would be up to the journey. Even with the convenience of the station at Great Falls the journey is long and can be very draining (that possibly isn't what you long to hear as I try to convince you to come!) I should love to have the time to undertake the journey to see her – but cattle need care at all times. This is why I have included the ticket for you. Much as I would like to be able to meet you in Boston it simply isn't possible for me to do so.

I do enjoy reading, though I rarely get time to finish an entire novel, so I enjoy the short stories they sometimes publish in the newspapers, and poetry. I am writing this having just seen a rather splendid play in the theatre at Great Falls, and I quite like music – though I have never been much for opera. But I am happiest when I am out on horseback, riding across this majestic land, enjoying the sun on my skin and wind in my hair.

Your letter, though short gave me so many questions I long to ask of you. I want to know if you have ever been anywhere other than Boston; have you any family; what truly makes your heart beat faster and makes you feel alive are just a few of the many things I long to know about you. You gave so little away – and I have to say for an inquisitive soul like myself that was too much to resist.

I do not want a wife to just take care of house and hearth, though my love of the land and being free may indeed sound that way. I long for a wife who will be a true helpmeet, a partner and, if I may be so bold, a lover. This is why I believe it so important that we meet, and soon to find out if such things could ever be possible for us and so I can begin to unravel the enigma that you pose my dear!

I look forward to your response, and pray that I shall be able to meet you at the station should you accept my invitation to Montana.

Yours Hopefully

Mackenzie Stott

Annie sighed and clasped the letter to her breast. He made it all sound so wonderfully easy. But though he was able to comprehend that a trip to Boston to visit with her would be impossible given his commitments in Montana, he did not seem to appreciate that should she request the time needed for such a stay that she would most surely lose her position here. It was a huge gamble to take, one she was not sure she was quite ready to take on such a short correspondence.

His letter had amused her, and his outpourings had made her realize what a passionate and exciting man he must be, and also so unlike his advertisement in truth. He would be more than disappointed when he met her she was sure; she was such a mouse after all. There was little interesting about her. She had never been outside of a three block radius, let alone travelled the high seas and traipsed across the country in search of adventure as he had. Reluctantly she put the letter down and accepted that the simple and straightforward man she had so longed for did not exist – and that she would have to write to him later to end their correspondence. It was not fair to him, or to herself to continue to live in a fantasy world. She could not lie to him, make out that she was more than she truly was. She would not set herself up for such potential heartache.

The next days passed in their usual drudgery, yet the sunshine seemed to beckon to her, coaxing her out to play and explore. Each day she tried to find the time to go for a solitary walk, to feel the wind and the warmth on her skin the way Mackenzie had written of it. She had never stopped to notice such things before, had never taken the time to really appreciate what was around her every day. Now it seemed his words echoed in her head, and she felt more, saw more, and heard more than she ever had until now. The birds in the trees, the chatter and giggle of children playing in the park, and the pleasure of lifting her face up towards the sun. It felt wonderful, as if there was an entire world that she didn't even know about, and the more she did it the more she knew she had to do so again and again.

She still hadn't replied to him, and knew that it might be that her letter may not now reach him until after the date her train should be arriving. She wasn't sure what had stayed her hand. She had been so certain that she could not take such an indulgent risk, yet here she was feeling nervous and agitated. She wasn't unhappy, not exactly, just discontented. It was as if she had been walking round with scales over her eyes obscuring her view, and that Mackenzie's words had sloughed them away, letting her see the world clearly for the very first time. It was interesting, and vast, and she found herself longing to see something more than the inside of another family's home, though that little voice in the back of her head wouldn't stop telling her that she didn't deserve such pleasure, such joy, such hope.

"Annie, the new governess will be arriving tomorrow. I trust you will ensure her room is aired and cleaned meticulously. I do not want her to get the wrong impression of us," Mrs Hepworth said haughtily from the end of the corridor as Annie was just taking off her coat and boots. She felt her little moment of bliss slip away from her as the demands of reality took over once more. "I shan't ask where you have been when you should have been here working. I have been calling for you for a quarter of an hour, and that simply isn't good enough. Really, I don't know what has gotten into you in the past few days."

Annie knew better than to respond, to argue or even to try and explain anything. Mrs Hepworth didn't care about anything other than putting on a show to the rest of the world. The pretentiousness of the entire house and the extravagant parties they threw just made it more obvious to anyone who had ever been around those from the genuine upper classes. Annie's first position had been in the Boston home of an English Earl. The house had been filled with old family treasures, most ugly but all worth more than the entire contents of the Hepworth house. He hadn't cared one jot what anyone thought of him, or his home. He hadn't needed to. His title had bought him access to every drawing room and ballroom in the city without any effort. She missed working in such a place, but she couldn't bear to think about why she had been forced to leave.

Mrs Hepworth was still standing in the service corridor, looking down her long nose disdainfully at her. Annie suddenly felt the mischievous and adventurous spirit that seemed to have overtaken her in recent days begin to exert itself. Unable, and even unusually unwilling, to keep it under control she decided to stand up for herself, just this once. "Ma'am, all of my chores were completed and so I took a walk. The park is quite lovely with all the flowers coming into bloom." Mrs Hepworth sniffed and the furrows between her eyebrows deepened as she frowned down at Annie.

"Your chores are complete only when nobody in this house has no further need of you. It is not for you to decide when you may take time away from your duties." Annie looked at her incredulously. She knew her place, did not need to be told. She had never so much as considered breaking a single rule in the five years she had been in this household. Yet, she could not remember a single time when this woman had ever complimented her on a job well done. The strong and determined young woman she had spent so long trying to damp down and keep under wraps decided to take control. Annie was going to do something for herself, something that would make her happy. Suddenly she was certain that the consequences were more than worth it.

"Ma'am, I am glad you have sought me out as I have needed to speak with you," she said hurriedly as Mrs Hepworth made to move away, clearly she believed that there was nothing further that needed to be addressed. But for once Annie was not going to bite her tongue, was not going to be so careful that she actually ran away from life.

"Annie, I have better things to do," her employer said impatiently turning on her heel. It clearly wasn't the best time to be broaching this, but for the first time in her life Annie felt reckless. It didn't matter what happened. She knew Myra would not let her be homeless, would help her to find a position either back here in Boston, or in Montana if she needed one, should things with Mackenzie not work out. She was still young enough to have a life of her own. She was not going to stay and take any more from this cold and unfeeling woman.

"I wanted to let you know I need to take a leave of absence. I will need to be away for at least two months."

"Is your Mother sick?"

"No. My Mother died three years ago. You attended her funeral."

"Then what possible reason could you have to need such a period of time?" Mrs Hepworth said, undaunted by Annie's words. "I cannot spare you for even a day right now. The new governess is coming and will need your assistance in settling in and we have Carolynn's coming out ball to arrange after all. No, you simply cannot take the time right now."

"Then I shall have to offer you my notice."

"Don't be so ridiculous girl. What would possess you to be so foolhardy?"

"I am going to meet the man I hope to marry, not that it is any of your business. I have a life separate from my work Ma'am, and if you will not release me from my contract and offer me a character, then I shall go without one and have to take my chances." Mrs Hepworth's face told Annie that for once, she had managed to finally penetrate this woman's cold façade, and had shaken her to the core.

"But Caro's ball? Mr Hepworth will be furious!"

"And I am afraid that shall be your problem to deal with and not mine Ma'am. I shall be catching a train on Monday, so if you could possibly ensure that my wages are ready at the end of the week?"

"Your impertinence is noted, and there shall be no character, you little slut. How dare you do this to me? I shall not ensure your wages are ready, you have given me no notice and will leave me in a position that is simply untenable." Mrs Hepworth's handsome face was screwed up with venomous anger, but rather than feeling cowed, Annie actually felt vindicated.

"Ma'am. I have been doing my own work and that of the governess for two months, I am sure that the new governess can do the same," she said cheekily. "And, I shall go and see the gentleman that so ably assisted Mr Green with his little matter if you insist on not paying me. I am sure that a judge would perceive your not paying me what I am owed as being most inappropriate." Mrs Hepworth didn't seem to know what to say to that, she made an odd noise, something between a harrumph and a snort, and Annie had to hold back her giggles. "Oh, I was going to suggest a couple of young women who may have been available to assist you in my absence had you agreed to it, but I am inclined now to just let you find your own new maid. I wouldn't recommend working here to a single soul now."

Before she could lose her nerve Annie ran upstairs to her room. She had never been so rude, had never stood up for herself and her own wants and it felt peculiar. She felt equal parts of elation, fear, excitement and guilt. But she had paved the way for a new life. She could only hope that Mackenzie would not find her too dull and boring when he met her and realized this truly was the most dangerous and undoubtedly the most foolish risk she had ever taken.

Chapter Four

The herd veered left at speed. Mack cursed under his breath, and wheeled his horse around to try and corral them into the pen before they stampeded through the yard and straight through his house. He hated to admit it, but he really needed to get some help now the numbers of cattle had grown so large. It wouldn't take much for him to be the unsuspecting victim of a panicked charge. He vowed to see if there were any cowboys hanging around the saloon the next time he was in Sun River. If he had some help then he could leave these dawn starts to them, he certainly wouldn't miss them one bit. "Whoah there girls and boys," he hollered as he managed to outflank them and shoo the bolting steers and cows back towards the holding pen.

As he dismounted and fixed the gate he looked up at the sky. A grey cloud had been looming, and he was pretty sure that the heavens would open long before he had them sorted. He needed to separate out the pregnant cows from the herd to make sure they were healthy and everything was progressing as it should for them and to mark up any expecting twins. They would need extra care, and he would keep them in the paddocks close to the farm so he could bring them into the barn easily when their time to calve came. The steers would need to go back up into the foothills to fatten up before the thankfully short drive across country to Great Falls and then on by train to every State in the Union.

"Mack, Mack, where are you?" his sister called loudly. He could hear a note of panic in her voice. "Mack, you have to get to Great Falls!"

"Penny, you aren't making any sense. I've nothing to do but sort out this mangy lot," he said as he ruffled the soft brown head of one of his pregnant cows who was nosily poking her head over the gate, his stomach growling the need for breakfast.

"There's a letter. It's from her. I'm sorry, I opened it by mistake, but she is coming. She will be on the train today!" She thrust the envelope at him and he took it and looked from it and then back to her.

"But, if she is coming why didn't she let me know before? I thought she wasn't coming," he repeated foolishly. Penelope laid a soothing hand on his arm, hearing the way his voice had cracked. He truly had given up hope of hearing from her. He had convinced himself that he must have come on too strongly, or expected more of her than she was able to give and so she had simply decided to end their correspondence. It had felt strange to him. Even though they had only shared a few letters he felt he knew her, and she didn't seem to be the kind of person who would do that. But it had been easier to bear that way, because he had already begun to anticipate when another letter would come. He had been downcast when nothing had arrived day after day.

He took out the letter and read the few short lines Annie had penned, clearly in haste.

> *Dear Mackenzie (I hope you do not think me too forward using your Christian name, I rather like it. It is a little raffish and mysterious!)*
>
> *I am on my way to Montana. I am so very sorry I did not write sooner – but I wasn't going to come. I thought I would lose my position if I asked to for the time needed to travel for an extended stay (and I was right, I have managed exactly that!). I wasn't sure I*

was ready to take the chance on so short an acquaintance. I was scared I would give up everything only to arrive in Sun River and to have you dislike me. You said you want a true helpmeet, a lover and not just a wife. I wasn't sure I could deliver that. You sounded so very full of life, and courage. I have none. I have done nothing in my life and am so terribly dull. But I found that I have a devilish little imp inside me that has awakened. She wants to take some risks, and so I am coming. I shall be with you very soon. I can only pray you will not be disappointed in me.

Yours in all hopefulness
Annie Cahill

"I'd better get to town!" Mack gasped as his heart soared. She was coming, and she had risked everything to do so – for him. He knew it was too soon to know, but he prayed that she would find him amiable, that she would be the gentle calming soul her letters seemed to convey to him. But he was also more than pleased to find that she too had a reckless side, and could take risks when she felt it right. She trusted herself, as he trusted himself and he could only hope they would learn to trust one another.

"I think she must like you too," Penelope said sagely. "No woman would take such a chance on a complete stranger if she didn't. Be careful, don't you hurt her."

"I see you already care more for her than you do me – what if she hurts me? You didn't think of that possibility did you?" His sister merely smiled at him, turned and walked away without comment. "Penny, please can you ride over to Carlton's place and tell him he's got a visitor on the way?"

"Why should I?"

"For Annie, not me. It will be strange enough just coming out here and she will be exhausted from the journey. It wasn't so long ago that we came out here, remember how tough it was? The least we can do on her first night in Montana is to ensure there is a friendly face that she recognizes watching over her."

"You didn't need to beg! I'm on my way right now," she said

infuriatingly and marched back towards him and untethered Blackie from the fence. In moments she was up on his back and racing across the fields to the Green farm. He couldn't deny it; she truly was an incredible horsewoman. He should have gotten her out with the herds rather than letting her keep house for him – she could outride and out jump him any day of the week.

Mack rushed across the yard, and lowered the bucket down into the well. He didn't have the time to have a real bath, he would already be late, most likely, but he was determined that he wouldn't smell too badly of horse and cattle when he met her. He wanted to make a good impression, not have her racing to get straight back on the train. He made his way over to the stable and pulled out the gig. It was covered in dust, it so rarely got used. He quickly ran an old cloth over it, removing the worst of the filth but it still looked terrible. He had no choice though, it was this or nothing. Carefully he pulled out the harness from the back seat, and prayed it would last the journey. It was worn in too many places, but Penny's old mare, Mildred, was docile enough and wouldn't strain between the shafts too much so they should be fine.

In just ten minutes he was on the road, and on his way into Great Falls. As he drove he kept on thinking about Annie and what she had given up to be here, to be with him. To think he might have not known, and that she could have been stranded in a place where she knew no-one. He shook his head, and clicked to Mildred to go just a little faster. He didn't want to push her too hard, the roads were a little rutted after the heavy rains and then baking sunshine they had seen recently. But the old girl took it well and they made good time, reaching Great Falls just after lunchtime.

The train was due at twenty five minutes past two o'clock. He glanced up at the big station clock and saw he still had twenty minutes. He rushed to the bakery on the main street and bought himself a meat pie and some dainty pastries for them both for the journey home. He devoured his pie whilst walking back to the station at pace. He wanted to be there waiting for her. He certainly didn't want her to think that he didn't care for her enough to be there to meet her. He paced up and down nervously, now wishing he hadn't bolted his repast so quickly – it had only given the butterflies in his belly fuel and they were making the most of it.

Finally he saw the clouds of smoke and steam coming around the bend and heard the whistle of the train. He watched avidly as the great iron beast pulled up. He was fascinated by the lumbering great machines. Their huge power and their ability to take you almost anywhere you wanted to go appealed to him greatly. He wondered if he would ever get the chance to go in search of adventure ever again. The ranch needed him now, but maybe one day he would be able to go in search of new experiences. He wondered if Annie would be keen to join him, or if her one experience of travel would be enough for her.

He suddenly realized that he knew nothing of what Annie looked like. How would he ever recognize her? Was she petite, blonde, a redhead? He had no clue, and as the smoke billowed around him he wondered if he would ever be able to find her anyway. He could barely see his own hand in front of his face. But as the smoke finally cleared he saw a small woman standing nervously a few yards ahead of him, biting her lip and clasping and re-clasping her hands. She had delicate features, a smattering of freckles across the bridge of her tiny, tilted nose, and a figure with curves any man would be glad to explore. She wore a smart blue hat that matched her coat exactly and clean white gloves on her small hands.

Mack was rarely lost for words, but seeing her standing there and looking so lost and vulnerable he was speechless. He felt his breath catch in his chest as he moved towards her, and he longed to hold her and reassure her that everything would be fine, that he would take care of her, that she had nothing to fear. Yet the words would not come, he stood gaping at her, sure his mouth was wide open like a cod fish.

"Mr Mackenzie Stott?" she asked him after some time had passed. He jolted.

"Sorry, yes, yes. Annie Cahill I presume?" he said trying desperately to cover up his embarrassment at being stuck for words at the very sight of her. "How was your journey? I only received your letter this morning – I very nearly wasn't here to greet you!"

"I am so very sorry, it was such a spur of the moment decision. I so very nearly didn't come. I was so fearful of what I would lose; I simply couldn't focus on the things I might gain." Mack was aware how quickly they were both speaking, how breathless they both were and laughed. "I'm sorry," Annie asked with a quizzical look, "did I say something funny?"

"No, I was struck by how we are both so very nervous that we are speaking so rapidly to cover it up," he said. Her expression softened a little. "I am sorry, this isn't going the way I planned it. Can we maybe start again?"

Chapter Five

Annie looked at his face. It was a kind face, but rugged and tanned from his work out on the land. His eyes were the most vivid hazel she had ever seen and she could barely tear her eyes from them to even take into consideration the rest of him. He was very tall, she had to crane her neck to look up to him, but the fine features and laughing eyes made it worth any ounce of pain. Reluctantly she tore her eyes away from his, and looked him over quickly. She didn't wish to appear rude, and so she made her passing glimpse swift. She took in his broad shoulders and the tapering hips that made her feel tiny and powerless. It was an odd sensation, she had never really thought of herself as being particularly weak, or even that feminine before, but he made her feel as delicate as a china doll. He truly was an impressive figure of manhood, and she would have had to have been half dead to not find him attractive – but that just made her even more nervous.

"Of course," she said, finally responding to his gently asked question. "It is a pleasure to meet you Mr Stott." Awkwardly she looked down towards her feet and held out her hand for him to shake. He clasped it and held it tenderly for a moment. She couldn't help but notice his large, strong hands with those long and tapering fingers. She could see tiny scars where he had suffered nicks and cuts as he undertook his work, and feel the hard skin from riding out on the land and pulling on ropes on board ships. They were hands that would always catch you if you fell, she thought as a bolt of electricity flashed through her entire body.

"The pleasure is all mine," he said, his deep baritone voice rippling through her like music. He bent down and raised her hand to his lips and, in a move she hadn't expected, turned the palm over and unfastened her glove. He pressed his lips slowly to the inside of her wrist, and then carefully buttoned her back up. Her entire body quivered. Nobody had ever done such a thing to her before; it was so intimate, so sensual. Whatever she might think of him as a man, her body was certainly more than happy to respond to his advances. She felt light, shivery, almost faint with pleasure as he took her arm and tucked it into his own.

"So, how was your journey?" he asked politely again.

"It was an experience," she admitted with a wry smile. She had never been so frightened in her life. "There was a gentleman in my carriage; he didn't say a word to a soul the entire journey. We were all sure he was some kind of gangster, or gun for hire. He certainly didn't seem the warm and friendly type. He had the most spectacular moustache, and was constantly chewing on a small piece of wood – and he stared at everyone as if he hated us all."

"He sounds horrible, but it sounds as if you managed to make some friends to at the very least discuss his peccadilloes with?"

"I did. There was a lovely older couple, they got off at Billings, were going to see their daughter. She married a banker apparently and is expecting. And then there was Mr Craven. He is a Minister, is going to be building a chapel somewhere near us I believe. They were all most kind." He stopped her by an old gig. It was sturdy, but clearly hadn't been used in some time. "I can only apologize for the gig my dear, as I said I only got word first thing this morning that you were coming and so it is a little dirty," Mackenzie said, as if he was reading her mind. She looked up at him, a smile on her face.

"I don't mind dirt. I've been a maid for over ten years Mr Stott, dirt I can handle in spades," she said bravely. She was rewarded with a huge grin. He had the cutest dimples and his eyes literally sparkled when he was happy. She let him assist her onto the dashboard of the gig, and watched as he heaved her trunk up behind her. He barely seemed to have to even step into the tiny carriage, his legs were so long, and it looked a little uncomfortable for him to be so cramped up as he clicked to the horse to get moving.

She didn't really know what to say to him, and suddenly she felt utterly exhausted. He smiled down at her. "You look about all in," he said as he pulled a blanket from under the seat and tucked it around her knees. "I know it's warm now, but as the sun starts to set it will get quite chilly – and if you are tired you'll probably need to sleep. Don't you worry if that pretty little head of yours nods its way over to lean on my shoulder, I'll take good care of you and have you safely tucked up with Myra in no time at all." Gratefully she tucked herself up against him, and as the waves of tiredness engulfed her she soon drifted into a light sleep. She hadn't felt so safe since she had left home all those years ago and she allowed herself to sink deeper into her dreams.

"Miss Cahill, Annie wake up! Are you alright? You were screaming and moaning," Mackenzie said, his face a picture of concern as she was jolted awake. She gazed around at the huge mountains and the unfamiliar scenery, but was completely disorientated by the feel of his big, warm hands on her own. It was entirely too delicious, and distracting and she pulled away quickly.

"Oh, I was only dreaming," she said dismissively. She wasn't ready to admit those dreams to anybody, certainly not a man she barely knew. She had never spoken of the reason why she had left the Earl's employ, and she wasn't ready to face up to it and speak of it now – or ever. But it was good that he cared for her, though she was left wondering why she should have the nightmare now, of all times. She hadn't had the dreams in years though they had once been a part of her everyday existence, torturing her and making her dread the nighttime hours. No, it was just because she was overtired, and that everything was so strange and new. She was bound to feel a little discombobulated, she would get over it all in no time, and she would never need to speak of it ever again.

"We can go on now, I'd like to rest properly and I can't wait to see Myra and Carlton again," she said determined to change the subject, though something in Mackenzie's eyes told her that he may let her off now because she was tired, but that he wasn't the kind of man to let such a thing go entirely. She would need to remember that, and to make sure he never suspected that it was anything more than just a bad dream because she was so utterly and completely fatigued.

"Well, if you are sure, but I'm here if you ever want to tell me anything. I am like a closed book – I never tell anyone's secrets to a soul," he assured her. "Now you're awake I can tell you a little bit about Montana as we go if you'd like?"

"That would be lovely," Annie said glad of the change of subject and the chance to bury her thoughts and fears where they belonged once more. "Can you tell me about the mountains please? They truly are majestic, aren't they?"

Annie barely heard a word Mackenzie said, but he seemed happy enough to give her the full guided tour of his home. She sat quietly and wondered why she had ever thought that this could be a good idea. She should have known that those memories would come back at some point. She couldn't bear it. She simply didn't know what to do. Mackenzie was such a nice man and he genuinely seemed to care for her. She couldn't drag him into her own personal hell; it would not be fair on him. Yet, she so desperately wanted to be free of it all, to be able to start a new life. Why should such a thing, one not of her doing, have the potential to ruin everything?

Chapter Six

Mack rushed through the sorting, he simply couldn't wait to be finished so he could ride over to Carlton's place and see Annie once more. She was such a petite and pretty little thing, and despite being so tired she had shown a real interest and appreciation for the landscape they had driven through the day before. He wanted her to meet Penelope, and to see his home and the ranch, to meet his cattle and see everything. But he had a feeling that he may need to take things slowly. The nightmare she had endured told him she was more fragile than she wanted him to believe her to be. There was something in her past she had buried, and he had to find a way to help her to move past it.

He had seen many men, mainly in his days at sea, that had allowed old memories to fester and to congeal around their hearts. It made them unable to trust another soul and left them lonely and unhappy. He would not wish such a bitter existence on anyone, much less on the woman he was determined he would make his wife. He had never felt such a pull towards another soul before. Something in her called to something in him and he felt powerless to resist it. She thought she was dull, and of no consequence – but he saw something so very different. She was feisty and full of courage. She was honest and caring. He didn't know why or how, but she had captured his heart right from her very first letter.

"I brought you your breakfast, I presume you will be tearing off across the valley as soon as you are done," Penelope said with a twinkle in her eye.

"Would you like to come with me?" Mack asked, knowing his sister well enough to know that she would be itching to meet Annie as soon as possible.

"I'll let you have her to yourself today brother, but I shall invite her to supper tomorrow. Maybe we could invite Myra and Carlton too?"

"That sounds like a wonderful idea and thank you for my breakfast." He bit down into the large hunk of freshly baked bread, and then took a bite of the cheese she had handed to him in a bright red kerchief. He munched contentedly, and looked out over the land. He truly loved his home. He could only hope that Annie would fall in love with it, even if she couldn't fall in love with him – at least that way she would stay.

His breakfast consumed, he saddled Blackie and Mildred and put her on a lead rein, then set out. The sun was peeking in and out of fluffy clouds, but a large storm cloud was hovering off to the East. He wondered if it would hit today or later that evening. The wind was light, barely a gentle breeze. Maybe they would be lucky and he would be able to take Annie to see the Falls? He was sure she would find them breathtaking, and he couldn't think of a more romantic spot to ask her to be his wife. He knew it was sudden, probably too sudden, but he knew he didn't want to wait – knew that she was the only woman he wanted to spend his life with. So, why wait?

"Good morning neighbor," Carlton drawled with a huge grin on his handsome face. "I was expecting you at the crack of dawn!"

"I had cattle to sort – got interrupted yesterday, otherwise I might have been here even before the sun came up," Mack joked.

"She's a pretty little thing. Myra and she have been giggling and gossiping all morning – but she works!"

"What do you mean?" Mack thundered, Annie was supposed to be a guest in their home, not unpaid labor.

"Hold your horses, she was up before us both and had the kitchen spotless before we even knew what she was at. Said she wanted to be busy. I think she's a bit nervous. Be gentle with her." Mack stared at his boots, what if she was nervous because she didn't like him? What if she had realized she had made a terrible mistake in coming here, and keeping busy was the only way to stop herself from thinking of it?

"What have I done?" he said, taking off his Stetson and running his fingers through his hair.

"Stop that right now," Carlton said. "She's fine. Tiredness can do funny things to a woman. Myra was up all through her first night too; fidgeting and moving things around. It takes people a while to settle to anything new."

"Of course, you are right. I can't expect her to just fit, to know that this is right."

"But you do?" Carlton asked curiously.

"I do. I knew from her first letter."

"Me too, with Myra. Though she was the only letter I got - unlike you! I feel for you my friend. It is hard when we fall –especially until the day you are sure they have too."

Their conversation was stopped as Myra appeared out on the porch. "Well good morning Mackenzie. I presume you would like to take Annie out today? Do you need me to come along as a chaperone?" she teased as she gave him a welcoming peck on the cheek.

"I don't know, do you think it would make her feel more at ease?" Mack said anxiously.

"I think you will be fine. She is a sensible woman, knows her own mind. I'll just go and get her."

Mack paced up and down on the creaking deck, he hadn't ever though that something so simple as taking a girl for a picnic could ever make him so nervous, but his stomach was churning. "Ow," he exclaimed, as he bit too deep at the skin around his finger nails – a habit he had thought he had long ago abandoned.

"Good morning Mr Stott," Annie said in her sweet voice as she came through the screen door. She was wearing a pretty floral dress and her hair was lying in rippling waves down her back. He longed to bury his hands in the silky tresses and pull her to him for a kiss. But, the amused looks of his friends stopped him.

"I think it's time you called me Mackenzie, or Mack," he replied. "May I call you Annie?" She grinned, and he smiled back at her. "So, would you like to go for a ride?"

"But, I don't know how."

"I can teach you. I brought Mildred, she's old and steady. Penelope learned to ride on her when we first moved here and she's a better rider than anyone I know now. Mildred will teach you in no time." She nodded, but he could see a touch of wariness in her eyes still.

"I shall pack you both a good lunch," Myra said generously.

"No need, I have a saddle bag full of goodies, and an invitation for you all to join us for supper tomorrow from Penny. Do say you will all come?"

"We would be delighted," Carlton said as he moved to stand beside his wife and put an arm around her waist. Mack couldn't help but wish that he could do the same to Annie, to simply take her in his arms and reassure her that he would never let any harm come to her. But instead he stood awkwardly and said nothing.

"Shall we go then?" Annie finally said as she moved towards him. She took his hand and began to lead him down the steps towards the horses. "Now, how on earth do I get up there?" He put his hands around her waist and carefully lifted her into place.

"I hope you don't mind riding astride, we don't have a side saddle and very few women out here ride that way. Maybe we could get you some breeches if you decide you like it – that is what Penny wears."

"You are babbling again," Annie teased.

"I can't help it," he whispered so only she could hear. "You make me nervous."

"I cannot think why. I am not the scary type," she confided in him, leaning down to whisper in his ear. The gentle touch of her breath against the sensitive skin of his neck made him shiver.

"Oh, I think you are far scarier than you could ever imagine." She laughed and watched him closely as he mounted. He had never felt so exposed, so anxious to please anyone. He gently squeezed his heels into Blackie's side, and keeping a tight hold on Mildred's lead rein they walked slowly out of the yard and up onto one of the gently worn trails.

"I'll keep you on the rein until you feel a little more confident," he said as he dismounted once they reached a beautiful meadow full of wild flowers. "Would you like to trot? You'll need to stand up a little in the stirrups as you do, rise and fall with the movement otherwise your backside will be sore as anything!"

"Why not?" she said, her pretty face lighting up with her determination. Carefully he showed her how to squeeze just so into Mildred's flanks so the old horse would pick up her speed just a little, and watched carefully as she began to bounce around in the saddle a little. "I don't think I've quite got it!"

"Just feel the rhythm, and then rise and fall along with it," he encouraged her as Mildred turned in a wide circle around him.

On her third go she got the movement just right and her face was alight with joy. He grinned idiotically at her, as proud as she was of her achievements. "Want to go a little faster?" he said with a mischievous chuckle.

"Uh-huh," she said and carefully did as he told her to bring Mildred to a gentle canter. On her fourth circle he let go of the lead rein, and Annie didn't even notice that she was riding alone.

"Now, squeeze her again and go a little faster," he encouraged her. Mildred responded and moved into a sedate gallop, She was too old now for much more, but Mack could see how much Annie was enjoying herself. "Now pull back on the reins very gently and sit back in the saddle and she will naturally come to a gentle halt." Annie's face was a picture when she did exactly what she had been told and the well schooled old mare did exactly as she was asked.

"I rode!" she exclaimed happily.

"You did indeed. And very well too. You have lovely light hands, you'll not hurt her mouth and you learn very quickly," he said admiringly. She suddenly flipped her weight, bringing her leg over and dismounted just as he had done, landing right in front of him, so close he could feel the heat coming from her body. "Really fast," he said with an appreciative whistle.

"This is wonderful. Will I get to ride a lot if I stay here?"

"You can ride all day every day if you want to. You can come out with me with the herds, we can get you your own gun and a neat little holster to put it in," he teased as he mapped out where it would lie against her hip with his hands.

"I'd like that," she said breathlessly. Unable to stop himself, he dipped his head and kissed her rosy lips. They tasted sweet, and he pulled her to him as she began to respond tentatively. Her fingers crept up and began to twine around the curls at his nape, and he allowed himself to bury his hands in her long blonde locks. Breaking away he gazed into her eyes tenderly.

"Annie, I know we barely know one another, but will you marry me?" he asked her, knowing his hopes and dreams were written all over his face – she merely had to look at him to see how she set him on fire.

She pulled away abruptly. He looked at her, confused. She had been right there with him. That kiss had been mutual, and he was sure she cared for him too. Her face had gone cold, closed – as it had been when he had questioned her about her dream the day before. "I'm sorry. I should never have come, should never have thought that I could do this," she spluttered as she tried to move further from him, but Mildred's sturdy body was in her way. "Please," she begged, then turned to bury her face in the horse's body to hide the tears that had begun to fall. Mack spun her to face him.

"No! Now, you are going to tell me what this is all about. You clammed up on me yesterday, and I will not let you fob me off again."

"It is nothing. I can't change it. You can't change it. So what difference would it make?"

"It is clearly making a difference, if you cannot even tell me what the matter is. I may not be able to change it – but I can hopefully put your mind at rest and let you know that it doesn't matter. Nothing could be so very bad that you cannot even tell me."

"If I tell you, you will send me straight back to Boston and there is nothing for me there. You will never look at me like that again, and you will certainly never want me to be your wife."

Chapter Seven

Mack stared at her, but his face was not angry –just terribly sad. She longed to reach up and kiss the little lines around his eyes and on his forehead until they softened and went away, but it was not her right. She should never have come here. She should have known that her past would catch up to her, that she would never be free of it. Mackenzie was a good, kind man and he deserved a good wife, a chaste wife, an honest wife. But she could not bring herself to admit to her deepest and darkest secrets to him, or anyone.

"Annie, I am waiting," he said firmly. "Whatever you think is so bad that you could never be my wife cannot be as bad as you think. Your past is your past. I am far more interested in your future – your future here with me." Annie so longed to believe his words, but he was making promises he couldn't keep. No man could. How could any man ever accept her as she was, as soiled goods?

"Mr Stott, please do not make this harder on us both. I shall get the first train back as soon as I can. You will forget about me in no time and will find yourself a wife worthy of the name."

"I think you are worthy of the name of Mrs Stott and I have yet to learn anything that tells me otherwise Annie – and my name is Mackenzie."

"Stop this, please. I just can't," she cried tearing away from him and running as fast as she could. She had no clue where she was going, but she just couldn't be so close to him and keep her wits. Everything about him overwhelmed her, and she longed to give in – to believe he truly could forgive her anything but she knew that men simply couldn't do that. Society couldn't do that.

"Annie," she heard his heavy footfalls behind her. "ANNIE!" She turned, he had tears pouring down his cheeks too. Without thinking she reached up to wipe them away. He held her palm against his face and just gazed into her eyes. "I love you. Whatever you have done, I am certain that I have probably done worse. If you will tell me of your demons I shall gladly tell you of mine." Mesmerized by the sincerity in his hazel eyes she nodded and then sank to her knees in the long grass. He collapsed beside her and took her hand firmly in his. He took a deep breath and then began to speak softly.

"When I was at sea, I was lonely. I was never anywhere for very long and so like many sailors I often used to go to the brothels. We would get drunk and sometimes the women were badly used. Not by me, but I did nothing to stop my shipmates from doing so. For a brief while I served onboard a pirate ship, and we did some unspeakable things – but it meant I could send money home to my family to keep them safe. Nobody is perfect Annie, and I doubt if you have killed just so you can take the cargo from another man's ship, or ever used another human being ill, or stood by while such a thing was done. You are too good and too kind."

Annie stared at him; his confession was not what she had expected of him. She had guessed from his last letter that he had a past that was possibly more colorful than anyone she had ever known, but to think she was sat beside a real life pirate was strangely exciting. She simply couldn't reconcile the sweet and gentle man who sat by her side now with her idea of a cut-throat privateer.

"I don't believe you."

"You don't have to." He pulled up his sleeve and showed her a brand on his arm. "It is the mark they give you in the Indies if you are caught as the member of a pirate crew. I was lucky I wasn't hanged – but the Governor benefited from an unexpected cargo of rum – enough to keep him soused for many years - and our lives were spared." Annie giggled nervously. It was her turn, and though she knew he would not be as understanding of her past, she had to let him know that it didn't matter to her what he had done.

"You would never do such a thing again?"

"Never. My life is here, and I am content. I could be happy if you would agree to stay here with me as my wife."

"We'll see. You were young. You did what you had to. It doesn't compare."

"As you say, we'll see. Now it is your turn."

"When I left home I worked in the house of an English aristocrat in Boston. He wasn't in the country very often, but he had land and holdings here and so he visited for about three months of every year. However, he often allowed his friends to stay and use the house in his absence so there was always work to be done. I worked as a scullery maid. I was the lowest of the low and some of the male guests did not always behave as the gentlemen they were supposed to be." She stopped, unable to say exactly what they had done. But she could see the truth dawning on Mackenzie.

"They forced you?"

"Some of them did. One even professed to love me, wooed me and convinced me he would marry me and take me away with him. I fell pregnant. I believed it would all be resolved as he had said he loved me and could not live without me. But when I told him I never saw him again. Earl Lightfoot fired me on the spot, and I had to go home to the tenements where my poor Mama was dying of consumption. My sister was trying her best to bring up my brothers and sisters on the tiny wage I had sent home – but it was not enough and without it we were in dire straits indeed."

"What happened Annie? Because I see nothing that you have to be ashamed of. I see men who should have known better, men who took advantage of your youth and your kind soul. I see a world where the person most in need of care and support was the one cast out. None of that reflects badly on you."

"I sold my child! I sold my baby boy so I could get back to work, because I couldn't care for him!" she cried, unable to take any more of his kindness, his understanding.

"Oh Annie," he said tenderly as he pulled her to him and cradled her and let her sob. "You did what you had to do. Is your child well cared for? Does he want for anything?" She shook her head. "Then you did what was best for him. What more could you have done?"

"I should have found a way," she murmured.

"How old were you when this happened Annie?"

"I was fifteen."

"Oh my poor, poor girl. Such responsibility, such hardship to bear when you were so young. Like you so easily forgave me for my youth and foolishness – and I was in my early twenties when I was being so reckless with my life and those of others – I can forgive you anything. But, the problem is not my forgiveness is it? You can never forgive yourself, but you have to – for all the reasons you were able to forgive me. You were young and you had no choice. You did what you had to, in order to survive a brutal world. If I were still the pirate I used to be I'd be on my way to Boston to punish the men responsible."

"But don't all men want a virgin bride?"

"I could hardly judge you on terms of chastity. I chose to be unchaste – you were forced. How could I ever punish you for a sin I have committed myself. Your past is your past. You have no intentions of being unchaste once we are wed do you?"She shook her head. "Then you will marry me?"

"You sneak," she said her eyes lighting up. "You caught me. Yes, if you truly can forgive me I will marry you and the sooner the better!"

"Would you like me to see if we can have your son restored to you?"

"You would do that for me?" He nodded. "No, he is happy and loved. It would break too many people's hearts to do so. But thank you for offering to do so. I do not deserve you."

"No Annie, it is I who do not deserve you – but maybe we can make a happy life together, a pair of old sinners!" He kissed her and she melted into his arms, glad to be free of her burden of guilt at last.

Epilogue

The church in Great Falls was brimming with gardenias and lilies. The scent was intoxicating, but even more entrancing was the sight of his bride walking towards him on Carlton's arm. Mack had never been so happy in his entire life. Myra helped Annie to remove the veil from over her face and he was glad to see that she was wearing the self same excited grin he wore himself. She was truly beautiful, and kind and good. He would spend the rest of his life gladly making her happy.

"Do you Mackenzie Gladwin Stott take this woman to be your wife," the Minister intoned.

"I do, with all my heart," he replied.

"And do you Annie Cahill take this man to be your husband,"

"I do, gladly," she said solemnly.

"Then I now pronounce you man, and wife!" Without waiting for permission Mack lifted his bride and kissed her, not caring who was watching them – just knowing he had to claim her for his own forever and always.

Putting her down gently, they began to walk back down the aisle of the little chapel, and he took her hand in his. He felt a piece of paper in her hand. "What is this?" he asked as he took it from her and began to smooth out the wrinkles. A picture of a small boy stared back at him, his face alight with happiness. "Apparently they couldn't get him to look solemn," she said. "The photographer was apparently furious, was worried the exposure wouldn't come out right!"

"He is a handsome young man. I am glad he was here with you my love. And I have a surprise waiting for you at the ranch."

"A surprise? Whatever could you have been up to?" she asked impatiently.

"You shall have to wait," he teased. But no matter how much she tried to coax it from him he was not prepared to utter one word more. He lifted her up into the smart open carriage he had hired for the day and drove her back home. Waiting on the porch for her was her beloved sister and her two younger brothers. "I hope you don't mind, but I need some strong young men to help on the ranch, I figured you'd like it best if I could keep it in the family." She took his face in her palms and kissed him.

"You pirate, still kidnapping folk I see! Thank you. You will never know how much this means to me." He watched as she leapt out, her veil billowing behind her and was engulfed in the loving arms of her family. He was certain he knew exactly what it meant, because not having Penny by his side would have been, until now, the worst thing he could ever imagine. Now, the two orphaned families could become one happy, large one and that made him happier than he could ever have imagined too.

The End

✶ ✶ ✶ ✶ ✶ ✶

A Bride for Ethan Book 3

Chapter One

"You look like you could take on a rattler, a mountain cat and still have enough anger left over to tackle Mrs Wainwright," Cook said as Maggie stormed back into the kitchens at Young's Hotel.

"Don't even get me started Ellen, and I think it might be best if I stay out of the way of our erstwhile housekeeper or I may find myself out on the streets without a character," she said thoughtfully. "I have about had it up to here with idiots today."

"So who was foolish enough to rile you this time?" Maggie sank into a chair by the fire and looked at her friend's earnest face. Ellen never got angry at anybody, but Maggie seemed to have been born furious. It was as if she had been born in the wrong place and at the wrong time. She seemed to want everything that her gender weren't supposed to - like a career and purpose in life. She had no issue with women who longed to be wives and mothers, but something inside her had always been crying out for more. Men were allowed to have both a home and a family, why should bright and capable women be any different?

Many years ago she had felt forced into making a choice, one that had cost her much, though it had set her on a path to the success she had achieved, becoming second in command in the vast kitchens of one of Boston's finest hotels. Though she was sure she had been right to take the risks she had, there was still something missing – and so her annoyance seemed destined to haunt her forever. But knowing something wasn't enough had never been something she could accept and so she was sure there had to be a solution. There had to be a man out there, somewhere, who could accept that she had as much ambition as he?

Her mentor looked at her with compassion.

"So you have placed your advertisement?" she asked. Maggie nodded. "And it didn't go well?"

"I am not a young woman in need of rescuing Ellen, you know that. How dare that little fool treat me in such a way, it isn't some pimply clerk's job to humiliate and belittle me because I am a strong woman prepared to take a stand to create the future I want."

"Oh dear, the poor lad. I presume his ears will be ringing for a week?" her friend gave her a wry smile. Maggie had to grin, Ellen knew her so very well.

"No I kept my temper for a change, but I was tempted. That little brat couldn't have been more than sixteen and he had the cheek to ask me to supper when he saw the advertisement I was placing. The horrible creature assumed I must be desperate!"

"You have to admit Maggie, very few women would take such a step. It is easy to misconstrue such an action."

"Oh stop being so kind. He was in no way being kind and charitable, nor did he actually want to take me to supper. He was being rude and offensive and thought it all a joke."

"Oh Maggie, are you sure this is such a good idea? After all, if the young man at the newspaper thought it all a joke had you not wondered what kind of responses you may be likely to receive? What if the only people who respond are reprobates and bandits?"

"Either would be preferable to that tow-haired little fool at the Matrimonial Times office," she said with a grin. "Of course I have thought about it, long and hard, as you well know. But I am never going to find a man here, and if I apply to an advertisement I have no control over whether he picks me and I have only a few lines to try and find out if he is good and kind. At least this way I am the one choosing, and I am the one who can decide yes or no." Ellen looked at her, skepticism in her eyes but she didn't say any more.

Maggie had been working at Young's since she turned fourteen. She was now twenty- seven and she had watched girls leave and find husbands who were less capable, far more stupid, and occasionally less pretty than her. She was fed up of it always being everyone else's turn and she was never going to find a man while she was tucked away where nobody could ever see her. She loved her work, and had risen to being second in command to Cook, who ruled the kitchens as if they were an extension of her own loving family. But she had deserved to do well and she wanted a family, and though she was self-sufficient she longed for a man to care for her, who she could care for too. So, when she had seen that women were beginning to place their own advertisements in both the Boston Globe now, and in the Matrimonial Times, she knew it was time to take a chance.

The days passed slowly as she waited for the first responses to arrive. She knew that she would only be likely to attract a certain kind of man – few would be strong enough in themselves to welcome a woman so independent that she would take such matters into her own hands. But she was prepared for the oddities that may respond too. She prayed that somewhere out there was a strong man who would be happy to let her be a strong woman – and wouldn't mind that she was a little bit older, a little bit more set in her ways.

* * * * *

Talented Cook, seeks a kind and honest man with a view to matrimony. He should be happy to let her be as she is, and not try and change her. He should enjoy laughing and be well read. To like children and to consider the possibility of a family would be welcomed. The subscriber is happy to make and maintain a loving home and would be happy to take on the responsibility of a child not her own. All Responses to Box 476, Matrimonial Times

Ethan looked at the advertisement his sister had circled in bright red ink. Annie would never be so crude as to tell him to his face that he needed a wife, but she had her ways. It made him chuckle to think of her poring over the newspaper just for him. He was more than happy on his own, and he simply couldn't understand why Annie was so insistent that he was lonely. He had never been happier since they had moved here to the ranch just outside Sun River, Montana. Herding cattle seemed to come naturally to him, and he had to admit he enjoyed the solitude of being away with the herd so much too. It gave him much needed respite from the demands of being part of such a huge family once more.

"Annie, you need to be a little more subtle," he said with a grin as she waddled into the kitchen, her swelling belly and happy face telling a story all their own. "You have to stop trying to get us all to settle down. We'll do it when we're ready."

"I can't seem to stop myself. Myra said I was nesting, that I want everyone around me settled and content, and life as stable as possible around me. It's something pregnant women do apparently. But, I think it is just because you always look so sad. Ethan, you are a wonderful young man and it would be good for you to have a wife. You're nearly thirty after all."

"And that is your criteria for when a man needs a wife? I have a full four years before I turn thirty, so come back and nag at me then. In the mean time, why not find John a wife – he seems to be much more inclined to go in search of female company than I."

"Which is why I don't need to give him a nudge you great galoot. And because at only eighteen he needs some of his rough edges smoothed off before any poor girl should have to be expected to take him on!"

Ethan shrugged. Maybe she was right. Maybe the fact he was always so tongue tied around girls was because it meant so much more to him than it did to John. His younger brother was one of those people who seemed to have more confidence than they should, but he wasn't arrogant or mean with it. He just knew who he was. Ethan had never felt so certain. He wondered if it had something to do with being the eldest boy in a family that was almost split into two generations. He and Annie were both so much older than Hannah and John because Mama had sadly lost a number of babies in between them.

The two of them had been forced to grow up early and take responsibilities beyond their years. Everything had changed for them after Papa had died, and Mama had taken ill. Both he and Annie had gone out into the world to do the best they could to support their family while Hannah and John had been left at home to care for Mama, despite their own tender years. It had been tough for them all, but Ethan and Annie had ensured that both of them got to attend school too – a luxury that neither of them had been so lucky to receive.

But consumption had finally taken its toll, and the family had fragmented; each going their own way. Ethan had started out working in Boston as Annie had, but as work for uneducated men became more scarce in the bustling city he had been forced to move further afield, and had taken jobs wherever he could find them. John had become a clerk at the local court house, and Hannah - well she was still so young when Mama had died, and with Ethan in Colorado by then and Annie in service nobody could take her in, and John had been too young. So she had been made a ward of the courts and had been taken against everyone's wishes into the Boston orphanage. But her siblings' continuing financial support had meant she could continue her education and she was as bright as a button.

At least, that had been the way it was right up until Annie had gotten married to Mack. The sentimental soul had tracked them all down, had paid for them to come as a surprise for Annie. He had even managed to get the court to award Hannah's guardianship to them now they were married and such pillars of their local community. Everyone had been delighted to be back together once more, but the close proximity of so many people living together after years of solitude could be tough at times too.

Ethan had been impressed by his brother in law's generous and thoughtful gesture when the telegram had finally caught up with him in Alabama, where he had been working as part of a logging crew. Annie had been the only one of his siblings who had written to him religiously as he had made his way across the country, trying all manner of different jobs in his attempt to find a home and a career he could love. He wouldn't have missed her wedding for anything – and then when Mack had offered them all work and a home together once more he had almost wept. But it seemed that his years of solitary wanderings had made it tough to spend so much time around others and so his work on the land gave him the respite he needed.

Annie kissed him on the forehead and bustled outside. He picked up the newspaper again and re-read the words highlighted so clearly. This woman didn't sound like any woman he had ever known. No, that wasn't true. This woman sounded exactly like the one woman who had captured his heart and held it tightly in her grasp ever since. But, it couldn't be. She had been so adamant that a husband and children were not things she wished to appear in her future. But he knew things could change, people changed. He knew he had. But that made it even more unlikely it could be her. He couldn't really be so lucky to find that she was still available, and more to the point looking for a husband, could he? But did he truly wish to see her again after the way she had so ruthlessly trampled over his heart?

But even if it wasn't her, it was someone like her and there could only be a small amount of women that feisty, that determined and that independent in the world. Maybe he might get lucky, and by applying he just mayfind himself someone capable of wrenching his heart away from the phantom grasp of his childhood sweetheart after all this time. Annie was right; he did need to settle down. He longed to be a part of a loving relationship just like the one she shared with Mack – but he wouldn't settle for second best and most women were just too darn insipid these days. He needed a woman not scared to speak her mind, a woman that took risks and fought for what she believed in. The woman in this advertisement sounded like she just might fit the criteria. But would she be able to live up to his memories, his dreams? There was surely only one way to find out.

Chapter Two

Maggie pushed the stray strands of hair back from her face and then returned her attention to the large mass of dough she was kneading. She loved baking. Just the idea of it fascinated her. How the simple ingredients of flour, water and starter could create something so fluffy and delicious and good never failed to astound her. As she felt the dough become silky under her hands she popped it carefully into a bowl and put it by the fire to prove gently, while she took up the next batch. Kneading was soothing. It helped her to get rid of the anger, the frustrations that seemed to bubble up within her all the time.

"Maggie, do you think you would be able to take responsibility for the kitchens for a couple of weeks?" Mrs Wainwright was suddenly standing by her side. The stern housekeeper had a tendency of moving so silently you didn't even notice she was there until it was too late, and it was more than a little disconcerting.

"Of course, is Cook all right?" she asked concerned. Ellen had been looking a little tired recently, and Maggie knew she was worried about her sister who lived on the family farm a little way upstate.

"Yes, but her sister has sadly passed away and Cook needs to arrange and attend the funeral. I have assured her that the kitchen will be in safe hands, but you know how she worries." Maggie was stunned. Mrs Wainwright had always appeared to be cold as ice, with no compassion for a soul. Yet here she was, clearly concerned for Cook. But, she supposed that the two women had worked together, here at Young's, for over twenty years and had both reached the pinnacles of their domain - it was to be expected that they should have some kind of relationship – even if it was never on show to the staff around them. Ellen could have confided in her of such a thing, especially when she thought of the amount of times she had berated the women who now looked so genuinely concerned. She had to admit, she felt a little ashamed of herself for doing so now.

"Tell her to take as long as she needs Ma'am, I can take care of everything here. I shall arrange something from the staff here in the kitchen for her, to let her know we are thinking of her."

"That would be kind. The hotel will, of course, send flowers on behalf of all the staff but I know she would be touched by something a little more personal from you all." Maggie was sure she saw the flicker of a tear in the steely grey eyes, but Mrs Wainwright had turned and left long before she could confirm it. Who would ever have thought that the old dragon had any feelings at all? But, that wasn't what was important now. She had to catch Cook before she left.

She ran up the back stairs to the senior staff's bedrooms and without knocking she barged into Cook's. She looked up, startled. Her eyes were red rimmed, and puffy. "Oh Ellen I am so very sorry for your loss," she blurted as she rushed forward to hug the woman who had been like a mother to her over the years. "You've been so wonderful listening to me moan and complain about the trivial troubles in my life, and barely said a word about how serious things were for poor Patricia."

"So Millie spoke with you then?"

"Mille? Mrs Wainwright is a Millie?" Maggie asked incredulously. "I had her down as something altogether more fearsome – maybe Ermentrude or Earnestine!" Ellen gave her a tight little smile.

"You are ever so naughty, even now. You need to try and curb that just a mite love," she warned.

"I doubt I'll change much now Ellen. But, other than taking care of things here, is there anything else I can do for you?"

"No, you just keep things ticking here. I'll be back in no time. There isn't much to sort out. Patricia wasn't a wealthy woman. Like me she lost her husband young, but she has a daughter and she will need my support."

"Take however long you need Ellen, don't rush back. We'll be more than all right."

"I know sweetheart. You're a good girl." Maggie gave her another quick squeeze, and turned to go.

"I've had some replies," she said suddenly. Ellen looked up at her and smiled.

"Now that is wonderful news. You know, I've always thought it such a shame you let that young man of yours get away when you first came here. He always struck me as the sort that would have been more than happy for you to have your career too."

"I know, but I didn't see that until it was too late and I had sent him packing. The world doesn't make many like him sadly. But let's hope that someone just like him will be hiding in the pile of letters I have to look through and I will be able to make amends after all." Ellen stood up and moved towards her. Patting her affectionately on the cheek she gazed steadily into Maggie's eyes.

"Don't be so stubborn this time." Maggie laughed wryly.

"That is like asking a light not to shine, or the sea to not be salt!"

"I know, but you can do it. Be gentle on him and yourself. Good luck and write to me about it all."

"I shall. Safe journey. Now I really must get back to the bread or there will be no loaves for lunch."

She ran back downstairs, wiping furiously at the tears pouring down her cheeks. Poor Ellen, she was being as stoic and brave as always – and dispensing good advice too. Maggie wasn't sure why she had confided in her, but was glad she had. Ellen was the only person who had known about her young man all those years ago – and that she had pushed him away because she had been so set on having a career and had believed that a husband would only hold her back. She had regretted it ever since, but he had disappeared and she was left wondering what might have been.

The pile of letters still sat on the kitchen table. She had been using the bread making as a distraction, too nervous to even look at a single one. But with Ellen's words of encouragement she sat down and began to sort them quickly. She was stunned to see that there were over thirty of them. Each had a neatly printed envelope and the return address of the Matrimonial Times. People had actually responded, and in such numbers. She hadn't expected there to be so many men interested in her. She had worded her advertisement so clearly – to make certain they knew she wasn't some simpering little thing and would not be an easy conquest.

She ripped open the first one and scanned the first few lines. The man sounded like a complete idiot. He clearly hadn't read her words at all, had probably just responded to every woman he could. She put it down and opened the next one. He wasn't any more suitable either. She opened and scanned, and threw each letter down getting more and more frustrated. Why had not one of them read her advertisement properly. Each and every one of them was only concerned with what she could do for him, and each and every one seemed to just want a woman to cook and clean and maybe have his babies. Well, that wasn't for her, at least it wasn't the only thing she wanted from her life.

She wanted to be married and she wanted a family, but she did not want it to be her only focus in life. She was talented and clever and she needed more of a challenge than that. She had to hold fast to the belief that there was someone for her, and not allow herself to just throw the remaining letters in the fire. It would be so easy to get dismayed, to believe that every letter would be the same, but she had to be strong. She knew that this would be like looking for a needle in a haystack when she had placed the advertisement. For once she had to be patient. She would save them until later, would read them in privacy in her room. Maybe, just maybe there would be one decent man in this sorry collection?

Her day dragged, and her mood did not improve. She was worried about Ellen and frustrated at life and the caliber of the possible marriage pool open to her. But once she was sitting quietly in her room after supper she took a deep breath and began to open the remaining letters. She knew not to have her hopes too high, but it seemed that even her low expectations had been too much - until she came across a letter written in a sloping script that was strangely familiar.

Dear Talented Cook,

I dare say you have had many replies to your rather unusual and very pertinent advertisement. But I pray that I will be the man you respond to. Your words reminded me of a woman I once knew and she was a real firecracker. I suspect that you may be just as feisty and if so, that would be a wonderful thing.

I do not long for a peaceful and doting wife. I would much rather one with her own ideas and opinions, and a desire to be whoever she wishes to be. If that is to be the mother of my children that would be wonderful, but if she would prefer to have a career of her own I would support her in her every endeavor.

I am a cowboy. I have been a logger, a stevedore, a trapper, a miner, and even tried panning for gold at one time. But my life here in Montana seems to suit me best. I currently share a home with my married sister and her husband. My younger brother and sister live here too. We have been separated for many years, and I would very much like to stay with them, for a time at least. We have missed out on so much in one another's lives.

The ranch I work on belongs to my brother in law, but with the new homesteading opportunities here my brother and I may be able to claim further lands nearby -and so, between us, we could own much of the valley and build quite the enterprise.

Strong women are much needed here in Montana, and those with good hearts and valuable skills are thought much of. I would be honored should you choose to correspond with me, to see if we might suit. I look forward to finding out more about you.

Yours most humbly

Ethan Cahill

Maggie's heart leapt at the sight of the name, so neatly written at the page's end. How could this be? How could kind, loving Ethan not be married and settled? And who was the mysterious firecracker he remembered so fondly? A shot of jealousy surged through her. But then she stopped and looked at his words once more. What if the firecracker was her? Could it be that he still harbored feelings for her? Surely that would be too good to be true? He had once been her very reason for being, but she had never wanted the life of a wife and mother that seemed to be the only path open to her should she remain with him. But, she remembered his gentle eyes and loving ways every day, and her memories of his strong, hard body and tantalizing kisses could still have her feeling flustered even after all these years.

But would he respond once he knew it was her? And if she didn't admit to her identity in her responses, how would she ever be able to explain why she hadn't been honest from the start? But she longed to find out about his adventures, to know how he was. She had to know if he truly was happy, that she hadn't hurt him so badly that he had been lonely ever since she had left him. She jumped up to get paper and pen from her chest, and began to write. The words flowed effortlessly, right up until she reached the point where she had to sign her name. She paused, chewing anxiously on the tip of her pen, still unsure whether to tell him the truth now or later.

Chapter Three

A pounding of hooves on the trail behind him alerted Ethan that he had company. He turned to see his brother's stricken face as he reined his horse in abruptly. "Ethan you've gotta come home," he said. "It's Annie."

"Annie? But everything was coming along fine when I left. She seemed positively glowing." He could feel the anxiety in him grow; they had only been together such a short time. He couldn't bear the thought of losing any of his siblings again.

"No, she's well. It's just the baby, it's coming!" John said excitedly. "She said she'd hang on as long as she could. She wants us all to be there." Ethan could tell by the look on his young face that John was not so happy about this idea.

"Never upset a pregnant woman John, if that is what she wants, then that is what we must do. The herd will be fine here for a few hours I guess. Come on, I'll race you back!" John grinned at him, and they both kicked their mounts to a gallop. John's new gelding was fast, but he was temperamental. Ethan had chosen a sturdy beast, bred by Penelope's new husband. Mack's sister now lived just across the valley from their ranch and Callum Walters, her besotted new husband, was renowned throughout Montana - up as far as Washington in the West and even down in Texas to the south for the quality of his horses. They were ideal for ranching. They could go all day, but they also had a turn of speed that could best any but the finest race horses.

When they returned to the comfortable clapboard ranch house the two men found it in uproar. Penelope had arrived, and she and Hannah were bustling between the main bedroom and the kitchen with hot water and plenty of linens. Mack looked almost distraught as he paced up and down on the porch, while Callum was puffing away on his pipe even though it was still unlit. "How is she?"

"Hannah said she was doing fine, but you hear such stories," Mack said distractedly. Callum's face blanched. He had yet to go through the birth of his first child, but it would not be long as Penelope wasn't too far behind her sister in law. But everybody knew of the dangers women faced in childbirth. It was a wonder they ever let a man near them.

"She is fine. Everything is going well," Penelope said firmly as she waddled outside to give them an update. "I think you will have a strapping son Mack, she's coming along so fast so long as none of you buy us troubles with your worrying!"

"It's being out here and knowing nothing," Mack said. Ethan could hear the frustration in his voice. He had to admit, he wondered why Annie had ordered him back from his work. It wasn't as if he could do a thing other than just sit and wait. "Why can't I come in and see her?"

"Because it isn't right. It's woman's work to do without men under our feet."

"Well you know what tradition means to me Penny. I don't give a fig for it. I'm going up to see my wife." Without waiting for her to react he stormed inside and ran up the steep stairs two at a time, Penelope following as fast as she could.

"Stop, you can't. It isn't right," she remonstrated with him as Ethan and John followed them up. Mack paid her no heed, and stormed into the bedroom. They heard a brief shriek, and then a deep murmuring.

"Penelope, I don't think he's going to listen," Ethan said to her as he laid a gentling hand on her arm. "You need to be calm too, you don't want your little one to come early now do you?"

"Men!" she exclaimed and shook her head in frustration.

"Sorry," Ethan said with a grin. Finally she smiled back at him. "We have seen much worse, it won't shock us one bit."

"I know, you boys are out with calves and foals – in all weathers. But it just feels wrong."

"Come on, let's all go in. If Annie wants us all gone, I will personally drag Mack out of there for you."

Annie was propped up in the bed, sweat pouring down her flushed cheeks. Her legs were spread wide, but covered with a sheet that looked sodden with her sweat. "New sheets for you my love," Penelope said as she began to quickly strip the bed, hardly needing to move Annie at all.

"Thank you." Annie gasped as another contraction rocked through her. "I think I need to start pushing now."

"Do you want me to banish them all?" Ethan asked nodding towards John and Mack who were holding a hand on either side of his sister.

"No, I'm glad you are all here. It feels right to have my entire family here."

Mack sat on the bed, and pulled his wife against his body. "You scream and holler all you want," he assured her as she rested into his solidity. "But, if you need to squeeze hard on a hand, I'd be glad if you made it John's!" he joked. Everyone laughed, but another contraction came swift and fast, and so the moment of levity soon passed.

Ethan was impressed as he watched Hannah and Penelope guide Annie through her ordeal. It was clearly painful, but thankfully it was swift. Almost as soon as Hannah told her sister to begin pushing they could see the head of the baby and with just a few good pushes he was out and hollering up a storm. Ethan was moved more than he would ever have imagined as he watched his youngest sister carefully swaddle the child and take it to its mother.

"Have you done that before?" he asked her quietly as she began to tidy away all the soiled linens.

"There were always women nearby having babies Ethan, it wasn't as if you can stand by and do nothing." He knew of many people who had lived in the tenements in which they had grown up who would have done nothing to help a single soul. "But, I also helped out at the orphanage. Often young girls would come to us, to have their child in safety and then leave the babe with us."

"I'm so sorry we had to leave you there Hannah."

"I don't mind. I was happy there, in my own way. I learnt a lot of useful things, and you and Annie made sure I could still go to school. I'd like to become a midwife. I think it would be wonderful to be able to help women as they go through this."

"You'd be wonderful at it, if this was an example of your skills. You kept Annie calm as anything," he said admiringly.

"Oh, Ethan," Annie said weakly from the bed, a look of absolute infatuation in her eyes as she gazed down at her beautiful new son, "there was a letter for you yesterday. I put it on the mantle, behind the pewter candlestick for you."

"Only you would remember a thing like that, at a time like this," he said giving her a smile. "Congratulations to you both," he added as he shook Mack's hand and moved forward to kiss Annie and the new baby on the forehead.

"Would you mind if we call him Henry?" Annie asked Mack cautiously.

"Not at all, but why Henry?"

"Because Henry was Papa's name," Ethan said, spying a tear in his sister's eye. John and Hannah all nodded, and he pulled them to him. "He'd be proud as punch Annie."

He ushered his siblings from the room, and found Callum waiting awkwardly on the stairwell. "You could have come in, none of us would have minded," Ethan said as he slapped the quiet man on the shoulder affectionately.

"It was a moment for family, it wouldn't have been right."

"You are family Callum." The shy man blushed beet red at the compliment and beamed at Ethan. "You are the proud uncle of a new baby boy called Henry, go on in and meet him."

He went downstairs and walked into the parlor, where the letter Annie had spoken of sat awaiting him. "John, could you maybe ride over and tell Myra and Carlton the good news? He asked as he sank down into the comfortable wing chair by the fire.

"Anything to get out of here!" his younger brother said, poking his head around the door. "Can I go up and check on the cattle once I'm done? It would be nice not to have to come back for a day or so while everyone goes silly over the baby."

"That is your nephew John, but yes. I'd be glad of a day or two back here and I don't think Mack will be leaving Annie for a while yet so somebody needs to be up there. Be careful, and any trouble you come right back here, d'you understand?" John nodded. They had never left him alone with the herd, but he was more than capable. He could just be a little too impetuous at times. But he could understand why an eighteen year old boy didn't want to be in a house with a new baby.

Ethan picked up the ivory handled letter knife from the table beside him and slit through the cream envelope. It had come from Boston, and he could only hope that meant he had received an answer from the mysterious advertiser. Other than Maggie, he had never really found women that distracting, but in recent weeks he had found himself continually wondering what the intriguing woman who had placed that advertisement might be doing, who was she, and why was she in search of a man?

"Dear Mr Cahill,

I was delighted to receive your response to my advertisement. You would not believe how many of the men who did respond were clearly complete imbeciles! To find at least one who knew how to construct a sentence, and who had clearly read my advertisement properly was most refreshing. I have been told by many that I am too forthright, and just a little bit too aggressive. But I am a redhead, and the passion inside just seems to leak out at times. I know what I want, and I have a tendency to not stop until I have whatever my heart desires.

I am a cook in one of the finest hotels in the city. I cannot imagine my life without my work. I enjoy it, and get great satisfaction from it. I hope that honesty does not affront you in any way – but I do feel it best to let you know exactly the kind of woman I am. However, I do want a family and a husband and so I advertised for just that. I won't sit and wait for a man to come to me!

Your past love, is she someone you are still in contact with? Do you still harbor feelings for her? I do not wish to be rude, but I will not diminish myself in that way. I am a woman in my own right, and deserve to be loved for the person I am – not because I may remind you of somebody you once knew.

I am glad for you that your family has found one another again. I would not wish to take you from that life now you have it. But this may leave us in a little bit of a quandary. I have my position here in Boston, which I have no desire to leave. You seem to be settling happily in Montana. So, do you expect me to come to you, or would you be prepared – maybe in time as I can entirely appreciate your need to be amongst family now – to come here to Boston? If we cannot settle this one fundamental issue, then maybe it might be best if we did not correspond further?

Yours Sincerely

Miss Smith

The wording was as forthright as her advertisement, and it made Ethan chuckle – until he reached the part where she was already suggesting that they stop their correspondence before it had even begun. A pang of anger grabbed his heart as he realized that she was pushing him away. But why? What offense could she possibly have taken from his letter? But, then he began to look back over her letter. She gave him no obvious clues as to where she was working, did not give her name, and bristled at the possibility he may be trying to replace his lost love with her.

He knew that there could be a thousand Miss Smith's in America – but two that had red hair and worked in a fine hotel in Boston as a cook? That seemed to be too much of a coincidence. This was his Maggie, he was sure of it. She must have realized who he was immediately and in her blunt, yet oddly evasive way she was telling him that she did not want him. He felt his heart sink, and knew the pain of losing her all over again.

But she wanted a husband. And she longed for a family. She had told him that she never wanted those things, though he had always been sure that she was lying. He had tried back them to find a way to convince her to let him prove he was the kind of man who would let her be, and would gladly help with keeping the house and bringing up the children so she could continue to do so. But it had not been enough for her then, and clearly it was not now.

He took the letter upstairs to Annie. She and Maggie had been close once, and he was sure that she would know if Maggie was pushing him away because she had never loved him, or if it was something deep within her that made her distrustful of any man. He had always been so sure that she loved him, yet her behavior then and now surely told him otherwise – but he didn't believe it, not even in black and white on the page.

"I know you should be resting, and I don't want to interrupt the time you have with Mack and young Henry, but I need you." The little family were huddled together on the bed, the proud parents beaming down at the tiny, perfect little creature they had brought into the world.

"Mack, could you take Henry and put him down for a nap?" Annie said and patted on the bed beside her, indicating that Ethan should sit. Mack took Henry from her arms, and kissed her on the forehead.

"Have a sleep yourself when you are done, I'll bring him in when he gets cranky for his supper!" Annie smoothed the downy hair on her son's head, and smiled at them both.

"Thank you," she said and then waited as they left the room.

"What is it?" Ethan gave her the letter. She read it, and sighed heavily. "You answered the advertisement then?"

"I did. She sounded so like Maggie and I hoped that maybe there were two of them in the world and I might be lucky enough to keep hold of one this time," he admitted sadly.

"Oh, Ethan you old romantic! I always knew you had never really gotten over her."

"It is her isn't it?" he asked, half of him praying she would agree with him that it was, the other hoping it simply couldn't be.

"I think so. I doubt they made another one quite like her. But Ethan, do not be downhearted. She has given you enough clues to know it is her. I think she is praying that you will forgive her, will go to her."

"Really?" he asked incredulously. "I just see her pushing me away again."

"She knew it was you. She also knew just how much she hurt you, and herself when you were younger. She would feel that she had no right to expect you to just forgive her, or to even ask for that forgiveness. Look, here," she pointed at the letter. "Weren't those exactly the words you said to her when she went to work at Young's?" He looked again. Annie was right, they were. The exact terms. He had called her forthright, aggressive, blunt and rude in that final, horrible encounter.

"Annie, what if it is someone else and they just aren't interested?"

"It isn't. It simply couldn't be. It is too like her in every way. She loved you, yet pushed you away. She is doing it again because somewhere inside she thinks she doesn't deserve you – she never did."

"But that is such nonsense."

"No, Maggie had a tough life too. But she was determined to never let anyone have the power to ruin her life again. That is what you have to find out. Who was it, and why she has never let herself trust a soul since."

"So you think I should go to her, and what? Just ask her? She won't tell me. She wouldn't say a word then, why should she now?"

"No, I don't think you should go to her at all. I think we should ask Peter, Myra's Uncle to see what he can find out. I think you should continue to write to her. Be your usual sunny and positive self. Keep telling her that it is who she is that matters most, and her happiness is all you desire. Try not to let on that you know who she is, flirt a little – woo her!"

"But…" he tailed off. She was right. Maggie would be spooked if he ran to Boston to confront her. It would back her into a corner and out of stubbornness it would ruin everything for them both. More than ever he was sure that she still cared for him – had never stopped loving him and he knew he had always held her in his heart. He just had to let her come to him.

Chapter Four

Maggie was stunned to see a thick envelope sitting in the box she had hired at the postal office to hide her location from Ethan. He had always deserved so much more than she could ever offer him and she would not hurt him again. She took it out and saw his looping script and couldn't stop herself from smiling. He hadn't given up on her! But, she had no clue what he had written inside and he may be furious with her for such a blunt and unpleasant response to his kindly letter. She hurried to the park, and found a quiet spot to sit and read it without prying eyes intruding.

Dear Miss Smith

I trust that this letter will find you well. Thank you for your very honest response to me, and your categorically unambiguous approach to life. I agree, there are potentially some issues we will have to consider at some point, but might it be possible for us to converse a while longer until we know each other well enough to know whether such changes may indeed be required?

I shall never be upset, or put off by a woman who speaks her mind. I have always had the utmost respect for the wisdom and capability of the fairer – but not weaker –sex. How could I not, when I have a strong and capable sister, who has ever been the one I turn to when I am in need of advice? I should also consider the backbone of my younger sibling, Hannah, too who deals with a crisis both calmly and sensibly. They truly are both quite remarkable human beings.

The most exciting news I have is that my older sister, Annie, has just given birth to a fine and healthy boy. They named him Henry for our Papa. He has certainly inherited his lungs, and can yell the whole house down when he so desires. Annie and Mack, her husband, are proud as can be – and secretly so am I. John is a little nonplussed by it all. I think he has enjoyed being the youngest boy – maybe he feels a little usurped. But, he is also only eighteen and I don't remember being particularly enamored of babies myself then. Hannah is over the moon. She is determined to become a midwife, and having seen how calmly and carefully she assisted Annie I do think it could be her calling.

There is a new hotel opening in Great Falls next year. According to the gossip, they are aiming to outdo all of the big establishments in Boston, New York and Chicago. There will be electricity throughout, and each room is to have its own bathroom – though I have no idea how he intends to afford such a thing! But, can you imagine? People will flock to it in their droves, and when people then get to see the beauty of Montana and feel the benefit of the clean air and wonderful scenery, the town will be set as a fashionable tourist destination forever.

Montana truly is blossoming, I shall hardly recognize it soon it will be so debonair! But, as long as they don't take away my mountains, and the glorious waterfalls that are all around us here then I shall be content.

Please do continue our correspondence, I believe there is no issue you have concerns over that cannot be addressed and dealt

with, when the time comes.
  Yours Hopefully
  Ethan Cahill

Maggie was almost in tears as she read his words. As always, he was so kind and thoughtful of her needs, her wants. She did not deserve such a kind and good man, she never had. But, she was also delighted for dear Annie. They had been inseparable as girls, and Annie had long dreamed of having her own family. That they had named him Henry was testament to a good man. She had always wished her own Papa had been more like theirs. But, that was in the past now. She was sure he knew it was her, and though she knew that she should probably end the correspondence now, he had made the choice. He had written back, knowing that she had hurt him once and probably would do so again. If he was prepared to take the risk, then surely she could too?

It wasn't as if he had jumped on a train and rushed to her side, no he had only required that they continue to correspond. What harm could there be in that? He was not professing his love through all eternity, nor even marriage. She did not have to ever meet with him, and could continue to hope that another response would come from someone who would pose less of a threat to her heart. She could have this brief interlude of happiness and pleasure, couldn't she?

She stuffed the letter into her reticule and rushed back to her room in the hotel where she re-read his words. Oh, he was so very clever and sweet and dear. To so carefully give her news of her friend's happiness – and even that there could be a job opening for her should they decide they did suit. He hadn't changed. He could still make her feel that she was the center of his world, and that all problems could be overcome – but she knew that some scars could never heal.

The next few weeks rushed by in a flurry of activity. Boston was hosting a grand exhibition, and the hotel was full to capacity. People were arriving from all over America, and she had met a few interesting people from Europe and even Africa too. Everybody was excited by the future. Progress seemed to be happening at such a rate. Young's was no longer unusual, many hotels now had electricity throughout, but they were still the first and this meant that many of the scientifically minded young men made a pilgrimage to see it firsthand.

Maggie was glad of the distraction. Being so busy gave her no time to regret the chatty and more open reply that she had sent to Ethan, nor to consider that she was being a fool to do so knowing that there could be no future for them. She had never baked so much bread, or so many pastries in all her life, but she found he enjoyed the singular focus on just one aspect this had given her. She began to wonder if she would even wish to continue to work in a hotel. Maybe there was an alternative. She began to dream of being a baker in a tiny town, tucked away in the foothills of the Montana mountains, and it was a good dream.

"Maggie love, thank you for all your help," Ellen said as she bustled past, a large casserole full of rich stew in her arms. "You have always had such a gift with dough of all kinds."

"I am just glad it is all over," she laughed, pulling out the cutlery to lay the table for the staff's supper. Cook plonked the large dish down, and Nat and Matthew arrived with tureens full to the brim with buttered peas and boiled potatoes. "That smells delicious." It looked it too. Her mouth began to salivate as everybody began to collapse tiredly onto their chairs around the vast table. She sank into her own, and accepted a ladle full of the rich beef concoction, and then piled the plate high with the delicious vegetables.

"Did you ever hear anything from your advertisement?" Ellen asked her quietly.

"I did, but nobody was worth considering."

"Your frown tells me something different Maggie. And don't you dare try and tell me you don't want to talk about it. I know you. I virtually raised you. You think you are so tough, that you can deal with everything alone, and you have pushed virtually everyone who has ever cared about you away. But, you need us and you need to talk before you end up lonely and bitter like poor Millie." Maggie looked over at the tiny room that Mrs Wainwright kept as a private parlor. She sat, ramrod straight eating tiny bites of her meal. Ellen was right; Maggie certainly did not ever want to end up alone like that.

"I shall tell you later, when all of this lot are out of our hair," she said, trying to smile and reassure her friend. "Now, I have barely had a chance to speak with you and find out how you are since your return from your sister's. How is your dear niece?"

"Samantha is well thank you. She has a sweetheart, and he has proposed. I told her to wait if she wanted, that she did not need to rush into anything because of her Mama, but I think they would have wed soon enough anyway. He is a nice young man. He reminded me a little of your Ethan. Same eyes, and same drive to make something of himself."

Maggie felt a tear welling in her eye, even at the mention of his name. She choked her feelings down and tried to look happy. She could not bear to have anyone feel pity for her. She had made the choice to be alone, to be without Ethan. She should at the very least try and be content with it. But his unexpected reappearance in her life had changed everything, and for once she was going to ask for help – she had to. She couldn't trust herself to make the right decision, because she had clearly been a fool for too long.

Maggie sat quietly in her room after supper, waiting for the knock she knew would come. Ellen did not let her down. She welcomed her in and they sat side by side on her narrow bed. "Maggie love, what is it? I hoped that finding someone to write to might make you happy."

"Oh Ellen, Ethan replied." Cook looked at her with her eyebrow raised quizzically.

"Ethan, your Ethan?"

"My Ethan. He must have seen the advertisement somehow, and he wrote – and keeps on writing no matter how rude I am to him!"

"But Maggie, why ever would you be rude to the only man you have ever loved? Are you trying to push him away again?" Maggie nodded. "But why? Does he know it is you?"

"I think so, though he has not been so crass as to say so. I don't know why I do it Ellen. I do it with everyone but you. I did it to Ethan, to his sister Annie who was my best friend in the world."

"Who hurt you Maggie? Who went when you didn't want them to?"

"I don't know!" she cried, but she did. She just didn't want to admit it. It had been buried inside so long, and she couldn't bear it if it came to light now, to torment her life once more. Ellen held her tightly, and let her sob. She hadn't ever done so before, she had been too afraid to show anyone that she had a weakness - that she cared about anything or anyone.

"Maggie love, you have to let these things out – they fester and ruin your life otherwise. You are a good girl and you don't deserve to be in this pain." But Maggie knew that she wasn't, she was so terrible that even her Papa hadn't loved her, hadn't wanted her, had abandoned her without a care.

Chapter Five

Maggie hadn't sent a reply. Weeks had gone by and Ethan was close to giving up hope of ever hearing from her. He had been sure that Annie had been right, and so he had been light and breezy in his letter and tried to take the pressure of Maggie as much as he could. She had always taken responsibility for everyone's trials and tribulations. He wished he could ease the burden for her, but he had no clue how to do so, given that he had no clue why she was as she was. He was determined not to lose her this time, and vowed that if he hadn't heard anything by Thursday then he would be on his way to Boston to find her and demand that she give him another chance.

He rode in to Sun River. The day was hot, and he was thirsty and so he stopped in at the Whistling Rock Saloon. It was just a long wooden shack, with a long wooden bar – but it did what was needed. Ethan didn't often drink alone, knew few men that did and certainly he was not a man to drink in the daytime. But his utter frustration at hearing nothing from Maggie, or from Myra's Uncle Peter had him kicking his heels. His instincts told him to take action – but there was nothing he could do. He simply wasn't good at dealing with that.

He walked up to the bar and he ordered a beer and a shot of whiskey. "Slow down young'un," Tom, the bar man said with a wink as he was about to down the shot. Ethan stopped and lowered the glass back to the bar.

"You're younger than me Tom," he said. "And, to be honest I don't really care how slow I take it right now.

"I know. I just like saying it! What's up? You aren't usually the kind to be in here at all, let alone before lunchtime. But I am glad you stopped by, not just for the coins in my cash register – but there is some mail here for you. Nobody from the ranch has been down for a while, I guess you've all gone a bit baby crazy," he teased.

"Annie, Mack and Hannah have definitely," he admitted. "But John, well he's his usual grumpy self. I think the lad may grow on me once he is old enough for me to teach him to ride! Thanks for these." He took the pile of mail from Tom and flicked through it. There were a few bills from their feed supplier, and two letters from Boston. One in Maggie's familiar hand and the other in a small, neat script he did not recognize. He checked the return address and saw it was from Judge Peter Walker. At last, he might find something out that could help him to make sense of this all. Quickly he downed the shot, and then the lukewarm beer and rushed outside. He un-hitched his horse and galloped up into the mountains.

He stopped when he reached a tiny cave. He had found it a few weeks ago whilst out hiking. He didn't get much time to relax and just be alone now, and it was quiet and peaceful, nobody seemed to even know it was there. He loved his family, but the house was always so busy and especially now young Henry was there and making his needs known , having a bolt hole had become ever more important to him. He settled himself on the little ledge outside, and let his horse graze on the long grass all around. He ripped open the letter from the Judge and began to read.

Dear Mr Cahill

I am glad to be of service to you, and hope that you find the following information useful to you. Myra assures me that I can trust you, that you will be discrete. I pray that will be the case as I should not be sharing this information with you without Margaret Smith's permission – even though much of it is available in the public court records.

Initially I came up against a bit of a blank when searching for her - that was until I realized that Miss Smith was not always called that. Once I discovered that she was actually born Marguerite Jeanette Kennedy things began to come a little clearer.

The records in the Boston Court House show that Miss Smith is the only daughter of the shipping magnate Charles Kennedy. However, the record shows that he left his family and set up home with a ballet dancer when she was a child. Miss Smith took her mother's maiden name at this time, as did her Mother. The divorce was kept very quiet, and he left them with only very little to live on. Miss Smith's Mother died some ten years ago, I believe you knew her at this time, so it will not be news to you. But Miss Smith was already working to support the income of her family at that time.

I do hope that this information may be of help. I am afraid I cannot offer anything further.

Yours Faithfully

Peter Walker

The information was not much, in truth. But knowing this made Maggie seem more real to him at last. The secrets he had always sensed, the lies she had often told. He had always known, her nostrils would twitch ever so slightly and her lip would curl just a little whenever she told an untruth. It was just one of the things that he had loved about her. But he knew now that he should never have let her get away with those lies, should have made her tell him the truth from the start rather than play along as if he couldn't tell.

She had never spoken of her Father, not once. But, where they lived in the tenements it wasn't that unusual. Many of his friends didn't even know who their Father was, few cared. Those that did have Fathers often complained of beatings and drunkenness. He knew that he and his family had been lucky. Papa had been a good man, though they had lost him too young. Maggie had just been like everyone else, a child with only one parent. But he did remember that she had always seemed to despise anyone with money. She had been scathing in her attacks of those who took their privilege for granted, and her Papa's defection from her could certainly explain that. Poor Maggie, to lose her Father and be left on the scrap heap of life to survive as she might, it just did not seem fair that she was the one still carrying the burden of guilt and fear for something not her fault.

In moments he was back on horseback, and racing towards the ranch. He would go to Boston now, this very minute. He would find her and demand that she tell him why she was always so determined to push him away. He would tell her that he would never leave her, would never toss her away because he had found something or someone else. He loved her, and he always had. He always would. He was determined that she would not do it to him again, would not leave him and condemn them both to a lonely life apart from one another.

He tore into the house and up the stairs. In his room he pulled at drawers randomly, stuffing things into a bag. He would probably find that he had three pairs of pants and no shirts when he arrived, but he had to be at the station in time to get that train. "Ethan, whatever are you doing?" Annie said as she came into the room to find him throwing garments onto the floor and bed in his haste.

"I'm going to Boston. I have to find her, bring her back and let her know that she has a family – she has always had a family."

"I saw the letter on the table, but you haven't opened the one from her. What if she doesn't want you to find her, to rescue her? If I remember rightly Maggie was not the kind of girl who dreamt of a white Knight racing in on his snow white charger to save the poor damsel in distress!"

"She has no darn choice," he growled. "There is nothing she can say that will change my mind."

"I guessed that, but remember to be careful with her. She can be so prickly, and she will do everything she can to push you away. She certainly managed it with both of us before. I miss her too you know – she was a good friend, but it was just so difficult to keep in touch after you left. She didn't seem to want any reminders of you anymore and so she stopped coming back to see me too." Annie sighed. "Here, take this," she thrust a number of ten dollar bills into his hands. "You will need every penny, and read her letter on your way."

Swiftly he hugged his sister and then was on his way once more. He got to the station in Great Falls with time to purchase his ticket and to find a lad to take his horse back home in exchange for a dollar, and he was just about to do so when he saw something he had never expected to see. A young woman was standing at the very front of the queue, asking for directions. She had the most vivid red hair he had ever seen, and an hourglass figure that he simply longed to take in his arms and hold forever.

"Maggie?" he asked incredulously, barging past the surprised people in the queue between them. She turned to face him and her beautiful face lit up with joy. It was her! He wasn't imagining things – though he had begun to wonder for just a moment.

"Ethan," she sighed as she held out her hands to him. He clasped them desperately, as if he were a drowning man and only she could save him. In a way he supposed he was. She was the love of his life, and he could only pray that she wouldn't let him go this time.

"However did you get here?" he asked foolishly, knowing he should have asked why she was here, if she loved him – anything other than something so utterly foolish. She chuckled, and her beautiful green eyes lit up. Unable to control himself any longer he pulled her to him, and crushed his lips to hers. They were soft and yielding, and he felt her hands creep around his back and caress him tenderly. The electricity that had always sparked between them was still there, and he lost himself in the scent of her, the taste of her, and the soft warmth of her against his tired and lonely body.

"I came on the train," she said with a grin when he finally released her. The people around them looked scandalized, but he didn't care. Maggie was here and, if that kiss was anything to go by, she loved him just as much as he loved her. It spoke of hope and possibility – and he was willing to grab onto as much of that as he could get.

"Yes, I know. Stupid of me. Why are you here? Sorry, that sounds pretty harsh, but Maggie you…" He couldn't bring himself to finish the sentence. He had felt a surge of anger course through his veins, that she could be here and so nonchalant. Didn't she know the torment she had put him through, then and now?

"I came to see Annie and to meet Henry of course. Thank you so much for telling me of her wonderful news in your letter," she said in a matter of fact tone. He felt his heart sink, he had so wanted her to be here because she loved him, and finally knew that she couldn't live without him another day. "Oh you lovely, silly man. I am teasing. I am here to see you. You did know it was me you were writing to didn't you?" He could feel the frustration within him rising, knew his eyes were flashing fire. She was teasing him? After everything else she had done?

"I did, but I could hardly believe it was true. How you can simply stand there and be so flippant I do not know? How much more pain do you intend to put me through? Haven't you been cruel enough?" he burst out, unable to keep it in any longer.

"So, you haven't received my last letter then?"

"It arrived this morning. I was going to read it on the train."

"Read it before we speak again," she said mysteriously. "I hope it will explain why I am here, being nervously flippant because I don't have a clue as to whether you still care for me, or could ever forgive me," she said suddenly looking utterly overwhelmed, and so very vulnerable.

"I have never stopped thinking about you Maggie. I love you. That is why it all hurt so darn much!"

"Shhh! Not here. We do have a lot to talk about, and there is much you should know before you make any such declarations Ethan." Her delicate features looked so stern, so unyielding. But, if she didn't love him, then why would she be here? None of it made any sense to him.

"I shall hire a carriage to take you and your luggage to the ranch. Annie will be delighted to see you. She has missed you too," he said finally, putting a protective hand in the small of her back and picking up her luggage. "Is this everything?" he asked looking at the capacious carpet bag. She nodded.

"I thought women always needed trunks of things – knick knacks, fripperies and the like" he admitted. "But then, you were never like any girl I've ever met." She smiled and allowed him to direct her outside. He took her to where the stage coach that passed through Sun River was waiting and went to assist her inside, but she ignored his supportive hand and boarded without it. He kicked himself for being such a fool. Maggie was still the determined and independent woman she had always been. The fact she had come without warning told him that.

He watched the coach set off, and then went in search of the lad he had paid to take his horse to the stable. He was still standing talking to a friend, eating a tasty looking pie. "You can keep the dollar," he said with a grin, certain that his money was how the boy had afforded his meal. He took the reins and then began to make his way back home where he quickly put Mildred between the shafts of the gig and set off into town to meet the stage coach. Main Street was pretty deserted as he pulled up outside the saloon, and he was glad of it. He opened the envelope and pulled out her letter, his hands shaking a little. He wasn't sure what he wanted to read, or what he didn't – but he hadn't been expecting what he did find.

Dear Ethan,

I am sure that by now you know who I am. You have never been a fool, and I doubt if that would have changed. I have much I would tell you, much to beg your forgiveness for – but yet I still do not know where to start.

Firstly, I must apologize for not being honest about my identity from the start. I was unsure if you would wish to continue to write to me if you knew, and did not wish to risk you cutting me off if you were still angry. Yet, I couldn't bring myself to pretend either and so I sent that cruel and ungenerous response to you in the hope I might make you wish to be the one to cease our correspondence. As soon as I saw your dear script, and your name at the bottom I knew nothing had changed for me, and nor would it ever be likely to do so.

But, I also owe you an explanation for why I pushed you away all those years ago. I remember you asking over, and over again why I was breaking our engagement and no matter what I said you were never happy with my answer. But, eventually I did manage to drive you away – and I have been sorry for that ever since. I was a fool. I didn't deserve you then, and I probably still don't now. But, I don't believe that I could ever have answered you sufficiently then – because I simply did not know myself.

I spoke with my dear friend, Ellen, before I wrote this. You may remember her as Cook, the women who taught me everything and loved me like a daughter. I was so scared of her on my first day at Young's, and you were so very supportive of me. To think how things can change, and in such odd ways! Well, Ellen helped me to understand why I pushed you away – and finally helped me to see that that reason was never my fault.

You know Mama died not long after I met you. She had been frail for much of her life. But, there was a reason for that. Mama wasn't born into the life we all led. She was brought up in a world of silk sheets and servants. So was I. But, when Papa decided he wanted a younger wife, who would be prettier on his arm at his soirees, he left us with nothing. He gave Mama barely enough for us to survive. It was why I was so determined to never be like my Mama. I could not ever consider the idea of being dependant on a man, could not leave myself to be so vulnerable should he ever decide to leave.

I hated myself for loving you, for even considering marriage with you – and yet I couldn't ever say no to you. I knew you would never treat me the way Papa had treated Mama – you are the best and kindest man I have ever known – but he had so damaged me that I could not allow myself to believe that then. I am still not sure I can allow myself to believe it now either.

I have built a life for myself. I need never rely on a man ever. Yet I am as lonely as my Mama ever was and my life just as empty – more so as I do not even have a child to care for and love. But I want that to change. I want to change – though I know it will be more than difficult for me to do so. I cannot ask you to give me the time I will need to learn to trust. I cannot ask you to forgive me for the way I treated you. I cannot even ask you to forgive me for trying to hold onto you once more, even if it was only for this very short while. But, you must know that I do love you. I always have. I am sorry, and I always will be.

Yours, forever

Maggie

"Oh you foolish girl," Ethan said as he brushed away the tears that were streaming over his cheeks. "I can forgive you anything, but I will not let you waste one more minute of the time we can be together." He chuckled as he jumped down from the gig as he saw the coach come into view. He was so glad she had finally learned to trust, and had come looking for him. He wouldn't let her get away from him again. Not this time. She had admitted she loved him, and he was going to make sure that she never forgot that.

Chapter Six

Maggie nibbled on her fingers throughout the entire carriage ride from Great Falls to Sun River. She had no idea what to expect when she arrived. Ethan would have read her letter by then, he would know what she finally knew. She prayed she had not pushed him too far, that he could forgive her for everything she had done. She was well aware that she did not deserve a second chance, and felt he would be utterly entitled to dismiss her and send her straight back to Boston – but she prayed that he would not do so.

The coach was full. A rotund man in a smart suit was taking up almost two seats beside her, wedging her tightly against the door and a wealthy looking woman had her two daughters sat opposite her. The lady sat opposite her looked at her ungloved hands and the calluses on them and gave a disgusted "Tsk," before peremptorily turning away. She gave her daughters a look that did not disguise her distaste. The two girls looked away shyly, not wanting to meet Maggie's gaze. She looked at her hands, they showed clearly that she worked hard for a living, but as far as she was concerned that was nothing to be ashamed of. But, her finger nails would be down to the quick if she didn't stop nibbling at them soon. Hurriedly she replaced her gloves and gazed out of the window.

The scenery was indeed just as lovely as Ethan had described it in his letters. She found herself hoping that she would be able to stay and explore it with him, side by side. She longed to trek up the mountains, to play in the snow at the peaks and to swim in the winding rivers and cool, clear lakes that rolled by outside. She felt a weight begin to lift from her shoulders and her heart the nearer she got to her destination, as if the place had magic that could heal her and make her whole at last. But the nearer she got, the more her nerves began to bubble deep inside her. She tried to distract herself by listening to the birds that sang so lyrically all along the route, and even by looking for patterns in the bright, fluffy clouds in the sky. But nothing could soothe the churning turmoil in her belly.

"Sun River," called the driver, banging hard on the roof. Maggie jumped almost out of her skin. It was too soon. She wasn't ready. She had no clue what to say, or how to deal with any of this. She peered anxiously out of the window and saw Ethan waiting for her as the stage pulled up outside the saloon. He looked so calm, so utterly handsome – as he always did, and she realized she had absolutely no idea of what he was thinking. She sat back and took a deep breath, then grabbed her things and took the first step into what she hoped would be her new life.

"Welcome to Sun River," Ethan said as he took her hand and assisted her to alight from the carriage. In the past she would have been furious at any man who did such a thing, but suddenly it felt natural and right to accept Ethan's assistance. It was a long drop, and there was no block to make it easier, and her full skirt made her clumsy. She stumbled a little, losing her balance. He held her tightly, stopping her from falling, and she thought of all the times he had done so in different ways. He had always been there for her, even though she had done little to deserve it. She gazed up into his handsome face, feeling his wiry and strong body pressed up close to hers and longed to reach up and kiss him. But, she knew she could not, not yet.

"I read it," he said, his voice calm and even.

"And?" she demanded, unable to take much more.

"There is nothing in it that could ever have changed the way I feel about you."

"Ethan, I am so sorry that I didn't let myself trust you. I should always have known that you were nothing like my Father. I should have known that you would never do to me what he did to my Mama. But, I was young and silly, and so very scared. I thought he had gone because I was a bad girl, that he couldn't tolerate my bad behavior any longer. It took me such a long time to learn that relationships fail, because people let them. He didn't want us, it was nothing either Mama or I had done.

"When he left, things did not change much - at first. We stayed in the house, and he had so often been away a lot anyway. Mama still acted as his hostess, and he would belittle her and humiliate her in front of everyone as he always had. They all knew he had left us – but they were all such hypocrites. They would gladly come to our home and accept my Mama's hospitality, and laugh at her behind her back. It was all so amusing to them. I think that was when I began to distrust anyone. How could I trust people who could be so cruel to a woman in so much pain?"

"That must have been hard to bear for her, and difficult to understand for you. You were so very young," he said gently. His eyes were so soft, so full of love for her. She had expected pity, but there was nothing but admiration for her written on his face.

"But, then when he decided he wanted to marry Brigitte, well he wanted the house too. He wanted his life to carry on as it always had, and so we were now surplus to his needs. He found us the apartment across from yours, and left us there. I don't think I even realized that it was my new home – not until much later. Mama would say he loved me, would come and see me – but he never did. And, so I stopped looking for him. I stopped looking for his love."

"But by doing so, you stopped allowing anyone else to love you too?" She nodded. She should have known he would understand. Ethan had always been so much more sensitive to others needs than any man she had ever known, more so than many women too.

"I am so glad you understand. I didn't know how to do anything else but feel that way," she sighed, the final wave of tension leaving her body finally. "Now, what is there a girl can do to earn her keep in Sun River?" she said, trying to ease the mood. She began looking around her. Ethan chuckled.

"There isn't much, but we are growing all the time," he said tipping his Stetson back from his forehead and escorting her, tucking her arm in his as they took a walk down the tiny main street.

"I see the saloon, and a hardware store. Is there a grocery store?"

"Nope, that is inside the General Store. It's getting harder for poor Will though, he's not ever got anything the women want these days. He much preferred it when he was only supplying men – they just wanted canned beans, and flour!"

"Do you think there are enough people to want a small bakery?" she asked curiously.

"More than enough, especially if you sold some of the more 'high falutin' stuff' I think it was Will called it!"

"Where should I have my bakery," she asked him, feeling dreamy. He hadn't even proposed, but she was sure he would – and well, if he didn't then she sure would.

"I think right here," he said as they walked up towards a site with a large wooden frame laid out on the ground. "This will be the church, we'll be building it over the next few weeks. We are all chipping in what time we can. A bakery right next door would mean everyone will know where to find you."

"That is a very wise idea," she said with a smile. "Then I shall have to find out how to go about buying this plot of land and building me a little shop."

"You want to stay?" he asked, she could hear the tension in his voice.

"If you want me to?" she said simply.

"I do," he admitted.

"We may have to wait a bit to say that," she teased. "No church!"

"Then we'd better get it built quick, so we can sort that out!"

"Ethan, will you marry me?"

"You never needed to ask that Maggie. You've held my heart since I was just seventeen years old. I've never considered giving it to anybody else." He pulled her against him and held her tightly, she melted into him and finally he felt as if his life was exactly the way it should be.

Epilogue

"Do you Ethan Cahill, take Marguerite Jeanette Smith to be your wife; to have and to hold, for richer and for poorer as long as you both shall live?" the Minister asked him. He looked at his radiant bride and laughed. So many of the vows they were making today did not feel right. He wished they could have written their own, but he dutifully made his response.

"I do," he said and squeezed her hand tightly.

"And do you Marguerite Jeanette Smith take Ethan Cahill to be your husband; to have and to hold, honor and obey as long as you both shall live?"

"I do," she said as she winked at him.

"Then I pronounce you man and wife, you may kiss your bride!"

Ethan bent his lips to his wife's, and kissed them tenderly. They turned and began a slow walk to the end of the church. "I promise to love you even when you are stubborn, to care for you even when you push me away, to always be there for you even when you expect me to leave," he whispered into her ear. She turned and smiled at him.

"And I promise to talk to you when I am troubled, to trust you to love me come what may, to know you love me just the way I am and always will."

"I know it is unlikely, but I wouldn't object to the honor and obey bit too!" he joked. She swatted at him playfully.

"I'm sure you won't hold your breath until I do though."

A crowd clustered around them, and Ethan felt as if his heart might burst. Maggie looked so very beautiful, her long auburn hair trailing down her back. Her green eyes were alight with mischief and happiness, and he wondered what life with her would bring. He knew it would be an adventure. He accepted the warm congratulations of his family, and was glad to see them hugging Maggie just as tightly. Annie had tears in her eyes, as she pulled her old friend to her.

"You take care of him for us," she said, wiping a tear from her cheek.

"I shall, but surely we will be staying at the ranch with you?" she said. Annie gasped, and Ethan looked at her, a stern look on his features. But he couldn't keep angry with her for long.

"Well, I guess I'd better show you your wedding gift then, as Annie has so wonderfully let the cat out of the bag," he said, picking up his wife and cradling her in his arms – despite the howls of protest, and flailing limbs.

"I am not this kind of woman," she told him. "If you'd wanted such a woman you should have found a meek and docile little thing. Now put me down!"

"Nope," he said glad to have her in his arms. "Now calm down little kitten, before you scratch my eyes out and make me no use to man nor beast!" Unwillingly she stopped her twitching and lay calmly in his arms, but the pout on her lips was just too inviting and so he bent his head and kissed her soundly.

He carried her along the street, past her brand new bakery and to a neat, clapboard house. He kept walking, and then turned onto a small trackway, barely big enough for a cart to travel along. "I must be heavy, you can't carry me all the way up the mountain," Maggie said as the path began to climb.

"Oh I think you'll find I can," he said in a low growl.

"I know you are strong, but you don't need to prove anything to me."

"Just be patient, and be quiet," he said as he shifted her weight a little in his arms.

"I'm too heavy," she said impatiently.

"No you aren't. Just stop wriggling!"

Maggie didn't say another word. Ethan had to admit that he was beginning to regret his gallant gesture, as his arms and back began to ache. But as they turned the bend it was worth every moment of agony. "Oh Ethan," she breathed. "Is this our home?"

"Yes my love, John and I have been busy don't you think?"

"I do. It's beautiful."

"And now, I shall carry my bride over the threshold and we shall have a happy life here, together at last. And, you'll notice that we are far enough away from town for us to live however we please – without nosy neighbors to tell us we are wrong."

"Oh Ethan, you truly are the most wonderful man alive," Maggie said as she cupped his face in her palms and kissed him soundly. He stomped up onto the wide porch and kicked open the door.

"I think we are going to be very happy here," he said as they went inside. "But I am truly sorry – I can't manage to carry you upstairs!" he joked as he dropped her unceremoniously into a plush armchair. She giggled.

"I knew you were just being stubborn. I love you Ethan Cahill."

"And I love you, Mrs Cahill – the most stubborn person I have ever known.

The End

* * * * * *

A Bride for Thomas
Book 4

Chapter One

"You will marry who I tell you to marry girl." Catherine's Father towered over her, his face beet red, sweat beading his plump features.

"No I won't," she said fiercely. "You cannot make me marry Elphias Garner. He is three times my age and four times my size. I shan't do it."

"No daughter of mine will defy me. You shall stay in this house until you see sense!" He stormed from the room and slammed the door so hard that the frame wavered. Catherine sank down onto her bed and sighed. Papa had always been so indulgent towards her before. This mean spirited and angry man was not the one she loved, was not a man she recognized at all. She knew that something must have happened for him to be so frightened. But marrying her off to that venomous snake was not the answer.

She had to find a way to get Papa to tell her what was really going on, what hold the cunning money lender had over him. Her Father had not taken her Mama's untimely death well, and this was the first time in weeks she had seen him up in daytime hours. He had taken to drinking and gambling, and Catherine was sure that he had borrowed money all over town to try and run from his grief. But, she was not going to be bought and sold because of his weaknesses. She was grieving too, but she hadn't spent every penny of their family wealth.

She had to find out what he owed, and to whom. Maybe she could find a way to negotiate with them, to make an agreement as to how to make reparations? But, she knew that while Papa continued to drown his sorrows and play cards every night she would only find herself with more people to beg consideration from next week, the week after and the week after that. No, she needed to find a way to get him away from Boston. He needed a fresh start in a place where there were no memories of Mama, and no temptations from liquor and the casinos.

He couldn't stop her from going out. He wasn't around to even know, or care so his words meant little. But where should she start? Papa was out all night, every night. His study here at the house was locked tight. He hadn't been to work in months, as he slept all day, but his clerk, Andrews, sent missives every day which her Father addressed before he left the house for the evening, after a bottle of claret and some of his best port. So, she had the daylight hours to go to his place of business, and the night time to find her way into the study. She just hoped that she had the time she needed to solve the problem before she found herself wed to a man she despised and who would only ever make her life a misery.

She sat patiently opposite Papa at dinner, making polite chit chat as if their earlier argument had not occurred. She watched disgusted as he guzzled at the fine wine, and picked at the sumptuous supper Mrs Minton had prepared for them. She did her very best to bite her tongue when he brought up the subject of her impending nuptials, merely nodding and smiling as she delicately cut her steak and chewed each bite carefully. The meal seemed interminably long, and by the time her Papa had retired to take a glass of port and to smoke his cigar in his study she could barely contain herself. Why could he not hurry and leave the house? He would normally be gone in no time, his desire to lose himself in oblivion too strong.

Finally she heard the door of the study click shut from her spot in the drawing room, where she was perched anxiously on the edge of her chair. Every sinew in her body felt taut, like to break if she moved too swiftly. She listened as Papa took his hat and cane from Wilson, his valet, and tried to pick out what was being said. The two men both had deep voices, and it was hard to make out their words. She moved to the door, keeping out of sight, but she could discern no more. But, finally he was gone and she could try and explore, and see what she could do to get herself, and Papa, out of this mess.

She tried the door of the study, unsurprisingly it was locked. She wished that her upbringing had been a little less genteel, that she had a few useful skills like picking a lock, or wielding an axe. But sadly, Society deemed such skills unnecessary for a young woman. She could dance elegantly, paint a passable watercolour, and play the piano and sing at the same time. But, thankfully she was clever and she remembered that Papa never smoked without opening the window. Maybe he had left it unlatched so she could sneak in that way?

Quietly she tiptoed across the hallway, past the heavy front door and made her way towards the dining room. The French Doors led out onto a broad terrace, and Papa's study was the next room along. It would be easy for her to stand on the parapet wall and try the window. She crept stealthily across the terrace, glad that her dance lessons had taught her to be so light of foot. She gathered her skirts and tucked them up in a most unladylike fashion and clambered onto the limestone parapet. Carefully she inched towards the window, and reached out to see if it might move. It was stiff, but to her great relief it began to rise. She almost lost her footing and had to take a moment to regain her balance. Then, excitedly she squeezed herself through the open space.

Once inside she paused for a moment to catch her breath. She was sure that Wilson, or the housekeeper would be able to hear, she seemed to be gasping for air and her heart was beating faster than she had ever known. Composing herself as swiftly as she could, she made her way to her Papa's old oak rent table. His own father had brought the great monstrosity with him from England when they had come to make their fortunes some seventy years previously. Grandpa had done well, though it was rarely spoken of how a pauper lad could have turned his fortunes around so completely.

She began to rummage through the tiny drawers. When it had been made, it would have had a drawer for every tenant's home or business. Annual rents would have been marked as paid or in arrears every quarter day. Her grandfather however had not been some great landowner, quite the opposite in fact. He had been a poor tenant laborer turned poacher on the estate of an aristocrat who had turned an entire village off his land when he wished to extend the run of his game park. Hunting had been more important to him than the people who had served his family for generations. Grandpa had stolen the table from the hall, though no-one was sure how, as a symbol to himself that he would never owe his life or his livelihood to another soul ever again.

She made her way around the table. Many of the old initials had now worn away, but she knew the drawer that her Papa would keep anything of any importance in. The drawer that had, all those years before, held the rent records of Grandpa's family. Finding the drawer with a large P upon it, she hastily pulled it open and found a stack of pieces of paper. Every single one of them had her Papa's name upon it, a sum of money, and the initials I.O.U. The pile of his vowels added up to a sum greater than any she could even have imagined. They owed thousands of dollars, to people all over town. But then, she found a sheet of parchment that made her blood run cold. Elphias Garner had purchased every single one of her Papa's debts, and he had given him a very generous three months to find the money. If not, he would take the prize of his choosing. Though it did not say so in words, the meaning of the document and subsequent events were clear. Her Papa had unwittingly sold her to the highest bidder.

Well, she would not permit such a thing to happen. If even the thought of having to sell his own daughter had not been enough to change his ways, Catherine knew that nothing she could say or do would ever make one iota of difference. He would continue to rack up his debts, and would finally end up alone, and in the gutter. When she thought of the fact that he had sold her before he had considered selling their possessions, or even considered taking out a mortgage on their house told her that her dear Papa, the man who had loved her and cared for her was no more. The man left behind was a selfish drunk; a gambler who rather than gamble his own life away had gambled hers. Well, she would not stay here and let him do so. She would not watch as he drank himself into poverty at best - or an early grave at worst.

She clambered back through the window and raced upstairs to her room, where she began to grab at her clothes and possessions in a misty haze of tears. Stuffing them hurriedly into carpet bags she found under her bed and on top of the armoire she packed up her entire life in less than a half an hour. She was not sure what to do, or where she might go – but she knew she could not stay here and await the fate laid out for her, and so, bravely, she wiped away her tears, picked up her bags and walked regally down the grand staircase, as if she was daring anyone to stop her. As she reached the door, she turned and looked at the life-sized portrait of her Grandpa that hung above the mantle. "Are you proud of him?" she asked it. "Would you have sold your own child to save your own hide?"

Sadly, she was sure he would have done just that, and more. Grandpa had been a hard man, made bitter by his experiences as a poor boy, turned out of his home. He had always claimed he had done what he had to do to survive, but to hear Papa tell it, Grandpa had been proud of every time he had cheated, or gulled an innocent person along the way. She had believed that Papa was a better man, that he had done things right. Maybe he had. But Papa was not Papa anymore; she had to stop feeling that she was letting him down by trying to save herself.

She made her way down the street, not sure where she might go. The evening was cool, but not unpleasant. She walked slowly, trying to think, but her mind kept going off in different directions, making no sense of what was happening around her, to her. She walked, and walked and finally found herself at the entrance of Young's Hotel. She didn't have much money, but she had enough to get herself a room for a few nights while she tried to figure out what to do next and so she went inside.

The lobby was brightly lit, and people were hurrying around with bright smiles upon their faces. A kind gentleman at the desk took her details, and gave a large key to a lad hovering behind her. "Please take this young lady up to room four-one-six," he said as the boy took her bags and ushered her away. In minutes she was inside a luxurious room, with a large bed and a comfortable area in which she would be able to relax, with plush chairs and a table. Newspapers were stacked neatly in a rack, and a bureau stood open with good paper, pens and ink inside. Exhausted, she collapsed onto the elegant chaise longue, and smiled wanly as the boy put her bags down. "Would you like me to get one of the maids to help you unpack?" he asked.

"No, I think I would prefer to just sleep tonight. Maybe someone could bring me up some chocolate in the morning, and assist me then? Though I am not sure how long I shall be staying." He nodded and disappeared.

She pulled out her nightgown, and washed her face in the large ewer at the washstand. The bed was delightfully comfortable, and she sank into the pillows, praying she would wake up in the morning and find that it had all been a bad dream. But, despite her exhaustion, her mind would not stop spitting emotions and thoughts at her. She tossed and turned, fidgeting and wriggling in the hope that if she could get her body position just right then her mind would quiet itself – but it was to no avail.

Reluctantly she got up and pulled on her robe. She took a newspaper from the rack and began to flick through it absent-mindedly. But, she soon stopped and stared. It was as if she was meant to be here, to find this simple paragraph, a paragraph she prayed would change her life.

A Gentleman of Montana seeks a woman with a view to matrimony. She should be polite and good, and not afraid of hard work. The subscriber owns a small business, in a small town, but both are growing and he needs a helpmeet. But he also longs for companionship, someone he can enjoy intelligent conversation with. A love of theatre and music would be most appreciated. Replies to Box number 231, The Boston Globe

Chapter Two

Tom sifted through the mail for Sun River. Most of the farmers and ranchers nearby didn't come into the tiny town often and so he kept their correspondence for them until they could. There were a few letters for him, mostly bills, but there was one that had come all the way from Boston. He tucked it into his vest pocket, and prayed it was what he had hoped for all these weeks. He had placed an advertisement in the Matrimonial pages after seeing his friends do the same. All of them now seemed to be not just content with their mail order brides, but head over heels in love with them. He couldn't help but feel a little jealous.

The Whistling Rock Saloon had been the hub of the community for years, and he had been amongst the first folk to settle here. Back then it had been just a few trappers, and a couple of hardy souls determined to make the land yield. Few of those early pioneers were still here, but he was and his business was doing well. But, he knew he needed to make things different. In the past he had been surrounded by men. They hadn't wanted much more than a place to have a drink and play cards. But, many of them were marrying now, bringing wives and bringing up children. His back room had already been commandeered as a meeting place for the Women's Suffrage group, and was the town's place of worship when the Minister from Great Falls came to deliver a service. But with the new church that had just been erected, and the meeting hall planned for the spring, the Whistling Rock needed to change, to adapt to fit the new needs of the community – and he was full of ideas. He was also lonely, and he wanted to find the kind of happiness that always seemed to pass him by.

He finished sorting the rest of the mail and tucked each little pile into the cubbyholes he had built for the purpose, then began to check the bar over to make sure it was ready for the day's trading. He noticed that he was short on bourbon, and that the beer would only last another couple of days. He'd need to make the trip into Great Falls today to restock. He wondered if there would be anybody free to keep an eye on the place for him while he went. As if God was answering his prayers a loud hammering started up on the door. With a chuckle he unbolted it and found Ethan Cahill standing there.

"Well my friend, married life seems to be suiting you well," he teased. The young man had only been married a few weeks, and the couple had barely been seen by anyone since.

"It is mighty fine," Ethan admitted, pushing his Stetson back up off his forehead.

"What can I do for you that needs you to break down my door at this time of day? I never had you down as much of a drinker?"

"I'm not. But, I need to pick up a parcel in Great Falls and wondered if I could borrow your cart? Our gig is in no state to cope with the journey ever again!" They both chuckled at this. The gig was in fact still sitting in the street outside, the axle broken clean in two, its wheels akimbo.

"How big is the parcel my friend?"

"Maggie ordered some fabrics and some things for the bakery. I don't think it is too big. Why?"

"Well, I need to go to Great Falls myself to get some supplies for this place – but I don't have anyone to keep an eye on things while I do…"

"And you'll pick up Maggie's things if I do you a favor?"

"Something like that," he said with a cheeky wink.

"Sure, why not?" The two men shook hands warmly. "So, show me what's what my friend!" Ethan said happily. It wasn't long before Tom had shown him how to tap the barrels, how to move them so they didn't get damaged, and how to use the cash register.

"I'll be back before supper time. Things should be quiet most of the day, we get the odd few in at lunchtime, but most folk come in after supper."

"I'll be fine," Ethan assured him. "Get going, sooner you head out, the sooner you'll be back."

It didn't take him long to hitch up his broad-backed cart horses into the shafts, and soon the three of them were ambling along the road to Great Falls in the sunshine. He patted at his pocket, reassured that the letter was still there. Suddenly a wave of impatience overtook him, as he realized he couldn't wait a moment longer to find out who had responded to him. He whipped the letter out and ripped open the envelope. A second envelope fell out. The paper was fancy, a thick creamy paper and the script upon it was neat, but had a gentle slope and swirl to it. He took a quick look up, and clicked to the girls to bring them back on course, then opened it.

Dear Gentleman of Montana,

I cannot tell you how fortuitous it was that I saw your advertisement. It sounds like you could use some help, and my hands are unfortunately currently sat idle here in Boston. I would very much like to meet with you, as soon as possible, to see if we might suit – though I am sure you will have had many replies and I must not assume that I am the only woman to see something worth writing to.

I have been attending the theatre and the opera house since I was a girl. In fact, my Mama – before she so sadly passed away – was on the board of one of Boston's finest concert halls. I used to very much enjoy the opportunity to go backstage to meet with the cast, and to assist the crew, though my Mama would have been distraught to hear such a thing!

However, please do not think that I am some spoiled little rich girl, just out for an adventure. I find myself unexpectedly alone, and with only a small amount of money to my name. I do not seek your pity, nor do I expect you to consider me because of this alone. I say it merely because it is true, and for some reason writing things in a letter seems to make the telling of confidences so much easier.

I do not expect flowers and romance, I am no naïve girl. But I do believe that I would make you a good wife, one who will work hard and will support you, if you will do the same for me – as a husband of course! I long to find someone who will treat me as an equal, not as some trophy, or thing to be bought and sold. I believe I could be the helpmeet you desire.

Please, write to me soon, tell me I may use my last funds to come to Montana and meet with you at least.

Yours most hopefully

Catherine Parker

Tom stared at the page, until a jolt made him look up. Molly and Dolly had managed to wander off the road and into a small ditch. It wouldn't take much to coax them out, but he sighed heavily as he dismounted. He should have been paying attention, not been engrossed in Miss Catherine Parker's letter. Gently he helped the girls to back up, and got them back onto the road. "I'll pay more attention," he promised them as he scratched their soft, velvety mouths and then got back up onto the dashboard.

But, what he had read troubled him. He had expected to receive all sorts of things, but a woman who sounded desperate to leave Boston had not been one of those things. Clearly something had happened to her, and she felt she had to flee. But should he trust her that she was the innocent party? Was it his place to rescue a woman he had never met? It was clear she came from a wealthy family, would she even be able to cope with the kind of life he led here in Sun River? He had big plans to turn his humble little saloon into a theatre. He would need a woman not scared to set foot in either – though she had confided that she already had experience of doing so.

He couldn't stop thinking of her as they made their way into the town of Great Falls. It was much bigger than Sun River, had a railroad station, a number of banks, three saloons and a grand theatre that attracted travelling shows from Chicago and even as far as Boston and New York. He stopped outside it, and took note of everything he could see, from the shiny brass door handles to the rich red carpet inside and the tasteful show bills. He pulled out a small pad and pencil and scribbled down the names he saw on them, and wondered how he might get in touch with them.

His curiosity sated, he drove to the brewers yard where he loaded up with everything he needed, and then made his way to the station where the parcel that Ethan had asked him to collect was waiting. He stowed it carefully in the back and then turned to look at the locomotive sat puffing at the platform. Impulsively he suddenly rushed across the platform to the ticket office, where he purchased a one way ticket from Boston to Great Falls. He scribbled a hasty reply to Catherine's letter and handed it to the station master, asking him if he might ensure that it was included on the next mail run.

As he drove home, he couldn't explain to himself why he had done such a foolhardy thing. He was a man who thought about things forever, sometime to the point of never actually doing a thing. He made plans, and lists. He considered the good and bad consequences of every action – and yet he had now sent an invitation to a woman he knew nothing about. She could be some kind of criminal, or a confidence trickster for all he knew. But something told him that her distress was genuine, and he could not bear the thought of letting her down. She needed him, she needed to escape and so he would help her to do just that. If they did not suit once she got here, then so be it, but he would not leave her alone and so fearful for her future.

Chapter Three

Weeks had passed and Catherine's meager funds were rapidly dwindling to nothing. She had been forced to move from the smart Young's Hotel to a boarding house, recommended to her by one of the chamber maids. It was clean, but her room had few homely touches. "Catherine, I have tickets for the theatre this evening. Would you like to join me?" Gwen cried happily as she burst through the door.

"I cannot possibly afford to pay you back," Catherine admitted. "I should so love to see the new production though."

"You ninny," Gwen said affectionately. She had truly been sent to Catherine from heaven. From the very first she had taken her under her wing, and Catherine, usually so taciturn and closemouthed about her troubles, had found herself confiding in her from the start. "The concierge at the hotel gets us tickets; we don't pay a penny for them. It will be up in the God's, and standing – but a night out is a night out! They will go to waste if you will not come with me as all my friends are working tonight."

"Then I should be delighted to accompany you." Gwen smiled at her gently.

"It might help take your mind off your troubles for a short while at least. I could maybe ask if they need anyone to work at the hotel if things get too tight?"

"Thank you, but it would be too hard. Being a guest one week and an employee there soon after. It would not be right and besides, I would be too easy to find there. I have to get out of Boston, though if one of those gentlemen I wrote to does not respond I shall be stranded here."

" How many did you send letters to Catherine?"

"Twelve. I was careful, picked those that sounded the most intelligent, affluent and kind – though it is hard to tell from an advertisement of course. But, I so hope one of them will respond soon. I know it can take weeks for post to reach places such as Texas and Montana, but I had penciled into my calendar that I might be able to expect replies this week – yet there is nothing." Catherine could hear the fear and anxiety in her own voice.

"Maybe they needed time to sort through their responses and make a decision," Gwen said placating her. "I am sure someone will write and will be determined to have you join him post haste. Now, shall we dress up tonight, or down?" Catherine allowed her friend to coax her towards the little mirror above the chest of drawers. She unpinned her long chestnut locks and began to brush them out. "You have such lovely hair Catherine. You should wear it down over your shoulders more. If I had such hair I would show it off."

"I used to," Catherine said. "I fear someone might recognize me if I did so." Gwen nodded and then carefully pinned it back into an elegant chignon.

"Hmmmm," she said then ran into her room next door. Catherine gazed at her reflection, wondering if maybe she had sounded too desperate in her letters, that in her need she had scared every one of the men away. She so desperately wanted to get away from here, the memories and the possibility of bumping into her Papa, or worse Elphias Garner or one of his cronies. She simply could not bear the thought of being forced to wed that odious man. However her father had gotten himself involved with such an out and out crook she did not know, but it was not fair of him to expect her to rescue him.

Gwen arrived back with a very pretty hat. It was red, with a smart little net veil. She pinned it carefully in place. It set off the warm tones in her hair. "Well, don't you look lovely," Gwen said admiringly.

"This hat, it must have cost you a year's salary," Catherine exclaimed. "I could not possibly wear it." Gwen laughed.

"Before I was a chamber maid I was apprenticed to a smart milliner. She made hats for everyone, Madame Giradis, you may have heard of her."

"I have indeed, then this hat would have been closer to three years' salary! Everyone I knew longed to have her make them a hat. She had a waiting list so long you could make your payment now and not expect to receive your hat for an entire year. Why ever would you leave such a position to become a chamber maid?"

"Because she worked her apprentices to the bone, paid us next to nothing and slung anyone with a soupcon of talent out before they could become any kind of threat to her. I just make these for fun now. I find it soothing. And, working at the hotel can be wonderfully good fun. Well, that is until so many of my friends' have just up and left to find themselves husbands of course." Catherine heard the reprimand, though it was gently given. She was another friend who would leave Gwen behind as soon as she could.

"Why not come with me? Take your chance at finding a husband? Maybe the women out West long for smart hats to make them as fashionable as their Eastern counterparts?" Gwen chuckled at the thought.

"I doubt that many men, even out West, would be happy to have a working wife. No, I'm happy here for now. Maybe one day," she mused.

"Girls, your supper is on the table!" Mrs Ellington called up the stairs. "I shan't be joining you this evening as I shall be going out with Mr Graham." Catherine could hear the girlish hope in their land lady's voice. She had been walking out with Mr Graham for a number of months, but he had yet to ask for her hand. The doughty widow was beginning to believe she might have to start another courtship, but she didn't wish to.

"Good Luck," she and Gwen chorused. "He'll pop the question soon, we are sure of it." They giggled.

"Your post is by your plates girls. The door will be locked at eleven as usual, I expect you to be in before then."

"And we expect you to be in before then too," they said cheekily as they clattered down the stairs to kiss the older woman's plum cheeks and wish her a good evening.

They made their way to the table, finding a tureen of soup and freshly baked bread. The scent of the rich mutton broth made her mouth water, and Catherine ladled them out huge bowlfuls as swiftly as she could. She took a dainty, ladylike spoonful and laughed as she watched Gwen spoon hers in, in great gulps. "They will never be able to accuse me of being a lady," she admitted ruefully. "However can you be so patient? I am always half starved, cannot imagine taking such time over every bite."

"My Mama insisted. She always said that there were few things that could never be forgiven – and to eat in a way off-putting to others was one of them. It often made me wonder how she ever tolerated my Papa's table habits. He was a guzzler, but she never let on." Catherine felt a pang at the thought of those happy days before her Mama had died, when they had appeared to be a loving family with all opportunity and hope ahead of them.

"Your letter, who is it from?" Gwen asked eagerly. Catherine was so glad she had met the young woman, she was almost as invested in her finding a new home and a husband as she herself was and it felt good to have someone to care, to confide in. Catherine put her spoon down carefully and picked up the letter. Her fingers began to shake as she saw the return address was Sun River, Montana. The envelope had clearly gone to Young's Hotel, and they had neatly crossed out their details and put her new address upon it. No wonder it had taken so long to arrive if it had been reposted.

She could barely open the envelope as the tremors began to take over her entire body, a cloud of butterflies jostled for space inside her still empty belly. She had only responded to one man from Montana, that very first advertisement she had read – the one that had given her the idea of how to escape and the one she had most hoped and prayed would answer her. "I can't," she exclaimed, a tear falling onto her cheek. Gwen took her hand.

"Yes, you can. It is going to be fine, you'll see. Would you like me to do it?" Catherine shook her head, and continued to try and prise the envelope open. Finally, admitting defeat, she handed it to Gwen and wordlessly begged for her help. Gwen took the butter knife and raggedly sliced through the stiff paper. A single sheet of paper fluttered out, and a train ticket. Both women gasped as Catherine grabbed for the letter.

Dear Miss Parker

I hope you do not think me rude, but I had the strangest feeling that your letter was written in the kind of haste that could only mean one thing – that you need to escape your current situation as soon as possible. I do not purport to guess your reasons for this, and pray that we shall build up a suitably close relationship that you may choose to confide in me when you are ready. But, in all good conscience I could not let you founder without recourse to some kind of safety. I enclose a ticket which will bring you from Boston to Great Falls.

You do not have to use it, you can choose to spend some time getting to know one another through our correspondence if your needs are not as I suspect, or if they have changed. If you choose to come, I will not hold you to a marriage you may not wish for – but will offer you a position as housekeeper at the hotel I am intending to build, or as my theatre manager whichever would be your preference. I can arrange for you to stay in a boarding house, or with friends of mine should you wish to come. I don't want you to compromise anything, and we can keep it all proper and right.

I am the owner of a small saloon at present. I know this may not seem to be the most respectable of positions to a young woman of your breeding, but it is a simple place where the local people can meet. There are no girls, or any bad behavior. I would not countenance such things. The Minister preaches here every other Sunday in my back room, and many local groups meet here too – or at least they will until the new meeting hall is built. Sun River is growing so fast. We have just finished building a church, and we have a new bakery opening in town too. We have a General Store and a few specialist farm supplies places. But, I think as more and more of the farmers and ranchers marry we will see dress shops and all sorts opening too.

You didn't tell me much about yourself, but I look forward to learning more. I myself am quite a tall man and I have brown hair in need of a barber and long limbs. I will admit I have been called gangly on many an occasion! I don't often have much time for leisure pursuits, but when I do I love to read and visit the theatre in Great Falls. It was why I decided to open one here in Sun River. I think it would be mighty fine to have one closer to home.

The landscape around us here is breathtakingly beautiful and I am sure that there is the potential of attracting visitors here from across the country to see it. The air here is so healthy too, maybe Sun River could become one of those spa places that attract the sick to come and recuperate. As you may tell, I am full of ideas.

I hope I shall be meeting you from the train very soon – but if not, I would very much like to keep writing to you. You intrigue me Miss Parker.

Yours hopefully

Tom Shandon

Catherine passed the letter to Gwen and picked up the train ticket. She could hardly believe a stranger had been so perceptive as to read into her hurriedly scrawled words that she needed to escape. She kissed the ticket, and mentally wished the caress be sent to her kindly benefactor. She would be free. He didn't even demand that she wed him straight off the train. He had offered her a job, and a home. She would have loved him for those things alone – but his gentle manner and his excitement about his plans made him seem somehow youthful and full of hope. She needed such positivity to make her believe in the goodness of others once more. She had been burned so very badly by the one person she should have been able to trust with her life.

"He sounds sweet," Gwen said putting the letter down on the table. "You could leave tomorrow." Catherine could hear the sadness in her voice.

"Then we had better make tonight a night to remember," she said bravely. Gwen nodded and brushed a tear away from her eye.

"I shall miss you."

"We can write, and I'll find you a handsome Montana man to marry so you can come and join me," she teased.

"No you won't. I told you I'm not ready for that. But I'll let you know when I am."

Chapter Four

Tom paced up and down on the platform nervously. If she was coming she would be on the train. If she wasn't, then he had wasted a day. Catherine Parker intrigued him, and the longer he had to wait to get his answers the more she fascinated him. Ever since he had responded to her letter he had been unable to banish her completely from his thoughts. She seemed so worldly, yet so naïve; so capable yet so troubled. He longed to help her in whatever way she might let him.

A distant whistle told him the train was coming, and the cloud of smoke and steam that came with it engulfed him, making him choke. He waited for it to clear, not knowing whether he wished to see a young woman standing in front of him or not. Finally it began to dissipate, and he glanced anxiously at the passengers disembarking: an elderly couple, a group of young men, a widow with a small dog. None of them looked like the image he had in his mind of Catherine. Then he turned to see a young woman with her back to him. She was dressed smartly in the kind of outfit he hadn't seen except in the newspapers, nobody he knew could afford to have anything so fine. She was instructing one of the young porters to find her luggage. "I have four carpet bags," he overheard her say. "Not a trunk." The boy scampered off and she turned.

His breath caught, and his heart began to beat so loudly he was sure she might hear it. She was beautiful. Her chestnut hair gleamed under her neat little hat, the tiny net veil doing nothing to hide her large brown eyes. She had small features, her nose tipped up a little at the end and her ears had tiny pearl studs in them. Though her travelling clothes were in a tasteful muted grey, the cut of the rich velvet hugged her slim figure perfectly, showing the curves to their fullest advantage. "Mr Shandon?" she enquired politely. Tom tried to speak, but his mouth was dry and he simply couldn't. He tried to clear his throat.

"Ahem. I am sorry," he finally managed. "Yes, and you must be Miss Parker?" She nodded. He watched as her eyes flicked up and down him. He was sure he saw a look of something approaching disappointment in her eyes, but she hid it quickly. She turned a smile on him so bright it could have lit up the entire town.

"I am so grateful to you Mr Shandon, I cannot tell you. Thank you, a million times thank you."

"Anyone would have done the same," he said flushing a little with embarrassment. He could feel the heat creeping up his neck and into his cheeks and prayed she wouldn't notice.

"No, they wouldn't – and didn't. Most people don't see what is right in front of them, so to find someone who saw what I hadn't written was a refreshing start to our relationship."

"You flatter me, but I simply sensed you needed a place to escape to – and there is none better than here."

"From the scenery I glanced from the windows of my carriage I would have to agree," she said with a smile.

"There is even more still to come," he told her and was glad to see her face light up at the thought of it. "But, we should get you home to Sun River. It is still quite a drive and I am sure you must be tired and hungry for some good food."

"Where shall I be staying?" she asked as they drove along the well worn road.

"I have arranged for you to stay with my friend Carlton and his wife Myra. She used to be a governess in Boston, I thought as you seemed to come from quite a genteel background that the two of you might have the most in common of any of my acquaintance. She is expecting a baby any day now, so could use a hand around the house so I hoped you might suit one another."

"That sounds wonderful. Do they live far from your saloon?"

"They have a farm in the valley; it's about an hour's ride from town. But, don't fret, if you don't ride yet we can soon teach you so you can come and go as you please."

"It was just that you said you wanted a helpmeet, and offered me a position working for you if we decided we did not suit - I thought I would be working with you?"

"You may do so if you choose – but I think you should let yourself settle in first, and let us get to know one another for a while." He looked into her eyes, worried she might not think it such a good idea, but she nodded.

"I think that is probably a very good idea, but I am so excited by your ideas. I should love to be a part of them if you will let me?"

"They may be some time in coming," he admitted. "I get ideas all the time, never do much about them. But I am going to have to. Things are changing here and the saloon must too. I don't want to find myself left behind."

"Then maybe I shall be the driving force you need to make you take action rather than simply plan," she said cautiously. "I am not much for dreaming. I like to make things happen."

"Then maybe we are a perfect match," he said unguardedly, then wished he had never said it. It was truly strange; he had never found it so easy to talk with anyone. But he knew he had to tread carefully. Just because he was enamored with her at first sight, did not mean that she would feel anything for him in return. He had to be patient, build her trust. He still did not know why she had run from Boston, and he was sure that was important.

Tom smiled as he watched Catherine's face fill with wonder as they drove through the snow-capped mountains, and along the wide road that was Sun River itself. The little town was just a handful of buildings, most of its inhabitants lived on farms in the surrounding valleys. "I know you said it was small, but... one, two, three...," she tailed off as she counted the number of buildings.

"Yup," he said with a grin. "Still manageable on hands right now. But just look at all the plots laid out! There'll be houses and shops on those in no time."

They continued on their way up a winding track out of the little town that turned a corner and then headed back downwards into the valley. A vast herd of cattle could be seen in the distance, and Tom could hear the calls of Mack and Ethan carrying on the wind as they herded them into the foothills for the rich grazing. "You'll be sure to meet them soon enough. Mack owns the ranch and is married to Annie, Ethan's sister. He just married a girl called Maggie. They are good people. You'll like them I'm sure. Maggie used to be a cook at Young's Hotel, where you were staying." Catherine went strangely quiet. "What is it?" he asked her softly.

"I had to leave the hotel. I couldn't afford more than a couple of nights there. But I was so lucky, my chambermaid, Gwen, she told me about the place where she boarded and there was a space there and so I had to move," she said shyly.

"Catherine, you do not have to explain anything to me unless you want to. I am not about to judge anyone because they can't afford to stay in some fancy hotel for weeks on end. I am a straightforward man, with simple tastes. Why, you saw the saloon as we went through. That has been my home for over ten years! It started out as just a tiny hut. I expanded as more people came, but it isn't exactly fancy!"

"But you have plans for it. You don't intend it to remain that way do you?"

"No I don't, but that is so I can keep a roof over my head and food in my belly. If I could leave it as it is, believe me I probably would."

"No, you wouldn't. I think there is an ambitious man inside of you Mr Shandon. I think that is why you came here in the first place, and why you are still here too." Tom was flattered by her assessment of him. She was perceptive, and her soft brown eyes seemed to miss little. He would have to be careful around her, because he was already starting to fall for her. He just prayed that she would find something in him to care for too.

He stopped the horses outside a smart farmhouse. He watched as Catherine took in the tidy yard, the neat strips of vegetables and the beds full of flowers. Two rocking chairs sat on the porch. "This is lovely," she sighed. "Is this where I shall be staying?" He nodded and bounded up onto the stoop, where he knocked loudly on the door.

"Keep your hair on!" a friendly voice hollered. "Tom, you don't know your own strength and I'd like to keep my door where it belongs." Carlton Reed said as he opened the door, a huge grin on his handsome features. "This must be Miss Catherine Parker? Charmed."

"Thank you, and thank you for your hospitality. I would never have expected strangers to take me in, would have been happy to find a boarding house somewhere."

"Well, Myra would have none of it and I must admit I am not sure that Mrs Greig's would have been the right kind of place for a young lady. Full of miners and cowboys – chancers the lot of them," he winked at her and Tom felt his shoulders relax. They were getting on fine, and Catherine seemed happy.

"Welcome," Myra said, waddling out behind her husband. "You could have brought the tea tray for me," she said as she struggled to bend and put it down on a nearby table. "Catherine you are most welcome," she said as she kissed her gently on the cheek. "Please forgive Tom and Carlton, they weren't brought up in the world we were."

"You were a governess?" Catherine asked curiously.

"I was, to the children of Mr and Mrs Hepworth. My family was once quite well to do, nothing quite like the Parker's of course, but things changed."

"Things do – even in the hallowed halls of the Parker's," Catherine admitted.

"You must be exhausted after your travels, so have a cup of tea and then off to bed with you. I've made up the guest bedroom with clean sheets, I'm sure you'll be comfortable there."

"I shall make my excuses and leave you so you can rest," Tom said with a little bow. Carlton laughed, but kindly.

"Your customers will be thirsty too, eh?"

"I certainly hope so. Shall I come and visit with you tomorrow?" he asked Catherine. She nodded.

"Maybe you could teach me to ride so I can come and visit with you occasionally too?" she said with a smile that could just be construed as flirtatious. Tom's heart leapt in his chest, and he had to try ever so hard to hide his hopes.

"I can do that," he said.

Chapter Five

Myra soon had Catherine settled in to her room in the warm and cozy farmhouse. Her room was simple, with a heavy wooden bed and a large armoire. A washstand with a smart china ewer and matching jug meant she could freshen up before bed without having to leave the room again. She fussed around putting her things into the chest of drawers and then sank gladly onto the bed. She lay staring up at the whitewashed ceiling, marveling at how so much had changed in her life in such a short period of time.

Such a short time ago she had been living in her family's handsome town house, the respected daughter of Cornelius Parker. Her place in society had been assured. She moved in all the finest circles, enjoyed the luxuries others could only dream of. Yet in just a few tiny acts, her world had collapsed around her. She was now living in the home of two complete strangers, on the other side of America. It might as well be the other side of the world. Everything seemed so unfamiliar, yet strangely the same. The dusty tracks instead of real roads, the wooden buildings that sat higgledy-piggledy up against one another on the main street in Sun River, and this lovely farm house, and the majestic landscape it nestled within.

Tom's face drifted into her mind. He wasn't every girl's dream of handsome, but he had the kindest eyes she had ever seen and they were a shade of the softest, smokiest grey. He had not lied about being tall either. He towered over her, and even over Carlton who was by no means a short man. But she kind of liked the gangly nature of his limbs. He was endearing, and a little bit uncoordinated, with his big feet and huge hands. But he was astute and had a big heart, she was sure of that, and that made his physical imperfections fade into the dust. He was a good man, and she was beginning to wonder if he was the first truly good man she had ever known. Feeling safe for the first time in too long, she curled up under the covers and soon fell into a deep sleep.

She awoke to the sight of sunbeams dancing on the panes of glass in her window, and moved swiftly to pull the drapes to enjoy the vista before her. The valley looked even more beautiful to her in this early morning light. She could not wait to get outside and explore her new home. She hoped that Tom would come early so she could begin her education in how to be a Montana bride. She had the distinct feeling that her current skill set might be quite redundant.

She made her way downstairs cautiously. She could hear no sounds in the large house, but she was sure she wasn't the first person up. She knew that only city dwellers like her slept in past sun up. She was right; there was a note on the table waiting for her alongside a pitcher of creamy milk, some freshly baked bread and a side of ham. She poured herself a glass of milk, and carved a thick slice of the delicious looking ham. She rolled it up in her fingers and delighted in not having to use a plate or a knife and fork. She took hungry bites as she read the note that told her that Carlton was out in the fields and Myra could be found in the barn with the chickens.

She finished her breakfast quickly and headed outside to go and make herself useful. She found Myra busy scraping at a perch. "Good Morning," she said brightly.

"Should you be doing that?" Catherine asked, surely a pregnant woman should not be around such muck?"

"If I don't nobody else will and then the hens will get sick, we'll get no eggs and then they'll die," she said matter of factly.

"You were truly a governess before you came here?" Catherine asked incredulously. "You seem as if you were born to this life."

"I shall take that as a compliment. I love being here, I love my husband and I don't miss Boston and its snooty folk one bit."

"I know just what you mean." They laughed together. "So, what do you know about Tom?"

"Ahh, a wise woman! He's a love," she said a slightly dreamy expression in her eyes. "Now, don't get me wrong, I love Carlton with all my heart. But Tom, well he always seems so young, in need of a bit of care and support. Not that he can't look after himself, he does. But, he has a real tender soul, would take in every waif and stray in the district. Not a bit of malice or vice in him."

"That is good to hear," Catherine admitted. His owning the saloon had concerned her a little; she did not want to marry a man like her Papa – or be employed by one. "Does he have family?"

"He's never mentioned any, but many of the men out here aren't the talkative type. It's a tough life, but they are good men. They just don't go round telling all and sundry their feelings. Now, we need to find you a riding habit, so that when he gets here you'll look the part and be all ready for him," she said excitedly.

When Tom knocked on the door, Catherine was wearing a smart pair of velvet culottes, in a burgundy red and a smart matching jacket with a light cotton blouse underneath. Considering Myra was a mite taller than her it fitted well, and she couldn't help admiring herself in the looking glass one more time before she ran downstairs to greet him.

He was wearing a Stetson, and a pair of Mr Levi Strauss's denim jeans. He looked every inch the cowboy. She felt her heart flutter a little as she took him in, and could barely speak when he bent down and kissed her lightly on the cheek. "You look lovely, quite the Montana lady," he said softly. She touched her hand to her cheek, still feeling the touch of his lips there.

"You look fine too," she mumbled.

"Shall we go and find you a horse?" he asked with a grin. She nodded. They walked over to the stable block, where three handsome looking mounts were happily chomping on nosebags full of oats. "Now, I think Midnight here might be a little too big for you and Marlin, though lovely and placid is about the strongest horse in these parts – she's happier pulling a plough than being ridden, so Emmy it is," he said as he moved to the stall of a sweet looking grey. "Now, you come here and meet her. She's a sweetie, and she loves a carrot or two." He pulled some from his pockets and gave them to Catherine. "Now, if you hold your hand just so," he showed her and then quickly adjusted the palm she showed him. Then he put the carrot in it, and she tentatively held it out towards the pretty pony.

Catherine gasped as her soft lips moved over her hand, but she could feel no teeth even though she could hear the pony happily crunching on its prize. She giggled. "That tickles," she said.

"It's kinda nice though," Tom said.

"Yes, can I do it again?" he nodded, a broad grin lighting up his face. She noticed he had the cutest smattering of freckles over his nose. It was yet another feature that had him look like an overgrown schoolboy. Tom gave her some carrots and then went to give some to the other horses too.

"I don't want them to feel left out," he said happily. She smiled. He truly was kind and straightforward. She liked that. She felt safe with him, as if he would never lie to her – and that meant more than she could ever say. "Now, it's time to show you how to put on her bridle and saddle." He lifted them down from the wall of the stall as if they weighed nothing at all. He went to hand them to her, and she dropped them immediately.

"However will she manage with that and me on top of her?"

"Horses are much stronger than they look. She's a tough little thing. Now, with the bridle, now come here, you take it in your hand like this." His big hand closed over hers and showed her exactly how to hold the mass of leather straps. "Now, you put the bit in her mouth, then swiftly pull it over her head, and make sure you don't catch her ears, she won't like that one bit." She could feel the muscles in his arm clenching against hers as he deftly maneuvered the bridle into place. Emmy twitched her ears a little, but didn't seem to be the slightest bit bothered. Tom patted her neck affectionately. "Good girl."

"Is every horse this easy?" Catherine asked.

"Nope, which is why we will leave Midnight right where he is. He can be a temperamental old soul when he wants. Emmy is a love, she'll let you make about any mistake in the book without getting riled."

"That is good, because I am already feeling a little overwhelmed."

"You'll be a natural. Just look at Myra, she came here like you – didn't know a single thing about life in the country, on a farm. But she's an excellent rider now, and manages this place so it runs like clockwork. Just give yourself time, and be patient."

"I've never been much good at patience I'm afraid," she admitted. "I like to be good at things straight away."

"Well, you shall have to curb that a little," he said playfully flicking his finger down her nose. It was the first outwardly flirtatious thing he had said or done, and she found herself fluttering her eyelashes at him just a little. He seemed to like her, and that was wonderful – because just his being so close that she could feel the heat from his lean body was doing all kinds of strange things to her senses.

The rest of the lesson in the stable went well, though Catherine was sure she wouldn't remember a thing Tom had said about how to strap the saddle on tightly or to adjust the stirrups. Her insides seemed to have turned to jelly, and she no longer wanted to learn to ride at all. All she wanted was for him to take her in his arms and kiss her until she forgot about everything that had brought her to Montana. But, he seemed determined to be a perfect gentleman, and so she found herself trying to think of ways to encourage him. Her upbringing simply hadn't covered such things. Young ladies weren't supposed to ever show desire, or even feel it. But she did, and she longed to find out more about the attraction that was building between them.

She got her chance though when they went outside and Tom took Emmy to the mounting block. Patiently he showed Catherine exactly what to do, taking each movement and slowing it down. It was funny watching his long limbs as they straddled the pony. He made Emmy look like a toy. She was nervous, he made it look so easy, but as she put her foot in the stirrup as he advised, she lost her balance. He was just behind her, and in a split second he had her cradled safely in his arms. "Whoah there," he said as she gazed up at him. "Take it slower."

"But I don't want to," she said wickedly as she pulled his head down to hers and kissed him full on the lips. He resisted, but only for the shortest moment. Then, his lips softened under hers, and he began to deepen the kiss, running his tongue gently across her mouth, encouraging her to open up to him. She was almost paralyzed by the sensations that rushed through her body. Every part of her seemed to be alive with electricity, tingling and sparking until she could hardly bear it. She snaked her arms around his body, feeling the interplay of the muscles in his back as he held her so tightly.

"Catherine, we shouldn't," he murmured against her neck, trailing kisses from her ear lobe to the collar of her jacket. "Especially not in broad daylight, in front of anyone who cares to look out."

"Myra is the only person here," she said dreamily. "She won't mind."

"But Carlton may, could come back at any moment. I don't think he would take kindly to my sullying a guest in his home."

"Sullying me?" she giggled. "If this is being sullied I wish I had learned about it much sooner. It's delicious."

"Yes it is, but you'll never learn to ride if we are both this easily distracted." She looked at him seriously.

"Hmm, you are right of course. Maybe I could ask Carlton to teach me? There'd be less chance of my being distracted then," she said outrageously.

"You are a minx. I should send you home on the first train out of here," Tom teased. She pulled away from him, a cold chill suddenly coming over every inch of her.

"You wouldn't?" she asked anxiously.

"No, of course I wouldn't. In fact I have every intention of doing the opposite, want you to marry me as soon as possible so that you can never do so."

Chapter Six

She stared at him as if he had said the most ridiculous thing in the world. Her face was pale, had blanched pure white when he had teased about sending her home. There truly was something terrible that had happened there and she was petrified of having to return. "Catherine, why did you want to run away to Montana," he asked before she could respond to his clumsy proposal. He didn't want it to be that way, she deserved romance and everything a girl could dream of.

"I didn't," she said, clumsily moving further away from him. "I just saw your advertisement and thought it might be an adventure."

"Don't lie to me, I think you applied to every man you could because you couldn't wait to get away. Now why?" Her eyes clouded over, their usual warm brown now looked almost flinty and hard.

"If I don't tell you will you send me back there? Will that mean you won't offer me a job? That you no longer wish to marry me?"

"No, of course not. But if you have any intentions of accepting my terribly timed proposal, then I want you to know I only ever wanted a true wife – one who would share everything with me, including her secrets."

"So will you tell me yours?" she spat angrily as if she expected him to keep his own past to himself. He wondered what kind of men she had known before, but he believed firmly that a relationship should be between equals. If she could accept his past, his mistakes then he could forgive hers.

"Yes, what do you want to know?" he said calmly. She sagged, and collapsed to the ground where she sat cross-legged like a little girl. He hunkered down beside her, and pulled her close, putting his arm around her shoulder.

"Why did you come here? Why do you run a saloon when you don't drink?" He chuckled.

"Ah, straight to the point. I came here because I was running away from the man I thought I might become. My Papa was an alcoholic and he was never faithful to my Mama. As a boy you want to impress your father, to make him proud and so I tried to be like him. He didn't approve of the fact that by my nature I was more like my sweet and gentle Mama. But I tried. The problem is, liquor is a demon, and soon it did have me under its thrall as much as it had ever had my father. I couldn't give it up. My Mama died, and I kept on drinking. My Papa was killed in an accident – he worked on the railroads. Accidents are common, especially to someone too drunk to notice an oncoming train." Catherine gasped, and put a hand out to comfort him. He pushed it down. "No, I don't deserve pity for that. It happened and there is nothing I can do about it now. My Papa was a fool – and I was one for treating him like a hero."

"I wasn't going to offer you pity. My Papa turned to alcohol after my Mama died too. I know it can be hard to lose someone you love, but it is so much harder to lose them when they are still alive. Alcohol is a cruel master." Her comment was pithy, but not hard. But he could sense that she had withdrawn from him a little. He could understand that, he had just admitted to using alcohol in the same way her father had, and it wouldn't surprise him if that scared her.

"It is indeed. My Papa's death woke me up to what might be my fate and I took the decision to change my life. I came out here to Montana. My hope was that as a trapper, in the wild, I would have no access to liquor and I was right. I was a terrible trapper, but the solitude and the privations helped me to move forward. I will never touch another drop as long as I live."

"I believe you," she said earnestly. Her eyes told him she believed him, but her pretty face was still pale though, and he wondered if honesty truly was the best policy. What if it meant he lost her? He had only just found her? But she had to know the truth, had to accept him for everything he was – not just the man he had become. It would not take much for him to slip backwards, he knew that. "So why the saloon?"

"Someone had to. There were growing numbers of men arriving. They wanted somewhere to congregate, to unwind after a hard day. As I said, I was a terrible trapper. Somewhere in my mind I think I convinced myself that it would be the ultimate test. If I could stay sober even when surrounded by my worst fear then I would be able to stay that way for a lifetime."

"It makes sense, I think." Catherine reached up and stroked his cheek. "You mustn't blame yourself. You achieved something many men can't, even when the most dreadful consequences are put in front of them if they do not."

"Your Father was tested?"

"And came up wanting," she said sadly. "He gambled too, and he had debts all over town. He signed a contract with a despicable man and still he couldn't pay. Elphias Garner made him sign a contract that said he could take the prize of his choosing if Papa did not pay in time. Then, out of the blue he started insisting that I marry Elphias. I can only assume that I was the prize and my dear, loving Papa was prepared to sell me to get rid of his debts once and for all."

Tom stayed silent, just letting her words sink in. He squeezed her in to his body even more tightly. He wanted her to know that he would not go anywhere, would always be by her side – but the anger inside him was raging that anyone could do such a heartless and cruel thing. He didn't dare speak. Did not want her to think he was angry at her. Finally he turned her head so that she faced him squarely. He looked deeply into her eyes.

"Catherine, your Father has done you wrong and I long to take him to task for doing so. But I will not do anything without your permission. I have a question to ask, and I want you to think very carefully about it before you answer." She nodded, and stared back at him just as intently.

"Catherine, I know you still love your Father,"

"No, how could I after what he has done," she cried.

"Because he is your Father and wasn't always as he is now." She sank back against his body, tears flooding down her cheeks. She nodded and bit at her lip in her anguish. "If I could pay his debts, and bring him here to Montana and help him to give up drinking – if he wants to do so – would you want me to do that for him?"

"But he won't, he'll just take the money and gamble and drink that away again too."

"He won't get the money if he isn't prepared to get sober," Tom said adamantly. "But, if you want me to try and help him I will go to Boston and seek him out – even though every part of me longs to do him harm rather than give him a second chance."

"Oh Tom, heaven sent you to me, I am sure of it," she cried as she covered his face in kisses. "I want to hate him, but you are right. I cannot do it. I love him and I know he is still in there somewhere, we just have to find him again. I often felt that if I could just get him to leave Boston, where all his memories of Mama were, that he would be able to move forward in his grief and rebuild his life. But I had no power to make him do so."

"I think we should get you inside. You will need to rest. When I get back we will both need to be ready to be strong, if he chooses to come back with me. If he does not, then we shall have a wedding to plan – the first in our brand new church!"

"You still want to marry me?" she asked him, her little face looking so delightfully surprised that he longed to kiss her and take away all her fears.

"Oh my love, your Father's sins are not yours. Why would I love you less for telling me that you were strong and brave and did everything you could to survive such a difficult situation? You silly moppet. I think I loved you from your very first letter. I always did want to rescue a damsel in distress!" She smiled up at him, and laughed weakly. He kissed her on the forehead and then picked her up and took her inside the farmhouse.

When he came back down the stairs having deposited her gently onto her bed where she had almost immediately fallen into a peaceful sleep, Myra gave him a quizzical look. "Take care of her for me while I am gone?" he asked.

"Of course. How long will it be before we see you again?" she teased him.

"It may be a few weeks."

"Sorry?" Myra looked completely confused. "I am sure I saw two people kissing, rather passionately in my yard not half an hour ago, so much so that you seem to have quite worn poor Catherine out!"

"You did, and I did not. But that is not why I will be away. Maybe Catherine will tell you, it is not my place to do so. But, when I return I will make her my wife, whatever happens."

"What of the saloon?"

"It can stay closed, or if Ethan has the time he can open it up. I don't care." He knew his behavior was impulsive, and out of character. But, for once he knew that the more he thought about this, the less likely he would be to do the right thing, and to find out what had truly happened to Catherine's Papa. He knew alcohol, and its wiles – but it took a lot to make a happy man turn to it as a solace, even when bad things happened. Either there was something more to the story than Catherine knew, or he had always had a problem and just hidden it well.

Chapter Seven

Tom was itching with frustration by the time the grand locomotive pulled into the station in Boston. The journey had done nothing to calm his anger, but he had at least managed to make some plans as to how to go about his business. He made straight for the imposing town house that had once been Catherine's home and knocked loudly upon the grand front door. A wizened old man opened it cautiously. "You must be Wilson," he said. "I am a friend of Miss Catherine's." The man's thin lips parted in surprise, as he opened the door a little wider and ushered him in.

"Miss Catherine is all right?" he asked cautiously. "We have all been so worried for her."

"Miss Catherine is fine. I am here to try and help her father, if he will let me."

"Mr Parker has barely left his room since Miss Catherine left. He has been beside himself with worry." Tom snorted in derision. "No Sir, whatever you may have heard of him, he truly has been sick with worry. Has even stopped asking me to bring up his claret in recent days. Tom's ears pricked up at this tidbit of news. Had Mr Parker already begun to try and change his habits? He prayed it was so, for Catherine's sake.

"I must see him, whether you believe him fit to see visitors or not. I have a message from Catherine and she insisted I give it to nobody but him," he said slyly. The old butler was clearly too tired, and himself overwrought with concern for his erstwhile master, and his errant daughter.

"Come this way," he said as he began to climb the ornamental staircase that dominated the hallway slowly. He halted in front of a pair of gilded doors and nodded. "This is the master's suite," he said. "If you need anything, just ring the bell by the mantle."

"Thank you Wilson," Tom said and watched as the poor old man made his way back to wherever his duties needed him most. He took a deep breath, and knocked sharply on the door before turning the handle and marching right in.

"Mr Parker," he said in an authoritative voice. I am here on behalf of your daughter Catherine." There was no response from the great, canopied bed and so Tom moved in closer. He could hear the man's heavy breathing. It was ragged, and came in fits and gasps.

"Who are you," the grey looking man in the bed said as he came closer. His voice was husky, and quiet. Tom remembered having felt this way. The first few weeks without alcohol had most definitely been the hardest. It had felt as if he had the worst influenza, diphtheria and typhoid all at once – but there was no peaceful end in death.

"My name is Tom Shandon. I came to ask for your daughter's hand in marriage." Mr Parker raised an eyebrow.

"I doubt that," he said. "My daughter has been missing for months."

"Yes, she has been in hiding here in Boston, and recently joined me in Montana. I wish to marry her and would like your blessing," he repeated.

"If you have ever met her, which I doubt, then you would not be here asking my permission to marry her. You would be here wishing to kill me."

"Well I must admit, when she told me that you had as good as sold her to pay off your debts I did want to do exactly that. But for some reason she still loves you, wants to help you. And so, I am here to pay those debts, and to ask if you would agree to return to Montana with me. There are conditions to this offer. If you are to come with me, you must renounce alcohol for all time. I shall help you, as will Catherine to do so – but I must warn you I do run a saloon so temptation will be great."

"Why would you do such a thing? I do not deserve your sympathy, your charity."

"No, you do not. But I was once bound to alcohol myself. I know how tight those chains can be. I have managed to purge it from my life, and I know that if you wish to do so, you can too. The question I am asking you is this: is your daughter enough of a reason for you to do so? I know she hasn't been in the past, but is she now?"

"I have not drunk a drop in days," Mr Parker said wearily.

"I know, Wilson told me. But was that from choice?"

"Yes. I couldn't bear being without her, and I knew that the only way I could make it up to her was to be sober, to have paid my debts, to tell her my secrets."

"I guessed there may have been more to it than just the loss of your wife. What has been tormenting you Sir?"

"I loved my wife, more than any man should ever love another soul. She was so much fun, so sweet and everyone wanted her to be theirs. I was so proud when she agreed to be my wife. But, the delightful flirt I had fallen in love with turned out not to be just an act; she used it to gain herself a wealthy husband. You might say it was her vice, like alcohol and gambling became mine. But I loved her, blindly and stupidly. It was not until her death that I found out that she had been cuckolding me throughout our marriage. The rumors flew. I raged at them, swore my life on her virtue. But there was one man, Elphias Garner. He turned up at my place of business, with some very incriminating proof of my wife's infidelities. I could not bear for Catherine's memories of her Mama to be sullied. Did not want her to think less of her, and so I began to pay Garner to keep quiet."

"But he kept threatening to expose what he knew?" Mr Parker nodded. Tom did not want to feel pity for this man, but he had to admit it must have been a hard thing to cope with. He had lost the woman he adored, and then lost her again as he found out that she wasn't the woman he had believed her to be either.

"Indeed. Garner had known my wife, I don't think he ever knew her carnally, but he knew her better than I did. That hurt me, but I had to keep the truth from Catherine. But, a secret only ever festers, and it began to eat away at my soul - that I could tell nobody of my sadness, my loss made it that much harder to bear. Especially when Garner told me in a sneering voice that my wife hadn't been sure that Catherine was even my child."

"I think it is time for you to tell your daughter the truth Sir. She will not love you less because of other's sins. However, you still need to explain why you wanted her to marry such a man?"

"Garner kept pushing, and the more I broke the more he pushed. He waited until I had nowhere to turn, and then he sprang his little trap. I will not deny that I should never have agreed to such a thing. I should have found any way to expose him for the piece of detritus that he is, but I was so scared, and I had nothing left to fight him with. This house has been mortgaged to the hilt, I owed money to everyone I knew, my business was failing. The only thing I had left was Catherine, and in my weakness I was prepared to lose her completely, to have her hate me as I deserved to be hated rather than tell her the truth."

"The webs we weave," Tom sighed. "I think even I can forgive you in such circumstances, though you will have a lot of work to do to prove to me that your contrition is genuine. But, Catherine is good and kind, she will forgive you. She will understand, and I doubt if she will feel that the possibility you may not be her Father is anything to be concerned over. She strikes me as the kind of woman who can deal with that, and who will understand that the man who loved her and brought her up is her Papa and nobody else." The older man had tears pouring down his craggy cheeks as

Tom spoke. "Now, do you think you can give up alcohol and learn not to keep secrets any longer?"

"I do, please, please take me to my daughter," he begged. Tom smiled at him.

"I will, but you will need to rest before we can undertake the journey, and I have some business to attend to with your Mr Garner."

Using the directions Mr Parker had given him it did not take Tom long to find his way to the dingy offices of Elphias Garner. The man was clearly a loan shark, and it made Tom wonder how a woman who had married someone such as Nathaniel Parker, had met him. There was more to this than Nathaniel knew, he was sure of it. But, as he entered the office a stench of decay hit his nostrils making him almost back straight out again. He looked up and down the street outside. Nobody was around, the tenements looked as if they could collapse at any minute. He went back inside, pinching his fingers over his nostrils.

He wandered through the maze of rooms, not sure what he was looking for but it was clear that nobody had been here in days. A large safe took up much of one of the little rooms, it lay open. Tom was surprised to see such a thing. A man such as Garner would surely keep both his secrets and his money locked up tightly. But, as he sifted through what was left inside he could see that other than any money that may have been in here little else had been taken. He found stacks of envelopes, each with a name printed neatly on the front, each stuffed with documents and even photographs. He rifled through them quickly and found the ones that related to the Parkers.

He leafed through the contents. In it was a record of the money Nathaniel owed him, and the money he had paid to keep his secrets. There were also details about his daily activities, and a large photograph of Catherine. Tom wondered how often the old lecher had taken it out to gaze at it, it was covered in sweaty fingerprints. But, the interesting information was inside the envelope with Catherine's Mama's name emblazoned over it. Snatching them all up, he rushed back to the town house, and began to prepare Nathaniel for his journey to Montana.

Who knew if Nathaniel would choose to stay out West with his daughter, or even if he would be able to make the changes he seemed to want to make. Tom wondered if either of the Parkers would ever see this house again, or if arranging its sale through the family's lawyers would be for the best so that they and their staff could make a new start. But Nathaniel and Catherine needed to choose whether to do that, it was not his place, though he would do whatever he could when the time came.

Epilogue

Catherine had kept herself busy after Tom had left. She couldn't stop herself from being anxious, both for her Papa and for the man she now knew she loved with all her heart. She had convinced Carlton to teach her to ride, and was now more than competent in the saddle and she had used her new found skill to ride into town and look around the place of work of her husband to be. She had taken one look at the rough wooden bar, and the dirty looking slatted walls and had decided that something had to be done. Sun River was now a place for families, and this place needed to adapt to fit that. She could see people choosing to dine here, and meet up for special occasions. But she didn't want to upset the men who might still be single and would still want a quiet place to enjoy a drink and a game of cards.

She had worked hard, whilst running the saloon as best she could, letting Ethan get on with his real work. But, she really needed Tom to come back before she began authorizing any actual building work, and so she was now kicking her heels praying for a swift return. She longed to be his wife, and for them to build a wonderful life here together. She looked up from where she was scrubbing the floor behind the bar when she heard the bell ring above the door. "Good golly," she heard a voice exclaim, one she had longed to hear for too long. "Catherine, are you in here?"

She stood up, and looked into Tom's sparkling grey eyes. She rushed out from behind the bar and flung herself into his arms. "Do you like it?" she asked as she kissed him all over his face.

"The bar, or the kisses?" he asked with a grin. "I have to admit, I love both!"

"I am so glad you are home. I think we should turn the meeting room into a restaurant. We could extend out back, to build the kitchens. We could be the first restaurant for miles. People could come to us for their birthdays, their anniversaries, their weddings…" she tailed off with a flutter of her long eyelashes.

"I take it you wish to have a big party for our wedding?"

"It would be wonderful publicity. We could invite everyone," she enthused.

"We could indeed. But, much as I love your excitement aren't you even curious as to what has been happening to me?"

"Well, Papa isn't with you, so rather than dwell on what can never be I thought it best to look to the future," she said bravely, but she could hear the emotion in her voice.

"Your Papa did come with me sweetheart, he's settling in up at Carlton and Myra's, though I think we will need to get you two a house of your own, Myra can only be days away and they'll need their peace then. I went there first, didn't expect to find you here running the saloon!"

"It is such fun. Everyone is so kind, and friendly. I feel I've gotten to know about the entire district now," she said with a grin. "He truly came? He wants to stop drinking?"

"He had already begun to before I even got there Catherine. He is so wracked with guilt. But, I think we should go home and talk about all that in privacy," he said softly, kissing her on her smooth forehead. She nodded.

"Marshall, will you be all right for the rest of the evening?" she called to a good looking lad who had suddenly appeared from out the back. He nodded eagerly and picked up the scrubbing brush she had so recently set down. Tom looked at her quizzically.

"Who is Marshall?" he asked.

"He works for us. He's ever so diligent. He's old Henry's lad."

"You really have gotten to know everyone haven't you?" Old Henry never comes into town!"

"He's been coming since I did the place up, he says he likes it now it looks clean and hospitable." Tom shook his head in amazement as he looked back at the refurbished, and altogether more elegant, bar he now owned.

"It looks like my bar, but it truly isn't now is it?" he asked her. "With those whitewashed walls, pretty drapes and polished tables. But, I have to admit it my love, I like it!"

They rode home swiftly, and Catherine burst into the house and ran into the parlor where her Papa was sat quietly, wrapped up in a warm blanket. He was shivering still, though the fire was roaring. "Papa?" she said as she kissed him and held him tightly.

"Oh my darling," he wept. Myra and Carlton politely left the room, and Tom told her everything her father had told him. She held his hand throughout, and when Tom was finished she kissed him again.

"You poor silly man," she chided him gently. "You will always be my Papa, nobody else could ever take your place in my heart." He held her tightly and they both sobbed.

"There was something else I discovered. I don't know if it is going to make you happy or sad, or maybe a bit of both – but you should know,"

Tom said cautiously. Catherine looked at him, wondering what on earth he could have left out.

"I also found this file," he said as he handed over the file with her mother's name on it. "It seems that Mr Garner had been blackmailing your Mama since her marriage to your Papa. He knew she came from the tenements, was not the Society Miss she made herself out to be. He helped her to create the persona she portrayed so cleverly all her life. But, when she refused to pay him any more to keep her secrets, he threatened to make it known that she was cuckolding you, Sir.

"I don't understand? He was blackmailing me about something that was a fabrication?" Papa asked.

"Indeed, I have pored over these files carefully. He has no such evidence. He only ever showed you the envelope and the list of places he believed she had been conducting her affaires in didn't he?" Papa nodded. Catherine sat with open-mouthed astonishment at the lengths Tom had gone to for her, for her family. She truly had chosen a good man. She could never be angry with her Papa when his actions had led her here, to this clever and funny man who loved her enough to risk everything.

"Garner followed your Mama everywhere. He was a constant shadow and so he was easily able to compile lists of times when she was not seen with anyone. He knew that the inability to account for her whereabouts accurately at those times would be enough to drive you mad. He knew this, because the times he knew she was with you drove him crazy with jealousy, he was in love with her, and never forgave you for being the man who won her heart Nathaniel."

"So he wanted to punish me?" Tom nodded.

"That was why he wanted Catherine. I though this picture was of Catherine, but when I looked at it more closely, I could see that it had been handled too many times and was too faded to be Catherine, plus I know you do not have that tiny mole under your ear," he pointed to the mark on the page. "This is a picture of your Mama when she was your age." Nathaniel nodded.

"She was so beautiful."

"Yes she was, and it would seem that she never betrayed you after all. Which means, that unequivocally you must be my Papa," Catherine said delightedly. She kissed him, then stood and flung her arms around her husband. "Now, I believe we said something about getting married once you came home?"

"But what about the advertisement for the new restaurant?" he teased her.

"I don't think I can wait that long. The new Minister arrives in town tomorrow, shall we ask him to do it the day after?" He bent his head and kissed her deeply. She knew that was a yes.

The End

* * * * *

A Bride for Matthew
Book 5

Chapter One

The gasp from the audience was incredulous, almost comical in its abject horror. Somehow it made everything seem even more unreal. Emily clutched at her throat, as if clawing for air but none seemed to be making it to her lungs. The air seemed hazy around her as if she was in a dream and not in the ring with Claude nuzzling at her gently, clearly wondering why she wasn't getting up to finish the act. She tried to reach out and pet his soft nose, to fondle his long ears, to reassure him that she was alright. But, he seemed so far away too.

"Emily, Emily!" Marcus the ring master cried as he rushed to her side. She turned to see the look of concern in his eyes and knew that something terrible had happened. "Stay completely still. Don't move. Claude, damn you, get away from her you stupid ass." Emily watched as Marcus tethered her beloved donkey away from her. He was probably right, but she wanted to tell him not to be so impatient with him. Claude was her family, as much a part of her as her long copper hair, or her flashing green eyes – and like them he was one of such a few things that she had left from her flamboyant and generous Papa.

She drifted away, remembering the wonderful childhood she had enjoyed. Being a circus child wasn't always fun, but for her it had been. Her parents had an Act. They were a big name in the circus world and people travelled from miles around when the circus was in town to see them and their bareback horses doing their tricks. Mama would ride, dressed in the most glorious of costumes, performing tricks while Papa would bounce from horse to horse, as if trying to chase her down and claim her as his own. Their acrobatic skills, their horsemanship and their dedication to one another had made for a heady mix. The crowds adored them. Their popularity had led them here, to Boston, to become a part of a Circus that never travelled. The giant arena was a permanent structure – yet it appeared to be just like the big tops of the travelling shows. Every night of the year it was full of the very best performers in the country: clowns and acrobats, aerialists and sharp shooters, magicians and novelty acts. It had meant that the little family had been able to set down some roots, and that she and her older brother, Evan, had been able to go to school.

Emily had so longed to be like them, but it had become clear very early on that she would never become a part of their Act unlike Evan who had inherited all their grace and skill. She simply wasn't able to emulate them no matter how hard she tried. She could do the tricks, and she loved the ponies, but she simply didn't fit the smoothly executed and almost balletic style they embodied. But, then Papa had found Claude. He was an abandoned pit donkey, and had been nothing but skin and bones. But, she had adored him from their very first meeting. He was clever and gentle, but he had a wickedly cheeky nature and that had given her an idea. In secret she had begun to practice the tricks she had learned from Papa, but aiming to be even more ungainly and clumsy. Their partnership was the antidote to the glamour of her parents' Act, and their antics never failed to make the crowds laugh. But, it seemed that this time she might just have gone too far.

"Emily, stay with me now. Wake up. The doctor is on his way." She opened her eyes to see Mama gazing down at her, tears in her eyes. She was in bed, at home. She wondered how long she had been unconscious. She couldn't deny that every bit of her hurt, she had never had such a fall. Emily tried to speak, she needed to know that Claude was alright, but the words wouldn't come. But Mama knew her so well, knew her agitation would never be for her own welfare. "Baby girl, don't you worry, Claude is in his stall. Evan is taking care of him for you." She relaxed. Her brother was just like Papa, he had a way with animals that put them at their ease and he would reassure Claude. The daft old creature would pine without her, but Evan would make sure he didn't suffer too badly.

A smart looking man in a dark morning coat entered the room, and began bustling around her. "She should not have been moved." He huffed, and looked at Mama in a condescending manner. "It could have caused damage to her spine."

"We know what we are doing Dr Bright," Mama said firmly. "We may be circus folk, but we have been caring for our own for generations. I doubt there is much we don't know about how to care for someone after a fall – they happen almost daily after all." Emily wanted to chuckle, but it was too painful. Mama was tiny, under five feet, but what she lacked in size she had always more than made up for in force of will. "We immobilized her as best we could and as you can see she is still strapped to the boards we used. I am sure she would appreciate your speedy assessment so we can take her from them so she can be a little more comfortable."

"Your ingenuity is impressive," the pompous doctor opined, "though possibly a little over zealous. But, always best to be cautious." He prodded and poked at her limbs, making Emily cry out. "Well, it would seem she still has sensation everywhere," he admitted. "She has a few broken ribs, a lot of bruising, a broken arm and leg, and her left foot is crushed."

"But will she heal?"

"Yes, but I don't think that was what you really wished to ask. I think your question was will she be able to perform again."

"You are right," Mama said impatiently. "That is what I was asking. I am a heartless fiend who only wants to see my daughter in the ring risking her life. Dr Bright, I can assure you that I only wished to know if she would heal. If I had wished to know anything else then I would have asked that." It often amused Emily that Mama was the only member of the family who was not a red head – yet she was the owner of the infamous red-headed temperament. Papa had been the most easygoing of men, and Evan and herself were both very calm, despite their shocks of copper bright hair.

"I'm sorry, I am sure. But, maybe she might wish to know what her future may hold, even if you do not?" the doctor added waspishly. "I think it unlikely that she will ever be able to undertake her tricks in the ring, though I am sure she may prove me wrong – especially if she has even half the fire of her Mama. I'll deliver my bill to the circus. Good day."

"What an absolutely horrible man!" Mama exclaimed as he swept from the room. Emily could only manage a weak smile. He may not have delivered the news in a caring manner, but it didn't change it. She would be unlikely to make a full recovery, may never be able to vault onto Claude's back again pretending to be intoxicated, or to fall from him and ride him upside down, clutching at his belly, her head only an inch or so from the sawdust beneath. She would probably have to accept that they may never make people laugh and smile at their antics ever again. She could feel the tears building inside her, the pain of that was overwhelming – far more so than the physical pain she was in. To be without an Act in the circus was to be no-one. She had worked so hard to find her niche, to build her place in this world. She had always known she would never command audiences as her Mama and Papa had done, and how Evan and Mama now continued to do, that she had her place in the show here because of who they were, and not entirely because of her own talents - but she was a good performer, and she simply didn't know how to do anything else.

"Mama," she managed to croak. "Mama, I'm tired."

"I know. Here, take some of the laudanum he left you, you'll be in dreamless sleep in no time my darling." Emily accepted the carefully measured drops her Mama gave her on a spoon, and was glad to feel the sleepy nothingness begin to overwhelm her. "You can do anything you want to," she heard her Mama say, as if she was a million miles away and not right beside her. "Doctors aren't always right, remember that."

The sun was streaming brightly into her room when Emily awoke. Mama was snoozing in the chair beside her, a newspaper clutched in her hand, about to fall to the floor. She looked like a tiny china doll. Emily had often wondered how someone so slight could be so very strong in every way, but she was indomitable. Even when Papa had passed away Mama had been stoical. Emily couldn't ever remember seeing her cry, yet today there were undeniable streaks in her stage makeup that she still had not removed - streaks that told Emily of the tears that had been shed on her behalf. She remembered the doctor's words, and wondered what on earth she would do if he was right and her own tears began to fall too.

"Oh Emily, don't cry," Mama said waking as she heard her sobs.

"I can't help it. It just all seems too much," she admitted.

"Just concentrate on healing for now my darling, we can worry about everything else later."

"I know, but I can't seem to get it out of my mind. Maybe if I were to read, or do something to take my mind off my woes?" she suggested hopefully.

"Here, take my newspaper, I'll get you some novels to read from the lending library."

"You may want to get changed and take off your makeup before you go anywhere," Emily teased weakly.

"You may be right, and if you can still joke there is always hope." Mama smiled as she left the room. Emily wondered whether she would be able to keep up the pretense that she could cope with this. She had no desire to be a burden to her family, and knew that Major Cranhorn would not tolerate having an Act that did not pull its weight. His Circus was run like an army battalion, and there was no room for either her or Claude if they could not be in the ring night after night.

Emily pulled herself upright as best she could, she found the newspaper a little difficult to manage with her sore arm, and the throbbing pain in her chest from her broken ribs, but she persevered. She had to think about something other than what might be her future. But, she was unable to forget even for a moment. There was an article about her accident, and it made her cringe to read about the moment that had changed her life forever. It sounded so fantastical, as if it couldn't possibly be real. One of the lions had a bad tooth, and he had been cranky for days, but he had chosen the moment when Emily had been leaping through a hoop of fire to let his indignation be fully known. Claude had panicked at the sound of the bellowing roar coming from behind the scenes and had bolted. Emily had been distracted, hadn't prepared for the fall. It sounded so foolish in black and white, not anything that could take away a person's entire career and yet it just might do so.

There was little else to interest her in the pages and so she cautiously turned to the Matrimonials page. It had always amused her to think that people would place an advertisement to find a husband or a wife, and she loved to try and imagine what the people behind the words might be like. Evan thought she was crazy, her Mama knew her to be a romantic. She had always dreamed of being swept off her feet by some glamorous man with a great Act, but now she looked at those advertisements through different eyes. This may be her only chance now, the only way she may find peace. If she couldn't be in the Circus she was sure she couldn't bear to be around it, a reminder of all she had lost. But a husband in the West could be a new start.

A number of them intrigued her, but one in particular stood out. They had travelled through the West when she was a girl, before the permanent job here in Boston. She remembered Montana as a beautiful place, and she was sure she could be happy there. But it wasn't just where this gentleman came from that she felt drawn to.

A Gentleman of Montana seeks a woman with a view to matrimony. She must be patient and kind, and love children as the subscriber is the father of a young boy who is bright and honest and in need of a Mother. A love of theatre and the arts would be ideal, and some interest in running a good home a benefit. The subscriber has grand plans, and someone to encourage him would be most preferred. Replies to Box 452 The Boston Globe

Emily read the words with fascination. Well, she had never been to an actual theatre in her life, but she had seen opera singers and plays put on in the Ring all the time. She loved children, and was usually good with them. She wasn't the best housekeeper, but she could learn and she could definitely encourage someone to be the best they could be. She would contact him as soon as she could, though she did not know how she would manage to do so without her Mama or Evan finding out. "Miss Wilkins, I've brought you some hot chocolate from your Mama," Maisie their maid said as she bustled into the room. Emily smiled, Maisie would be perfect. She was the most discrete person she had ever known, and more of a romantic than Emily herself.

Chapter Two

Matthew was busy. He barely had a moment to himself, but he liked it that way. He knew he was taking a huge risk, but he was sure that it would be worthwhile. Sun River was small, but there were many farmers and ranchers living in the valleys nearby. Many were cultured men and women and often travelled into Great Falls or even as far as Billings to attend plays, and concerts. A small theatre was just what the town needed to brighten up the long winter evenings, and he was the man to deliver it. He pored over the plans, sweeping his hand through his long hair to keep it out of his eyes as he did so.

"We can't do that with the timber that has been delivered," Ardloe said gruffly as he pointed at the sweeping arches that were intended to make up the grand hallway.

"Why not?" Matthew asked slightly distractedly.

"Because, the planks aren't long enough and it has been cut the wrong way. It'll break before you put any weight at all on it, let alone the entire roof."

"What way is the wrong way? No, don't answer I don't need to know. Are they what we ordered?"

"No, I ordered what we needed."

"Then leave it with me, I'll go into Great Falls and complain. Write down exactly what it is I need and I'll bring it back with me. No, better yet, they could still bamboozle me as I don't have a clue what you are talking about - you'd better come with me." Ardloe nodded, and began to load the wood up onto a large wagon.

"I'll get the men to keep on with the main structure. They should have it raised by the end of the day, and then you'll at least have a building by the end of the week," Ardloe chuckled. Matthew looked at the frames currently lying out on the ground, and wondered how Ardloe was always so optimistic. But, he was also always right. Most of the buildings in the rapidly growing town, including the brand new church had been created by the talented master craftsman. They seemed to appear almost overnight, and he'd yet to hear anyone complain about shoddy workmanship.

"I'll just nip to the Saloon, I need to see if Tom has any mail for me, then we'll be on our way," Matthew said as he ran down the wide main street. He could hear Ardloe grunting with the exertion of loading the timber, and knew he should have stayed to help him, but he always seemed to be more of a hindrance than a help. He was ridiculously clumsy. As if to prove his point, he tripped over the step as he rushed into the Saloon, and landed face first on the highly polished floor.

"Well, hello Matthew. How lovely for you to drop by, I do enjoy having a man at my feet ready to indulge my every whim," Catherine, Tom's new bride, teased him. She offered him a hand to help him to rise, and he dusted himself down.

"Hello Catherine. Well, I can see marriage is suiting you well by the glow in your lovely cheeks," he said as he kissed her gently on the cheek in greeting. "Is Tom about?"

"No, your cousin is out with my father. They have been taking some very long walks into the mountains. They seem to have much to discuss, though I am sure poor Tom might find getting blood from a stone easier than getting to the important things with my Papa."

"How is he doing?" Matthew asked, genuinely concerned. Nathaniel was a sweet and gentle man, but he was struggling with the demons of drink and gambling.

"Very well, and he looks so much better than he did when Tom brought him here. But, what can I do for you?" she asked, a twinkle in her eye as if she knew exactly what he was there about. "And how is dear Christopher?"

"He is well, an absolute hellion, but I suppose that is how a five year old boy should be," he smiled as he thought about his tousle-headed boy. "Has there been any post for me?"

"Yes, about twenty letters, all from Boston. If I didn't think you were still in mourning for Martha, I would have to assume that you have followed in Tom's footsteps and placed an advertisement?" she said cannily.

"Martha has been gone three years. Even if I do still miss her terribly, it is not right that Christopher should grow up without the love of a mother."

"Be careful," Catherine warned as she walked behind the bar to collect the letters from one of the mailboxes there. "I know there are a number of lucky souls here in Sun River who have found love that way, but you have to be sure that who you choose truly will love that boy as their own."

"I know, and I have every intention of being certain. I could not dream of marrying anyone unless Christopher loved them too." Catherine handed him the large bundle. He looked at it surprised. "There are so many!"

"I know, good luck," she said as she hugged him.

He wandered slowly back to the wagon and got up on the dashboard beside Ardloe. "Ready?" he asked as he tucked the letters into his pocket carefully.

"Yup," Ardloe said as he cracked the whip lightly and they set off towards Great Falls. The men travelled in companionable silence, the letters piquing Matthew's curiosity at every pace. Finally he could stand the suspense no longer, and he yanked them out and began to read. Most were full of frothy and frivolous prose. The women seemed to think he would be interested in their love of fashion, and their accomplishments as singers or musicians. Hell, he was looking for a wife, not an act for the theatre. Not one of them seemed to mention a word about his son, and none seemed to care about him or his plans.

Frustrated he put the remaining letters down, and sighed. "No luck?" Ardloe asked.

"It isn't looking hopeful."

"Keep on readin'," he said wisely. "The right 'un'll be in there."

"How do you know?"

"Because all the others have found someone doin' the same thing! Tom, Carlton, Ethan, Mac – they've all found their gals through them advertisements. There'll be a good 'un for you and young Chris too."

"I wish I could share your optimism. We haven't exactly had the best of luck over the years."

"Nope, 'n young Martha was a love. But she's gone 'n she wouldn't want you to be lonely out there on that farm of yours."

"No she wouldn't. But, I'm not sure I want to be there myself either. That's why I want to build the theatre. It all seems so lonely out there without her. I've tried, but I just can't bear it. Mac or Carlton'd take my land in an instant."

"Yes I'm sure they would. But, you built that place with her, you sure you wanna leave her behind forever?"

"I'm not sure of anything anymore. But, how many women would want to live in another woman's home anyway? We've kept it like a shrine to her - nobody wants to compete with a ghost."

Ardloe nodded, and just kept his eyes on the road. Matthew thought about what he had said, and the things he himself had revealed. He had never been so open about anything, with anyone – not even Martha. He wondered what it was about this crusty old timer that had made him do so. He picked up the bundle of letters once more, and continued to read. Maybe Ardloe was right, there would be someone in there, or maybe in next week's post, or the week after that. He could be patient if needs be. But, then he found her letter.

Dear Gentleman of Montana

Firstly I would like to express my condolences to you, though I am being presumptuous that you must be a widower. It must be hard trying to bring up your son alone, and you must miss his Mother terribly. It must be very difficult for you to have taken such a decision as to consider another wife, and I want you to know how much I admire your courage.

I have recently found myself having to rethink my life, and the plans I had made in it. I was in an accident, and it means I will need to change most everything I have ever known. It is quite frightening considering starting all over again, so though I cannot imagine your grief, I can understand the fortitude required to place that advertisement.

I would love to hear more about your son, and your wife should you wish to confide in me. I love children, and am told I have a knack for entertaining them. I must confess to you now my deepest, darkest secret – I am a circus performer, or rather I was before my accident. I know that in many people's eyes that makes me less than respectable, but I can assure you that my Mama and Papa brought me up to be a good Christian woman.

I have not spent my entire life on the road. Mama and Papa were such big names in our world that they were able to get us a place in a permanent circus here in Boston. I have lived here since I was about seven, and have attended school. I enjoy history and literature very much. When I was not practicing my Act, I could be found with my nose in a book somewhere. Now reading is the only joy I have as I convalesce. I have never been to any of the smart theatres here in Boston, though I would have liked to – but when you are a performer yourself it is difficult to get a night off. However we often had troupes that came and did turns in the Ring.

I would very much like to hear more about you, your son

and especially about how you ended up in Montana. We performed there once when I was a little girl, I remember it being very beautiful indeed. I would love to return and see it again.

Yours Hopefully

Emily Wilkins

She sounded more interesting than anyone he could ever have imagined, with her plain name and exotic life. He wondered what her Act had been, where she had travelled to in her short life, and if she might be even a little bit interested in someone as dull as he. He had no clever tricks, was a simple farmer - though he had grand ideas. But, Emily may just have the expertise he needed to deal with performers, to make sure his venture was a success. But, he could not choose a mother for Christopher just because he was lured by the glamour of the Circus; he had to be more practical than that. He knew he would never love anyone as he had loved Martha, and did not want to – yet Emily intrigued him. He had fond memories of nights at the Circus when he was a boy, back East in Boston. Maybe he had even seen her, and admired her from afar. But, was he truly ready? Could he learn to love again?

He pondered those questions throughout the rest of the journey to Great Falls, and they were still playing on his mind when he finally made it home and kissed Christopher's soft curls goodnight. His son always slept so peacefully. Matthew couldn't help but be envious; he hadn't slept a full night since Martha took sick. So much depended on him making the right choices, this little boy needed a mother that would love him. He thought of the vapid responses of so many of the women, and then Emily's gentle and simple letter. It filled him with a warmth he could not explain, but it was as if his heart were aglow. He gently caressed his son's cheek and then made his way to the kitchen, to respond to her. He couldn't help but wonder how bad her accident could have been that she could even consider leaving the only life she had ever known. If she was crippled, Montana was not the place for her. This land needed a strong hand. But there was something determined in her missive, he couldn't help but think that she was a woman who could take on any challenge and win – if she chose to do so –

and that made him wonder why she wanted to leave the circus.

Chapter Three

Maisie entered the room and gave Emily a wink. At last, he had written to her. Now, all she had to do was to find a reason for her Mama to leave the room. It seemed to be getting harder and harder to do so. Ever since the accident she had become so over protective, it was quite stifling at times. "Mama, shouldn't you be rehearsing with Evan today?" she asked. Her curiosity wasn't just in order to gain a few quiet moments alone, she was genuinely worried that Mama wasn't practicing enough and that would cause her to have an accident too.

"Evan is working the horses. It will be fine. I have been doing the tricks my entire life."

"But we both know how quickly we can get stiff; our muscles need to be supple. You cannot risk your wellbeing to be by my side every hour of the day. I am quite well enough to be left alone for more than a few minutes Mama."

"I know, but I worry that you will be bored and I am your Mother. Worrying is what I am here for!"

"The time to worry is over. Everything is healing well. Even my foot is strong enough for me to begin to walk upon it according to the doctor. You have never been so concerned about our falls in the past," Emily tried to reason. Mama chose to ignore the concern in her voice and immediately changed the subject.

"That quack! He wouldn't know good health if he came face to face with it in broad daylight." This too was something Mama did not usually do. She was usually kind and generous to others, and had previously respected the bright and capable Dr Bright. Emily was sure that Mama was hiding something, but what it was she had no clue.

"Mama, you have to stop being so overprotective or I will never be able to walk at all. Whatever is the matter? You have always extolled Dr Bright's virtues, why is his judgment suddenly so circumspect?" Emily gazed earnestly at her Mama, but it seemed the older woman had no intentions of having her secrets drawn out in such a way..

"What are you up to?" she asked as her eyes narrowed suspiciously.

"Nothing! I'm just trying to understand why you are being so peculiar – and to please give me a few minutes alone! Truly, I do not need you to be by my side, holding my hand all the time. And, I do need to start walking. Maisie can help me and you can go and make sure that the new routine goes perfectly so that neither you nor Evan ends up where I am! You don't have to tell me why you seem to think that only you know what is best for me, but you have to let me at least try and walk soon." Mama sighed heavily, and kissed Emily's cheek tenderly.

"I hate to leave you my darling, and if you insist on trying to walk I shall send Evan up. He is stronger than Maisie after all." Emily could see just how hard she found it to say the words, though she was trying to look as if she didn't have a care in the world. But, Mama could be like a locked vault. If she did not want you to know, that secret would go with her to the grave. Emily grabbed at the lifeline, and did not push to find out what was playing on her mother's mind. If she wished to tell, maybe one day she might. But it was clear that she had no intention of doing so now.

"Then you would still be unable to practice!" Emily said as gaily as she could manage. "Mama, Maisie is more than strong enough to support my weight and you need to get out of this room. I need to too – so I know you need some air, to feel the sun on your skin."

"Why don't I get Evan to bring you downstairs? We can set you up in a chair near the practice ring and you can tell us where we are going wrong!" Mama cried suddenly, a tone of triumph in her voice that she would be able to get her own way and not let Emily out of her sight. Emily sighed.

"Mama," she said with a warning tone to her voice. "I love you, and I know you are only being so protective because you love me so much, but I need some privacy – a bit of time to myself. Please, go and practice. Let me try my first steps up here with Maisie. Then, maybe when you take a rest Evan can bring me downstairs and I can tell you exactly where you are both getting it wrong?" She hoped that her Mama would accept the compromise. She needed to read the letter she knew Maisie had in her apron pocket. She wanted to take her first steps, but not with her Mama or Evan there. Both would be too worried if she stumbled, would bundle her back into bed before she could even try again. But she also longed to go outside, the weather had been glorious in recent days and she missed Claude too. She couldn't remember having ever gone a day without seeing him, and it had been weeks now since she had scratched his funny head.

"You aren't going to let me win are you?"

"No Mama. I think you have already kept me in bed longer than you ever would have stayed there yourself. I have to get my strength back."

"I just don't want you to get hurt again. You're right though. I need to let you stumble a little and get yourself back up. Your compromise is accepted. I shall go and practice with your brother. You have two hours. Take your first steps with Maisie, but do not over tire yourself. Get some rest and then we shall see."

"No Mama, Evan shall bring me down so I can see Claude and tell you both off!" Emily said with a smile at her Mama's weak effort to try and go back on her own suggestion.

Maisie handed her the letter as soon as Mama had left the room.

"I'll leave you to read it alone. I have to finish making supper anyway. I'll be back up in half an hour."

"Thank you." Emily whispered as she gazed at the gentle sloping script on the thick parchment envelope. Finally alone, for the first time since she had taken her fall, she breathed a sigh of relief. It was wonderful to have these few moments. Mama had insisted she have company at all times, so even when she and Evan had been performing Maisie or one of the roustabouts had been sent up to watch over her. It was lovely to have her room to herself, to be able to be happy or sad and not have to worry about how everybody would react to a change in expression, or even her breathing rate.

She opened the letter gingerly. She wasn't sure that she was ready; her rash response to the advertisement had been fuelled by the recklessness that laudanum had brought. But, she couldn't help but be excited that he had written back. It had been so long that she had almost begun to wonder if she truly had even done such a thing as to write to a complete stranger. But, here it was. His handwriting was simple, with few flourishes – except on his capitals. She decided she liked that, it was simple and straightforward – but just showy enough to let her know that this man was not dull.

Dear Miss Wilson

I hope you will not think me too presumptuous but I would very much like to invite you here to Montana. I have a farm and I am in the process of building a theatre, so cannot leave right now, and I couldn't possibly leave my son, Christopher. I am sure you can understand this. Also, I hope that it may be the perfect place for you to recuperate from your accident. My cousin has recently married a young woman from Boston himself, and I know that Catherine would love to meet you and welcome you into her home. I have enclosed a return ticket, should you think it a good idea. I think that the best way to get to know anyone is to meet them, and that is obviously a little difficult for us as you are in Boston and I am here. But, it need not be an impediment for long. Please do let me know that you will consider my proposal at least?

My son, Christopher, is now five years old. Sadly we lost his Mama, my Martha, when she contracted tuberculosis some two years past now. I miss her every day. I know that I am not enough for my boy. He needs a woman's hand, a woman's love. He has the bonniest blonde curls. I don't know where he gets them from, as both Martha and I have hair as straight as a poker. But he is friendly and charming. He can be a little boisterous, but I think that is something to be encouraged – as long as he remains polite and knows when to stop!

I am an ambitious man. I have a farm, though if my little gamble does well I hope to sell it and move into town. My wife and I built it together, and it seems very lonely without her now. It is hard to see her things lying around, the tools she used and the furniture we picked or made together. But I hope you will not think that I am some hopeless soul unable to move on as I am not. I loved my wife, and I will always have a piece of my heart devoted to her but I know that I am ready now to allow someone else into my life.

My gamble is taking up most of my savings, so I am afraid that I am not a wealthy man – though I do most fervently hope to be so one day. I am praying that my neighbors will long to see entertainments on a daily basis. I have always loved the theatre, plays and spectacles of all kinds. I remember attending a circus once, many years ago now. The Kiriakov Circus I believe it was. They were spectacular. I couldn't help but marvel at the elephants, and the big cats. That a man can control such huge beasts seemed impossible. But I especially liked the acrobatic acts. There was this one couple who rode and tumbled. I have never seen anything like it before or since. Incredible they were. If I had not loved Montana so much I would have run away with them then and there, though I was only a boy.

It must be very difficult for you to imagine a life without it, and I will understand if now that things have maybe healed a little,

*that you may have regretted responding to me – but I do pray you
will come out and meet with me. I cannot deny it, your letter made
you sound so very interesting, fascinating in fact.*

    Yours Hopefully

    Matthew Simmons

Emily read his words with interest. The world was so vast, and yet
in some ways it could be so very small. He had seen the Kiriakov Circus,
and remembered her Mama and Papa's Act. She did not know how old he
was, or how long ago it had been – but his description could only be of
them. If she had needed a sign, here it was. The link that connected them,
despite the miles and differing lives.

Even more than that, he was offering her the chance to escape the
shackles of her Mama's overprotective regimen, and to travel to Montana
where she would be able to rest and recuperate – and more importantly
rebuild her strength without such scrutiny and control. She longed to reply
then and there and just say yes, she would be on the next train. But her
current circumstances would make that more than a little difficult. She
could not walk, and though she had some meager savings, she did not have
enough to hire a nurse to care for her during the long journey.

But they were small, easily remedied concerns. Her greatest worry
was how to tell her Mama of such a thing. Mama would not understand.
She would do everything she could to keep their little family together,
would try and persuade her that recovery was possible, or that it didn't
matter that she could no longer perform. She would cajole, and beg, and
outright demand Emily's obedience - and she would acquiesce, as she
always did. She didn't know how to say no to anyone, least of all her fiery
mother.

Emily knew that she would have to accept that she would not be
able to go. She stared at the letter, and ran her fingers over the lightly
embossed train ticket and felt a tear trickle down her cheek. It was
hopeless. She had been a fool to think that there was a life for her outside of
the Circus, that she could even consider leaving her family. But he sounded
so good and so kind, and even a little reckless. She liked him. She wanted to

find out more. She wanted to go to him, and give herself the chance to find out if she could be happy somewhere as she had never been here.

"Miss Emily, the doctor is here to see you," Maisie said brightly as she came back into the room. "Your Mama must have forgotten to tell me he was due."

"No, I just dropped by," Dr Bright said solemnly as his tall frame filled the little doorway. "I wanted to see if you have been getting up and following the exercise regimen I prescribed." Emily looked at him openmouthed. Mama had told her of no such thing. She had been forced to barter with her to be permitted to even take just a few steps today.

"How long should I have been following this regimen?" she asked curiously.

"For the last two weeks, since I saw you last." Emily could feel her cheeks flushing crimson with anger. It was one thing for Mama to want to care for her, but to deliberately ignore the good doctor's advice, and make her have to bargain to be permitted to do what he had prescribed weeks ago was a step too far. She was an adult, not a child and it was time her mother began to accept that. She took a deep breath and tried to steady her voice.

"I am sorry. I did not know. I have been trying to get Mama to let me get up for days, but she has been so insistent that I should rest a while longer."

"Shall we see what you can do?" he asked her with a smile as he took off his top hat and laid it and his coat neatly on the chair. She smiled back, glad he had chosen to be so diplomatic, and to not labor the fact that Mama had over-ridden his treatment.

"Yes, I think we should," she said eagerly. He rolled up his sleeves, as she shuffled to the side of the bed. Tenderly he helped her to drop her feet onto the floor and put a supportive arm around her to help her up. Her legs felt like jelly, and she gasped as pain shot through her as she put her damaged foot to the floor. He adjusted to take more of her weight, and she felt the pain ease a little.

"Do you want to carry on?" he asked her, watching her features carefully. She nodded and pushed down through her legs once more. The pain was not as bad this time, but she couldn't remember having felt so weak and incapable before. Very carefully Dr Bright helped her to take her first steps, but three was all she could manage. "Emily, I would have expected you to be hobbling around on crutches by now. I am disappointed that your mother has completely ignored all of my advice," he said sadly. "You have the strength, or at least you did, to be able to be well on your way to a complete recovery.

"She was doing what she thought best," Emily said, agreeing with him but not wanting to betray her Mama. She had no clue what her reasons for babying her so might have been, but she knew that they would have been there. However, his concerns did give her an idea. "Dr Bright, do you think that I may progress better if I were to convalesce away from my family?"

"From what I have seen thus far, I would have to admit that I do think that. Why? Is there somewhere you might go?"

"There is. A friend has invited me to Montana. I know it is a long way to go, and I know I am not yet up to a long train journey but I think it might do me good."

"I think it would be perfect. I can arrange for you to borrow a rolling chair, so you could make the journey tomorrow if you wished. You would need a nurse to assist you, as your muscles are weak, but your health could stand the journey."

"Would you please speak to my brother and maybe even to the Major? There is no point in talking to my Mama, she will dismiss every word you say, but if the Major and Evan were convinced then she would have to give in." Emily could hardly contain her excitement, her face lit up from within. Dr Bright smiled down at her, clearly glad to be of assistance to her – and eager to have her be able to follow a suitable plan of rehabilitation.

"I shall do what I can for you Emily, but if I do so I expect you to follow the regimen I have laid out for you to the letter."

"I shall be happy to!" she assured him, shaking his hand enthusiastically. "Thank you."

Emily could hardly believe her luck as she watched the Major and
Evan trying to convince Mama later that day. The statuesque owner of the
Circus had come in at the end of their practice session, his face solemn. Dr
Bright had clearly kept his word, had spoken to the man whose opinion
mattered more than anyone's in this rag tag world. Mama kept shaking her
head, and Emily knew that she wasn't far from tears, but in the end even
she could not deny that she had ignored the doctor's advice, and Emily's
recovery was lagging because of it. "Well young lady, I would like to know
who your mysterious friend is in Montana," Mama demanded as she
marched towards her, her eyes flashing with fury. Emily gulped. She had
known that this would be coming, but she had decided that nothing other
than the truth would be a suitable defense.

"Mama, I answered one of those Matrimonial advertisements."

"You did what?"

"Please, don't get so upset. Matthew is a kind man. He has a young
son, and he has offered me a place in his cousin's household to
convalesce."

"You do not know if he is a good man, or a killer! How could you?
No, I shan't allow it."

"Mama, yes you will," Evan said as he moved swiftly towards
them. "The Major cannot afford to keep paying the wages and expenses for
an Act that may never be able to walk again, let alone fall off a dumb
donkey. Em needs to be away from us so she can heal, and so she can work
out what to do next. Can't you imagine how difficult it must be for her to
see all of us around her, life going on as usual when at best all she can hope
for is that she will walk with a limp for the rest of her days?"

Mama's face fell, Emily wanted to reach out to hold her and
comfort her. She was more devastated by Emily's injuries than she was
herself, and as she took in Evan's blunt words, the tiny woman crumpled.
"Mama, please do not feel sorry for me. I was never so good at what I did as
to be so upset at losing it," she assured her. "Claude and I will be glad to go
into retirement, I will be able to take him with me won't I?" Evan grinned
at her.

"Just like my little sister to be more worried about whether you can take that damned ass with you than to have to change your entire life!"

"Claude is my responsibility," she said stubbornly.

"Yes, he is. I'll arrange for him to be sent first class," the Major said in his gruff voice. "I'll upgrade your ticket too Miss Emily. My Circus owes your family much, it is the least I can do for you and for your dear departed Papa, my friend. Now you get well and strong out there, and if you ever decide to come back, there will always be a place for you here."

"I know," she said with a grin as she beckoned him to come down to where she was sat for a kiss on his cheek, "if I can come up with a good Act that will make you money!" He rubbed at his full moustache, twirling the ends awkwardly, as if she had caught him out. "Mama, please I would like to have your blessing."

"I know my sweet, but I shall miss you so terribly. I have never been apart from either of you for so much as a day. I don't know if I can bear it."

"Papa will keep an eye on me," Emily said, knowing her Mama believed that Joe Wilkins was in heaven watching over them all. "He'll take care of me." Mama sniffed and then flung her arms around Emily. She curled her arms around the slight body that was so fragile and doll like – yet was all sinew and muscle. "Mama, both you and Papa taught me to be strong, capable, determined. Let me go and find out what my life is to be now. I can't do it here, Evan is right, it is too hard watching everyone do everything – it always has been. I am not a circus girl at heart and you have always known it. I am happier with a book than I have ever been in the ring."

"Evan, carry your sister upstairs. She must be tired. We'll talk about this tomorrow," Mama said firmly, trying to reassert her dominance over the situation.

"No Mama, the decision is taken. I shall leave for Montana the day after tomorrow. There is nothing else to say." Evan lifted her up, and Mama squeezed her hand tightly. "I will be fine Mama, I'll write every week, I promise. It'll be as if I am right here beside you telling you all my stories just as I always have."

★ ★ ★ ★ ★

Evan and Maisie took her to the station. Mama had suddenly found a pressing need to be with the horses, one had apparently gotten a limp in the evening performance. Evan had told her the truth - that all the horses were quite well - and it had hurt a little that her mother could not bring herself to be here to say goodbye. The rolling chair was heavy to push, but it did mean she could move around much more easily. The Major had hired a nurse to accompany her and she was smart and efficient. Emily was sure that once they were acquainted that they would become good friends. She had a kind face, and the loveliest blue eyes. "Mama wanted to come, it is just difficult for her. Everything has happened so suddenly," Evan said lamely as he settled her in her carriage.

"No she didn't, or she would be here. She has barely left my side in weeks. She could have come to see me off. I know she loves me, and I know she is worried about me – but she cannot cope with the thought of my growing up and not needing her."

"We'll always need her," her brother said sagely.

"Yes we will, but don't ever tell her that!" Emily joked. "I shall miss you."

"I'll miss you too little one. Now, be careful out there. Don't go getting yourself into mischief, and if you need anything let me know straight away. I'll come and rescue you!" He hugged her tightly, and kissed her on the forehead. She smiled and squeezed his cheeks together, like she had when she had been a little girl. He grinned.

"I'll just check on Claude, make sure they've settled him in. I wonder what your young man will think when you turn up with that useless donkey in tow!"

"Claude is not useless. He is clever and good at tricks, and I am sure I can teach him some new ones so he can continue to earn his keep," she retorted.

"I'm sure you will. Love you little sister, but don't let your pride get in the way." Emily knew what he meant about Mama. But she had already

209

written a letter which she had left with Maisie. She had known right from the start that she wouldn't be able to bear the thought of either of her babies leaving the nest. Evan would never leave, but she had already stayed longer than she should have. It was time to find out who she was, and what she might be without her famous family. It was time to find Emily at long last.

Chapter Four

Dear Matthew,

I do hope you will not think me presumptuous to call you by your Christian name, but your kind offer will have us become acquaintances soon enough, it seemed foolish to continue with formalities!

Thank you for the ticket. I am on my way. As you receive this I should be changing trains in Chicago, and will be bound for Great Falls in just a few more days – on the 9th. If you are not there to greet me I shall understand – I just hope this gets to you before I do so. You will be looking for a young woman (twenty-seven is still young, at least I certainly feel it), in a rolling chair with hair as bright as a copper kettle. You may be please to know that I do not have the temper to go with it!

I have never done anything so impetuous, but circumstances at home had meant that getting away from my family for a period is necessary, and I had nowhere else to go. If your cousin cannot put me up, I shall be happy to check into a boarding *house or hotel. I have some savings and the Major has been kind enough to give me a small sum to fund my convalescence.*

The Major has known me since I was about five years old when he saw Mama and Papa in the Kiriakov Circus and decided they were just the Act he had to have for his show in Boston. I always thought he was crusty and bad tempered, but he has been nothing but kind since my accident. I was amazed when you said you had seen the Kiriakov Circus, and you therefore must have been describing my Mama and Papa when you did so in your letter. That they made you want to run off and join them made me feel that fate maybe has a hand in our meeting.

I do not wish to be a burden to you, or your family so I have a nurse who will be attending me. Ellen is sweet and very efficient and I have no doubt that she will wish to have me back up and on my feet in no time. She has a fiancé in Boston she longs to return home to!

I cannot thank you enough, and hope you will not regret your invitation. I shall try my best to be less bother than your young rascal!

Yours gratefully
Emily Wilkins
P.S. I have donkey called Claude, he shall be accompanying me. Is there anywhere I would be able to stable him, or put him out to pasture nearby? I am happy to pay whatever it takes. He is my oldest and dearest friend.

Matthew read the letter, and took note of the date she expected to arrive. It was just three days away. He couldn't keep the smile from his face as he thought of her speeding across the country in her rolling chair, her beloved donkey trailing behind her. She was unique, and truly on her way. Like her, he had never been so impulsive either, but he also couldn't help but think that the Circus he had seen all those years ago had been the one her family had been a part of was a sign. They had been destined to meet, to know one another. He knew of the whims of women, that they liked flowers and romance – but one that took a donkey with her across the entire country was someone he simply couldn't help but admire.

Her news made him look around his home with new eyes. He had no time to waste, must make it somewhere that a young woman would wish to become her own and that meant finally removing Martha's old things. He and Christopher made a game of it. He would tell Christopher a story about every item that they found, and then they would decide if it was important enough to keep. He was sure that someone with a good heart would understand that they could not completely banish Martha from their hearts, but it did them both good to remember the happier times as they went about their task.

With a small pile of items they could not bear to part with, and a larger one of things they were happy to give away they sat on the floor, leaning against the bed. Christopher snuggled into his chest, and Matthew twined his fingers absent-mindedly in his curls. "Papa?"

"Christopher."

"I don't remember Mama much."

"You were so very young when we lost her."

"Thank you for telling me the stories. She seems more real now. Can we talk about her like this again?" Matthew looked down into his son's huge blue eyes and smiled.

"Any time you wish. Your Mama loved you so very much. Christopher?"

"Yes Papa?"

"I have a friend coming to see us. I shall be fetching her from the station in a day or so. I want you to promise you will be polite and good to her."

"Will she be my new Mama?" he asked, his eyes filled with hope. Matthew felt a lump in his throat form, and he tried to gulp it away before he responded.

"Maybe. Would you like a new Mama?"

"If she can make cakes like Aunty Catherine I think I could like it."

"I don't know if she bakes or not Matthew, but she is bringing a donkey with her." The little boy's eyes widened even further. "She was in the circus, so I'll wager he can do a few tricks."

"Really Papa?"

"Truly," Matthew said chuckling. "But, you must be gentle with her, as she had an accident and cannot walk very well."

"Like when I fell and hurt my ankle?"

"A little bit. But, she cannot walk at all at the moment. She is coming here to learn again in peace and quiet."

"Will she be staying with us, here?"

"No, she'll be in Sun River staying with Uncle Tom and Aunty Catherine for a while. Then, if we decide we suit then maybe she'll come and live here and be your Mama."

"I'll be good. Everybody else has a Mama. I'd really like one too."

Over the next couple of days Christopher got progressively more excited, and was telling everyone they saw that he was getting a new Mama and that she was arriving on a big train. Matthew wondered if he had done the right thing in telling his son so much, but he was so happy. He had tried to insist that Christopher stay with Catherine while he went to the station, but the young lad had been insistent upon accompanying him. He had been glad of the company, his son's lively chattering had made the miles to Great Falls pass quickly. But, he could see how tired Christopher was, and prayed he would not get too cranky.

"Wow Papa, the train is so big!" Christopher enthused as the giant engine loomed around the bend puffing smoke and steam like a great dragon.

"It certainly is. Now, hold tight to my hand. When it comes into the station, it will be difficult to see because of all the steam and smoke. I don't want to lose you."

Christopher clung to his hand, and Matthew could feel his son's anxiety by just how tight his little grip was. He had to admit he felt more than a little nervous himself, could feel his stomach churning. He wanted them to make a good impression on this young woman, did not want her to feel she had made a terrible mistake. His head itched, and he slid a finger under his hat brim to scratch, and only then remembered that he had intended to get his hair cut. Tom constantly teased him about his long hair, and he wished he had at least tied it back with a ribbon to keep it tidy. Everything was happening so fast, and he simply hadn't had time to even think about it.

But, as the steam began to clear he could make out the silhouette of a large chair, a young woman and a porter leading an animal moving slowly towards them. He gulped nervously, and fidgeted with his shoe string tie. He felt strangely unready, but as the strange little group became clearer, he could see that the young woman in the chair was smiling, and waving at them shyly. She was not pretty, not delicate, but she was striking. Matthew felt his breath catch at the sight of her. The chair hid what he was sure was a fine figure, with curves where they should be and long, lean muscles honed by years of acrobatic stunts. Her hair glinted in the sun like fire, and her emerald eyes had him mesmerized.

"Papa, why are you just standing there?" His son was tugging at his hand, his little face bemused. "Papa, come on, I want to meet the donkey!" He broke free from Matthew's grasp and ran forwards, beaming all over his cherubic face.

"You must be Christopher," the seated angel said as the little boy came to a halt in front of her. "Hmm, good control for your age," she said thoughtfully, almost under her breath. "This," she indicated to the gentle looking beast by her side, "is Claude." She clicked to him, and the animal dropped into the most comical of bows. Christopher burst into peals of giggles and bowed back. As he did Claude quickly nipped his hat, and somehow flipped it up onto his own head. It landed over one ear, and dangled precariously. Matthew couldn't help but be just as amused as his son. "Would you like to ride him?" Emily asked. He nodded eagerly. Matthew picked him up and placed him carefully on the donkey's back. Christopher took his hat and put it firmly back on his head. Matthew couldn't help but smile at the determined set of his small features.

"I'm Matthew," he said. "You must be Emily, and you must be Ellen?" he asked of the two women. They nodded. "Does he do anything else?"

"Oh yes! He is rather a talented creature," she said with a broad smile that lit up her eyes, she was clearly very proud of him. "Your son seems to have very good balance and muscle control for one so young. Maybe you will let me teach Christopher to do some of the less dangerous tricks with him so he can stay fit while I recuperate?"

"As long as Christopher will be safe," Matthew said warily.

"It wasn't Claude's fault I fell. He is the safest, gentlest creature alive," she assured him as the donkey nuzzled up against him amiably. He scratched between his ears, and could have sworn that Claude winked at him.

"I think he would like that," he said as he took in the sparkling green eyes, and glorious mane of gleaming copper. It would be hard to ever say no to someone so gentle, so beautiful. Emily was quite simply the most perfect woman he had ever seen, and it didn't matter to him one bit that she was stuck in that ugly chair. He couldn't help but think that finally Fate had been kind to him and had delivered him the kind of woman who would make sure that their lives would never be dull ever again. He couldn't wait to find out if he was right. "Welcome to Montana, I hope you'll be very happy here."

Chapter Five

Emily observed Matthew as he drove the open-topped carriage he had borrowed from a friend to collect her in. "I thought that you might like to see some of the scenery, and feel the air on your face after all that time cooped up on the train," he said thoughtfully. He had the brightest blue eyes she had ever seen, like a perfect sky, or the plumage of a kingfisher. No, neither color was quite right, they had a shade all their own, but they didn't pierce through you in the way some could. They were soft and yielding, making her feel utterly at ease. He had a strong back and soft hands. He wielded the reins gently, and his horses were well schooled and reacted to his lightest touch. His hair was long, and looked silky soft. She couldn't help but wonder what it might feel like to touch it, to run her fingers through it. But it was his full lips that she could not take her eyes from. She had never really been impressed by the physicality of a man. There had been many good looking, muscular men in the circus. All had been good people, yet she had rarely felt many yearnings towards more intimacy with any of them. Yet something in her had stirred, awoken at the very first sight of this tall man.

"I have been cooped up for too long since my accident," she admitted. "Thank you for thinking of such a lovely treat for us all. Christopher, is your Papa always so considerate?" she asked the boy sitting in her lap.

"You can tell him to take his seat properly," Matthew said with a grin. He had the cutest dimples, just like his adorable son's.

"He is fine where he is," she said as she brushed a wayward curl from his temple. "He is a very handsome boy, you must be very proud."

"I am. He made us both very happy." Matthew's voice went quiet, and a contemplative look came over his face.

"You must miss her terribly. I want both of you to know I do not wish to try and take her place in any way. You must take me as myself, and I will take you both as you are."

"You are forthright, aren't you?" he said, a slight smile reappearing on his deliciously full lips. Emily shivered, unable to stop herself. "Are you warm enough?" he asked as he saw the tiny shudder.

"I am perfectly well," she reassured him. It was nothing that being held in his arms and kissed wouldn't cure, she was sure. But she couldn't ask him that, at least not yet.

The journey was over too soon, and Emily found herself wishing there was a way to make it last longer, to be able to spend more time with this man. After the initial awkwardness they had found much to talk about, and for the first time in her life she had felt that someone was truly listening to her. He wanted to know how she felt about things, to know about her – he seemed to have no desire to make her into something she was not. She loved her family dearly, but they had never understood that she didn't feel the same way about things as they had. They were happy in the world of the circus, and though she had tried, and though she adored Claude, she had never fitted into it. She wanted to experience more than the Big Top, knew there was a big world to be explored and understood.

They pulled up outside the saloon, Emily looked at Matthew quizzically. "You have a drinking problem? Cannot go a few hours without it?" She tried to make the enquiry lighthearted, but she had seen drunks and knew she could not bear for this lovely man to be one.

"No," he chuckled. "This is my cousin Tom's business. Catherine will be inside. I promised to pick her up on our way through to their place. They have a lovely house just a little way out of town." He hopped down from the dashboard and hurried inside. Emily sighed with relief, and looked around her. The little town was a simple street. But, she could see there was a lot of building work going on. There was a new bakery, a general store, a small church and a number of other buildings. They were all smart, with brightly colored clapboard, making the town seem cheerful and welcoming.

"Welcome to Sun River," an elegant young woman cried as she rushed to the carriage and standing on one foot on the step leaned in to plant a kiss on Emily's cheek. "I saw you in the circus in Boston. We used to visit all the time. To think you will be staying here with me." She jumped back down and moved to the back of the carriage where Claude was standing and flung her arms around his hairy neck. "And the infamous Claude too! You are heartily welcome," she said as she planted a kiss on his nose and then gave him a carrot.

"He will now be your adoring slave for all eternity. You must be Catherine," Emily laughed. "I know Matthew said you came from Boston, but that you saw our Act," she added incredulously. "It isn't often we have adoring fans, is it Claude, and we certainly weren't expecting it out here in Montana!"

"If it bothers you, you may need to keep a low profile. There are a number of us in town now who came from Boston and every one of us is excited that we have Mademoiselle and Claude living amongst us. You could have taken your pick of any of our homes to stay." Emily didn't know what to say, she had hoped to come here to get away from the Circus, but it would seem it would follow her wherever she went. She wasn't sure if she was happy or sad about that, but it was a little unsettling.

Matthew appeared, with a lanky young man by his side. "This is Tom," Catherine said proudly linking her arm through her husband's arm. "He will be home later, but he has to work right now. We should get you home and settled. You must be exhausted."

"I am a little tired," she admitted. Catherine jumped up onto the dashboard, and Matthew plucked Christopher from Emily's lap. "Are you not coming with us?"

"I must attend to some business here in town, but Catherine has kindly invited us to supper tonight. I will see you very soon," he reassured her. She knew he was a busy man, he had a farm and the new theatre to take care of after all, but she couldn't help but feel a little lost as they pulled away. She had felt so comfortable in his company. She had never before felt so at ease with another human being. She would miss him, even though it would only be a few hours at most before she saw him again.

✶ ✶ ✶ ✶ ✶

Her room was simply furnished, with whitewashed walls and a big, comfortable bed. She was glad to sink into it, with Ellen's assistance. It was peaceful here, and she suddenly felt utterly weary. The excitement of the past weeks caught up with her, and overwhelmed her as she sank back against the pillows. "Sleep Miss Emily. I shall wake you in time to bathe and dress for supper," Ellen assured her.

"I don't think that will be hard to achieve," she admitted. "Will you check on Claude for me?"

"I will. Mrs Shandon said that her father was settling him in. Mr Parker seems a good man, and he was just as excited as Mrs Shandon to have Claude staying here. I wish I'd seen your Act now, I have no idea why they are all so impressed."

"Neither do I. I wasn't ever very good at anything. But Claude was. He is ever so funny."

"Like when he met young master Christopher?"

"And more. He used to have everyone in stitches Ellen," Emily said wistfully, but she was too tired to talk any longer and was glad when the young nurse left her in peace. She fell asleep, a fat tear falling over her cheek as she wondered if she had done the right thing in bringing Claude with her. She may not miss the Circus, but what if he did?

Chapter Six

Every day they spent together was a pleasure. Matthew watched as Emily grew stronger, her steps more secure and her limp less pronounced. He couldn't help but be proud of her. She was so determined to recover. Nothing stopped her. She took impossible circumstances, and made them work. It was a skill so few people embodied. But, as she was able to do more and more for herself, he realized that the time was coming when they would have to decide if she was to stay or go back to her home. He didn't want her to leave. They had built a good friendship, they laughed all the time. He had discovered himself again and it was a gift he was more than grateful she had given him.

A day was not complete without seeing her. No matter what he had to do, how busy he was, he made sure that he spent time with her. Christopher's easy acceptance of her had made this easy, and she had offered to take care of him when Matthew had to work. He watched her with Nathaniel and saw her patience and kindness towards him. When he struggled she was there to tell him stories, or to let him talk if he needed to. She had sent Ellen home to her sweetheart just a week into her stay, as she felt the benefits of the mountain air and the lack of constraint from her family.

Each day brought a new adventure, a new piece of knowledge and another string that tied her more securely into his heart and into his life. They had gone on family picnics up by the Falls, had taken leisurely walks, him pushing her rolling chair so she could get to know her neighbors and so he could spend the odd moment alone with her. They had attended suppers with Catherine and Tom, with Mac and Annie, and Myra and Carlton. From the first she and Myra had gotten along, and he often found the two women together planning and plotting – though he did not know what they were up to.

Christopher adored her, and she spent hours with him every day teaching him how to do tricks with Claude. He watched now as his son stood on the patient animal's back and carefully leapt through a paper hoop. He could do all kinds of simple tricks, and his confidence had grown with each one he learned. He was happy in a way he hadn't been since Martha's death. Matthew was overjoyed to see his son blossom in such a way. "Papa, did you see? Emily says she will make Claude trot next time!"

"I did, it was well done," he said as he swept up the happy child into his arms.

"He is a natural," Emily said as she moved towards them using only the cane he had made for her.

"Your walking is almost perfect. How long before you are back doing your tricks?" he asked cautiously. They had discussed many subjects in the past weeks, but she often clammed up when he broached her life in the Circus, or what she intended to do next. He wished she would let him in, he longed to help her to take the decisions he knew she was concerned about. But, he hadn't wanted to press, had been determined to let her come to what she truly wanted in her own time.

"I will never be able to do what I did. I don't want to," she said slowly. "I'm not even sure I want to go back," she said, her eyes lowered. He tilted her head up so he could look into her eyes.

"Does that mean you do not wish to leave Sun River too?" he

asked her hopefully. He held his breath, he had tried so hard not to pressure her. He wanted her to make her decision, but he had fallen for her in that first instant at the train station. Her funny, direct letters and those eyes with depths he had yet to explore held his heart.

"There is much about Sun River I like," she admitted cagily. "But, I would not want to stay where I am not wanted."

"Emily, you have to stay. You have to teach me more tricks," Christopher interjected, his little face full of worry.

"Darling Christopher, I will teach you all the tricks I know," she reassured him. "Maybe we should talk about this later," she added turning back to Matthew. He nodded and watched as she headed inside for a rest.

Claude walked over to them in his gentle loping gait. Matthew held Christopher so he could scratch the spot between the donkey's ears that made him happy. He brayed gently then Christopher fell from his arms. Matthew gasped and went to grab at him, but the boy did a neat tumble, and ended up sat facing backwards on the ass's back. Claude bucked his back legs gently, and Matthew watched open-mouthed as his son did a quick, jumping turn to face the right way then somersaulted off, landing squarely on his little feet. The two bowed deeply, his son grinning at him wildly while Claude bared his teeth. Matthew could almost swear that he was laughing. He scooped his son up into his arms, and covered his face with kisses. "I will have to have words with Emily for teaching you such things and not telling me!"

"Did I not do it right?" Christopher asked anxiously.

"No, I think you probably did it perfectly, that is what is so frightening," he added with a smile. "Come, we have to go home now. We both have chores." Christopher pouted, but took his hand and the two made their way to Matthew's horse. He clutched his son against him tightly as they rode home. He had been absolutely petrified as Christopher had fallen, but his amusement and the relief he felt that he was safe were still warring inside him. Emily was right, the boy was a natural. Clearly he had a gift, one that should be encouraged – but did Matthew have the courage to watch as he learned such things? Did he have the courage to ask Emily to stay? More importantly, did he have the courage to tell her he loved her?

He arrived back at Tom and Catherine's that evening, dressed smartly with his hair tied neatly back. He was nervous. He had decided that he couldn't wait any longer to know whether Emily felt the same way about him as he did about her. He had to know, and that meant he had to take her somewhere where they could be alone. He could only think of one place, and it was the only place he hadn't yet taken her to see. He hadn't known if it would be a good thing, or a bad thing for her to see the theatre that now stood so proudly, the largest building in town, on the main street just waiting for the first shows to take place inside.

"You look different," she said as she came slowly down the stairs towards him. "More serious."

"I'm just the same," he said. "Are you ready? You look beautiful."

"I am ready," she said blushing furiously at his compliment. It made him smile that she still didn't know just how stunning she was. "Who is looking after Christopher?"

"He is staying with Myra and Carlton tonight. Shall we?" He offered her his arm, and she took it gratefully, leaning on him a little heavily. "Where is your cane?"

"I am doing rather well without it don't you think?"

"You are. I think you and my son have been working on more than just his death defying stunts!"

"I'm sorry if I overstepped my bounds. But, he is just so good at everything. He reminds me of my brother Evan. He was always so quick to learn everything. Christopher is the same, and he is such a joy to be around," she gushed as he helped her up into his gig.

"I don't mind. As you say, he has a talent for it. It scared me half to death when he 'fell' from my arms, but what followed was spectacular."

"So, where are we going tonight? I still haven't met Maggie and Ethan, are we dining with them tonight?"

"No, tonight we dine alone, if you think you can manage to keep your hands off me without a chaperone present," he teased awkwardly. "I think it is time we talked about some things, don't you?" She nodded at his more serious tone, but the happiness in her eyes seemed to dissolve into the night air. He hoped he was not pushing her into a decision. He knew that she had felt pressured to be something she wasn't her entire life. He didn't want to be yet another person who put his own expectations onto her narrow shoulders. But, for his sake, for his son's sake he had to have answers.

He pulled up the gig in front of the theatre and helped her down. "So I am finally allowed to see inside," she said with a wink. He could tell she was trying to lighten the mood once more, and for the moment he was happy to play along.

"It is finally all finished and I need your opinion on the drapes!"

"I am not the girl for that sort of thing. You need Catherine. She is the one with all the taste. I'm just a gaudy Circus girl."

"Catherine did help," Matthew admitted. "So, what do you think?" He flung open the doors and watched as Emily's eyes widened, her face was filled with wonder as she took in the brass rails, the plush red carpet and the sweeping staircases in the grand lobby.

"It is rather grand," she said finally. "But, what about the theatre itself?" He took her hand and led her towards the doors. The entered the auditorium at the back of the stalls. She gasped at the banks of velvet covered seats, and the vast stage. "Oh Matthew, it is magnificent. I would give everything I have to come here and see a play!"

"That is good, as our opening night is next Thursday and I would very much like you to accompany me and Christopher, to sit in that box there," he pointed to the luxurious private box that would normally be reserved for visiting dignitaries, "as my wife to be."

She turned and stared at him, her eyes wide. "Your wife to be?" she asked. "Isn't there a little question I should have been asked before you can make such a presumption?" she teased. He took her hand and led her up onto the stage, opened the curtains where Claude stood patiently as always, with a tiny gift box suspended from his mouth. She laughed. "Well, it wouldn't have been right if he wasn't here to give his permission!"

"Emily Wilkins, will you marry me?" Matthew asked as he took a large ring from the box and took her hand in his.

"I will, you know I will."

"I do?" he asked. "Then why have I been utterly petrified that you would want to return to your old life?"

"Is that why you didn't want to bring me here? Were you scared that the greasepaint and limelight would beckon me back?" He nodded sheepishly. He had indeed been worried about just that. It was a lot to give up, he wasn't sure if he would have been able to give up such a large part of his life so easily. "Matthew, I have learned much about myself since I have been here. The most important thing is that I am a teacher. I am far better at telling others what to do than I ever was at doing it myself. Myra and I have been discussing it for weeks. I should have told you, but I didn't want to worry you that I wanted to stay, in case you didn't want me to stay with you. I didn't want you to feel you had to marry me. But, Myra and I are going to open a school. She has wanted to since she moved here, but had nobody to assist her. I think I can be a good teacher."

"I think you can. You should have told me! It is a wonderful idea. But, it might be an idea not to teach all the local children the skills you have taught Christopher!" He bent his head to hers, and touched his lips to hers. He felt her body quiver, and pulled her closer to him. She reached up and untied his hair, running her fingers through its lengths and sighed contentedly.

"That is much better," she said happily.

"You like my hair long?" he asked, surprised. Most people told him to cut it, said it made him look like some kind of bandit.

"I do, it reminds me of my Papa. He had lovely long silky hair too. His was copper though like mine, and used to billow out behind him as he rode in the ring."

"I remember. He was my hero when I was a boy. I could never decide if I liked him because of the way he rode, or because he reminded me of the lions. Maybe it was just because Fate knew he would one day bring me to you."

"I forgot you saw their act," she said thoughtfully. "Quite a hero for a boy!"

"Indeed. I doubt I will ever quite live up to him."

"I think you do, you are a better man than he was. You are happy for others to have their own dreams. He couldn't understand a life not his own."

Claude was clearly feeling left out, and had moved towards them. He pushed his nose between them, forcing them apart. Emily laughed. "You will have to get used to this, Matthew will be sharing me with you now," she said to him solemnly. He looked at her with his soulful eyes as if his heart was breaking, then brayed softly. She hugged him tightly. "I think you already have a new partner in crime anyway," she said. "I saw what you did with Christopher. The pair of you will suit one another perfectly, you are both rapscallions!" Matthew laughed as the gentle animal hung his head, as if ashamed, then looked up with his toothy grin.

"I think we have his blessing."

"I think you may be right," Emily admitted as she melted back into his arms.

Epilogue

The theatre was quiet, tonight's show would not be held inside the auditorium. Matthew looked around at the business he had built from the ground up, and marveled at how wonderful the past few months had been. It could so easily have been a mistake, but he had been right. His friends and neighbors longed for distractions, and he was blessed to have found them spectacles that they enjoyed and had made his money back already. He walked outside, and marveled at the throng of people who had come to tiny Sun River. He could see people he knew from both Great Falls and Billings in the crowds, and felt his chest puff up just a little bit in pride that he had brought something so spectacular here.

"Be careful, you will burst your buttons," Emily said as she walked up beside him.

"Is everybody ready?"

"Yes, and eager to give me my wedding gift!" Matthew took her hands in his, he still marveled that this perfect woman wore his ring upon her finger.

"Not many girls get an entire circus," he admitted happily. "I cannot wait to see your Mama and brother perform. I wonder if they will be as good as I remember your parents being when I was a boy. Christopher is going to love it so much. Where is he? I thought he was with you?"

"He is with my Mama, enjoying being backstage. He and Claude have been poking their noses into everything," she chuckled.

"I hope he hasn't been upsetting anyone," Matthew worried.

"They love him. He's one of them in some ways."

"You think he might run away with the circus one day?"

"I think he just might, like you wanted to."

"But he will actually do it. Just not yet. I'm not ready for him to leave home at just six years of age."

They took their seats, and waited for their son to join them. But the lights were dimmed, and the show began and still Christopher did not appear. Matthew began to get concerned, but Emily seemed completely calm. Then he saw why as Claude appeared in the ring, a small boy running after him. He vaulted onto his back, landing backwards, then did his clever turn to go forwards but overshot and had to cling to Claude's neck. The donkey suddenly stopped dead, and Christopher fell to the ground. The clowns ran forward, as the boy lay prone fussing around him. Matthew felt his heart almost stop, fear filling his heart, but then Claude began to trot around the ring and picked up a bucket of water which he returned to the boy and flung it over him. Christopher jumped up spluttering, and chased after the cheeky ass, vaulting back onto his back and then leaping though a paper hoop held by one of the clowns as they left the ring to wild applause. Emily looked at him, her eyes full of love and he smiled. "He may be leaving sooner than I would like," he said wistfully. "He's very good."

"He's much funnier than I ever was. They suit each other perfectly. But, he still has a lot to learn before the Major would accept him as an Act. I'll drag out his training, I promise!" She squeezed his hand as they watched the rest of the show.

After the climax, they rushed to the performers' area and found Christopher sitting proudly on Claude's back, his face alight with happiness. "He's better than I was at his age," Evan said as he reached out his hand and shook Matthew's warmly.

"That is quite a compliment," Emily's Mama said as she moved towards them. Her strong body made her move with a feline grace. "Evan is one of the finest horsemen his Pap or I had ever seen. But he is right, Christopher has a natural talent for it." She embraced her daughter and kissed her cheeks. "You look positively blooming my darling."

"I feel it. Montana suits me."

"Marriage and motherhood suit you," her Mama said sagely. Matthew had to agree. Emily seemed to be much more confident and happy than when she had arrived in Montana, and he was glad of it.

"Mama, thank you for convincing the Major to bring everyone here. It has been such a wonderful wedding gift. To see Christopher in the ring with Claude, and you and Evan. It was wonderful."

"I needed to come and see you. I needed to explain why I behaved as I did. Why I tried to stop you from doing what I knew you needed to, to get well."

"Mama, you did what you thought was best."

"No, I didn't. I didn't want to let you go. I couldn't bear the thought of losing you and I knew that if you healed – but not enough you would leave. I was selfish, and I was cruel. I thought if you were too weak to walk you wouldn't be able to go."

"Oh Mama, you were scared. But, you will never lose me. I may be here in Montana, and you may be in Boston but I will always need you."

"I know that now, and seeing you so happy I am so glad that you defied me and did what you knew you had to." The two women embraced, tears pouring down their cheeks.

"Women can be crazy," Evan said raising his eyebrows. Christopher nodded his agreement as Claude dropped his head as if he was astounded by the revelations.

"Emily, this is just one more reason why I will always love you," Matthew said, laughing so hard that his ribs felt they might burst. She raised an eyebrow and looked at him expectantly, waiting for him to elaborate. "Even when you have an emotional and dramatic revelation it is still utterly theatrical! It is as if you rehearse this to make it the most ridiculous and bizarre spectacle ever seen."

"Well, life is never dull when you choose to be part of the Circus," she said as she moved to his side and kissed him passionately. "We just need to find a way to make you a part of the Act too."

The End

✶ ✶ ✶ ✶ ✶ ✶

A Bride for Daniel: Book 6

Chapter One

Alice sighed. Whenever she received a letter from her friend, Maggie, she felt that her life was somehow not exciting enough. Her vivid descriptions of the new world she had found herself in were so enticing. The rugged mountains, the handsome farmers and ranchers, and the wonderful friends she was making were torment enough, but when she regaled the tales of how perfect her new husband was it just made Alice feel very lonely indeed. Her life was not supposed to have turned out this way. When she had moved to Boston to take up a position as a chambermaid in Young's Hotel, she had thought that she couldn't possibly want for anything more. Sadly, years of cleaning up after the guests, working long hours and barely having a moment to herself had disabused her of the glamour of her position.

Maggie had been lucky. She was one of those women who hadn't been afraid to take her future into her own hands, had placed an advertisement to find herself a husband. But, Alice read the newspapers, most women who answered such advertisements, let alone those that took the risk of placing them, were not so lucky. She had come upon lurid tales of ambush, kidnap, and much worse when she had first learned what Maggie intended to do. But now, it seemed that Sun River was becoming a haven for contented and even loving pairings. Alice was pleased for her, but she couldn't help being more than a little jealous as she read Maggie's latest news – it seemed that a loving husband was not enough, she now had a child on the way too.

A knock on her door made her jump out of her skin. "Alice love, could you possibly help me today?" Cook's voice called through the closed door. "I know this is your day off, but the owner's coming by, bringing a whole party with him. That man is the devil for late notice. But, what can I do?" Alice opened the door, Ellen looked almost frantic. She grinned at her, and gave the older woman a quick hug.

"Ellen, of course I will. I know you still haven't found anyone suitable to take Maggie's place, and the amount of work doesn't change. Mr Reed-Whipple I presume?"

"Yes. Mr Hall at least has the decency to give me a day or two's notice!" Ellen looked frazzled. Alice wished there was a way to reassure her, but they had little to no influence over their employers, and she was sure that if anyone tried to point out to the indomitable pairing that they needed to be more considerate that the person would find themselves out of a position – and without a character. They would be unlikely to ever find work in Boston, or along much of the East Coast, ever again.

"Just give me five minutes and I shall come down," Alice told her friend. Ellen nodded, and looking a little soothed made her way back to the kitchens.

Alice tidied away her letter, and changed out of her smart muslin dress, and into a plain grey work one. She slipped a crisp white pinafore over the top and wondered if she would ever be permitted to have an entire day to herself. She couldn't remember the last time she had been able to enjoy her day off. There was always some kind of crisis that desperately needed her. She didn't blame Maggie for wanting something more at all. She couldn't help but think that there had to be a better life than the one she was living.

Ellen had her up to her elbows in flour within moments of her setting foot in the kitchens. A game pie had been requested, and there was bread to be made too. While Ellen's assistants got on with the daily requirements for the guests and the dining room, the two of them would prepare an entire banquet for thirty-two people. Ellen had been the Head Cook at Young's for almost ten years now, and had worked for the inimitable Mr Young, and now for the two gentlemen who had come from Parker's Hotel to take over. She was used to the demands, but it didn't stop her worrying. The hotel had a reputation to uphold, and she didn't ever want anyone to think her standards had slipped. Alice knew how much of a blow Maggie leaving had been to the older woman, but she also knew that she begrudged none of them their own lives.

"Did Maggie write to you of her news?" Ellen asked her, as she looked over the pastry crust Alice had just finished rolling out. "A little thinner, I think," she added. Alice took up the rolling pin once more. The pastry eased out under the pressure.

"She did. Isn't it wonderful that everything has gone so well for her?"

"It is. I loved her like she was my daughter, like I do you. The pair of you came to me when you were so young. I've seen you both grow up and become such beautiful, kind young ladies."

"You miss her don't you?"

"I do, and not just here in the kitchen. But, as I said to her, I will not be here long – so don't make decisions about your lives because you don't want to upset me." Alice was surprised by her words. She had never confided to anyone that she was considering anything other than her life in the hotel. She had barely even acknowledged it to herself until she read Maggie's letter just now. But, Ellen was wise and had seen many a young girl grow up, marry and move on here at Young's.

"You are too astute for your own good Ellen. How did you know I have been feeling restless?"

"I don't know exactly. I just know that there comes a time when even the most eager and the most ambitious of girls start to consider if there is something more. I know you covet Mrs Wainwright's position, and I have no doubt that you would make a fine housekeeper – but she will not be leaving these halls for many a year to come."

"I know, though many of the younger maids would be glad to see the back of her!"

"You are more like Maggie than you think you are Alice. I know you believe that you couldn't just up and leave everything you know – but you have done it before, and you have thrived. You were just a farm girl, and now you are second only to the housekeeper in one of the most prestigious hotel's in Boston. That took as much courage as leaving here to find a husband would."

"Are you trying to get rid of me?" Alice asked, trying to make her tone teasing.

"Not at all. I would miss you terribly – as I do Maggie. But I will be retiring next year, and I want to know that you are happy."

"I am." Ellen looked at her searchingly. "No, truly. I am happy. I won't lie to you Ellen. I do want marriage, and babies – what young woman does not dream of such things – but I want something more too."

"I often wonder what women mean when they say they want more. What more is there?"

"I don't know. Maybe it is because men get to have work and a family. They get to continue to pursue their interests, while a woman is frowned upon as unnatural, if she shows that she has anything more in her life than her family. Somehow none of it seems fair." Ellen laughed.

"One day, you will understand that having a family becomes everything to you, if you are blessed enough to have one." Alice chided herself silently. She shouldn't have made little of motherhood. Poor Ellen had lost her husband and children in a tragic fire, many years ago. She missed them every day. "Don't you go feeling sorry for me," Ellen said, spotting the look on Alice's face. "I was blessed to have a family, and then gain a new one here. You have all been my babies," she said as she looked around at the young men and women scurrying around, hard at work.

"I think I am beginning to understand it now. Nothing seems to be enough anymore. I don't think that getting the housekeeper's position would be enough either. Oh, I am a foolish ninny – but maybe I am just starting to feel it may be too late if I do not do something soon."

"Well, try not to make it too drastic a change!" Ellen laughed. "You will work it out, and will have my blessing whatever – so long as you are happy."

They continued to work companionably through the day. When they were done there was a fine spread just waiting to be delivered to the dining hall. Alice couldn't help but feel that maybe she was in the wrong position. There was something altogether very satisfying about seeing your work lined up on the tables in front of you. She enjoyed ensuring that every guest's room was spotless, but because she did such a good job at it there was rarely a tangible difference between a room that needed cleaning, and one that she had just finished. As she looked at the crisp golden crusts of pies she had made, the elegant desserts and inhaled the scent of the loaves of fresh bread she felt at peace. It had been a good day's work.

"Alice, I know this may be a difficult thing, considering our conversation earlier today – but would you consider taking Maggie's position?" Ellen asked as they took off their aprons and sank into chairs by the fire. "You don't have to tell me now, but think about it. You are a very talented cook, and I do believe that you would be happier here than under Mrs Wainwright. It would be an increase in salary, and you would get your own room and be able to share my parlor." Alice looked at her friend. She was in earnest, and she knew that Ellen was hoping to take someone in the position that could take on her own role when she retired. Maggie had been the obvious choice, but she was no longer here. Alice wanted to say she was happy to say yes, that it would be the new challenge she was looking for – but something held her back.

"I will think about it," she said. "But I need time."

"I know." Alice turned to leave the kitchen, and began to head up to her bed. She was more than tired, and she had an early start the next day. But she had barely set foot upon the stair when she heard her friend's voice. She turned. "Alice? Take this. See if there is anyone that makes your heart leap," Ellen said as she thrust a copy of the Matrimonial Times at her. "If a promotion doesn't get your heart racing, maybe it is a new life all together that you need."

In the privacy of her room, Alice pondered the conversations she had shared with her friend. She had not known just how unhappy she was, how much she felt was missing from her life until they spoke of it. She re-read Maggie's letter, marveling at the joy and happiness she could hear in every word. She didn't envy Maggie her happiness, did not begrudge her it in any way – but she did long to have something of her very own. She picked up the newspaper and began to flick through the advertisements. She didn't think that marriage was the salve for her discomfort, but as Ellen said, it wouldn't hurt her to explore the possibility.

Many of the men who were in search of wives seemed good and kind, though it was clear why so many more of them had need to advertise. Even in their few words they came across as coarse and unpleasant. But there were at least half a dozen that she thought could be worth corresponding with. Until she read the last advertisement in the entire newspaper, it made her laugh. This was a man who knew his imperfections, and who would accept that a woman would have her own too. She was sure she would like him, and that he was in Montana made her feel reassured. She would have someone to run to, in Maggie, if he turned out to be less than he at first appeared.

A Gentleman of Montana seeks a wife: I have little to offer, a small farm and a lot of hard work. The subscriber seeks a woman to talk with, walk with, share and grow with. If you love music, dancing, and can cook and clean I can offer you nights at the theatre, two left feet and a lot of mess. All responses to be addressed to Box 348, The Matrimonial Times

Chapter Two

"Dammit!" Daniel cursed as he lost his grip on the wrench. The rust on the wheel and upon the axle were making a difficult job even harder, but he couldn't afford a new cart and so he was forced to persevere. The sun was warm on his back, and he was sweating hard from the exertion. He rolled up his sleeves, and wiped his hands on his denim jeans. He liked the hard wearing pants that Mr Levi Strauss sold. He certainly had need of them being able to cope with everything he threw at them. Taking a deep breath, he tried the nut again. He gasped as he used all his body weight to try and get some kind of traction, but it was determined not to budge.

"D'ya need a hand?" Ardloe asked as he drove into the yard. Daniel had never been so glad to see the crusty old carpenter. He stood up and stretched out his back as Ardloe jumped down from the dashboard of his wagon. "Here, let me."

"Be my guest," he chuckled. Even Ardloe would be unable to shift this particular nut, he was sure of it.

"It's tight. You got any oil anywhere? Bit of grease – preferably warm?"

"Sure, but what'll that do?"

"Just you get it, then watch." Daniel went off to find an oilcan in the barn. He took it outside and watched as Ardloe carefully let the oil drip in behind the nut. He was patient. He wiped the nut again and then took the wrench, the nut slipped off into his hand as easy as anything.

"I shall remember that little trick," he said admiringly.

"Want me to get the rest of 'em off?" Ardloe said pointing to the remaining bolts. Daniel nodded. "The new wheel is in the back of my wagon, just you bring it over fer me?"

The new wheel was a piece of craftsmanship. Ardloe truly could do anything with a piece of wood. Daniel lifted it up and brought it over to the axle. Ardloe had removed the old wheel and was inspecting it carefully. "Shouldn't take too much to patch this up, if'n ya wanted a spare."

"It might be useful. Thanks for doing this so quickly for me. I have so much to do, and can't afford to fall behind."

"I know Danny lad. My boy, Frank, is in town looking for work. He don't need paying much, but he might be help to ya?"

"If he can work for free, I'd gladly accept his help – but until I get the harvest in I barely have enough to keep myself," Daniel admitted reluctantly. He liked Frank too, he was a good man and he worked hard.

"Hell, we can keep him fed an' he don't pay us no rent for his board. If ya agree to a share of the profits once ya are sold I'm sure he'd take it. Poor boy's bored out of his brain – and drivin' his Mama crazy."

"Well if he is happy with that, I'm sure I can be. There'll be no crop unless I can get the seeds in the ground after all!"

"The two of you'll have everythin' up and growin' in no time. I'll send him up when I get back."

"Thank you Ardloe. I appreciate it." The two men fixed the new wheel in place, and Ardloe tightened the nuts. He took a step back, and admired his work. Daniel took a small fold of dollar bills out of his pocket and pressed them into his gnarled hand. "Don't argue; you always undercharge me."

"That'll give Frank enough to have an occasional drink in Tom's saloon, so I will thank you. Oh, talkin' of which, he charged me with bringin' yer post." The old man wandered back to his wagon, and took a pile of letters from a box in the back. He hopped up onto the dashboard, and clicked to his old pony. They began to trundle back down the path towards Sun River.

Daniel took his mail and sat in the rocker on his porch. He flicked through the bills from seed companies and the place in Great Falls where he had purchased his plough. He had arrangements with them to pay at harvest, and so did not need to worry about them. But there were three other letters, all of them with the neatly typed address of the Matrimonial Times. He stared at them for a long time. He was still not sure what had possessed him to advertise for a wife. He could barely support himself, but he was lonely. True, he had made some wonderful friends since he had moved here to Sun River and claimed his parcel of land. But, everybody lived so far away from each other. He was a boy who came from the tenements of Chicago, he wasn't used to such peace and quiet all the time. But, he did love the mountains and the fresh air. He wouldn't swap Montana for anything.

He ripped open the first of the letters, and almost immediately threw the missive down in disgust. The woman who had responded seemed so terribly sure of herself, but she had obviously misconstrued his comment about visits to the theatre to mean in New York and Boston – he had no intention of going so far afield, not when there was a perfectly wonderful theatre right here in Sun River itself. She seemed far too eager for the finer things in life, did not seem to understand he needed a woman that could work – and work hard.

The second letter was marginally more encouraging. This woman came from Deadwood. But, by the final paragraph that he read he had already decided that she may be a whole different kettle of trouble. She spoke of an angry ex-husband that she had to escape from. He had no desire to become any woman's knight in shining armor, nor did he want a jealous man turning up on his doorstep and demanding what he believed was his. He didn't like to think of himself as old-fashioned, but he believed in marriage vows. He truly felt they were for life and that anyone who could either say them to a man or woman not worthy of such pledges, or who was prepared to give up on them was not a woman he wished to consider wedding. By the sound of it, this woman had every reason to get as far away from this man as she could, but he only had her side of the story.

He was sure that the third would be just as unsuitable, but was pleasantly surprised by the light and breezy tone. This was a woman he could indeed consider, he thought, as he read her letter with growing pleasure.

Dear Gentleman of Montana,

I want you to know that I have never considered doing such a thing as this before, and nor have I written to any other man. I am not even sure why I am writing at all, except that your advertisement amused me, and my friend insisted I explore some avenues outside of my normal life to try and find out why I feel that something is missing.

I am a chambermaid, but I also help out in the kitchen's here at Young's Hotel. I have just been offered a position as the assistant to our Cook in truth. Six months ago I would have said that a promotion would be everything I could ever dream of, and yet it did not give me any pleasure, and I am not even sure that I intend to take up the position.

Gosh, writing letters truly does make it easy to reveal things, doesn't it? Sorry if I am boring you, but I seem to have found that scribbling about my worries is most helpful!

You said you have a farm. I grew up on a farm, a little place outside of Boston. We worked hard, and Mama and Papa made it yield well. But I wanted more. Thankfully my brother was happy to stay where he was, and he and his wife seem more than content to stay there and take over when my parents pass on. They are good, Christian people and I love them, though I barely see them anymore.

Do you have family? Sorry if that seems impertinent, and if you do not I am ever so sorry for your losses.

Montana always looks so beautiful in the pictures I have seen. Is it truly as wonderful as it appears? I would imagine it can be quite tough to make your way there. I have a friend I used to work with here at the hotel, Maggie, who lives in a tiny place called Sun River. Is that near you? I understand that she is very happy there. Her new husband is quite perfect from everything she says in her letters.

Sorry, I am rambling a little. I shall leave you to make your decision, but I should very much like to correspond with you. I am not looking for wealth, or security. I would like to make a true friend, maybe explore a new part of the world, and find a new challenge. If you think that corresponding with me could bring you anything in return, I shall look forward eagerly to hearing from you.

Yours most hopefully

Alice Springham

Daniel brought the paper to his lips, deep in thought. A waft of roses greeted his nostrils. "By God, she scented the paper," he cried, laughing. He couldn't help it, he liked her. He was sure that this was the woman that would suit him. Certainly she was head and shoulders above the other two responses thus far. But, she did not mention a word about marriage, only about having an adventure. He wasn't sure if it was because she was trying to be polite, to not push him into a commitment they were neither of them ready for yet – or if she was merely using him to explore her options. He did not want to be used by anyone. He longed for a true meeting of minds and hearts.

He was an old-fashioned man, and romantic to the very bone. He believed that you should treat a woman right, with respect. He knew that he should not be corresponding with a woman that he had no intentions towards, or who had no honorable intentions towards him. It seemed altogether frivolous to just correspond for the pleasure of it. But she seemed so funny and warm, and so unguarded. It would most definitely be a lot of fun getting to know her. He did not understand why Society frowned upon friendships between men and women. He had always found them much easier to converse with than many of the men of his acquaintance.

But he also had too many memories of his intentions being misconstrued. He would never make the same mistakes again. He would only correspond with Miss Alice Springham if they were both looking for the same thing. It would be too difficult to bear the sadness if he invested his heart in their correspondence, only to find that she did not have any inclinations towards coming to Montana and being Mrs Daniel Havering. He needed a wife. He needed her to want a husband. Her letter did not make it clear if she did – in fact, it seemed that she had a career that could drag her from him before he had even begun courting her. If she just longed for a friend, or some kind of new experience to help her to make up her mind about what to do next he was not prepared to be that for her.

Quickly he gathered up pen and paper from inside the house, and returned to the porch to write his reply. There was so much he wanted to know, and he prayed that he would not sound like some old stick in the mud, but he would not be responsible for a young woman losing her reputation, and he could not bear the thought of having to make a home, again, if things did not work out the way he had planned. He could already feel a part of him warming to her sweet words, and almost breathless nature. He did not want to lose his heart. He had to protect himself – but he also did not want to scare her away.

Chapter Three

Alice waited anxiously for a response from the Gentleman of Montana. She wasn't sure if she had been too forward, or not forward enough, in her first letter. She was finding it harder and harder to make even the simplest of decisions, and she was sure it was because she didn't know if there was an alternative. But she knew, in her heart of hearts, that it did not matter if he wrote to her or not. The simple fact that she was waiting, and praying that he would told her that her goals and dreams had clearly changed.

She began to trawl through the Matrimonials page in every newspaper she read, cutting out the pages with men who sounded interesting. Yet, for some reason she could not bring herself to write to any of them. She kept telling herself it was because she was being polite, that whoever the man was in Montana that she had written to deserved to have sufficient time to respond before she entered a correspondence with someone else. After all, she could hardly be in love with a man she knew nothing of. She had read only a few lines about him. It wasn't sufficient evidence to base a future upon.

"Alice, love, there is a letter for you in my parlor," Ellen said, giving her a quick squeeze as she entered the kitchen as she leant up close to her ear and whispered, " I thought you might like a bit of privacy."

"Thank you," she whispered back. "Is Mrs Wainwright around?" Ellen shook her head.

"No, she is in a meeting with both the owners. I think she will come back with word that I must fill Maggie's old post. I don't think I can give you much longer to make up your mind."

"I understand," Alice said. "Maybe the letter will help me decide."

She hurried through to the little room beside the kitchens, and sank down into the seat that had once been Maggie's. She wondered if she had read her first letters from Ethan there, and if maybe it might bring her some luck. She sliced open the envelope carefully, and took out the paper. She could feel her belly churning, and was surprised that a letter could cause her so much anxiety. After all, the worst that could happen was that he was saying he did not wish to correspond with her.

Dear Miss Springham

Thank you for your delightfully scented letter. I was honored that you chose to correspond with me, but I have a few questions I must ask. I do not wish for there to be any confusion, or unhappiness between us.

I am looking for a wife. Are you truly looking for a husband?

I do not have time to waste on courting, nor do I have sufficient funds to spend on searching for a bride. If you are not serious in your pursuit of a husband, I would prefer to know now. I do not wish to sound harsh, and certainly do not wish to put you off – as I read your letter with much pleasure, and truly think we could suit. But I will not waste your time or mine, if I am merely a distraction you require to help you to make a decision as to what to do with your life.

Alice put down the letter unfinished. Her butterflies seemed to have turned into angry birds. She was fuming. How dare he be so rude?

She had written to him in all good faith, had laid her predicament out on the line and here he was, doubting her veracity? Never had she read a person so wrongly. She had thought he would be fun, and engaging. But he sounded like a petty tyrant.

"I brought you a cup of hot chocolate, love, thought you might need it," Ellen said as she popped her head around the door, the steaming cup of chocolate filling the tiny room with its rich vanilla and cinnamon scent.

"I could certainly use the comfort," she admitted sadly.

"Does he not wish to correspond?"

"I think he does, but I simply couldn't read the whole letter. His first words were to admonish me as a frivolous chit who didn't know her own mind."

"But that is exactly what you are," Ellen teased. Alice glared at her.

"I know that, and you do too – but what right is it of his to point it out to me?"

"He is looking for a wife, someone to share his life with. That is his right. He wants to know you are serious before he gives his heart to you."

"Read it Ellen, I don't think he intends giving his heart to anybody."

Ellen sat down beside her and took the letter from the table. Alice sipped at her chocolate, and watched as her friend read his words. It seemed to take forever. "Well, I agree the first page is a bit of a rant, but by page two he sounds like he is absolutely charming. I truly believe he is only trying to protect himself from hurt. Give him a chance, read the rest of it. I think you will be pleased you did."

Alice took back the proffered pages and set the chocolate down. She skimmed over the bit she had already read, the annoyance quick to ignite when she saw his bald question to her. But she bit it back down and continued to read.

I am sorry if I sound like the worst kind of tyrant, but I did not advertise for a wife lightly. I am a cautious man; an old fashioned man. I had hoped that I would one day just meet a girl, fall head over heels in love with her and that would be that. But my life has not run so smoothly as that, I am sad to say.

I find myself living here, in the most beautiful place in all the world with nobody to share it with. I do not wish to be alone. I wish to be a part of a family, with a loving wife and well-behaved children (though I would accept unruly and naughty!)I want to create a bond that is as solid and unshakeable as the mountains around me. But, there are not enough women here, and so I must resort to other means.

Writing, though a most pleasant pastime, is not an easy medium through which to get to know a person, though as you so rightly say it can make it easier to open up about some things we might not ever say in person. I am sure you will misconstrue my earlier words, for instance, and think that I am maybe trying to push you away or being overly demanding. But, your lovely letter made me feel that I have known you forever, and could therefore confide my fears.

I am not a wealthy man. I have had many responses from women who seem to expect me to be able to keep them in a manner I most certainly cannot. I have enough land to make a good living, but it will take many years to get my farm to be profitable. I need a partner, who will understand that this will be tough. I will need to rely on her strength and certainty, her trust that I will be able to make things come good.

I think you may be that woman. I think you have the right blend of fun, adventure, and hard work running through you or you would not have achieved what you have so far. This means everything to me. I have to choose wisely, and I am scared. Scared that I will do it all wrong, will not be able to make things right for any woman. And I truly like you. Something inside me simply sang out as I read your letter. I need to meet you, I need to know you are not toying with me in order to then change your mind and remain in Boston, and take your promotion.

You asked in your letter if I lived near Sun River, indeed I do and I know your friend Maggie too I believe. I also got the feeling from your letter that you are uncertain about much in your life. You seem to enjoy your work, but I noted that it no longer gives you the pleasure it once did. You think you may want a relationship, but seem scared to admit it even to yourself. And so, I have an idea. I truly hope that you will consider it, as I think it could possibly help us to calm our fears about this giant leap into the unknown.

Maggie has opened a bakery. I understand that she is expecting her first child with Ethan, and that he is concerned as to the hours and the difficulty of much of her work. I appreciate that if you leave Boston you will be doing so without any kind of guarantees that you would have work to return to, and so this way you could come here and have a position – whatever were to occur between us.

Maybe you could come and help her out, build a new life for yourself here - and we could see if we suit? I would love to court you properly. We could go to the theatre, and on picnics. I want to show you my farm, and the lovely stream that flows through it where I fish occasionally. I wish to show you the incredible mountains and the waterfalls and the wildlife that surround us.

Don't come to Sun River for me. Come to Sun River to build yourself a new life. If anything happens between us, then that would be down to fate. But, I truly feel you need a new start somewhere and this could be it.

Yours Hopefully
Daniel Havering

Alice could feel her eyes fill with tears. How had he seen so much from just a single letter? He had managed to pinpoint her dilemma exactly. She didn't know what she wanted, but she did know it wasn't what she had. It was why she had resisted the opportunity to take the promotion, and it was why she had leapt at the chance to write to a complete stranger. "I think he truly sees you," Ellen said sagely. "He is offering you the chance to change your life, if you want to."

"Without marrying me! I cannot travel across the country as a woman alone. It would be, I don't know, unseemly."

"Are you so sure that is what you want from him? It sounds to me that he is offering you a solution to your discontent, not attempting to sully your virtue. You would be going across the country to take up a position. It is no different to your coming here when you were a girl."

"No, he is right about that too. You are right, as always. I do like him. But I think you both may be right that I just want to get away from here, to do something different."

"It would do my heart good to know you are with Maggie. She seems to be so much happier since she moved to Sun River, and to know you are by her side as she has her baby would put my mind at rest," Ellen admitted, wringing her hands. Alice gave her a quick hug. She knew how much the older woman cared for both her and Maggie.

"Why don't you come with me?" Alice said suddenly. She could hear the wistfulness in the older woman's tone and she knew that she loved both her and Maggie as if they were her own children. In her heart of hearts, Alice was sure that Ellen would like nothing more than to be by Maggie's side as she had her little one.

"No, I should stay here. The hotel would fall apart if we all just up and leave."

"No, that shouldn't be your concern Ellen. You have given your best years to this place. Isn't it time you thought about what you want, what you need for a change? You should come and be with us. You are our family, and we both love you. Just think how incredible that bakery could be if you were a part of it. People would come from miles around!"

"Alice, it will be a small bakery, in a small town. It will not need three of us."

"But Maggie will not be there soon," Alice cajoled. She suddenly felt anxious about heading across the country alone. She needed Ellen there too, and she was sure that Maggie would be glad of her presence too. "Why don't I write to Maggie and see if what this man says is true? We can decide then."

"But you will write to him too?"

"Yes I shall. I shall be honest and tell him I am unsure, but that I do wish to come to Montana. I shall start to make my arrangements, and will wait until we have word from Maggie to finalize our plans."

"Our plans!" Ellen snorted. "Your plans, my girl. I am staying right here." Alice knew that Ellen longed to accept the invitation. She was tired of the hard work and lack of recognition she received here too. And they both missed Maggie so much. She wouldn't push, but she also would not set foot on that train without her friend and mentor by her side. She didn't doubt for one moment what Maggie's response would be to them both joining her in Sun River. She would be delighted.

Chapter Four

Daniel worked himself into the ground over the next few weeks as he waited for a reply. He knew he had possibly been too harsh on her. It wasn't Alice's fault that she was a little confused and did not truly know what she wanted. He had been in exactly the same position himself once, and never wanted to return to such a confused state ever again. To be so sure of yourself, and yet have no idea of what you wanted from life had made it difficult to make sensible choices, and he had almost made a few that would have ruined his life. But, he knew he liked Alice and he prayed daily that she would learn to like him too, in time. There was something about the way she wrote her letters that was touching, endearing almost. He liked that she wasn't guarded. She wrote what she thought, did not edit it or worry that he might not like what he saw. It was refreshing to find someone who appeared to have so little artifice.

Sauntering along the rapidly growing Main Street he caught the smell of freshly baked bread. The little bakery had been an instant success. Maggie baked daily, even on Sundays and the townspeople, farmers and ranchers were all grateful for it. She didn't just prepare bread, she made exquisite pies and pasties, and would even take in stews and casseroles for those who didn't have their own ovens. Many now wondered how they had ever managed without her. He decided to stop by and to say hello. The little shop had a bright display window, filled with tempting looking breads. Some were too pretty to even consider eating, but they showed how talented the young woman was.

"Good morning Maggie," he said smiling broadly at her as the scents of yeast and vanilla swamped his nostrils.

"Well hello," she said, grinning back at him warmly. "How are you today?"

"I am well. This all looks wonderful," he said looking at the artfully displayed loaves and the pretty looking pastries.

"You have been in here a dozen times Daniel Havering. You know I pride myself on how wonderful everything looks – as well as how good it tastes. You didn't pop by to say something so trite! You want to know if I have heard from Alice, don't you?" she asked perceptively. "You aren't interested in my buns at all!" He blushed. He didn't like being caught out, but he had to admit he was transparent to read these days.

"I am sorry. They do look delicious though. So, have you?" he asked her eagerly.

"I have, and I believe Tom is holding a letter for you too. They came this morning. She is definitely thinking about coming. But, she wants to bring our friend Ellen too."

"Is that possible?" he asked. He didn't want to make things difficult for Maggie. She was doing him an incredible favor as it was, but if it was the cost of bringing Alice here then he would be prepared to find a way to pay the woman's board and wages if need be. .

"It would be wonderful," Maggie admitted, a huge smile all over her lovely face. "If you think my baking is good, then you have not experienced anything quite like it. Ellen could double my trade in a week once word about her pies gets out. All of you lonely bachelors would be here every day to buy your suppers!"

"Many of us already are. If they are any better than yours then she will have the entire state falling at her feet! So you think it could work, that there is enough work for three of you?"

"It could indeed. I have already written back, told Alice to get on the train immediately. We could open up bakeries all over the county if they were here too. If nothing else it will mean I can take some time when the wee one arrives to get to know him, or her."

Daniel found her enthusiasm contagious; he had forgotten what an ambitious woman she was. He could barely fathom the idea of opening one store, let alone thinking in terms of a store in every town. But, if she truly thought it was possible, and that having Ellen and Alice here would make it happen then he was glad to have played a part in it happening. He made his way over to the saloon, his hopes high. Maggie had insisted he take a loaf of bread and a lamb pasty with him, and had refused to take a cent. He wasn't sure how that was good business, but was grateful as he had nothing so tasty back at the farm. He collected his letter and raced back home to read it on the porch.

Dear Mr Havering,

Thank you for your letter. I will be truthful, I almost did not read it all as I got so cross! But, thankfully my dear friend Ellen was on hand and made me read the rest.

I am truly astounded that you could so easily pinpoint things I did not see, or accept in myself until I read your letter. You are right, of course, that I am unsure of what I want. I am sure, now that I think on it, that my uncertainty was why I responded to your advertisement at all. I would not have been looking if everything in my life had been as perfect as I tried to tell myself it was.

Things have changed here at the hotel in recent years. We have had new owners, and they have changed things a lot. Staff seem to come and go a lot more quickly than they ever used to, and we seem to be expected to do so much more as we fill in for those who have left. It seems that nobody gets replaced any more. I also miss Maggie very much, and I think my unhappiness here without her was a prompt to me that I needed to change my life, if I wanted anything to be different. But like the stubborn mule that I am, I resisted that change, trying to make myself believe that I was happy.

I think, that as a woman, it is hard to just decide to up and leave. We have to have another position, or a marriage to go to. To just start again somewhere completely new is frowned upon still. I let myself believe that I could not make any kind of move without a man endorsing that change, rescuing me from my unhappiness if you like. As I think on it now, I can see just how ridiculous that is. I have never been one to wait for permission to do anything. I think that pioneering spirit has always been a part of me. It is why I left my family to come to Boston, and why I will now be making the journey to Montana.

I have written to Maggie, and I pray she will agree with me that I should bring Ellen (the wise lady who insisted I read the entirety of your letter). She will be lost without us, and I cannot bear to think of her being lonely and unhappy. She has been like a mother to me, and I know that Maggie and I hold places in her heart alongside those of her dearly departed children. Sadly, both of them and her husband were in a terrible accident involving a hansom cab and a phaeton, it was dreadful – was in all of the newspapers. Nobody had ever seen anything so tragic. How she ever managed to recover from something so terrible I do not know, but she is a marvel. I am sure you will like her, and that she will like you too.

I am excited about coming and working in the bakery, and I am so grateful that you had such a wonderful idea. I look forward to getting to know you better too, and will hold you to those trips to the theatre and to explore Montana. I am sorry if you believe that I am not serious about the possibility of being your wife. I want to assure you that my reasons for contacting you may have not been entirely due to that desire, but our correspondence thus far most definitely has made me realize that it is something I could most eagerly anticipate, with you.

Yours Gratefully

Alice

His memories of the scent from her last letter were still vivid, and so he raised the paper to his nostrils and took in a deep breath. This time there was a strong hint of cinnamon and vanilla. The scent reminded him of the smells in Maggie's little bakery. He wondered what she had been doing before she wrote to him, and lost himself in a daydream of her making dainty delights, that would melt on the tongue and leave just a memory of perfection lingering. He was so glad that she would be making the journey – was more than happy that she had taken up the challenge. He did not want her to feel beholden to him; he did not want to be her refuge. He wanted to be her partner, her lover, her friend. He wanted her to come to him because she wanted to, not because she felt she had no choice, and he prayed that this would be the start of something wonderful for them both.

Now his crops were planted, things on the farm were a little calmer. He was always busy and there were always a thousand things to be done, but nothing was urgent as he waited for the little green shoots to emerge from the soil, grow healthy and strong, and ripen into a bountiful harvest. So, he used his time wisely, splitting it between the chores he had to do on the farm, and making sure his home was fit to be visited. Alice would live in town when she arrived; she and Ellen would take the tiny apartment above the bakery. But, he wanted his home to be the kind of place a wife would be proud to call her own. He wanted to make a good impression, and so he asked Maggie and Catherine to give him advice. Catherine had only recently refurbished the saloon, and she was full of very useful ideas that he could implement without much money.

When they had completed their task his cabin looked like a home. It was no longer just the place he laid his head, and left in disarray. It would make a wonderful place to bring up children, and was a pleasure to live in. He wondered why he hadn't paid any attention to it previously. Like so many men, he had only cared that there was a bed to sleep in, and a chair to rest by the fire. Anything more than that had seemed unnecessary, but now he had drapes and armoires, a neat kitchen with everything in its place and he couldn't have been happier. He took pride in folding his things and putting them away carefully, rather than simply leaving them strewn across the floor.

The day of Alice's arrival finally dawned, and he hitched up his horse to the wagon and made his way towards Sun River. The train was due at midday in Great Falls, and he was determined to be there early. He stopped outside the little bakery on the High Street, and Maggie leapt up on the dashboard beside him. She was starting to show, the gentle swelling of her belly testimony of the life inside. "You look positively glowing," he said warmly as she settled herself down.

"Thank you. I am starting to get tired and cranky, so I'll apologize now just in case!"

They drove in companionable silence, and arrived at the station just as the sound of the train whistle sounded in the distance. "Just in time," he said wryly.

"That is all we need to be. Now, come along. I cannot wait to introduce you properly to my friends."

Daniel followed Maggie. He felt an unexpected reluctance to go any further forward as they reached the ticket office. "I can't," he said, feeling foolish.

"Of course you can," Maggie encouraged him. "There is nothing to fear from either of them, I can assure you."

"I know, I just… What if she hates me on sight?"

"She won't. I am sure she already likes you more than she would ever admit or she wouldn't have left a good job, with prospects in Boston to come here. Women don't do such things unless there is a bit more than just intrigue driving them."

"You think she has feelings for me?"

"I know she does. Now, straighten yourself up. Put your hat back a little so she can see your handsome face, and do your top button up!"

"Yes Mama," he said with a grin.

"Just relax and be yourself. There is much to like and I know I am glad to call you my friend."

Daniel wasn't sure if he could be calm, and doubted that he would be able to utter another word as he felt his heart leap up into his throat as the train arrived in the station with a loud hiss of steam and a plume of dirty grey smoke. He coughed a little, and tried not to focus on the torrent in his stomach. The last time he had been this nervous everything had ended in disaster. He placed his faith in Maggie, she was sure that all would be well and he had to cling on to that.

Through the smoke he saw the train doors begin to open. He held his breath; the woman he was sure held his heart would soon emerge from one of them. Suddenly Maggie shrieked, and ran towards two women disembarking the very first carriage, right behind the vast engine and the nearly empty coal wagon behind it. "You're truly here," she yelled as she flung herself into the arms of the older woman, and then the younger. "Oh Alice, you look wonderful and Ellen I cannot tell you how wonderful it is that you came!"

Daniel wanted to move forward to greet them, but found that he was pinned to the spot. He could only watch the delighted reunions with an emotion that felt akin to jealousy. He wished he could be so open, so relaxed as to rush over there and sweep Alice up into his arms. The petite blonde with the smile that could light up an entire city took away his breath as she smiled cautiously over at him. She had the cutest dimples, and wore the prettiest dress he had ever seen. Maggie pushed her over towards him. "This is Daniel," she said and then backed away so they could be alone.

"Hello," she said. Her voice was soft and sweet, like Maggie's cakes. She looked up at him, and held out her hand. He noticed it was quivering a little.

"Hello," he said as he took it between both of his. "I am so glad you came."

"I am too," she admitted. "I am petrified, cannot seem to stop shaking!" She giggled nervously.

"Me too," he admitted as he raised her hand to his lips and kissed the back of it tenderly. "You are quite lovely."

Chapter Five

Alice could hardly tear her eyes from the handsome man who stood, as nervous as she was, but more handsome than she could ever have imagined in front of her. She didn't know how to ease his awkwardness. All she knew was that she had never seen eyes of such a delightful shade of hazel, or a man of such height and strength. Even through his soft flannel shirt she could see his rippling muscles, and his denim jeans were pulled tight against his thighs. He was beautiful. She drank in his sculpted features, the strong jaw line and his soft brown hair. She wanted to speak, but she seemed to have lost all capacity to do so. She could still feel the gentle touch of his lips on the back of her hand, and couldn't help wishing it had been more. She longed to be scooped up into his arms, to have him whisk her away and do whatever he would with her.

But their moment was to be brief. "You must be Mr Havering," Ellen said cheerily, as she came up and put an arm around Alice's back.

"Yes, I am so sorry. Daniel Havering, this is Ellen McGraw," Alice said, feeling foolish for stating something so obvious. She couldn't remember ever feeling so flustered, but just a moment in this man's presence and she felt as giddy as a schoolgirl.

"It is a pleasure to meet you Ma'am," he drawled, bowing a little and sweeping his Stetson from his head gallantly. Ellen laughed. Alice was glad, it was clear that she liked him already. Ellen's opinion, and Maggie's too, mattered to her greatly. But, she was distracted again, his voice was deep and had a hint of rawness to it. She could feel it rippling through every part of her, like a gentle summer breeze, or the feel of silk against her skin. "We should get you both home to Sun River. You must both be quite tired after the journey."

"I don't know about Alice, she has been bouncing almost the entire way, but I will be glad of a soft bed and a hot bath," Ellen joked. Alice flushed, she hadn't wanted anyone to know just how nervous and excited she had been about coming here to Montana, especially not Daniel. What if now he had seen her he decided that he didn't want her after all? What if he chose to write to some other woman, and brought her here to marry him instead? All she could think about was him, and now he was here in front of her she knew that was only going to get worse.

"Well I am afraid there will be a little more bouncing to get us home," he said with a wicked glint in his eyes. "My old wagon is not the most comfortable of rides, but it will have us all home in no time and you girls can settle yourselves in to your new home."

"We shall be glad to be there," Alice said nervously.

"Not when I come in and start up the ovens at the most ungodly of hours," Maggie said with a wink.

"We shall be joining you. In fact, you won't need to be the one to do so any longer. Come in when you are ready, we can do that as we will be on the premises," Ellen said firmly.

"We can take it in turns," Maggie said diplomatically. "I shall insist that we all get at least one morning a week to enjoy the comfort of our coverlets!"

They made their way to the wagon and Daniel effortlessly hefted their trunks into the back of the wagon, and then helped them all up inside. He jumped up onto the dashboard and they were on their way. The weather was fine, and so he had pulled back the thick canvas covering so the cart was open to the sunshine. Maggie pointed out all sorts of landmarks as they drove, and Alice and Ellen looked on with awe as the beautiful landscape seemed to grow before their eyes. "It is so beautiful," Alice breathed as they crossed over the meandering river, and caught sight of a herd of cows off in the distance.

"That is probably a part of Mack's herd. He has a lovely wife called Annie, she's from Boston too. In fact it seems that Sun River men have a thing for us Boston girls," she said digging Daniel in the ribs affectionately. He smiled at her, but kept his attention on the road. The track was clearly well used, but it was a little rutted in places and it made for a slightly uncomfortable ride in the back. But Alice could see he was trying his best to keep it as smooth as possible.

"So, let me see if I remember this properly," Ellen said. "Now, it was Myra who was a governess and she married Carlton who is a farmer, like young Daniel here?" Maggie nodded.

"Yes, she is just about to open the new school."

"And Annie was the maid in their household, and she came out here and married Mackenzie, who is a rancher?" Alice said.

"Catherine, who was from some fancy family, married Tom the saloon owner and you, of course, married Ethan who himself comes from Boston, but is now working on the ranch with Mack." Ellen sounded quite proud of herself for remembering all the intriguing combinations that had occurred in recent years in the little town.

"And of course there is Emily, the circus girl who married Matthew, who owns the theatre, just a few months ago," Maggie added. "You have to meet her. She and her donkey, Claude, do the very best tricks."

"It sounds like Sun River has quite the collection of eccentrics," Alice said quietly. She wasn't sure if she would be able to fit in amongst such a group. They all sounded educated, and brave. She couldn't imagine ever even thinking of running her own business, as Maggie was doing, or setting up a school. And, to be a circus performer seemed completely beyond her imagination. She was just a simple maid, there was nothing special about her. However would Daniel find her interesting when the other women of his acquaintance were such formidable and intriguing characters?

"I prefer life a little quieter than my friends, I think," Daniel said softly, as if he was speaking only to her and he had heard her thoughts. "I just want a good home, fertile land, and to feel loved."

"Such simple tastes," she said, praying he wasn't lying. The way he said it made her long for it too.

"I've been eating bacon and beans for three months. It doesn't take much to please me," he said laughing.

"A strapping man like you, well we shall have to change that," Ellen said briskly. "You need some good home cooking."

"Don't believe a word of it Alice, I feed him every time he comes into town," Maggie laughed. Daniel winked at her and Ellen grinned.

"Well, you can't blame a man for trying to win a little good feeling," he said shrugging his shoulders, though he was clearly unrepentant.

"We're here," Maggie said as they began to trundle along a wide Main Street. An imposing theatre stood at one end, with a smart chapel and rows of shops on either side. Daniel drew the wagon up outside one of them. The little bakery had a freshly painted sign, and everything in the window looked good enough to eat. "Salt dough," Maggie confided. "So I don't have to change the display every day!"

"It is a good idea, and it looks wonderful," Ellen said as she and Alice gazed in admiration at the elegant sheaf of corn that Maggie had fashioned and the range of loaves and other goodies.

"Come upstairs. I can show you round the bakery tomorrow. Today should be all about you settling in to your new home." Maggie ushered Ellen upstairs, as Alice went to help Daniel with their baggage.

"You go on up, I'll be fine," he assured her. "Welcome to your new home. I truly hope you will be very happy here."

"You know, I think I will be," she replied. "It already feels right."

She was rewarded with a grin. "Thank you, for everything."

"I did nothing but make a suggestion."

"You did more than that, and I am more than glad you did Mr Havering."

"Please, call me Daniel," he said. "And might I call you Alice?"

"Of course. I would like that very much."

She made her way upstairs, and sank into one of the comfortable chairs by the fire in the tiny parlor. She smiled to herself as she watched Maggie and Ellen bustling around. Her fears had turned out to be unwarranted. Daniel was a lovely man, and she was sure that there was at least a tiny spark of something between them. She was sure she had seen his eyes light up, and she liked it that he felt confident enough to tease her. She didn't care about which would be her room, or how well appointed the tiny kitchen was. She hoped above all things that this would not be her home for long. She just sat and let everything happen around her, watching for Daniel as he brought up their things, glimpsing the way his muscles strained against the flimsy cloth of his shirt. Something primal seemed to be awakening within her, despite her exhaustion.

"May I call for you tomorrow?" Daniel asked her quietly when he had brought up the last of the trunks. She stood and moved to where he stood at the top of the stairwell.

"I would like that," she admitted. "Do I need a chaperone?" They were so close, almost touching and both were speaking quietly so the women in the other room would not hear.

"That depends on you, and your intentions I suppose," he said nonchalantly. But she knew he was flirting with her, as much as she was with him.

"Well, I think I can control myself..." she teased. His lips were only inches from her own. She longed to have the courage to reach out and touch them, to taste them. But, she had barely met the man, she was tired and disoriented, and maybe she was just misconstruing all the signs.

"Maybe you should bring Ellen," he said stealing a kiss. His lips brushed softly against hers, it was the barest glimmer of a caress, yet it shot bolts of electricity through her body. It was the most thrilling and exhilarating moment of her entire existence. Her eyes opened wide as she stared into his. "You may be able to control your baser urges, but I'm not sure I can."

She was still in a trance when her friends finished their tour and joined her in the parlor. "Oh dear, I think our girl is smitten," Maggie teased.

"I think our girl may well be," she admitted. "Isn't he dreamy?" She swooned into the chair once more where she lay, barely able to speak.

"Well, that went well then," Ellen said. "Thank you Maggie, but I think I had best get this young lady into a bath and then into bed before she gets herself into the worst kind of trouble!"

Chapter Six

Daniel spent the next weeks in a daze. He looked forward to seeing Alice, and found an excuse to do so every single day. He had never been seen so often in the little town of Sun River. But, he couldn't seem to stop himself. It was as if she had some kind of magnetic pull on him, and he was helpless to resist. The memory of that single kiss had embedded itself in his mind, and he longed to take her in his arms and make her his own, for all time. But, he knew he had to give her the space she needed and so he found himself taking picnics with Ellen, meandering walks with Maggie and rowdy suppers amongst all of his friends so he could spend time with her, without running the risk of forcing himself upon her.

He had never known anyone so delightfully sweet and kind. Everyone loved her instantly. Sun River seemed to come alive with the addition of the young woman, and of course gentle Ellen who took everyone under her wing and cared for them as if the entire town was her family. But, with each passing day he knew he longed to make Alice his bride more and more. Yet he was unsure as to whether she was any closer to knowing what she wanted. Their friendship was building, and he knew he had confided in her things he had never told a soul, but there were still things he hadn't said. He knew he had to; he could not, in all good conscience, ask her to be his wife if she did not know of his past – but he did not know how to do so. Every time he was with her he forgot all about it, got so lost in the present that what had gone before seemed to no longer matter. He did not want to presume there was more to their relationship than friendship – and if he were to talk of Amelia it would make it all too real once more.

"Are you ready?" Alice's girlish voice called from outside. "Hurry, the falls will not wait for us!" He grabbed at his oilskins and made his way out onto the porch. A cart, filled with his friends was awaiting him. Mack was driving, Annie by his side; Carlton and Myra were sat on one side of the wagon in the back; and Catherine and Tom were sat on the other. Alice was perched at the end, her face lit up as he appeared.

"No Ethan and Maggie?" he asked as he clambered up to sit opposite her.

"Maggie was tired, and Ethan wouldn't come without her. Her time is drawing nigh. I think she did not wish to be so far from home. And Matthew and Emily have the new show starting tonight, but they gave us all tickets," she added breathlessly.

"Their loss," he said, smiling at her excitement. He had never known a woman from a big city to be so easily pleased. Amelia certainly hadn't been. She had wanted the world, and had often pouted when she did not get it. But, today was about Alice and his future. It did nobody any favors for him to keep thinking back on past loves.

Mack drove the cart expertly up into the mountains. "I am so thrilled we are going to see the falls," Catherine said. "I have seen so little of the region since I arrived. What with the Saloon, and my Father needing our care it has been a tough time. But, it would seem that good things come to those who are patient." She smiled at her husband conspiratorially. Daniel looked at them, non-plussed.

"She is trying to make you guess their news," Myra said with a chuckle. "So when can we expect your little one to join us?" she asked.

"Was it that obvious?" Tom asked, grinning from ear to ear.

"It was the most likely news, and I am happy for you – though I will miss your skills at the school Catherine."

"I could help out," Alice volunteered. "I am not as educated as both of you, but I am good with little ones. I can teach them the more practical skills of how to run a home, how to sew and so on. They are skills everyone should have."

"I should be most grateful, but doesn't your work at the bakery need your full attention?"

"I have time off, and it would be nice to use it in such a useful way." Myra shook her hand solemnly, as if agreeing terms.

"Then welcome to Sun River School," she said. Alice nodded just as seriously, and then everyone giggled as if someone had told the best joke.

Daniel was pleased how easily Alice and Ellen had fitted into the community, and this was yet another indicator to him that she intended to stay. He just wished he knew if she just longed to stay because of the friendship she had found, or if there was something more. If he was even a part of her decision making – but he did not know how to ask. He seemed to get so tongue-tied in the few moments they did manage to snatch alone. He had so much he longed to say, and no idea how to say any of it.

"Oh my," she gasped as the cool, damp air greeted them as they neared the first of the falls. He moved forwards and wrapped her in the oilskins he had brought. "Thank you," she said quietly as she clasped them around her tightly. "I didn't think to bring anything."

"I didn't think you would," he said tenderly as they watched everybody else do the same.

"You should wrap up too," she said, concern in her cornflower blue eyes. "It wouldn't do if you were to catch a chill."

"No it wouldn't. Poor Frank would never be able to cope without me."

"I am sure he would, but I am not sure I could," she said boldly. He was taken aback. It was the most direct flirtation they had shared since

Alice's first night in town. He gulped, unsure how to respond. "I would miss you terribly, have gotten too used to seeing you every day."

"I would miss you too, though you could always mop my brow and feed me broth?" he asked tenuously, hoping he was reading the signals correctly.

"I could, but I would need to bring Ellen. It would be most improper for a young, unmarried woman to be alone in your home with you."

"It would indeed," he admitted, then almost fell into her lap as Mack pulled the cart to a halt.

"Anyone want to take a closer look?" he yelled, turning back and grinning at his passengers, all of whom were scowling at him.

"I would like to," Alice said, and made to stand. Daniel was not going to let her go alone, it could be slippery on the rocks, and he was determined to keep her safe. He jumped down and lifted her down onto the damp grass. As he lowered her, he could feel the warmth of her lithe body and the touch of her breath on his skin. She shivered a little.

"Are you warm enough?" he asked anxiously.

"Yes, I am quite warm," she said, gazing into his eyes. Unable to stop himself, he pressed a quick kiss to her damp forehead, and took her hand.

"Come with me, there is a wonderful point to view the falls from just downriver a little."

"Should we not wait for the others?" He could hear movement in the cart behind them, but he longed to have her to himself for a few moments. He shot a look at Mack, and at Tom. Both of them simply grinned maliciously at him, and continued to prepare to follow them. Then he caught Myra's eye and sent her a silent plea. It seemed she understood him, as she put a hand to her husband's chest, and frowned at Tom.

"No, I think we'll wait here," Myra said firmly. "I'd like to just sit here and take in the view, wouldn't you Catherine?" Catherine gave him a searching look, and then patted Tom's knee.

"I think I am with Myra. I almost turned an ankle last time you brought me up here, have you not forgotten?"

Daniel thanked them silently, he would be sure to do so properly later. But, now he had Alice to himself. He led her to the rugged path that led downstream. She followed him carefully. He couldn't help but find her look of intense concentration adorable. He was sure that at one point he had even seen her tiny pink tongue poking out of the side of her rosebud mouth as she focused all her attention on the slippery slope. He reached the vantage point first, and stood marveling at the power of the falls. But, his attention was soon back on Alice, who stumbled on the last few steps and fell against him, almost tumbling them both into the frothing water. "Whoah there!" he said gently as he held her tightly.

"Thank you," she said, her eyes wide with her fear. "I didn't see that rock, and I just slipped. Thank the Good Lord you were there to stop me." She snuggled in against him, her body shaking. He held her close, stroking her hair and making soothing sounds. "I think I am well now," she said cautiously. Reluctantly Daniel released his grip, it had felt so good to have her body pressed against his own. But, she stood up on tip toe and planted a determined kiss on his lips. He was shocked, had not been expecting it, nor did he expect her to be standing in front of him, her eyes full of fire as if she was tempting him to kiss her back.

"Alice, I..." he started.

"Do you not like me?" she asked. "I have been trying to build up the courage to ask you if you did for weeks."

"I do, more than I probably should. I can barely stop thinking about you – but..." he stopped. How could he explain his reticence? Would she understand how much it had hurt when Amelia had so hurt him. He couldn't bear to lose Alice in such a way.

"But, did you not advertise for a bride Daniel Harding?"

"I did. But, I am not sure if I had thought it all through when I did that. I was just so lonely."

"I thought it was just me who had things to work through," she said gently. "I have you know."

"Truly?"

"Yes. I came here to escape my unhappy and unfulfilled life. I now have a wonderful job, working with people I love. I am part of this wonderful community, and have made some marvelous friends. There are opportunities for me to give more to my community in a way I never could in Boston. But, I now know what I was truly missing from my life."

"And that is?"

"You." Her gaze was unwavering, but he could tell it had taken an immense amount of courage for her to admit that. She was breathing rapidly, and her words had been breathless, and hurried. He wanted to crush her to him and kiss her until both of them had such labored breathing. She was offering him everything he longed for. But, now she had he knew he simply couldn't say yes. The fear that was ever present in his heart and mind reared its ugly head and he pulled away from her.

"Maybe this isn't the time, or the place to discuss this," he said awkwardly. "We should get back to the others, before they worry."

"Daniel?" Alice said trying to take his hand. He turned from her. He could see the tears forming in her eyes, and could not bear the thought he had caused her pain. But she would thank him for it. He was not good enough for her. Had never been good enough for anyone, and was certainly not good enough for Alice. She was so kind, so sweet, so gentle. She deserved nothing but the very best – and he was not able to give her that. "Daniel please, don't be this way. I am sorry. I am so sorry. I did not mean to be so bold, did not intend to make you unhappy with me. But I truly thought you felt the same way for me as I do you. You brought me here, because you wanted a wife. I am trying to tell you that I want that more than anything in the world."

"I know. Please, do not speak of it again Alice. I cannot. I am so sorry. I truly thought that I could – but it just cannot be. Please know it is not your fault. I am sorry."

Epilogue

Alice took out her unhappiness on the bread dough each day, but it still seemed that there was more inside her. She hadn't seen Daniel since that terrible day at the Falls. Thankfully the sharp-eyed Myra had seen her pale face and unhappy eyes, and had suggested they head home rather than continue their day out. She couldn't have found the strength to pretend to be happy, as if nothing had happened. She had been so sure that Daniel cared for her as much as she had learned to love him. Now, she wished she had never laid eyes upon him.

The little bell above the door in the store rang, telling her there was a customer. Reluctantly she wiped her hands and made her way behind the counter. An elegantly dressed young woman stood gazing around her, a young boy at her side. He couldn't have been more than four. He had the curliest soft black hair, and bright hazel eyes. It was a startling combination. He reminded her of someone, but she couldn't place it for the moment, though such an unusual countenance should have been obvious. "I am looking for Daniel Havering," the woman said briskly. She wasn't rude, not exactly, but Alice was sure that she was used to getting her own way. But, the mention of Daniel's name set her on edge. Whatever could this woman want with him?

"He owns the farm just south of the town. Just keep heading along the Main Street and then turn left at the crossroads." The woman swept out, her little boy though stayed, his nose pressed up against the glass. His gaze was fixed on the funny little gingerbread men that she had made for the local children. "Would you like one?" she asked him. He nodded, his beautiful eyes clearly overwhelmed by her kindness. It made her wonder if he had ever seen much gentleness in his young life. He may be well dressed, but he was clearly far from happy. She handed him the gingerbread. His mother returned, her face tense with anger, but her voice was cool.

"Put that down. How could you be so naughty?" she scolded him. The little boys face fell and his entire posture slumped as he accepted the inevitable.

"I offered him the gingerbread. He is welcome to it," Alice said firmly.

"I shall thank you to stay out of our business," the woman retorted. "Come Louis, we have much to do."

"Take the gingerbread," Alice said pressing it back into the boy's hands. "I have just remembered I have to deliver some bread to Mr Havering's farm. I can offer you a lift in my gig if you would like?" She wasn't sure what this woman wanted, but she was sure it couldn't be good news for Daniel. He may not wish to see her, may not wish her to be a part of his life any longer, but that would not stop her from caring about his weal. She grabbed loaves from the shelves and one of Ellen's pies and piled them into a basket. "Shall we?"

"That would be most kind," the woman said through gritted teeth. "But I cannot trouble you."

"Ellen, I just have to pop out," Alice called out to the kitchens. "It is no trouble. I am glad to help. We can't have you wandering around out there with no clue as to where you are going – and it is a long walk for such little legs," she added smiling at Louis. Ellen appeared with flour all over her cheeks. Ellen looked their visitor up and down, Alice could see that she was sizing her up and that the fashionable clothing hadn't hidden a thing from her wise eyes. "I shan't be long."

"Take all the time you want. I have everything under control here."

Alice directed the pair to the little gig outside the bakery. "My name is Alice," she said.

"Amelia Sedgely, Louis," the woman replied curtly. Alice almost sniggered. It was clear that this woman believed a mere shop girl to be below her. She drove the gig skillfully out towards Daniel's farm. It was one of the skills she had once possessed, back on her family's farm that had thankfully come back to her quickly upon becoming reacquainted. She enjoyed driving along the roads and trackways, she found that the majestic scenery did much to help her heal her hurt.

But, she felt her heart skip a beat as they approached Daniel's farm. She had avoided it, had not wanted to face the pain of seeing him and not being able to hold him, or be with him. But, she had the oddest feeling that his reason for pushing her from his life was sat beside her now. She had worked out as they drove who it was Louis reminded her of, and it was his eyes. His eyes were Daniel's eyes. But how had someone so gentle and kind, so humble ever been involved with a woman such as this? Amelia Sedgely was ice cold, there was no give in her. She did not seem to be the kind of woman that Daniel would have ever sought out.

Daniel was chopping logs in the yard. Alice almost sighed as she saw his muscles bunch and ripple with each swing. He truly was beautiful, and she wished that things had been different between them. He turned as he heard the approach of the gig. His face lit up, and then fell just as quickly. "Alice?" he asked as she drew up beside him.

"This young woman came into the bakery asking where to find you. I offered to drive her and her son out here, as I had to deliver these," she handed him the basket. "But, I should get back and help Ellen." Amelia was sat primly, clearly waiting for Daniel to help her down. Louis was bouncing up and down.

"Mama, may I go and see the horses in the field," he asked excitedly.

"Louis, do be quiet," Amelia said firmly.

"Why don't I take Louis to meet the horses," Alice offered. "Then the pair of you can talk in private." Daniel nodded, though he looked reluctant to be left with the striking beauty.

Alice lifted Louis from the gig, and set him down. She took his hand and led him towards the field where Daniel kept his horses. She didn't want to intrude, expected Daniel to take Amelia inside to discuss their business, but when she turned the two were still exactly where they had left them. Finally Daniel spoke, and his voice was loud. It was almost as if he wanted her to hear every word.

"Why have you come here Amelia? You made it perfectly clear that the life of a farmer's wife was beneath you when I last saw you."

"Can a woman not have changed?" Amelia simpered. Alice snorted. She prayed Daniel was not such a fool as to fall for such a blatant act. Louis tugged on her hand.

"What is his name?" he asked her of the bay mare who was nuzzling at his pockets hoping for a treat.

"Her name is Blaze, because of the white stripe down her lovely nose."

"She is very pretty. Might I ride her?"

"Why not?" Alice was sure that Amelia would disapprove, but right now she was feeling reckless. She lifted the lad up onto the cart horses broad back. His legs barely stretched down her sides, but he looked so happy. Again, she found herself wondering how much happiness or love the boy had seen.

"But the child isn't mine," Daniel exploded behind them. "Why should I be the one to take care of my brother's mistakes? Or yours." So that explained why Louis had Daniel's eyes. Relief flooded through her, the man she loved hadn't been so foolish as to father a child out of wedlock with this minx.

"I have the chance to marry. He does not know about Louis, and nor do I want him to. I cannot care for him. You wanted him before, why not now?"

"Because he is not mine. I wanted him when you had me so ensnared as to believe he was mine. When I thought I loved you so much that I wished you to be my wife." Alice gasped. So he had been involved with her, had even asked her to marry him. But she had duped him. No wonder he was so loathe to give away his heart again. Her heart went out to him. She wished she could think of a way to make this better, to let him see that she didn't think he had been a fool, that she loved him no matter what. But then, she had an idea.

She lifted Louis down from Blaze's back, and took his hand. She made her way across the yard, and put her free arm around Daniel's back. She gazed up at him lovingly. "I am sorry, I couldn't help but overhear the more explosive parts of your conversation. I understand that you wish to leave your son here, with his Uncle?" Amelia nodded, a look of incredulity over her patrician features.

"Indeed."

"You wish to leave your son, flesh of your flesh, so you can marry a man who would think less of you if he knew you had a child?"

"Yes." Amelia's voice was curt. "Are you going to let this chit speak to me in such a way?" she asked Daniel.

"You know what, I think I am," he said smiling down at Alice. He kissed the top of her head, and she felt her knees almost give way. But she had to stay strong for him, for Louis.

"Louis is welcome here if he would wish to stay with us," Alice said smiling down at the boy. He grinned at her.

"Can I ride every day?"

"Yes you can."

"Do you have his things?" Daniel asked Amelia. She nodded and indicated a small case beside her in the gig. "If I take him, you never come here again. I never hear from you in any way – and neither does he. If you are so heartless as to give him up for your own pleasure, then he deserves to have a family that will truly love him. You will never be able to provide him with that, as you have only ever loved yourself." Alice was so proud of Daniel. He looked so determined, and his words echoed the way she felt inside.

Amelia nodded. In fact she looked relieved. She did not even say goodbye to her son when Daniel drove her back to town where he left her to find her way back to Great Falls. He rushed back to where Alice and his nephew were settled in by the fire playing a game of cup and ball. Louis was quite adept, but often missed the catch to make him feel even better at the game. "She is gone," he said softly. Alice stood and moved to his side.

"Why did you not tell me?"

"I wanted to, but did not know how to. I believed myself to be in love with her for such a long time. She said she loved me, wished to be with me. When I look back now I should have known. She almost insisted upon our being together, even before I had put a ring upon her finger. My brother was married, but it didn't stop him from taking whatever he wanted. I could have maybe felt sorry for her if she had been anyone else. But, you saw her. She is selfish and self-centered. She intended to keep the wool over my eyes and continue her affair with my brother."

Alice reached up and kissed him tenderly. "So, young Louis is going to need a Mama. Now, I have no other ulterior motive but to love you and him for the rest of your lives. Will you marry me Daniel?" He looked down into her hopeful face, and her heart sang. She knew the answer even before he spoke.

"You are too good for me, but I love you desperately. If you can forgive me my foolishness, I will love you until the end of time." He kissed her deeply.

"But is that a yes?" Louis piped up from the fireplace. Alice and Daniel broke apart, and the little family laughed together.

"Yes, that is most definitely a yes," Daniel said emphatically as he moved to the boy's side, and swept him up into his strong arms. "Would you be happy being our son?" Louis nodded and flung his arms around Daniel's neck.

"Then everyone is happy, and all is well." Alice ruffled Louis's soft curls and ducked her head into Daniel's chest. Somehow everything felt perfect, and she knew that they would be happy together and would make a good life for their little family together.

The End

* * * * * * *

A Bride for William Book 7

Chapter One

The gavel fell. It was finally over. Maddy sighed with relief as she left the courthouse for the final time. Everything that happened to her since January seemed unreal. The months had dragged by, every day bringing a new pain, a new humiliation as she had been forced to sit and watch as others decided her fate. But it had been decided, and she was exonerated. Yet as she listed to the catcalls of the apprentice boys, and saw the way her old friends continued to cross the street, or disappear into stores so they did not have to suffer the indignity of conversing with her, she knew that nothing would change. It was too little, too late.

She clambered into the carriage that awaited her, and accepted Papa's kiss on her cheek. "Are you quite well?" he asked, concern in his eyes. "You look so pale. Maybe we could send you to the Spa at Bristol Springs? Or why not at Saratoga? Your Mama says it is just the place."

"Papa, I am quite well, just tired and glad that it is all done. The last place I wish to be is trapped in a Spa with the women who have been gossiping behind my back about all this."

"You have been ever so brave my darling. We shall punish every newspaper and admonish anyone who has sullied your good name."

"Papa, no. I would rather just let it all die down, so I can move on with my life."

"If you insist," he said pompously. Madelaine knew that tone. It meant he would placate her now, but would ignore her wishes completely. But, if it made him feel better to extract revenge on her behalf, then she could do little to stop him. But, she could do something to ease her own burden. It would be the hardest thing she had ever done, harder even than fighting to clear her name had been. But she was determined. She would never again be responsible for hurting her family so badly.

The carriage pulled up, and she ran inside. She could hear Mama weeping in the drawing room, her heavily pregnant sister comforting her. She would let her Papa inform them of the good news. Maddy had grown weary of her mother's fits of the vapors, the constant tears – as if everything was happening to her, and not Madelaine. She had no doubt that Papa would be successful in packing Mama off to the Spa for a month or two. She was never happier than when she had teams of doctors fussing over her. As she raced up the grand staircase, she wondered if she sounded somehow ungrateful to her parents. She did love them both very much, but they could be so very exasperating at times. She envied her sister having escaped their clutches, but she would do the same – even if her method was a little more unorthodox.

A trunk sat at the end of her bed. She emptied it of the piles of bed linens it contained, and began to thrust dresses and skirts, books and papers into it, not caring about being neat and tidy. She just wanted to get away from Boston as quickly as she possibly could. She was tired, and it had been the worst time of her life. The sooner she could put it all behind her the better. "Papa told us you…" her sister cried as she burst into the room, "won."

"Yes," Maddy said turning to face her. She had kept her plans secret, and was not ready for the confrontation about to come.

"You can't just run away, without anywhere to go?" Carolynn said angrily, as she took in the evidence of Maddy's intended flight. "I know you want to hide, to lick your wounds and start again, but where can you go?"

"I don't know," Madelaine said sadly, sinking onto the bed. It felt as if she had deflated, as if all of the fight in her had been used up in the past months and there was nothing left to even keep her breathing. She had endured enough, and the idea of having to face Society as if none of it had happened was simply too much for her. "But Boston will not forget this. Oh, they may pretend that nothing happened, because of who you are, who you are married to, who Father is even. But they will not ever let me be, in their own way."

"I do understand Maddy, but please don't do anything rash. The girls would miss you terribly, and my time with this one is nigh," she stroked her heavily pregnant belly and looked at her sister with hopeful eyes. Madelaine loved her, but was not prepared to allow anyone to emotionally blackmail her into staying. The simple truth was that if she stayed all she would ever have would be her nieces. There would be no dynastic marriage for her now, nor even one with a young man of even moderate means. She would be infamous.

"I love you Caro, but I will not stay – not even for that. I cannot. And I will not bring our family into even further disrepute by doing so. You have all had to bear such scrutiny, such unpleasantness, because of me."

"Not because of you," Caro exploded. "The charges were dropped. The proof is there that this was some kind of spurious attempt to discredit our family somehow. They chose you, because you... oh I don't know why they chose you."

"Because they could. They cannot touch any of the rest of you. But, I am different. I stand out. My work with the slum children hasn't exactly endeared me to the great and good of the city."

"I just don't want you to leave us. We love you, and we need you."

"I know. But this will not be their first and only attack at us. If I go, I take away their easiest target. Things will settle down for you all. They would not dare come against any of you. And I want a family and a husband one day. I want a quiet life, where what I do is not front page news and a man who is honest and good."

"There is no such thing," Caro joked weakly.

"There is, just not in our world. I'm not afraid. I shall write often, and you are more than wealthy enough to visit me whenever you wish once I am settled."

"So you do have somewhere to go?"

"Not yet, but I will. I replied to this," she tossed a small pile of newspaper cuttings towards her sister. An advertisement was circled in red on each.

A Gentleman of Montana seeks a good woman to correspond with, for the purpose of matrimony. A gentle disposition, good education and a loving heart are all the subscriber desires. He in turn will offer security, a good home and a bright future. All Replies to Box 38, The Matrimonial Times

"He does not give much away does he," Caro said wryly as she read the first one.

"No, but neither of us ever expected hearts and flowers. We both knew we would make marriages of expedience. I am just taking matters into my own hands, rather than waiting for Papa to find some horribly ambitious fool, who might be prepared to take me. As you can see, his was not the only advertisement I responded to, but it was as good an example as any."

"Oh Maddy, any man would be blessed to have you as his wife."

"I know, but my character and my abilities will never again be a part of the reasons why any man here would ever consider wedding me. I have to make my own luck now."

Carolynn looked so sad. Madelaine wanted to reassure her that everything would be fine, but everything had changed for her now and she had to face that. Her sister's happiness had been secondary to the benefits both Papa and her husband, Blake, had gained from the union. She had brought him an old family name, and immediate entry into the highest echelons of East Coast Society. He had brought money, and a mercantile enterprise that had gone from strength to strength because of the merging of the two families. But, Caro had been blessed in that she had fallen madly in love with her betrothed, and he with her. They were an indomitable force, and their futures looked bright, as long as no further scandals were linked to them. It did not take much for Boston's elite to turn on you, and older and wealthier families than their own had been ruined before and would be again. But, it would not be over her, not if she could help it.

The scandals that had been linked to her name in recent months had threatened to ruin everything, Maddy was wise enough to know that. The flurry of gentleman callers had stopped almost overnight, the possible match between herself and one of the wealthiest bankers in Boston had vanished as if he had not been courting her assiduously for months. But she did not mind any of that. She did not want some preening peacock, who believed what he read in the newspapers and did not have the courage to ask her what was true. But she did not wish to become a lingering embarrassment to her family either. It would be best for everyone if she were to vanish quietly, never to return and so she had made her preparations, ready for when she found the right man.

"But, if you are still waiting to hear from them, however many of them you wrote to, why must you leave now?"

"Because if I don't I will burst!" Maddy exclaimed. "I have been kept, pent up inside this house for months. My only contact with the outside world has been within a courtroom. I am sick of the sight of everything within these walls. I am sick of the jibes, the snide comments everywhere I go. Even walking from the door to our carriage I have heard the whispers, and even worse at times. One lad called out the most obscene things to me. I am tired of being brave. I cannot pin a smile to my face any longer. I just wish to be somewhere, anywhere, where nobody knows me, or my family, our history. I need to get away before I go mad Caro, can you not even try to understand that?" Her sister sat quietly for a moment, then pulled her in close.

"I do understand. I am sorry, I am being selfish. I had not considered the torment you have been through, or that will continue to be flung at you even though it has been proven to be untrue. I just cannot bear the thought of you being far from me."

"I know. But I shall write, every day if you wish me to. I shall want to know all your news. I love you Caro and I will miss you."

"But you have to go and find a new life, one you can live freely and fully." They clasped each other tightly, tears pouring down both their cheeks.

Once Carolynn had left her, Maddy collapsed onto the bed, sobbing into her pillows. She did not want to leave her family, she loved them all so very much even when they were being infuriating, but the pain she felt every day, the shame and fear she felt when even walking outside of their elegant townhouse was enough to propel her forwards. This was not the way she wished to live her life. She wanted to be back with the children, teaching them their letters and helping them to learn the skills that would help them to escape their poverty and misery. She longed to be assisting gentle Doctor Hailey as he administered to the sick, but she could not do any of that any more.

She gazed down at the pile of advertisements. She had been responding to them for so long. She was beginning to give up hope that anyone would ever write back. Maybe the scandal had made its way out of Boston, and now no man anywhere would consider her? But, as she re-read the words of the Gentleman of Montana she allowed herself to dream. She had only written to him a few weeks ago. He should have received her letter by now. She would have to wait a little while to hear from him, but she still held onto hope that this time she would find the man she needed to save her from her misery.

She pictured him as a rugged type, most at home on the land. His Stetson perched forward to shield his eyes from the sun, a well-bred stallion between his strong thighs. Out on the land from sun up to sun down, he was tanned and lean. But, she also pictured him sat by the fire, reading a book or showing his children how to form their letters. Their home was not luxurious, certainly nothing like the home she had lived in her entire life, but it had everything they needed, and was cozy and warm. She had added a few touches to make it more homely, and they were well liked by everyone nearby. She taught Sunday School and helped the local doctor with his rounds when their two boys were in school.

It was a lovely picture, but it was becoming more and more faded as time went on. Each man who did not respond to her correspondence broke her heart just a little more, making her wonder what her options might be if she could not secure herself a husband. She could always become a governess, but nobody on the East Coast would hire her to care for their children, and she wasn't sure if she had the courage to head West alone.

Chapter Two

His office was full. William Butler wasn't sure if he should be happy about it or not. That the people of Sun River had grown to trust him and sought him out to tend to their needs was a good thing, but that there were so many people in need of his medical expertise was not. He called in his first patient of the day, and settled in to the routine of stomach aches, ear and throat infections and other minor ailments that plagued the townsfolk. He teased the children gently, coaxed their Mama's into agreeing to give them more regular baths, and tried to find ways to make vegetables more appealing. But, every day they fought him. He smiled as he thought of the multitude of disgusted faces he was privy to when he dispensed his wisdom, but he persevered.

So much of the illness he saw could be prevented with such simple measures, he was convinced of it. He spent much of his free time poring over the new studies that were being published about hygiene and the differences in health outcomes between the rich and poor. He was convinced that the biggest difference between rich and poor was in the food they ate. Rich people ate a broader range of foods, and considerably more fruits and vegetables and they most definitely suffered from less petty health concerns. He wondered if there was a way to prove his theories, but as a small town doctor he did not have the resources to do such a thing. He was sure though that there were ways in which he could encourage people to take care of themselves better, and he hoped that there were people within the community now that he could convince to assist him. He knew that both Catherine and Myra would be glad to help with the children, but their parents would be harder to convince.

"Doctor Butler?" He looked up. Tom stood in his doorway, waiting politely to be invited in.

"Come in, what ails you my friend?" he asked.

"Nothing Will. I brought your post – and wondered if you would care to join us for supper tonight?"

"Thank you, that is kind of you – on both counts!" Will grinned.

"Catherine would like to discuss your ideas for teaching the children how to grow things more, and I am glad to be of assistance." The two men smiled at one another. Will had been at Tom's side as he tried to banish his troubles with alcohol. They had built a close friendship, and their combined experiences in that field had helped when Catherine's Father had come to stay in order to give up his own demons. They had waved the old man off on the train, back to Boston, just a few days ago and were hopeful that he had the strength to resist now, even when back in his old life.

"How is she, now that Nathaniel has gone home?"

"Concerned I think. She has been throwing herself into every project that comes her way. Until she has regular reports that he truly is doing well, I think she will find it hard not to be."

"I have referred him to an old friend of mine. He is an excellent physician, and a good man. I am sure Nathaniel will find him good to confide in."

"Thank you for that, I know she appreciates it."

"So, what time should I come?"

"Around seven?"

"And who is in charge of the Saloon?"

"Ethan. He is a good man, and a good bar tender. I look forward to seeing you tonight, Doctor," he said as he dropped the letters on the desk and made his way out.

"Indeed," Will said, staring at the pile of envelopes. Three bore the return address of the Matrimonial Times, and he sighed. He had hoped there might be more. So many of his friends in Sun River had made successful matches by placing advertisements in the press and he longed to emulate their happiness. He wasn't sure how many responses any of them had gotten, but the women they had chosen all seemed to have been perfectly suited to them. He had pondered long and hard before he had chosen to follow their lead, but he still had doubts that it would be possible to find the perfect woman in such a calculated manner. But, he did not have time to open them now. He had a waiting room full of people, and so his own future would just have to wait a little longer.

Finally his day was done, and he made his way upstairs to his tiny apartment. He lit a fire, and washed himself carefully. After putting on a clean shirt, he sank into his chair and opened the first of the letters.

Dear Gentleman of Montana,

> *Firstly, I would like to say that I hope that this letter finds you well. There has been the most horrible outbreak of diphtheria in the tenements and slums here in Boston. I work there when I can, and so every time there is some kind of issue there I worry about everyone I know, and even those I do not.*

> *I would very much like to hear about the bright future you plan for yourself, and your bride-to-be. It must be wonderful to hold your destiny in your own hands, knowing you have a good home and the security upon which you may build. I would very much like to hear about your work, and about you. I picture you as a rugged mountain man, though I am sure that the truth is probably much less romantic! I do so hope you won't mind my imaginative tendencies.*

> *I was not entirely sure what kind of a woman you were*

praying might respond to you, but hope that I will suit. I am lucky enough to have a fine education. My Father is quite wealthy, and therefore I had the finest governesses, and tutors his money could buy. As all young ladies are, I am also able to draw and paint, play the pianoforte and to sing. I find these pursuits can be most soothing, especially when my work has been hard. But, I would gladly give them up, if required. I appreciate that not everyone can afford the time for hobbies.

I do not highlight my abilities and extreme good fortune in order to crow, or boast. I wish to leave my privileged life behind me forever, should I be lucky enough that you choose me to correspond with, and hopefully in the fullness of time to become your wife. I mention it, because it was one of your few stipulations, that respondents be educated. I am.

I have also been told that I am good hearted. As I mentioned above, I often work in the tenements and slums. I teach the children their letters, and assist a friend of mine who is a doctor to bring them medicines and knowledge on how to care for each other best when sick. My love of such work is frowned upon by many in Society, but I do it because it is so wonderful to see these people's lives change. It is not fair that some have so much, when others have so little, do you not think?

I am never happier than when I am there. I find such joy amongst people who should in all honesty be miserable. Their lives have so little color, or pleasure and yet they find much to celebrate. They love so passionately and fiercely, and truly seem to grasp life in a way those in my own circle do not. I see too much privilege, and it has made people complacent. They believe they deserve such luxury, simply because of their birth. My sister married a merchant, and for some time the match was deemed to be beneath dear Carolynn – but Blake has continued to prove himself, making more and more money and of course that has endeared him to all.

Yet everything feels like a prison. We must act a certain

way, dress a certain way, follow a calendar of events that never changes. Worst of all is the belief that we must only marry amongst our own. However, I do not wish to make a dynastic marriage. I have no desire at all for such a marriage. I truly wish to wed for love, to have a family and to be my own person. I wish to take my destiny into my own hands, and so I am writing to you. I do hope that I will be considered. I am sure that you will have many responses to peruse, and I understand that I may be waiting some time for a reply – but I pray you will look upon me kindly.

    Yours With Utmost Hope

    Madelaine Crane

Will pondered the heartfelt words. He was unsure. She sounded quite genuine, but he couldn't help but wonder whether a woman of her background could possibly be ready for such a different life. True, he was no rugged mountain man, as she dreamed, nor a rancher or even a farmer. But life as a small town doctor here in Montana was tough. Life for women here in Sun River was not easy. There were risks that even the most prepared of women would struggle to cope with. He put the letter down reluctantly. He couldn't deny there was something about the way she wrote that was truly alluring, a combination of hope and realism that he had not expected.

The other two letters left him feeling more than a little disgusted. Both seemed determined to insist upon their needs, their wants and did not care one jot for his. Neither was suitable, and the way they wrote had been harsh and unfeeling. Their education had taught them the basics, but not any refinement. Yet, Madelaine seemed to be too refined. He did not know what to do. Maybe he should just continue to wait. Hopefully there would be someone more suitable in the next post.

The clock chimed, and he realized he was running late. He grabbed his hat and coat, and for some unknown reason picked up her letter and stuffed it into his pocket as he rushed down to the public stables, where he kept his stallion, Harper. He saddled him up swiftly and galloped out to the lovely home that Tom and Catherine had made for themselves just outside of town. "I am sorry I am late," he said sheepishly as Catherine gave him a peck on the cheek in welcome.

"That is not a problem in this house," she chuckled. "I don't think Tom has ever been on time for anything in his life."

"Unfair my love," Tom said as he came through from the kitchen and shook Will's hand warmly. "I was on time for our wedding. You were the one who was late for that!"

"That is a bride's prerogative," Will said. They all laughed.

"I am so glad you could come. Tom let slip you had some letters from a certain newspaper," Catherine probed gently. Tom looked at her as if he could murder her on the spot. "Oh don't be a ninny, nothing stays secret in Sun River for long."

"So it would seem. I am not ashamed. It would be foolish to be so when so many men in town have found wives that way."

"That is true," Tom admitted. "So, did anyone make your heart pound?"

"It is only a first letter," Will said.

"I knew from the first," Catherine said dreamily.

"Me too," Tom admitted. "There was just something about the way Catherine wrote that just let me know it was her.

Will thought for a moment, unsure if he should tell them of Madelaine. He still wasn't sure about her himself, but like Tom had found, there was definitely something about the way she wrote that made her intriguing. "Will you read this for me?" he finally asked them as he pulled out her letter from his pocket. Catherine nodded, her face serious.

"Are you truly sure? This is something only you can decide."

"I know, and yes I am. There are just a few things, I just want to know if you see them too."

Catherine took the paper and began to read. Tom perched on the chair beside her, reading over her shoulder. The room was quiet, but not silent. Will could hear the gentle ticking of the clock, and even the in and out of their breath.

"You are worried about her coming from a wealthy background?"

Catherine asked perceptively. "You like her, but fear she will not be able to fathom the dangers and difficulties here?" He nodded. There was little point in denying it. Tom simply laughed. Will looked at him, shocked.

"What?" he asked.

"You do know that Catherine was a Parker, do you not? I mean, you do know that Nathaniel was once one of the wealthiest men in America?"

"No I did not," Will admitted. "I never asked for his surname. He was introduced to me as Nathaniel, and I don't know why but I never asked for more than that!"

"So, do you think that I am unable to cope out here alone, should anything ever happen to Tom?" Catherine asked him.

"I would never be so foolish. You are more than a match for him."

"Then I think that if you like everything else you should find out more. She is already less sheltered than I was, has spent time working in the slums. She understands hardship."

"Did you know her?"

"No, the Crane's moved in circles way above ours. We probably would have known them once. I could ask Papa if he does – men seem to be much less rigid about these things. But, we weren't moving in the more elevated echelons of society after Mama died. First we were in mourning, and then Papa had begun to drink and gamble and we slipped slowly downwards. Standards had to be maintained, but the Cranes moved to Boston from New York once we were out of favor."

Will tucked the letter back in his breast pocket, close to his heart. He had much to think on, but Catherine was probably right. Women were so much stronger than men ever gave them credit for. He would not hesitate to place his trust and faith in any of the women he knew here in Sun River. That Catherine had enjoyed a similar upbringing, protected and sheltered, and yet was the indomitable force that he knew definitely made him reconsider his earlier thoughts. Then he thought of Maggie, Alice and Ellen, all women who had worked, but had lived in Boston their whole lives; Myra and Annie who had been in service; and even Emily who had travelled the country in the circus as a child, and settled in Boston. The city seemed to have influenced them all, and all were women he admired and would be honored to call his wife.

Chapter Three

Maddy made her way to the postal office every day. She had not wanted her family to know her business, and now with Caro constantly filling her with horror stories of what could go wrong she wished she had maintained her silence. But, every day there was no reply and she felt just a little bit more desperate. She simply couldn't stay here in Boston any longer. She would buy herself a train ticket, to the first place she could, if there was no word from him. She would build a life alone if she had to.

"Miss Crane, good morning," the postmaster said brightly. "I believe there is a letter for you this day."

"That is wonderful news," she said as she signed for it. The handwriting on the envelope was scruffy, each line drifted downwards and the letters hard to make out. But strangely it did not put her off. In fact it made her smile, that her Gentleman had been in such a rush to respond, that he hadn't worried about something so irrelevant as ensuring his script was immaculate.

She strolled across the street and entered the park. She could see the usual people, wandering hand in hand, a few gentlemen on horseback, ladies in carriages – all hoping to see and be seen. She snuck away from the paths, and into the carefully manicured woodland. It was peaceful and quiet in here. Nobody would disturb her, and she found an old tree stump to sit on and settled down to try and decipher his words.

"Dear Miss Crane

I cannot tell you what pleasure I felt as I read your letter. Something in it spoke to me, and I was quite unable to dismiss you from my thoughts.

I am sorry to upset your fantasy, but I am not a rancher or a farmer. I am a small town doctor, and though I believe my opinion is respected, I do not fit the romantic ideal I know modern novels portray! I have a thriving practice, and I hope one day to build a hospital here, that will serve the entire local region.

As you can imagine, knowledge that you already assist a doctor in his rounds, and often in such trying circumstances, filled my heart with happiness. A doctor's wife is as important as any medicine I believe. Their commitment to their husband is almost secondary to their ability to put others ahead of themselves. This is why I required someone with a loving heart. My work often has me out late, and up early. My wife will need to understand this, to not be jealous of the time I am forced to spend away from her. So your having pastimes that you enjoy is a blessing, I will at least know that you can entertain yourself when I am busy!

I do not know what else to say, I feel oddly tongue-tied as I write this. What do you ask of a woman who so freely offered up such knowledge of herself? I cannot imagine there is anything much more to say and so, as I am finding this so difficult I think it best we meet, and soon. I am much better at talking in person, and am sure we would find out quickly enough if we will suit. So, I have enclosed a train ticket to Chicago. I have arranged accommodation there, in separate hotels, for us both. I will book tickets to the theatre, and maybe we could go somewhere for supper? I am happy to arrange a chaperone should you require one. Please write to me quickly to let me know you are coming?

    Yours in abject hope

    Dr William Butler

Maddy almost jumped for joy. She would be able to escape Boston, and so soon. The ticket was for Friday! She had barely any time to let him know that she was on her way. She tucked the letter away in her reticule carefully and then hurried back to the postal office. "Do you have paper and an envelope?" she asked the Postmaster. He smiled at her indulgently.

"Your sweetheart?" he enquired. "No, don't tell me. Here, take these." He handed her paper, an envelope and pen and ink. "If you hurry I can send it on its way today."

She didn't think about what she should write, she just scribbled five little words, shoved the paper into the envelope, addressed it hurriedly and then handed it and the pennies required to send it to the kindly Postmaster. "Thank you," she said as she tried to control her breathing. Her chest was heaving, and she felt quite overwrought. "I think I need some air."

Once outside she tried to control herself. This did not mean that he wished to marry her. It was only a meeting, but that he had given her the means to leave Boston, and that it was so soon, meant more to her than she had ever realized it would. Her trunk had been packed now for weeks, she simply needed the encouragement his short letter had offered. She did not care one jot if she did not love him on sight. She only cared that he know that she was everything he had ever wanted when they met. She had to make him marry her and take her home to Sun River. She had never been the most accomplished of flirts, and so she knew she needed help.

Rather than heading home, as she usually did to avoid public scrutiny, she made her way to her sister's imposing mansion. Helden, their butler, opened the door when she knocked. "Miss, what a surprise! Mrs Cavendish was not expecting visitors today I do not think."

"No, she wasn't, and especially not me Helden. But I am sure she won't mind if you show me in, whatever condition she may be in. I am her sister after all." He smiled awkwardly.

"Indeed," he agreed. "She is in her chamber I believe."

"At this time of day?" Maddy looked up at the grand clock above the stairs, it was showing midday. Carolynn was an early riser, was never in bed past nine. It was a standing joke that her servants hated her for it, as it meant they never got a moments peace.

"The last few days she has been feeling a little weary I believe, Miss Madelaine."

"Well, she does not have long before her confinement I suppose. I should think she is entitled to feel a little weary. I shall show myself up."

She ran up the stairs, not caring if anybody thought her a hoyden. Boston's opinion mattered not a jot any more. She would only be here for just a few more days after all. "Caro, darling Caro, he answered!" she cried as she rushed into her sister's rooms. Caro was propped up in bed, cushions all around her. She looked pale, but her face lit up with pleasure as Maddy threw herself into her arms.

"Who wrote? Which one?" she teased.

"The Gentleman of Montana," Maddy cried, over the moon. "He is a doctor, and wishes to meet me. He has sent me a ticket to Chicago, to see if we suit." Caro's face fell just a little. Most people would never have spotted it, but Maddy knew her sister too well.

"When do you leave?"

"Friday." They sat in silence, just holding each other's hands.

"Oh Maddy, I am pleased for you – I am," Caro said eventually. "But, I shall miss you terribly."

"I know, and I am so very sorry that I shall not be here to see this one into the world," she caressed her sister's protruding belly. "Are you sure you are quite well? You are never so late abed."

"The doctors are a little concerned, that is all. I am to spend every day in bed until the little one arrives."

"I shall stay if you ask me," Maddy said, feeling terribly guilty. Her sister needed her and she was thinking only of her own needs.

"I shall never ask that of you. I know how hard it is for you, I agree that it is unlikely things will ever change. You have to go. I have to know that you have found your place, your happiness once more."

"Thank you. I shall stay here, help with Mina and Hattie until I leave if you would like?"

"I would like that. I know they are running poor Helden ragged with their tearing around the house like demons!" Maddie patted her sister on the hand.

"I shall go and teach them how it is done properly then," she joked.

"I am sure you will," Caro grinned. "But, if you could at least teach them to do it quietly for the next few days it would be much appreciated."

"Your wish is my command."

Maddy left her sister to rest and made her way to the nursery. Her nieces were terrible tearaways, but she adored them. They both reminded her of herself, though they had Caro's beauty. "Aunt Maddy!" they cried as they rushed to hug her. "Where have you been? It has been forever since we saw you last!"

"I know, and I am sorry for that. I have been like poor old Catpuss over there, curled up by the fire, licking my wounds."

"Catpuss was in a fight, were you in a fight?" they asked curiously.

"Of a sort – but not quite like Catpuss. Mine did not involve scratches and bites, at least not physically."

"But you won didn't you? Catpuss always wins," they said proudly. "He is feared by all the other cats."

"As he should be," Maddy said. "I did win," she said. It was true enough, though it didn't feel that way most of the time. "Now, I shall be staying with you for a couple of days, to help your Mama out."

"How wonderful," Hattie said. "Will you play with us?"

"I will." Maddy was determined to spend as much time as she could with her beloved nieces. She wanted to embed herself in their little memories, so they never forgot her – as she knew she would never forget them. She would miss them terribly, but life was not contained within the walls of this well-appointed nursery, and she could not continue to live only half a life hiding from the world. She had to do this, for herself.

She picked up a story book and began to read to the two girls, who curled up beside her. She looked down into their rapt faces, and wondered what it might be like if she had her own children to read with and play with. She had rarely been envious of Carolynn, but as she thought of the happiness her sister had found with Blake, and that she was mother to these two bright and beautiful girls she couldn't help but feel she was missing out on so much that should be hers. She had never intended to be unmarried, yet for some reason Papa had not once approved of any of the young men who had come calling for her, and she hadn't been much impressed by them either.

As the little girls began to nod off she wondered if she would ever find love. She was more than happy to settle for companionship and was sure that she would find it with Doctor William Butler. They appeared to have much in common, a desire to help others less fortunate than themselves for one. She stroked Hattie's hair and carefully moved Mina's head from her lap and stood up. Whatever it took, she would make this gentleman like her. She was not prepared to wait any longer to have a home and a family, and she couldn't wait to be away from the gossips and the cruelty of the people she had once called her friends. But, more importantly she looked forward to being a doctor's wife. She was sure that together she and William could make a difference to many people's lives, and that together they could build that hospital, and ensure that everyone received the care they needed.

Chapter Four

I am on my way!

William looked at the short note again, and grinned, inanely. He couldn't describe the pleasure he felt at the five simple words written in her exquisite script. He tucked it back into his pocket, and looked out of the train carriage window. He loved watching how the terrain changed as he crossed the country, though even as he had barely left them behind he found himself missing the snow-capped mountain peaks of his adopted home. He had not been to Chicago for many years, but he hoped that the city would not have changed too much. He was sure that it would be bigger and busier as most towns and cities seemed to be these days, but he prayed that it would still be welcoming and friendly. He wanted to be able to show Miss Crane a wonderful time, wanted her to be charmed and intrigued about travelling further.

"Excuse me, Sir?" A young woman, with a cheeky looking boy sat opposite him. He was surprised to hear her speak, she had been silent for much of the journey.

"Yes, how can I help?" he asked her.

"I am sorry to be any trouble to you, but I couldn't help but notice you have a doctor's bag with you?"

"Indeed, I am a doctor, is there something wrong?"

"Not with me, but with my boy. The doctor in Great Falls told me he could not help, but that his friend in Chicago might be able to. I don't know, I just don't think Edwin is as sick as the doctor made him out to be, at least not now at any rate. I know I am here, on my way to see this gentleman, but he seems so much better now."

"Did the doctor tell you what he thought was wrong with your boy?" Will asked gently. The woman was clearly upset, and she wouldn't be the first person, nor the last, to be given a wrong diagnosis, and cheated by a man she should be able to trust.

"He didn't give me a name, said it would mean nothing to me and might only worry me. Please, could you examine him for me? Tell me if I am doing the right thing?"

"But, Madam, I could be as much of a fraud as you suspect your own doctor to be," he said with a smile. She looked at him intently.

"I doubt it. I have seen how much you cherish that letter, you seem overcome with happiness whenever you read it. I doubt any man who can feel that much for someone – I presume it is a woman you will be meeting when we arrive in Chicago – could be so cruel as to gull me."

"You would be surprised," Will said wryly. "I once heard of an old colleague of mine, we studied medicine together, he most certainly loved his wife and children – yet he was forced to leave New York because of his mishandling of patient's cases. I am afraid it does happen."

"You are right, I should not be so trusting. But you are the doctor from Sun River are you not?" He nodded. "Then I know that you are as good a man as you are a physician. Your reputation spreads even through the corridors of a railway train! There is always talk in the sleeping cars, and there is many a young woman who would be more than happy for you to cast your eyes her way."

"It is a shame I never met any of them before this," Will joked. "But to business. Tell me about your boy."

The young woman sighed, her relief was palpable. "Well, it started with what I thought was a bad cold. He had watery eyes and his nose was terribly runny. He began to rub at his eyes and they became sore, and red. He could hardly tolerate even the weakest sunlight. He became tired and irritable, and he is usually such a sunny boy."

"Did he ever have any grayish-white spots in his mouth, on his tongue? Any fever?" Will asked. She nodded. "And then a few days later he got a rash?"

"Yes, however did you know?"

"Your son has had measles," he concluded. Her face fell, and Will was quick to reassure her. "Though measles can indeed be fatal, he seems to be lucky that it was not a particularly virulent case. As you say he is healing, and should be quite well again in a week or so. He is obviously a very lucky little boy, and has a particularly strong constitution."

"So the other doctor?"

"I suspect he and his friend have a little scam I'm afraid. They send a boy, who appears to be healing anyway to the second doctor, who claims a miracle cure down to some particular tonic or treatment regimen, and you pay them a large sum of money because you are so grateful your boy did not die."

"But, what if he had gotten worse?"

"Then I am sure that they would have both been very grave, and terribly sympathetic to your loss. My advice to you is to take your boy home. We shall be stopping soon, get the first train back and get him into bed. Keep giving him plenty of fluids, bathe him in lukewarm water, with oats in it to help the itching and in no time he will be his usual sunny self."

"Thank you Doctor, I cannot thank you enough for putting my mind at ease. I know of so many women who have lost their children, I would have done anything to ensure I didn't lose him."

"I think you should find a new doctor." He scribbled the name of another physician in Great Falls that he knew was trustworthy. "I think you will find Doctor Gregson will be much more trustworthy."

"I am so sorry to have troubled you, it is not right of me to have done so – and in a railway carriage of all places. But I cannot thank you enough. How much do I owe you for your time?" she asked pulling out her purse.

"Nothing. It doesn't count unless you are from Sun River," he said with a wink. "I am just glad to have helped. Now, one final thing, the names of the two doctors please? I think I should pay them both a visit, don't you?" She nodded and told him, and as the train pulled into the station he helped her to get her bags ready to disembark. "Get well Edwin, and try not to worry your Mama so!" He ruffled the lad's hair, and the two left him with a wave.

The rest of his journey was thankfully much less eventful, and passed swiftly. He was soon standing on the platform in Chicago, waiting for Miss Crane's train to arrive. The porter at his side was bored, and stood nonchalantly smoking a cigarette as Will paced nervously up and down. Finally the huge locomotive arrived in the station, and once the smog cleared Will went in search of her. But, he could not find a young woman alighting from any of the carriages. He began to panic, maybe something terrible had happened? Maybe she had decided not to come after all? Maybe she had taken one look at him and decided to hide?

"Doctor Butler?" a soft voice said as he felt a light hand tap him on the shoulder. He turned, surprised to find that she was almost as tall as he. He took a step back, as he took in her cascade of long blonde hair, and the elegant outfit she wore with such grace. The blue velvet set off the vivid blue of her eyes, so deep it was almost violet. She was quite beautiful, and he could hardly believe that this young woman was here to meet with him. Surely she should have had hundreds of young Boston men falling at her feet?

"Miss Cccrane?" he stammered, feeling more nervous than he could ever remember.

"Please, do call me Madelaine, or Maddy if you'd prefer."

"Mmmm Maddy. That is lovely. I am so sorry, I do not normally make such a complete fool of myself at first meetings, but I wasn't expecting you to be…"

"So tall? So blonde?" she asked mischievously, her eyes sparkling.

"So beautiful," he admitted. "I do not know why, but the way you write it gave me the impression of someone maybe more handsome, than pretty." He could feel the heat rising up his neck and into his cheeks, knew that he looked and sounded a complete fool. "I am sorry, that sounds as if I believe that an intelligent and eloquent person cannot also be so stunningly lovely. If I ever did, I will never believe so again." She smiled at him again.

"I am so pleased that I am not the only one of us to be nervous about this," she confided. She pulled off her gloves to show him her nails. "See, I have quite bitten my nails to the quick with anxiety!" Unable to stop himself, he took the proffered hands, and kissed each fingertip. Her eyes were wide when he looked back up into them.

"I am too forward. I am sorry. I can arrange a chaperone, do not wish you to ever feel uncomfortable," he said, feeling utterly flustered. She laughed, the tinkling sound was like music, it flowed through him, as life giving and wondrous as water to a man dying of thirst."

"I do not mind one bit, and a chaperone could be so terribly tedious. We are both adults Doctor Butler, shall we not be able to take care of our own interests? I doubt you would ever force yourself upon anyone."

"No I most certainly would not, and please if I am to call you Maddy you must call me Will."

"Will," she said softly. The word seemed to sound completely different in her dulcet tones. "I shall be honored."

She gave him her hand, and he tucked it under his arm, escorting her happily to where a line of carriages awaited. The bored porter scampered along behind them, his trolley now filled with her trunk and his valise. Will tipped him gratefully and assisted Maddy inside. "I have arranged for you to stay at the Great Northern Hotel, and I shall be staying at Tremont House, though if you would prefer we can swap?"

"I do not mind where I sleep, as long as I get to spend as much time as possible with you. We have much to discuss, and I do not want to waste a moment of our time together," she said breathlessly. He had to admit, sitting so close by her in such a confined space was making it hard for him to breathe too, or concentrate on anything other than the sensation of warmth that emanated from her body.

"I have booked us a place for supper at a delightful restaurant, and thought that we could maybe go to the museum tomorrow, and take in a play at the theatre in the evening?"

"That sounds wonderful," she said, not taking her eyes from his. "I am sure that it will all be wonderful."

Will had never believed in love at first sight, yet he had never before met someone like Maddy. Her sheer physical impact was overwhelming. He simply could not understand how she could still be unwed, and how lucky he had been when he had chosen her to write back to. He reminded himself to send Catherine gifts every single day in thanks for her assistance in making up his mind. He was sure he would never regret it.

When they reached her hotel, he was loathe to leave her there alone. "I shall be quite alright," she assured him. "I have faced much worse than the wagging tongues of hotel staff." She laughed, but he was sure he detected a touch of strain in her tone. But, she must be tired, he admonished himself. He must not be the doctor here. It was not his place to analyze every symptom as if she were a patient, rather than a woman he intended to court. He watched as she and her trunk disappeared up the stairs, and wished he could follow her, but the hansom cab was waiting outside, and he must go and check in to his own rooms if he was to be refreshed and back here to collect her for supper.

As he bathed and dressed for the evening he tried not to read too much into the fact that she had brought such a large trunk with her. He was sure that most women probably travelled with more accoutrements than men, and their dresses must take up considerable room with all the petticoats, corsetry and other undergarments women seemed to be so enamored of these days. He was not sure that the fashion for such a tiny waist was altogether healthy. Young women, supposedly in the peak of health should not be so prone to fainting, he was sure.

Maddy was waiting for him in the foyer. She wore a dusky pink gown that had an exquisitely embroidered bodice and full flaring skirts. Her hair was pinned artfully so that it draped over one shoulder in elaborate coil. She looked quite simply magnificent. He quickly asked the bellboy to dismiss the carriage he had waiting outside. He wanted to see and be seen with this beauty by his side. He bowed gallantly to her and offered her his arm. "The evening is fine, would you care for a stroll?" She nodded.

"So, where are you taking me? I hope the food is good – I am absolutely ravenous," she admitted cheekily.

"I should have asked, do you like fish?" he said, suddenly feeling concerned about his choice of restaurant. So many people did not enjoy it, but Rector's was one of his favorite places and he always tried to eat there at least once when he visited Chicago. She gave him a long and serious look, and he began to feel hot under the collar. He ran his finger around it to loosen it a little and even mopped his brow before she put him out of his misery.

"I love it, especially oysters."

"That is wonderful news as we are to go to Rector's Oyster House. They also do the most wonderful cocktails, the concoctions are quite unexpected!" She licked her lips in anticipation, and the simple gesture almost made him lose control and kiss her right there in the middle of the street. But, he pinned his eyes forward, and tried not to think about the light touch of her hand on his arm, or the feel of her hips as they ever so gently swayed against his own.

Chapter Five

Maddy rolled over in her vast bed as the maid came in with her morning chocolate. She felt quite deliciously decadent, having slept in until almost ten. She was to meet Will at the zoological gardens at midday, so she had time to luxuriate in the pleasure of a real bed and plenty of pillows. The past few days had flown by, too quickly as far as she was concerned. Will would have to return to Sun River tomorrow, and she was still uncertain whether he intended to take her with him. She prayed he would, but he was not an easy man to read. She was certain that he liked her, he enjoyed her company and did not seem to object to her more forcibly expressed opinions as so many men had done in her past. Yet, since that delightful moment at the train station when he had kissed every one of her fingertips he had not made any kind of physical gesture towards her.

She had to admit it was quite frustrating, as she most certainly would not rebuff his advances if he were to try. She had come here, resigned to the thought that she would marry him if he wanted her, that her own feelings for him did not really matter. Yet, from the very first she had been smitten with his deep brown eyes, slightly scruffy and overlong hair, and his tendency to worry about how everyone else around him was feeling. He was quick-witted, and funny yet his humor was self-deprecating and endearing. She wondered if he knew just how good a man he was.

Her breakfast completed, and a delightfully warm bath, scented with rose petals, later and she was ready to join him. She picked up her parasol, as the sun was hot, and walked slowly towards the gardens. A young bellboy from the hotel was her guide, and he delighted in pointing out the kinds of sights that only the young in a city like this ever get to know. She smiled at his eagerness and was happy to give him a dollar for his troubles as they reached the gates. Will was standing, his jacket slung casually over his shoulder, he turned and the glint of his pocket watch in the sun made her blink for a moment. "You look lovely," he said softly as he took her hand.

"Thank you. So, what is on our itinerary today?" she asked, trying to hide the way that his innocent touch was making her feel. Just the sensation of his skin on her own was sending shivers through her, and when he bent to kiss her hand, she gasped as he turned the palm and kissed that, before closing her fingers over the spot, as if sealing it. It was intimate, a lovers kiss. She glanced around, wondering if anyone else had seen the look of pure ecstasy she was sure must have crossed her features. She blushed.

"Well, I have a date with the tigers," he said, innocently as if he had missed every moment of her delight. She wanted to scream out loud, and beg him to see her, truly see her – to see that she was smitten, and longed for him to make her his wife. But she was too well bred, and so she kept her own counsel and tried to reconcile herself to the thought that tomorrow, this wonderful man might just walk out of her life forever.

As always he tucked her arm through his, and escorted her proudly to their destination. A keeper was awaiting them at the enclosure and he gave them the most interesting lecture on the big cats. If she hadn't been so on edge, Maddy would have been utterly entranced, but she could barely drag her attention from the man by her side. "So, shall we go and see our newest acquisition?" the keeper asked. Startled, she looked at him completely confused.

"I'm sorry, I must have lost track. The heat," she said vaguely.

"Mr Moss has a special treat for us," Will said gently, as he urged her forward. Still feeling a little bewildered, she followed the stocky little keeper inside a nearby building. Inside she could see the cages that the beasts slept in at night. It was fascinating, and she could hardly believe her luck, that Will had arranged something so wonderful for her.

"This is Tilly," Mr Moss said proudly as he stopped at a cage that seemed to have no access to the outside pen. "Isn't she beautiful?" Maddy moved to his side and looked down, looking up at her was a tiger cub, with the biggest eyes she had ever seen.

"Oh my," she gasped. Will moved up close beside her, slipping his arm around her waist.

"Isn't she wonderful? Just look at the size of her paws!"

"Would you like to go in? She is due for her feed," Mr Moss asked. Maddy was stunned. Surely this was a wild animal, they should not be allowed even near to her. "Don't worry, she is quite harmless, is more than used to us keepers. Thinks I am her Mama!"

"She will let me feed her?"

"I think she would be more than happy to. Oh, and she likes having her nose scratched while she eats," he added. Will grinned at her as Mr Moss led her into the enclosure. She looked at him, trepidation being outdone by excitement and interest as she knelt down and took the bottle and offered it to Tilly.

The little cub took it happily, clearly not worried in the slightest who was holding it. Mr Moss indicated that she should sit down on a box he brought her, and she did, her skirts spreading around her. Tilly lapped at her milk, occasionally batting at the bottle with her paws. She was strong, but gentle, and her claws were tightly sheathed. Soon she was climbing up into Maddy's lap, and she was able to stroke her nose as Mr Moss had told her to do. It was soft and furry, like velvet. The cub chuffed gently in pleasure as she lay sated on Maddy's lap, her bottle finished

It was magical; she could have cried it was such an incredible thing to have been able to experience. Whatever happened between herself and Will, she would never ever forget this – nor anything else they had enjoyed together over the past few days. He had gone out of his way to make every moment special, and she was overwhelmed by his generosity.

"We should leave her to sleep now," Mr Moss said as he gently eased the young cub from Maddy's lap and settled her into her straw bed.

"Thank you, for everything," Maddy said ecstatically as they parted company with the kindly keeper, and let him go about his duties.

"It was my pleasure. Take care Will, best of luck," he said enigmatically.

She and Will began to walk back through the park. "I have a feeling you know Mr Moss quite well," she said to him.

"Indeed. He is my cousin," Will admitted. "He was more than happy to do me a favor when I told him why I needed it."

"And why was that?"

"Well, I have something to ask you, and I wanted to ensure you were in the best mood I could possibly manage."

"That sounds quite ominous," Maddy said with a rueful smile.

"I shall just come out and say it," he said, fidgeting with his pocket watch, and barely meeting her eyes. She began to feel her fear rise once more, that he would not want her to accompany him back to Sun River - that all this had just been to make her trip worthwhile.

"Then do," she said impatiently.

"Maddy, darling Maddy, will you marry me? I adore you, and want to spend the rest of my life with you!" he gushed.

Maddy could hardly believe her ears, he was saying everything she had been dreaming of, even before she had known how much she loved him, yet for some reason she could not answer. Her words got tangled up in her throat, and she found herself gasping for breath. "Maddy, please are you quite well?" he asked anxiously. "I would never have asked you if I did not think that you cared for me too. Please tell me I have not been a complete fool?"

"No, you have not. Could never be," she finally managed to force out. "Will, I would be honored to marry you, cannot think of anything I could ever want more."

She had barely caught her breath when he picked her up and whirled her around, clearly not caring for the stares of passing strangers. His face was alight with joy, and she could feel tears pricking in the back of her eyes as a lump formed in her throat. It had been so long since she had caused anyone to be so happy, and all because of her. "Shall we go and find a minister right now?" he asked her eagerly. "I do not wish to hurry you, but I cannot bear the thought of having to part with you, want you to come home with me tomorrow and do not wish to do anything to sully your reputation before I whisk you away."

He set her down, and Maddy felt every bit of joy ebb from her body. He could never ruin her reputation, it was already in tatters and he did not know. She had not mentioned her reasons for searching for a husband once since they had met. She suddenly felt as if she had been lying to him, had been leading him on. Yet, she truly did adore him. She wished to be his wife because of that love, no longer because he was the answer to her dilemma. She could not continue to take advantage of this kind and generous man. She had to tell him, but how? It simply wasn't something you could slip into a conversation that easily, and she had no clue as to whether he would understand.

But, could she consider taking the risk that he might never find out? Was that even fair? She wanted to be wed to him so very much, but how could she ever offer herself to him fully knowing of the secret she was keeping from him. News travelled quickly. She did not doubt that there was nowhere on earth where her disgrace would not catch up with her. But, was she selfish enough to take the happiness he was offering her now, and let what would come occur in its own time?

"Maddy? Whatever is the matter?" Will asked, concern written all over his face. "You have gone as white as a sheet! I shall escort you to the hotel immediately, you must rest. I shall send word of the arrangements for our marriage, if that is still what you wish?" She nodded, unable to speak – too scared of what she might say. "Come my darling, it is just the sun and the excitement that has left you overwrought. I cannot tell you how happy you have made me." His words did nothing to assuage her guilt, only made it harder for her to ever admit the truth of her past, and her flight from Boston. But would he ever understand? Would any man?

Chapter Six

Will sat nervously in his hotel room. He had found a Methodist minister happy to marry them that very evening, but he was concerned as to whether Maddy was well enough. She had seemed to be so happy, and then it was as if all the blood in her body had disappeared. He had been impressed, thus far, with her ability to keep up with him as he had set them a punishing schedule of sightseeing and activity. Clearly it had all been too much for her. He wondered if he would be able to prolong his stay a little, to give her time to rest before they made their way back to Sun River, but he knew it would be impossible. He had already left his patients without a doctor for too long, and did not want to be responsible for anyone dying because of a lack of care.

The clock ticked slowly, and he did not know if he was anxious about waiting for the ceremony, or if he expected her to send him notice that she would not be attending. She had seemed so over the moon at his proposal, and then so utterly dejected. He wondered if there was something in her past that had given her pause, but she didn't talk of her family or her life in Boston and so he had no clue if it might be that, or if she had simply not known how to tell him that she did not wish to be his wife.

Unable to bear the silence, he grabbed his jacket and made his way downstairs to the bar. He ordered a single shot of whiskey for his nerves. He nursed it tentatively. He wasn't one for alcohol usually, but each sip seemed to help as it burnt its way down his throat and warmed his chest. "Newspaper?" the bar tender asked him, brandishing a copy of one of the newspapers from New York. He took it; it would help to pass the time. He looked up at the ornate clock above the bar and sighed. Two hours and thirty seven minutes. He began to read. It amused him that so many of the stories revolved around money and politics. Everything in the East did. He was glad he had made his way West once he had completed his medical training. The vacuous and vain people of his acquaintance in New York had never been to his taste.

He skipped past the classifieds section, smiling at the pages of Matrimonial advertisements. Secretly he wished them all the luck that he had been blessed with, that their unions would be as happy as he knew his would be with Maddy. He had advertised looking for companionship, but he was sure that he had found in the elegant Bostonian a true partner, a woman who he could love and who would love him in return. She was just so honest and straightforward – attributes he had rarely assigned to such women in the past.

He began to read through the pages of news from around the country. Various new laws were being proclaimed in Virginia, and there had been a series of murders in Washington. He applauded the former, and was aghast at the details of the latter, but it seemed that the authorities had managed to capture the culprit. The next story was concerning a trial in Boston. A young woman had been fighting to gain her release from a mental institution, having been incarcerated against her will for being attracted to other women. The woman had claimed that it simply was not true, and her husband and family had stood beside her throughout the trial. Thankfully for her she had been released, but the newspaper details were lurid and clearly designed to stir up public sentiment.

Will read them, and felt his own anger rising. The poor woman had done nothing wrong, and even if the allegations had been true it was hardly as if her preferring the company of women to men was such a seditious thing. He knew he was a tolerant man, that many were not so liberal in their views, but even as a doctor he did not understand the idea that to be attracted to someone of the same sex as yourself was a medical issue. No amount of counseling or medication seemed to ever make a bit of difference in such cases, though many of his peers claimed to be able to cure both men and women of such ailments.

But then he stopped. The story continued with the details of the woman she was supposed to have been intimate with, who had not been institutionalized. The insinuation of the article was that this was because of her family connections and wealth, but Miss Madelaine Crane had also testified at the trial, and had vowed under oath that she and the accused had never shared such carnal relations as was alleged. Will's heart stopped. His brain suddenly went into turmoil, and he found himself gasping for air. Why had she not told him of this? Did she think that he would not understand? Was this why she was so eager to meet with him, to wed him?

He glanced back at the page. Both women had been exonerated, and the courts had insisted that the press be fair and impartial when reporting the case, but all Will could see was the sensationalism of speculation in the journalist's summation. He all but spelled it out that he thought that both women were guilty as charged, and that a terrible injustice had been done. While Will could condemn his opinions, and even his prejudices, the entire case left him with too many questions, and he knew he had to see Madelaine before they were to meet at the chapel. He could not marry her if she did not care for him as he did for her, would not marry her if she was prepared to lie to him about something so very important.

He rushed to her hotel, and ran up the stairs to her room. "Sir, you cannot just enter a guest's rooms without us announcing you," the manager cried, puffing and panting as he chased after Will.

"Sir, the woman in question will be my wife in one hour. I have every right to enter her chambers," Will said firmly.

"Sir, please. It isn't seemly. You are not yet wed! This establishment has a reputation, please do not tarnish that."

"Who is here to see me, and who knows my business?" Will retorted, his patience frayed. The door opened, and Maddy stood there, a filmy robe over her shift. Will felt his body react, as it always did to the sight of her, but he could not let his passion get in the way now.

"Mr Marchant, it is quite alright. Come in Will," she said standing aside so he could enter the room. "I shall be checking out shortly anyway. We have no desire to sully the reputation of your hotel."

Will watched her carefully. She was so calm. But, then she did not know why he had come tearing across town. He wondered if she would still be so in control when he told her that he knew all about why she was here, that her wonderful acting skills would do her no favors any longer.

Mr Marchant retreated and she shut the door and turned to face him. "I can see by your face that something is the matter William, so please do share it with me," she said, her voice quavering a little as she did so.

"Is there not something you should have shared with me, before you allowed me to propose marriage?" he asked angrily.

"Yes," she admitted frankly. Her candor surprised him. He had expected her to try and deny everything, to claim that nothing but love had brought her here. "I should have mentioned it to you long ago, but it was one of those things that seemed just too difficult to drop into polite conversation."

"I read about the court case in the newspaper Miss Crane. It is not something one wishes to find out about their fiancée from an external source – especially one so damn biased!"

"Yes the press did rather enjoy making it all out to be so much more sensational than it truly was," she admitted. "Unfortunately everybody in Boston took their word as truth, rather than the ruling of the court. But, I cannot change other people's opinions. I can only hold on to what I know was the truth."

"And that was?" Will said coldly.

"Francesca is a qualified lawyer. She has been my friend for as long as I can remember. We have worked together on a number of charities, and she has often undertaken work for them when legal assistance was required. She always had to get a friend to undertake her court requirements as judges are still reluctant to let women argue motions and fulfill the role completely, but she was getting under the skin of the establishment. She is very talented, but she crossed one too many of the people that matter. A suit she was working on accused one of Boston's finest and he was not happy about it – especially when he lost the case. He blamed her, rather than taking responsibility for his own wrongdoing."

"And so he came up with a charge of lesbianism? It seems rather absurd."

"It was. But he had already tried everything else. It was the only charge his lawyers could come up with in the end that did not need proof. It is very easy to have someone committed to a mental institution, and almost impossible for them to obtain their own release."

"You seem very knowledgeable about it all," Will said bitterly.

"Francesca was my friend. Is my friend. I was in court, to support her every single day. Thankfully she had friends who were prepared to risk their careers for her. Most of them left Boston immediately after the trial – none of them will ever be able to practice law there again I am sure."

"But why were you named?"

"Your guess is as good as mine. Maybe Granville Healy wished to ruin my Father for some reason, or my brother-in-law Blake. Either would make sense as their companies are in direct competition. But it was because I was there. I spent a lot of time, with my friend. We were close, we were often seen embracing in public – not anything untoward of course – but we were as close as sisters. I was easy, and my family connections would mean that I could not be touched. Healy could cause a scandal that would be enough to cause my family problems, but would be unlikely to face any kind of legal fallout from it himself."

"So, why did you stay and stand by her side? Surely that must have only fuelled the rumors?"

"William, I think I know you well enough to know that you would stand by a friend in need, that you would stand up for what is right? Please do tell me if I am wrong, for it is something that could definitely affect my reasons for marrying you."

"Of course I would. My honor would demand I do what is right – not what is easy," he said staunchly. But, he was a man. It was different. She could have saved herself and her family such trouble if she had simply kept out of the way.

"Why should a woman feel any differently?" she asked, as if she was reading his mind. "I could not have stood by and let anything happen to Francesca, could not let such a ridiculous lie tarnish my own reputation, and ruin her life?"

Will sank down onto the bed. He perched there, his hands balled into fists. The entire situation was so wrong. Yet, Maddy seemed so in control and so resigned to what had occurred. "Was it why you wanted to marry me?"

"Oh, dear Will," she said as she sank down to the floor in front of him. "When I responded to those advertisements I just wanted a way out, to get away from Boston. So, yes in a way it is. But that wasn't why I said yes this afternoon."

"I don't understand," he said looking down into her beautiful face. He reached out and stroked her cheek. The skin was so smooth.

"I came here because I needed to get away from the scandal, the gossip. But I fell in love with William Butler once I was here. I know everyone will tell us it is too soon. How can I know how I feel after just a few days? But I do. I loved you from the first; that stilted advertisement and your curt little letter. I longed to be with you, to have you do to me all the things a husband does to his wife from the moment you kissed every one of my fingertips at the station. And when you arranged for me to pet and feed that tiger cub, I knew I would walk on water for you if you asked me."

"So why could you not trust me? Why did I have to learn about your past from a newspaper?"

"Will, seriously? You have told me everything there is to know about your past? Good and bad?" she asked curiously.

"I suppose not, but anything bad in my past was a minor misdemeanor, at worst an indiscretion!"

"And mine was unfounded, speculative gossip. I did not do the things that Francesca and I were accused of having done. I have had to fight for months to clear both our names of such slander – only to find that no matter what we do, it will follow us everywhere we go. Even to this very room." She turned her head from him sadly, as if she had hoped for better from him. She was right to have done so, and Will knew himself to be the one at fault. He could not blame her for wanting to put aside such things, that were obviously still so very painful for her.

"I am so sorry," he said taking her chin and turning her face to his. "I should have had faith in you. I was just so very afraid that it might be true. That you could never love me as I love you. That your heart belonged to her, that I would never be enough for you." She laughed awkwardly.

"Oh dear Will, there has never been anyone in my heart until I met you. You have no competition." He sighed, her words acted as balm to his wounded pride and he bent his head and claimed her lips tenderly.

"Can you ever forgive me for my jealousy and mistrust?"

"Always, but on one condition," she said as her fingers entwined in the hair at his nape.

"Always do what you have done now. If you have questions, queries, doubts – come to me, talk to me, trust me."

"I swear," he said as he pulled her into his arms and kissed her passionately.

Epilogue

The little church in Sun River was full to bursting. Will smiled at his friends and took comfort from the presence of Tom standing by his side. "What made you choose to wait until you were here?" he asked quietly. "Remember you cannot lie, you are in the house of God!"

"We missed our date with the minister," Will said with a grin, as he remembered the passionate argument and even more passionate reconciliation that had followed it.

"So not only did you travel alone with your intended, you took advantage of her innocence too?" Tom teased.

"Not at all. She just decided that she didn't really have a reputation that could be sullied, and took advantage of mine!"

"Phew, you have a firecracker on your hands Will that is for sure."

"I know, and I am more than glad of it. Life will never be dull with Maddy in my life."

The organ struck a chord, and then began to play a wedding march. Will turned to watch his bride make her way down the aisle towards him. He had been so sure of her presence that he had felt no fear.

But as she approached him he felt his stomach begin to churn as the butterflies began to fly. She looked stunning, in her traditional blue gown. He had wanted her to wear the more fashionable white, but she had insisted that she wished their life to be without such artifice. Her Father was by her side, looking proud and he was glad that they had waited. It had been more than difficult to do so, he had found it harder with each passing day to resist Maddy's many charms -but this special day, surrounded by everyone they loved had been worth the wait.

Her sister, Carolynn sat surrounded by her young children, her handsome husband, Blake, by her side. She held their infant son, whilst the girls clambered all over their Papa. It was delightful to see such a loving and happy family. But, he was sad that there were so few faces on her side of the church. Few of her friends had made the journey from Boston, but as she had admitted she wasn't sure that she had ever really had true friends until she came to Sun River. He was touched that some of his friends had chosen to sit on her side, to offer her their support on this important day.

As she reached the altar, he stepped down to take her hand. A young woman he had not yet met smiled at him as he approached and took Maddy's bouquet of wild flowers, and pulled back the long veil that hid her luscious lips and wide violet eyes from his view. He could only presume that this was Francesca, her best friend. Of all the people who had said they intended to attend he had been most nervous about meeting her. He was still a little uncomfortable and angry too when he thought of what had happened to the two women. But, his fears disappeared when he saw the warmth in her eyes, and he looked forward to being able to get to know her better in the days to follow.

Will took Maddy's hand and they turned to the Minister. He couldn't remove the smile from his face as they listened to his homily, and he was happy to see that Maddy seemed to have a permanent look of joy on her face too. The Minister looked at them, pride and contentment on his kindly face. He guided them and spoke the words of the service eloquently in his rich baritone.

"Wilt thou, William Edward Butler have this woman to be thy

wedded wife, to live together in God's holy ordinance in the Holy Estate of Matrimony? Wilt thou love her? Comfort her, honor and keep her in sickness and in health, and forsaking all others keep thee unto her as long as you both shall live?" the minister asked in a loud clear baritone.

"In the name of God, I, William Edward Butler, take you, Madelaine Annabelle Crane to be my wife, to have and to hold from this day forward, for better, for worse, for richer, for poorer, in sickness and in health, to love and to cherish, until we are parted by death; and thereto I pledge thee my troth."

Maddy smiled at him as he spoke the words of his vow, and he knew that he meant every single one of them. He squeezed her hand as she pledged herself to him.

"In the name of God, I, Madelaine Annabelle Crane, take you, William Edward Butler to be my husband, to have and to hold from this day forward, for better, for worse, for richer for poorer, in sickness and in health, to love, honor and obey, until we are parted by death; and thereto I pledge thee my troth."

He kissed his bride, and was overwhelmed as the congregation began to cheer and clap. He wiped a tear from Maddy's eye. "I won't hold you to the obey part," he promised.

"That is good, I am sure I would never be able to abide by it," she said with a grin. They laughed together, and Will knew that their lives together would be full of such moments of happiness and joy.

"So, what do we do now?" he asked her as they made their way out of the church and into the bright sunshine.

"We go to the wedding breakfast that my Papa has so generously paid for. You cannot imagine how happy he was when he found out that the cooks from Young's Hotel lived here in town now. He used to eat there all the time!"

"Ellen and Maggie are rather special," Will admitted. "But I doubt if we will all fit in the bakery," he glanced across the street at the tiny store.

"No, it is at the Saloon," she said with a smile.

"How long do you think we have to stay to be polite?"

"I suppose we should at least stay until after the meal. We will need our strength after all," she said with a flirtatious look in her eyes. Will picked her up and spun her around.

"I love you Mrs Butler."

"I love you too Doctor Butler, but put me down – you'll rumple my dress!"

"Well, we can't have that," he teased as he gently set her down and took her hand, leading her to the Saloon. "Do you truly believe that you can be happy here in this tiny little town? That you won't miss the excitement and drama of Boston?"

"I am happier here than I have ever been Will, I will not desert you – unless I manage to somehow involve myself in another scandal!"

The End

* * * * * *

A Bride for Aaron
Book 8

Chapter One

Deep, booming laughter and rapturous applause filled the air as young Christopher completed a new trick his step-mother, Emily, had taught him to do with Claude and bowed deeply. Aaron, having only arrived at the farm a few moments before had found himself marveling at how calmly Matthew had watched as the boy tumbled off the donkey's back, had been apt to go and pick the boy up and dust him down. But he had soon realized it was just a part of an act when his brother put a hand out to stop him, and Claude had wandered over, nudged the lad and then taking his shirt in his teeth picked him up and carried him towards them where he dropped Chris unceremoniously into his Papa's lap. "I cannot believe how clever that mule is," Aaron said to Emily.

"He was always far better at being a circus performer than I was," she admitted. "Chris is so talented, has learned tricks in moments that it took me a lifetime to master."

"He certainly seems to enjoy it," Matthew said. "I can't tell you how scared I was the first time I saw Christopher roll off his back and onto the floor!"

"All I had to do was to teach Christopher how to land," Emily admitted. "After that he and Claude have been developing their tricks alone. I know my family will be very impressed when next they visit, will try and whisk them off to Boston to be in the circus, but I think we should keep them both here a while longer," she said, ruffling Chris's curls as Matthew hugged his boy close.

Claude nudged at Matthew, and Aaron laughed as the donkey seemed to grin at them as though he was proud of his antics. "You know where it is," Matthew said to him. Claude went straight for his coat pocket, and extracted a carrot. Content, he wandered back towards his paddock and crunched his reward. He clearly believed his work was done for the day.

"I can imagine they would. They truly do make a good partnership and I am sure people would be glad to pay out their hard earned pennies to see them perform. But, Chris does seem a little young yet." Aaron agreed.

"Emily was performing years younger," Matthew said proudly. She blushed.

"But I grew up in the circus, and my family were all around me. It can be a hard life, and he should be old enough to choose it for himself – though I know he would be much loved and taken care of by his Uncle and his Grandmama. But, we are too selfish, want him to be here with us – he has an important role to fulfill soon after all." She looked down at the boy who grinned at her.

"I am going to be a big brother," he announced proudly, his little chest all puffed out.

"Well, that is news indeed," Aaron said. "I am sure you will be a very good big brother, you have a wonderful example to follow. Your Papa is the best big brother in the world."

"But Claude will always be mine. Mama says the baby will be too little to play with him for a long time, but I don't think Claude would mind. He is very gentle." Aaron smiled at how grown up the little boy was trying to sound.

"Claude really is a character isn't he, and as much a part of the family as any of us?" Aaron marveled. Emily smiled. She was obviously proud of the animal, and he truly could understand why.

"Come Chris, you should wash and change before supper," she encouraged the boy. Matthew reached up and kissed his father before he got down. "We shall leave you two to catch up a little. You must have much to talk about."

"Uncle Aaron?"

"Yes Chris?"

"Will you be staying long?"

"I don't know. That depends upon a lot of things, but I certainly hope to," he said looking into the boy's serious little face.

"I hope so too. I like having you here, and so does Daddy. We have been very excited ever since we heard you were on your way."

"Well that is good to know."

He hadn't ever thought of himself as the paternal type before, but seeing his brother so settled and happy was having an effect on Aaron. As a journalist he had travelled the length and breadth of the country, and had always believed that he enjoyed his life that way. But, even in the short time he had been here with Matthew and Emily, in Sun River, he was beginning to see that there were positives to being settled too. He adored his young nephew; he was so full of life and curiosity and wanted to know everything anyone was prepared to teach him. He had begun to consider what being a father might be like, whether a child of his own was something he wanted. He was almost certain now that it was. He truly had expected that being in the same house as the boy for more than a few hours would have had him tearing his hair out in frustration, but the opposite was true. He couldn't wait to spend more time with the lad.

"Well, would you stay?" Matthew asked once Emily and Chris were inside. "I know you only intended to be here for a few days before heading off to find a story somewhere, but I'd love to have my little brother nearby."

"I hadn't thought about it Matty, I've been on the road so long it is what seems normal to me. But, you have a wonderful life here. I have to admit you are making me a little jealous. I never thought I would yearn for hearth and home, but if it contained a talented donkey and a woman as good as Emily I think I could be convinced," he joked. Matthew looked at him, staring deep into his eyes. His brother had always been able to read him like a book, and Aaron was used to the scrutiny, but today it made him feel a little self-conscious.

"Aaron, I miss you," he said finally. "And I think Sun River needs someone like you. We don't have our own newspaper, and it would be good to have something more up to date with our local news than the newspapers from Great Falls and Billings."

"You truly think there is a need? Sun River is pretty sleepy. I can't imagine much happens here," he said with a rueful grin.

"Are you sure? Just because things appear to be quiet it doesn't mean it is – you of all people should know that!"

"I do. Often the quietest places hide the best stories, but other than an influx of Boston wives, there really isn't much happening here."

"Other than the rumors that Sheriff Partlin is crooked? Or the unexplained disappearance of three actors from the theatre this week? Or the possibility that we may have the next Governor of the State living in our midst? None of that enough for you?" Matthew chuckled.

"Well, when you put it like that, then yes, I suppose there possibly is scope for a weekly newspaper I suppose. But, a man cannot make a living from such a small print run as would be required here."

"I can always use help here. In fact the farm will be up for sale as soon as I have paid off the debts I took on to build the theatre – though the sooner I could sell it the sooner I could pay those off too!" Matthew said. Aaron snorted.

"You do not want me here. I would have your farm in tatters in no time. I am not cut out for a life on the land and you know it!"

"Neither was I when I came out here, but I learnt. There are good people all around and they help each other out. I'd be nearby to give you advice." They both sat quietly, thinking for a moment. Aaron was grateful for his brother's support, but it was not right for either of them for him to accept it without taking his share of the responsibility and he was more than sure that owning a farm was not something that was right for him.

"There is always MacAlpine's campaign for Governor?" Matthew said suddenly. His face lit up. "The more I think of it, the better it is as an opportunity for you. You have contacts all over the State, you know all the people who would need to know him, and see him. You understand how politics works."

"I do, and it is why I have spent much of my life reporting it, rather than getting involved in it. I could never support any of the politicians I have met. They seem wonderful to your face, but dig only a little way beneath the surface there is always something unpleasant."

"Gideon is a good man. I wouldn't suggest you support anyone I don't believe in – but that is his problem."

"What do you mean?"

"He is too good. He genuinely wishes to seek election to make changes that benefit us all. He hopes to win because he is the best candidate."

"You and I both know that the best candidate rarely wins. You cannot win if you have scruples," Aaron said sadly.

"Indeed, but we need men like him making the decisions that matter. Good men can make a change."

"There aren't enough of them, that is true, but that is because even good men become bad men once they are in positions of power and influence."

"I know you are cynical, and I don't blame you given what you have seen. But will you at least meet him?"

"Of course, but meeting someone and agreeing to help them are two very different things." His brother nodded. But though he had misgivings about all of his brother's suggestions, he was glad that there were at least options should he decide to stay. He hadn't come here thinking of it, but the more they sat out there, on the broad porch, watching the sun set over the mountains he felt at peace for the first time in too many years. He could live here, in Sun River. It already felt like home, and the only people in the world that he cared about were here. But, there would be much to think on if he were to do so.

Emily emerged from the screen door, Chris trailing behind her. "Supper is ready," she said. "I'm sorry, I did not mean to eavesdrop, but I overheard your conversation from in the kitchen. Have you considered the school? Myra is looking for a schoolmaster."

"I think I would prefer teaching to entering politics," Aaron said with a smile. "But I have no experience, and am not sure I could cope with more than one child at a time."

"You will never know unless you try," she said with a grin. "Chris seems to have taken to you, and he is not always so outgoing. If you can win over our stubborn little man then the other local children would be easy. But come on in and eat, you can think about it for as long as you like. We will be seeing Myra and Carlton tomorrow at the Harvest Supper, you can talk to her then."

"If I did not know better, I would say that the three of you are conspiring to tether me down," he said, picking up Chris and raising him high above his head. The little boy squealed his pleasure.

"We love you Uncle Aaron," he said in his sweet and clear voice. Aaron squeezed him tightly against his chest.

"That is very good to know lad."

After supper he made his way out onto the porch alone. He sank into one of the rockers and thought about the conversation they had shared earlier. He was surprised to even be considering staying here. Sun River was so small. He was used to big cities. He loved winkling out corruption and laying it bare for all to see. He simply couldn't see that there would be that much here in Sun River for him to investigate. But, he also had to admit that he had begun to find the monotony of people's depravity was becoming dull. He found himself reporting on the same things, done by different people, in different places. Scandal seemed to be anything but shocking to him after all his years working in the newspaper trade. He was never surprised, never stunned by the things people could do to one another.

He could hear Emily and Matthew laughing together inside. He could see just how much pleasure their relationship was giving them. Their work together at the theatre gave them both much pleasure, and their skills and knowledge seemed to complement one another perfectly. The little touches, and soft looks they shared when they believed nobody was looking spoke volumes about the passion they shared and he was envious. Even here at the farm, they worked in tandem to ensure work got done and the land stayed in good heart, though he knew they hoped to move into Sun River itself as soon as they could.

He stood and stretched. His body felt tired. Too much travelling and uncomfortable beds in hotels had left his body feeling less than its best. He could already feel the difference in his health that the fresh mountain air was making to his wellbeing. Good food and a comfortable home would build him back up. But even now he wasn't sure he wished to return to his old life. He needed a new challenge, and he needed to feel as he had since he had been here: welcomed and loved. His life had become so lonely.

When he heard about the friends that his brother had made here in Sun River, the bonds that he had built so successfully, Aaron began to doubt the choices he had made in his own life.

He wandered over to the paddock. Claude plodded over to the gate and allowed him to scratch his nose. "Claude, you were a big city boy, how did you make the change? It must have been quite a shock, a big star like you." Claude brayed softly. It sounded as if he was laughing. Aaron looked at him. The animal often seemed so clever, as if he truly understood everything his family said. "You think I'm being a fool to ask such a question? What do you suggest? Should I stay?" Claude nodded vigorously. "You're biased. They've set you up to work on me," he joked. But though it seemed such a simple decision to make, there were things in his past that could make it hard for him if he chose to remain in one place, and the last thing he wanted to do was to put his family in danger. The donkey nuzzled at his chest, encouraging Aaron to stroke his cheeks and his neck. It felt so wonderful to be accepted, to be wanted though, and he knew he had even more than that here. He had love. "It's working Claude. You've done well."

"He really makes a lot of sense," Emily said, walking softly towards them. "I've always told him my troubles."

"He is definitely a good listener," Aaron said with a grin. "Gives good advice too."

"Always," Emily chuckled as she hugged her old friend around his hairy grey neck. "We would all love you to stay Aaron, but it has to be your choice."

"I am considering it. I do find it harder and harder to stay in my profession. I would very much like to believe in the goodness of people again. I sadly see precious little of that in my work."

"Aaron, forgive me if this is a little presumptuous, especially given how short a period of time I have known you – but I think you may be looking for your place, and most especially for love." He began to protest, but she shushed him quickly. "I saw you watching us, you had a look I recognized all too well – it was the look I often had as I watched my family and friends in the Circus. I wanted what they had so desperately, love of what they did and of each other. I never felt I fitted in because I didn't share their passions. But I found it here, that love and the feeling of being a part of something. Maybe you might too. So here." She thrust a newspaper at him. "It's how Matthew and I met. Maybe there is somebody in there for you too." He looked at the page she had left it open at. The Matrimonials advertisements. He laughed out loud.

"You think I should advertise for a wife?" he asked incredulously.

"No, I think you should respond to this advertisement, here," she said pointing at one she had circled.

Young Woman of Boston, seeks educated man to correspond, with a view to matrimony. The subscriber is strong, a capable cook and fine housekeeper and is good with children. Respondents should be kind and gentle, with a good heart. A sense of adventure would be most highly valued. All responses should apply to Box 643, The Boston Globe

"She sounds most practical," he said wryly.

"I think she sounds ideal for you. She can make you a home, and teach you how to live in it - but I think you will also need a wife who will understand that you are always going to be haring off to investigate something - whatever else you may decide to do in your future. If she already appreciates a sense of adventure, I think it may be a very good start." She winked at him and sashayed back inside.

Aaron shook his head in disbelief. The woman was incorrigible. No wonder his brother adored her so much. He re-read the advertisement, and found himself wondering what kind of a woman would write such a thing, would set herself up to potentially move across the country just so she could be wed. He had so often scorned the people who advertised in such a way, had believed it impossible to build a genuine relationship from such inauspicious beginnings – but his brother and sister-in-law and so many of their friends gave him the proof that he was wrong. Maybe he should respond, it would at least help him to answer his questions? Maybe he could write an article about it and submit it to the Globe? At best he might find the love of his life and at worst he would be able to make a few dollars from the experience. He gave Claude one last pat and headed back inside to write a response. He was intrigued as to what he would receive in return.

Chapter Two

Frederica kneaded a large mound of dough at her Aunt's kitchen table. Usually she found making bread to be an experience that helped her to clear her mind, but today as she pounded the dough and shaped it into loaves she couldn't help wondering if she would ever receive a response to her advertisement. She loved Uncle Frederick, for whom she had been named, but Aunt Marian was a hard task master. She seemed unable to understand that Frederica could still be devastated by the loss of her Mother and Father. She was always so terse and curt whenever she found Frederica looking anything less than content.

It had only been twenty-three long months since they had been lost at sea; their bodies never found after the sinking of the boat they had been enjoying a pleasure cruise in around Boston harbor. Aunt Marian did not seem to think there had been anything unfinished about burying empty caskets, the thought that without their bodies it was so much harder to accept. But Frederica still struggled to understand why her loving and kind parents had been taken from her in such a way, to be at peace with her loss. Every day it got a little easier to bear, but it never stopped hurting.

Her Aunt and Uncle were her only relatives, and had been kind enough to offer her a place on their upstate farm following the tragedy. She had nowhere else to go, and her family had left her with little; they had not been wealthy people. She had adapted as best she could to the new rhythm of life on the farm, and had become adept at milking the herd of dairy cows, making butter and cheese. It helped her to keep herself busy, to stop her mind from pondering her losses. She had surprised herself to find that she actually enjoyed it and did not miss the hustle and bustle of the city at all.

"Well my darling girl, "Uncle Frederick said jovially as he entered the kitchen. His vast girth took up much of the doorway, and his ruddy cheeks were always stretched into a happy smile. "Who is writing to you from the newspaper?" She almost dropped the tray of bread she had been about to pop into the oven.

"There is a letter for me?" she asked nervously. It was strange, she had been waiting for this moment, yet now that it was here she could hardly bear it. Butterflies began to beat their wings mercilessly in her belly, and she could feel her breath getting shorter and more shallow.

"No my darling, there is stack of them a foot high!" he chuckled.

"No!" she gasped. "Do not tease me so."

"I would not. But, I cannot help but be intrigued. You have lived here for almost two years now, and barely received a thing from anyone. "

"Will you promise not to tell Aunt Marian? I could not bear the snide comments she would be bound to make," she admitted. She knew that Uncle Frederick would do so, he always appeared to be a happy man but he did not have the happiest marriage. He and Aunt Marian had married because their families' farms had been adjoining and Grandfather had been determined to gain the lush grazing land their neighbors held. They had not been blessed with children, and this had made the already unhappy Aunt Marian become bitter. Frederica was determined that she would not be sold off in marriage in the same way, though she knew Uncle Frederick would never force her to anything. But, she had determined that she would make her own life, and this was the first step towards that.

"When does she ever speak to me, other than to call me for supper?" he asked and she could hear the sadness in his voice. Frederica was sure that he loved his wife, and struggled to cope with her ambivalence, but he was too kind to ever push himself upon her. The sadness in the house was tangible. She vowed to make sure that whoever she chose, her ' husband would have to possess the courage to speak up and tell her his troubles. She did not want to be alone in her own home.

"I placed an advertisement, in the Matrimonials section," she confessed. She found herself unable to look him in the eye, and fussed around checking the bread was correctly placed in the oven before she turned back to him.

"I should be surprised, but I am not. You are a woman of uncharacteristic courage my darling, I should have known you would take your destiny into your own hands. I am sorry our home is not more welcoming to you."

"It is not that," she said, trying to placate him. "I do long for a family of my own and I have nobody to speak for me but myself."

"I will always speak for you, would give you everything that is in my power to do so – and though I know that you believe your Aunt would not, she would. She loves you in her own way. You just remind her that she was unable to have children of her own and that is hard for her."

"I can understand that, and I do try to remember it always. Now, where are my letters," she said feeling oddly sad, and very excited all at once.

She dusted the flour from her hands, and followed him into his study. The pile was indeed much larger than she had ever expected. She prayed that somewhere in there that there would be a man she wanted to know more of, a man she could consider. Her Uncle's assurance that Aunt Marian did care for her did not change how hard it was to live under her roof. She wasn't prepared to take the blame any longer for the hardships Aunt Marian had been forced to bear. None of them was her fault, and it was unfair of her to take her unhappiness out on Frederica.

She sank into her Uncle's elegant leather chair and began to leaf through them. "I shall leave you alone," Uncle Frederick said kindly, patting her affectionately on the shoulder. "Choose well, and if you wish my advice I will always be here for you." He kissed her on the forehead and shut the door behind him. Frederica was astounded, as she counted under her breath. Twenty-eight men had written to her. She leaned back in the chair, and raised her hands to her face. Now she was faced with the reality of the situation it seemed completely unreal. She simply did not know where to start. However would she be able to choose between these men? What criteria mattered most to her in a future husband? What was she looking for? She suddenly doubted her reasons for ever placing the advertisement, her judgment and her sanity.

She opened the first letter in the pile, and began to read. She felt it only right to read every word that these men had labored over, it was only fair she give them an equal chance to impress her. But it was soon clear that many of the respondents could barely write a sentence, let alone make it interesting enough to make her wish to write back to them. She began to despair as she worked her way through the first ten letters. Not one of them asked her about herself, or cared enough to have even read her advertisement carefully. They seemed to have simply responded, thinking she must be desperate, and would therefore consider anybody.

She threw the growing pile of rejected suitors into the fire, and leant wearily against the mantel as they curled up and burst into flames. Why had she ever thought that she could change her life this way? It was hopeless. She moved back to the desk and picked up the remaining, unopened, envelopes and began to feed them into the fire. There was no point in reading them, they would all be the same, she was sure of it. "Frederica," her Aunt called. She wiped a tear from her eye and put the remaining letters back on the desk. She opened the door.

"Yes Aunt Marian?" she said to the haughty looking woman standing in the hallway.

"Your Uncle said you were in here. How much longer does the bread need to be in the oven?" she asked. Frederica looked over her shoulder at the large hallway clock.

"Oh my, thank you for reminding me," she gasped and hurried to the kitchen. "It would have been burnt had you not called." She pulled the loaves out and turned to place them on the cooling racks on the table, expecting to see her Aunt had followed her to give her a lecture about wasting expensive ingredients. But Aunt Marian had not done so. "Aunt?" she asked as she headed back towards the office. She blushed, and felt ashamed as she saw the older woman fingering the pile of letters.

"You have many friends at the newspaper?" she asked, her face icy.

"No, none."

"Then why so many letters?" Frederica sighed, she would have to tell the truth and so she did. Aunt Marian's face remained impassive, aloof. "I see," she said finally. "Have you found a suitable match? I presume there must have been something that intrigued you sufficiently to make you forget your chores."

"They were all terrible. In fact I was about to burn the remaining ones as I have given up hope that there will be anybody worth responding to, if the first eleven were anything to judge by."

"I think that rash. What if the man you are destined to be with is amongst these?" Aunt Marian asked. If Frederica hadn't known her so well, she would have sworn that a smile was playing around her thin lips, but that couldn't be. Aunt Marian never smiled.

"I doubt it."

"Nonetheless, you should continue to read them. I shall go and make a start on the milking for you." Frederica was now stunned. Her aunt never offered to help her out with her chores, and she certainly hadn't set foot in the milking sheds since Frederica had come to live on the farm.

"Why?" she said. "I am sorry, that sounded terrible. But, you have always seemed to dislike me, seen me as a burden you were forced to bear, yet you are being so kind now?"

"Dear Frederica. I am not heartless, though I know I may seem that way. I was once a young girl with dreams of a happy marriage myself. I suppose I could have tried harder to make the one that was forced upon me work better, but I wished to punish everyone for making me wed a man I did not choose. I think it quite possible that the only people who have been hurt by my actions are myself and your Uncle. He is a good man, and I have made his life a misery – when I wished to hurt my own Papa and his."

"Aunt Marian, it isn't too late. Uncle Frederick loves you – I am sure of it. He would welcome you with open arms if you were ever to show him the slightest indications of affection."

"I cannot. It is not proper for a woman to behave so," Aunt Marian said primly.

"Nonsense," Frederica said. "You are married, hardly a young virgin awaiting her first beau. If you want your life to be better then you have to make it so." The words were barely out of her mouth before she wished she could unsay them, but her Aunt did not react in the way she would have expected to her bluntness.

"As you have?" Aunt Marian asked, raising a single eyebrow quizzically.

"As I tried, yes."

"Then, will you take your own advice and continue to see that attempt through?"

"I shall, if you will try and make your marriage a better one for both you and Uncle Frederick. If I find a husband, it would be reassuring to know that I have not left you both here, unhappy and alone when you both wish for something else, something more, something better."

"You are a good girl. I am sorry I have been unkind. I was just so jealous of your mother. Everything seemed to come so easily for her."

"I can assure you it did not. She and Papa worked hard to make their marriage work. If it looked differently on the outside, then that showed how good they both were at hiding the cracks."

"I suppose we never know what is truly happening between closed doors do we?" Aunt Marian mused. "I shall go and milk the cows." She turned and hurried from the room. Frederica was sure that she had seen a tear in her eye, and that though she had admitted to much in their short conversation, that was just a step too far for Aunt Marian. She found herself hoping that what she had revealed was true, that her Aunt and

Uncle would find that it was never too late to reconcile and even build a wonderful and loving marriage. She sat back down and with a sigh opened the first letter.

It took her a further seven to find a man who sounded even vaguely interesting, and another five to find a man she wanted to respond to. His elegant script sprawled lightly across the page. He sounded perfect.

Dear Young Lady of Boston,

I am writing in response to your intriguing advertisement in The Globe. I can only hope that your situation is not a desperate one. I would hate to think that you find yourself in a predicament that forces you to take such drastic measures as to advertise for a husband. I prefer to hope that you are rather searching for love in some new and unconventional way. I admire women who take responsibility for their own lives, their own happiness and I am blessed to know of many people who have been successful in finding wonderful relationships this way.

I am a journalist. I will confess, when I first considered responding to you I did it with a view to maybe writing an article about my experience, but each time I read your words and then try and form my own I feel less inclined to do so. I am a lonely man. I have spent much of my life travelling up and down the country in search of a good story. It is time to stop searching and recording other people's lives, and to start experiencing my own.

I have a brother, and I am currently staying with him here in Montana. Sun River is a lovely spot, with mountains all around and I find myself eager to stay – though if you would prefer I can move back East to be near your family and friends if you would prefer. (Of course, this is presumptuous of me, that you would pick me and marry me! I apologize most profusely for my arrogance.)

He is in the process of selling his farm, and though I confess to knowing little about it, I find myself considering purchasing it from him. He did not know anything when he came here, so how hard could it be to learn? It is in a goodly spot, and has good yields.

He has kept in good heart, whatever that means!

I do pray that you will consider corresponding with me, I am eager to get to know you better and hope you will think we might suit.

Yours most humbly

Aaron Simmons

Frederica sighed contentedly. He sounded perfect, with the intelligence she craved and the desire to make a new start to a life no longer fulfilling him – as she was searching to do herself. She reached automatically for a sheet of paper from her Uncle's drawer, and began to compose a reply. With every word she wrote, she prayed that she had chosen wisely.

Chapter Three

Aaron had discovered that he was a fast learner. As he pitched hay into the barn, he couldn't help humming happily to himself. His body had never ached so much in his entire life, but he felt clean and content in the honest toil he undertook each day. "We'll make a farmer of you after all," Matthew teased him as he entered the barn and took up a pitch fork himself.

"You just might," he admitted, leaning against his fork, taking a breath for a moment. "Matthew, I'd like to discuss buying the farm from you after all. I've led a frugal life, most of my earnings I have saved over the years. I think I could afford to purchase the place from you."

"You should look into gaining the land adjacent too," Matthew said. "The Homestead Act means you can claim land – up to 160 acres. There are two ways in which you can gain legal title to it, proving up or outright purchase after six months. It is how I got this place."

"I shall have to look into that indeed," Aaron said. "What does proving up the land entail?"

"You have to work and live on the land for five years. It can be tough. The first five years are the hardest, as you are taking land never before put to the plough, or to grazing and making it good. But, you still have to do the work if you take the purchase option too, so I think it is wisest to prove up."

"How much would it cost to buy, do you know?"

"When I moved here the cost was $1.25 an acre and a $10 filing fee."

"That sounds more than reasonable, but would I be able to claim if I have already purchased land in Montana?"

"I do not know, but there is a lawyer in Great Falls who specializes in Homesteading. I can take you there so you can talk to him. We can wait for you to buy the farm if you want it too."

"I could not ask that of you, what if I have to wait the full five years?"

"You can still work the farm, just not own it! We can share the profits. But are you truly sure you want to become a farmer?"

"No, but I am beginning to come around to the idea. I like working outdoors, but I noticed that there is no dairy herd nearby? Maybe I could fill that gap. I am just exploring the options right now. The work at the school would be only a few hours a week at most, and the costs to set up a newspaper are prohibitive, and with such a small area of distribution it simply wouldn't be cost effective yet – though if Sun River continues to grow it might be in time. I do not wish to enter politics. I have met enough crooks in my life and have no desire to mingle with them by choice – even though your man is one of the rare few that is not yet corrupt."

"So, staying is a definite possibility?" Matthew asked hopefully.

"I think so," Aaron admitted. "I like it here, and I am tired of having no place to call home." His brother clapped him on the back and then pulled him into a bear hug.

"I am so glad," he said beaming. "We did not want to have to say goodbye."

The sound of a cart pulling up outside made them both turn. Emily was busy at the theatre, a new production was in rehearsal and so she was in town most days to ensure that the director had everything he needed. She often returned home exasperated, and it would appear that today was not any different. She stormed into the barn, her face as black as thunder. "How is dear Mr Lafarge today?" Matthew asked, trying to suppress a grin.

"The man is impossible. I shall be glad when he is gone. Thankfully the play only has a short run, otherwise I should be in fear for my sanity," she said, clearly infuriated.

"What does he demand today?" Aaron asked. So far he had asked for fresh flowers in his office every day, an entire roast fowl to be prepared for his lunch each day – and never the same kind to be served two days in a row, and numerous other little things that were simply ridiculous.

"He wishes me to hire some rigging from one of the theatres in New York, apparently ours is not suitable and he does not trust Ardloe to be able to create something suitable in time."

"Did you not explain that it would take longer to have something shipped from New York?"

"Of course I did, and that Ardloe is a genius, but the man will not be told. I am going to have to fire him. The theatre will go bankrupt simply because of his demands on this one production."

"But, who will we be able to hire at such short notice?" Matthew said anxiously. "We only have a week until curtain up."

"I will have to do it, otherwise there will be no profit at all," Emily said.

"But you do not have the time," her husband said, "and have you ever directed anything before?"

"No, but I do know the play well and the actors know what they are doing. It cannot be so hard. Maybe if I had some help?" she said flirtatiously, reaching up and kissing him.

"I could pop down from time to time, but…"

"We both can. Matthew we have both attended the theatre often, we can see what works and what doesn't," Aaron said. Emily smiled at him.

"Thank you, I would be ever so glad of your support and

suggestions." She turned to go inside. "Oh, I almost forgot. A letter from Boston, for you Aaron," she said turning back and giving him a wink.

"Thank you Emily," he said, amused at the pride in her voice that he had taken her advice.

"I hope she is lovely," she teased. Matthew watched the interplay between his brother and his wife with interest, but could not stop the look of confusion it brought about. They laughed at him, but neither bothered to enlighten him. Aaron could not testify as to Emily's reasons, but for now he personally wished to be able to get to know the mysterious advertiser without his brother getting too excited on his behalf. "Will you both excuse me for a while?" he said, and disappeared out of the barn before either could gainsay him.

He had long since discovered a quiet copse of trees at the end of the main paddock. He often made his way there when he longed for a little peace and solitude. He sank down onto the soft grass and lay on his back for a moment gazing up at the sky. It was not long before Claude came to investigate, and he was happy to spend a few moments fondling the curious animal's nose, and scratching lightly behind his long ears. "Well, she wrote back my friend," he said to the animal showing him the letter. Claude harrumphed softly and began cropping away at the grass. "You are right, why should it matter to you?" Aaron laughed.

He had expected to feel excited, maybe even a little anxious if he were to receive a reply, but he felt peculiarly calm – as if this was just another part of the puzzle of his life that was about to slot into place. He couldn't explain why he had such a good feeling about it, or why he was sure that this young woman and he would suit, but he did. He opened the envelope slowly and eased out the letter.

Dear Mr Simmons,

I cannot tell you how grateful I was to receive your letter. You would not believe the caliber of many of the responses I received. I was astounded that so many people would reply without having even read my advertisement carefully. I can certainly testify that very few had any education, let alone a good one!

I was intrigued when you said you are a journalist. I took a day and went to Boston where I went to the library to try and find as many of your pieces as I could. You have led a most exciting life if you have truly been chasing such stories across the country. To be so acquainted with a world of vice and danger must have been both thrilling and more than a little frightening I would imagine. I would imagine you have probably made some enemies along the way too, though I do hope that is not the case. Your writing is both eloquent and highly detailed. I found it most enjoyable, though often macabre!

I am glad that you think you may have found a place where you wish to rest, somewhere you may learn to call home. To have family is a blessing too precious to waste. Sadly I lost my parents in a tragic accident, but my Uncle Frederick was kind enough to take me in. For much of my time here I have not seen eye to eye with my Aunt Marian, but in recent weeks she seems to have thawed – not just to me but towards my Uncle too. I am glad of this, I think they may finally be learning to love one another, though they have been married for over twenty-eight years.

I have no siblings. I envy you a loving brother. I always wished to be part of a large family, but it was not to be. I hope that one day I will be able to have many children of my own. I never want a child of mine to feel the loneliness I did as a child. But, I am not unhappy I do hope you will believe this, though my words may make you think otherwise.

My Uncle is a dairy farmer, and I have grown to love living in the countryside. I have won awards for my cheese and butter making, and I find I truly enjoy the simplicity of milking and churning. My mind can so often go off on tangents, and I am prone to worries. I find that such tasks help to calm me, to soothe those thoughts away. I thought that I would miss the city when I moved here, but I was happy to find I did not. I got the feeling from your words that you are finding much the same thing.

Whilst in the library, I looked at pictures of Montana. It does indeed look most beautiful, the mountains so majestic. I can entirely understand why it had begun to work its magic upon you. I do hope that it continues to do so, that you choose to settle in Sun River with your family. I got the strangest feeling that being with them is making you much more content than your career has. I am most sorry for my impertinence!

I should very much like to meet with you, would like you to consider me as a possible bride for you as you begin your new life. My Uncle would happily escort me to Montana. I think he wishes to retire, and is looking to find somewhere beautiful to do so. I would not be surprised if he sold up the farm here and followed me if I were to move to Sun River!

I do not wish to scare you with the idea of me and my family turning up on your doorstep, will await your invitation should you wish to meet with me.

Yours most hopefully

Frederica Milton

Aaron smiled as he imagined this young woman sitting at a table, writing this effervescent missive. It amused him that she had investigated him, had found some of his articles and was more than flattered that she had liked them. But, he was stunned at her perception, that she had spotted the potential his work had for creating enemies. He certainly had made his fair share over the years. But, he was sure that none of them would pursue him further if he were to leave his journalism behind. None would follow him to Sun River, they would not even think of such a sleepy backwater as being his home he was sure.

He liked that she was inquisitive, that she so clearly adapted well to new things and that she already had skills in dairy farming. The more he thought upon his future, the more he was sure that it would be the most lucrative option available to him if he were to remain here. There were many farms, many ranchers, even a number of large sheep herds in the area – but there was no dairy herd. He had spent some time with Mack, herding his cattle, and he had found an unexpected tenderness towards the gentle creatures with their liquid brown eyes. But ranching did not appeal to him. He did not want to spend days, even weeks out on the trail taking his animals to and from markets, did not want to have to worry about where to find them. He liked the idea of neatly fenced fields full of happy cows, near to home.

Frederica could bring him the knowhow he needed, and if her Uncle did indeed follow her to Montana, he would have a fount of knowledge on his doorstep. It should not be a reason to marry a woman, but he couldn't help thinking that Fate had taken some steps in his direction for once. He wanted to meet her, wanted to know if they would suit – because so far everything was telling him that she might just be his perfect woman: practical, though clearly passionate; skilled and able to learn quickly; enthusiastic and fun. What more could any man ask for?

Chapter Four

Frederica nervously awaited a response. As soon as she had mailed her reply she had been hit by a torrent of anxieties. She hoped that she had not scared him away with her talk of wanting a large family, or that her Uncle was considering moving to stay near her. She had been surprised herself when he had taken her aside in the dairy one day and told her so. They had both wept as he spoke of his sadness at losing his last link to his beloved brother. But she did not know if he had even mentioned his proposal to Aunt Marian and that worried her. The pair had been showing signs of an improved relationship in recent weeks, and she did not want him to jeopardize his own chances for a happy marriage because he wished to be near to her.

She almost pounced upon her Uncle when she saw him entering the kitchen, brandishing a letter at her. "Thank you," she said, suddenly feeling giddy.

"I shall hope the man has sense," Uncle Frederick said softly patting her on the arm, then sitting himself down for breakfast. Aunt Marian served him his eggs, and even smiled at him. Frederica couldn't help herself, she kissed them both on the cheek.

"I am so happy that you are getting on so much better," she said as she ran out of the room to the privacy of her Aunt's parlor. She sank into the comfortable armchair her Aunt sat in when doing the darning, and felt the warmth of the fire through her plain muslin gown.

Dear Miss Milton,

I am so glad that you chose to correspond with me. By the sound of it you were inundated with options!

I will not beat around the bush, I confess I should be delighted to meet you. I have enclosed tickets for you, and your Aunt and Uncle, to come to Great Falls where I shall meet you. I have to meet with my lawyers there soon anyway, so have arranged to do so on the morning your train should arrive. I do hope that you will come.

I can understand your desire for family. Matthew and I lost our parents when we were young, but like you went to live with our cousins. My cousin Tom in fact lives here in Sun River, he runs the local Saloon. If he had not come here I doubt Matthew would have considered the place. It is small, but growing rapidly. Even since I arrived a further three homesteaders have arrived, and two more stores have opened in town. I like it a lot here, I hope you will too.

I find I do not know what else to say to you, and pray that I will not be so tongue-tied when you and your family make your visit. It would be a terrible waste of money to come all that way only to find I am a stammering imbecile!

Yours Most Hopefully
Aaron Simmons

Frederica smiled and clutched the letter to her breast. Her heart was pounding. He was delightful, funny and smart. She glanced at the tickets, the train left in just a few days. She couldn't ask her family to drop everything at such short notice, whoever would take care of the farm whilst they were gone? She would have to write and decline, maybe he would understand if she tried to reschedule the tickets?

"Frederica, was the letter from your beau?" Aunt Marian asked as she entered the pretty parlor and sat opposite her. She nodded. "You look sad, I do hope he hasn't snubbed you."

"No, quite the opposite," she admitted. She didn't want to show her the tickets, but Aunt Marian's sharp eyes rarely missed anything.

"He has sent you a train ticket? That is quite serious. I presume he intends to ensure all proprieties are taken care of?"

"He sent tickets for us all," Frederica said sadly.

"How wonderful. It would be rather nice to see Montana. I hear it is quite beautiful." Silently Frederica handed her the tickets, expecting her to gasp at the inappropriateness of the date of travel. She was simply too deflated to care what her prim Aunt might think of his being so presumptive. "Ahh," she said once she had read them carefully. "That may pose a slight problem. Give me a moment my dear." Frederica looked up. It seemed that there was something for her to be stunned by every single day with her Aunt these days. It sounded like her Aunt truly was on her side, and she had headed straight for the barn outside where she knew Uncle Frederick would be with the cows in calf.

Curious to see what was happening, under her nose, she got up and followed her. "Freddy, can we find someone to take care of the place while we do this? I should so like to make it up to dear Frederica. I have been such a shrew to her at times." Uncle Frederick laughed and put his arm around his wife. Frederica stared, open-mouthed as he bent down and kissed her gently on the cheek.

"My dear, I am sure I can arrange something. There is a gentleman who once enquired about buying the land. He wasn't sure if he wished to have a dairy herd here, but I am sure he could be prevailed upon to care for them until we can make arrangements. I shall contact him and find out if he is still interested."

"We do not need to sell up in just a few days, but we do need someone to mind it while we are gone," Aunt Marian said, her face a little stricken at the speed in which her husband was making such plans.

"Marian, do you truly wish to remain here? The site of all your biggest pain? You said just the other night that if you could leave tomorrow you would be glad to do so. This is such an opportunity for us all. I am tired, have worked hard my entire life. We have good savings, and the price we could achieve for this place could mean we could live a very comfortable life in somewhere like Montana, if we decided we liked it there. You hate this farm, it is the very reminder of everything that has been bad in both our lives. Why should we not move quickly to put it all behind us?"

"We have been making such progress together," she admitted. "But it seems so much to give up. Both of us have never lived anywhere else, and know nothing else but this life."

"I am sure we can learn, adapt. And it would mean that if darling Frederica marries her young man we could be near her, to see her little ones born."

"I should certainly like that," Marian admitted. "I do hope she will allow us to be involved in her life though. What if she wishes to escape from us completely?"

Frederica was so touched at the lengths both of them were prepared to go to for her, and she emerged from her hiding place in the shadows. "I will admit, when I first advertised that was my purpose," she said frankly. "But things have changed here since then, we have all changed. I would be honored to have you nearby, a part of my life and my children's, if I am so blessed. But I am not sure I can ask you to give up everything you have worked so hard for all your lives on a whim."

"Neither of us has been happy here Frederica," Marian said.

"There was too much history, too much pain here," Frederick added. "I think we shall both be glad to see the back of the old place."

"Then I should send word and pray that it reaches Mr Simmons before we do!" Frederica said happily. She rushed forward to hug her Uncle, and then her Aunt. "It will be a new start for us whatever occurs."

The next few days passed in a flurry of packing. She and Aunt Marian flew through the house, marking the things they wished to keep; those that they needed to take with them to Montana now, and those which were to be kept in storage if Uncle Frederick could organize a buyer for the farm. They also threw away more things than they could have imagined, the old farm house was filled with the possessions of two families after all. Most of the items they discovered in the attics bore no familiarity to either of them. Uncle Frederick spent his days in Boston, at his club and with his lawyer as they tried to find someone who might wish to purchase it.

"My darlings, the gentleman I spoke of is still interested. We finally found him!" he cried as he burst through the door, the night before they were to leave. He had clearly indulged in a few too many glasses of port, but neither she nor Aunt Marian scolded him. It was wonderful to see him so happy. "We signed the papers today, and the funds are with my lawyers as we speak. They will hold them until we decide what to do next."

"Splendid news, but now we must all get a good night's sleep," said Aunt Marian. "We have a long journey ahead of us." They all nodded, and meekly followed her up the stairs. Frederica was about to head into her bed chamber when Aunt Marian stopped her. "Are you sure this is what you want?" she asked kindly.

"I am," she admitted. "Are you?"

"Oh, I am sure I shall learn to live with your Uncle as well in Montana as I would here. I think he is right, that we need somewhere completely new – with no bad memories – so we can have the very best chance."

"I pray it will be so for us all. Goodnight Aunt," she said and reached out to hug her Aunt close. Marian resisted for a moment, but Frederica was over the moon when she felt the older woman relax into the embrace, and hugged her back.

"Good night, my dear. I am sure I shan't sleep a wink. I am not sure if I am excited or petrified," her aunt confessed.

Frederica closed her door, and leant her head against it. She felt much the same way. She longed for a new start, prayed that Aaron was as good a man as she hoped. But she had fears too. He was a clever man, used to a way of living that was fast and exciting. She was not sure that he truly would be able to adapt to the quiet life he professed to desire. But, she admonished herself, she had requested a man with a sense of adventure. Yet, she had not expected that a man whose entire life had been made up of the kind of experiences that his had, would ever respond to her advertisement. There was much to be fearful of, not least that he might decide upon meeting her that she was too dowdy and not for him at all.

Slowly she prepared herself for bed. This would be the last time she ever slept in this bed, in this house. She gazed around the large and airy room, at the trunks tucked neatly against one wall and wondered what the next chapter of her life might hold. She sat on the bed, her knees tucked up under her chin, unable to sleep as thoughts ran amok in her mind. She found herself wondering what Aaron might look like. They had not shared any details about themselves in that way in their letters. What if he thought her ugly? She knew she was not fashionably pretty, but her long blonde hair had been commented on by many. But she knew that many men wanted their wives to be demure, dainty and a little needy. She was none of those things. Her years on the farm had given her strong muscles, and a lithe and capable body. She was not one to wait for anyone to rescue her and she was all too opinionated. Well, she had not said she was anything else in her correspondence, and so she could only pray that he wanted such a bride. It would be altogether too humiliating to be rebuffed now.

Chapter Five

Aaron paced anxiously up and down the station platform in Great Falls. His meeting with the lawyers that morning had been most productive, and he was now the proud owner-to-be of one hundred and sixty acres of land adjacent to his brother's farm. It would not belong to him for five years, but when it did he would have some of the best grazing land in the region for his dairy herds to roam on. The train whistled, a long and loud hoot as it approached the station. He couldn't help but think of all the journeys he had taken himself upon these great iron beasts. He felt a pang at the thought that he would never again be setting off to explore pastures new, to investigate and report on dangerous and ruthless people. A part of him was glad of it, but there was still an urge to do so even now.

As the train came to a halt, the brakes screeching and the pistons groaning, he took a deep breath. He almost choked as his lungs filled with smoke and steam. Spluttering, he narrowed his eyes and tried to make out the people as they disembarked in the haze. He didn't know what he was looking for. He knew only that she was coming. He had never been so nervous, not even when he had faced down Johnny Malone, the hitman sent to kill him. But that was his past, and today was all about his future.

A tap on his shoulder made him jump. "Mr Simmons?" an elderly gentleman beamed at him. He nodded. "Sorry, didn't mean to scare you. I am Frederick Milton. This is my wife Marian," he indicated to a slender woman with a thin-lipped smile and wary eyes, "and my dearest niece, Frederica." Aaron turned a little to see the young woman he was indicating. She was struggling with a large trunk, and trying to bat away a porter who was offering to assist her. He smiled. He had expected she was determined, and independent from her having placed the advertisement, but he had not expected her to be so very beautiful. He moved towards her, as if drawn there by magnetism.

"Miss Milton, it might be best to let the porter help you," he said with a grin. "It is their job after all."

"What business is it of yours," she retorted. Clearly she hadn't seen her Uncle and Aunt approach him. "I am more than capable."

"I am sure you are, "Aaron chuckled. "But, if you were hoping that dealing with your luggage might put off the fateful moment when you meet Mr Simmons, then I am afraid you are too late." She looked up at him aghast.

"You are Mr Simmons?"

"I am, and do call me Aaron Miss Milton."

"Oh my, whatever must you think of me. I just got so nervous. I wanted to just get right back on the train," she admitted, glancing down demurely. She had the longest lashes, and they swept along the line of her cheekbone delightfully. He tilted her head back to his, and she opened her mouth as if to speak, but then stopped.

"I am nervous too, if that helps at all," he admitted. "But I still think we should let the porter do his job. They really are ever so good at it!" She smiled at him, and he felt a pang of desire for her light up inside of him. She had the most adorable dimples. He longed to be able to kiss them both, then her luscious pink lips until they both forgot all about being scared of one another. "Your Aunt and Uncle are waiting for us," he said stepping back from her. Standing so close he could smell the lemon in her hair, and a scent of lavender soap. It was quite delightful and very distracting. "We should make our way home."

The drive back to Sun River was slightly less uncomfortable. Uncle Frederic turned out to be a wonderful raconteur, and he regaled the stories of the people they had met on their journey across the country wonderfully. "Sir, might I spend some time with you once you are settled, to write some of these down?" Aaron asked. He was sure that many editors would love to have such a series of tales to print in their newspapers, about the types of people who made the move from East to West. Interest in such pioneers never seemed to wane.

"Of course my boy. Would be delighted," Frederick boomed. He was a charming and colorful character and Aaron was sure that he and the older gentleman would become fast friends.

Frederica and Aunt Marian sat quietly in the back, clearly they were used to being Frederick's audience but Aaron found himself wishing that Frederica would speak just a little more. She had a lovely lilting voice when she did, slightly deeper than most. He found himself bizarrely wondering if she sang at all, was sure if she did that her low alto would be most pleasing. Though he needed to keep his eye upon the often rutted roads, he took his chances to sneak a glimpse of her whenever he could. She seemed utterly overwhelmed by the beauty of the landscape; her face was a picture of pleasure. It made him happy to see it.

He pulled up, finally, outside his cousin's house. Tom and Catherine had agreed to put the trio up until something more suitable could be found. "Welcome," Catherine called as she stood up, their newborn baby in her arms. "I am so glad you have made it safe and sound."

"The journey was most interesting, if Mr Milton's stories are to be believed," Aaron said with a grin.

"You must not mind Uncle Frederick," Frederica said as she jumped from the wagon, not waiting for anyone to assist her. "He likes the sound of his own voice, and he does tell a good tale." He chuckled at the deftness of her movement, and the lightness of her landing.

"You must meet Claude," he said, not thinking that she wouldn't know who he was talking of. "I think the pair of you may get on well." She looked at him quizzically and Catherine laughed.

"It is a compliment, I think," she said. "Aaron was admiring your elegant jump. Claude is a Circus donkey. He does all sorts of tricks, and his owner, Emily does all kinds of acrobatics on his back."

"Oh, I see," she said, but Aaron could see she was still puzzled.

"You shall meet him later," Aaron said softly. "You are all invited to supper at ours tonight."

"That will be lovely," Aunt Marian said firmly. "But, I do not know about my dear niece, or my husband, but I am getting on in years and am quite fatigued from our journey. Might I please be permitted a few hours rest before we do anything else?" Her family smiled at her.

"Of course," Frederick said putting an arm around her and lifting her from the wagon as if she were as light as a feather. "I should think we could all benefit from a good wash and a lie down."

"Follow me," Catherine said, a gentle smile playing over her lips.

"Well, that was the most romantic gesture I have ever seen between them," Frederica said. Her happiness was tangible.

"You said in your letters that they hadn't always gotten on so well?"

"No, in fact I thought they hated one another until recently. To be fair I believed Aunt Marian hated everyone, but it turns out they were both just unhappy. They are trying very hard to build a new life together. I have high hopes."

"I think you may be right to," he assured her. "Do you not wish to rest?"

"I have been sat on my derriere for weeks. I have done nothing but rest. Could we maybe go for a walk? I have been beginning to wonder if my legs even work!"

"I should be delighted. There is a charming stream behind the house, it leads up towards the river and there is a lovely little falls. I have been known to bathe there occasionally, as there is a delightful pool."

"That sounds perfect, and a swim sounds quite the thing on such a hot day." He gulped, just the thought of Frederica in the water, her hair slicked off her face, rivulets dripping down over her skin was enough to have him almost lose control. But he was determined not to scare her, wanted her to know that he was a gentleman and would never rush her into anything she did not desire.

"If you think you truly might like to swim, I can get Catherine to give us some bath sheets so we may dry ourselves? We could at the very least paddle, I think that could be seen as harmless enough," he teased.

"I am a grown woman Aaron. I have come here with the intention of marrying you, I am not concerned for my reputation," she said bluntly as she set off in the direction he had pointed. He stood, marveling at how forthright she was, then rushed after her. Yes, he had been more than right to respond to that advertisement, and he found himself in a position he hadn't expected: he longed for her to be his bride, the sooner the better. He had liked her on paper, found her physically alluring, but this ferociously feisty young woman was more than he could ever have hoped for.

The scenery they walked through was stunning, but Aaron could barely tear his eyes from Frederica as they made their way up to the falls. She had a tiny waist, one he was sure he would be able to span with his hands if he were ever close enough to try, and gently curving hips that swayed as she walked. But she was also clever, and fascinating. She didn't just talk of clothes and hair and the other meaningless things so many women did. She was opinionated, like Catherine and Emily and she did not hold back on letting anyone know how she felt.

"Aaron," she asked him as they reached the pool. "Do you think we might suit? I know you have barely known me for five minutes, but I find myself oddly impatient." He stopped, and looked around, he could barely bring himself to look her in the eye. This was a question he should be asking her. "I am sorry, I do not mean to emasculate you," she added.

"Damn, woman!" he said. "How do you do that?"

"Do what?"

"Read my mind so easily. I was just thinking that I should have been the one to ask such a question!"

"I am terribly sorry, I am forthright – but even more so when I am nervous. You do not need to answer now, can wait until you know me better. I should not have asked."

"No, I don't mind," he admitted, surprised to find that he really didn't. She was refreshing. "But, we have shared only a few letters and a few words in person. There is more to a marriage than that."

"Whatever do you mean? Surely, the fact we get on is more than is evident in many marriages."

"I know you have seen unions that have stemmed from less than romantic beginnings, but I do not wish to be wed to someone I can merely tolerate," he said as he moved closer to her. She looked up at him, and he felt his heart beat faster. "Especially as I have a sneaking suspicion that I already feel a little more than that for you." He bent his head to hers, was delighted when she moved her lips to meet his. The kiss was soft, gentle but he could feel the heat inside him growing. He pulled her closer to him and ran his tongue across her lower lip. She breathed out in a heavy sigh, and parted her lips so he could plunder her mouth with his tongue.

"I have a sneaking suspicion I may feel a little more for you too," she whispered against his lips. Her arms wrapped around him, pulling him closer to her. He could feel every inch of her pressed against him, and it felt wonderful.

"Then I had best go and take a quick and cold dip before I take you back down to Catherine, so I can arrange a wedding with the minister as soon as possible," he said reluctantly pulling away from her.

"There is nobody here," she said wickedly. "Nobody who would see us."

"You are a temptress and a tease. Get away from me, I will not," he said trying to keep his tone light. "I will wed you first you little minx." She smiled at him, and he knew that he had just agreed to a life that would be more than exciting, every day would be a new adventure.

Chapter Six

Frederica wrapped her arms around herself and smiled. Every time she thought of Aaron, she pictured him dripping wet, emerging from that pool. His smile had been rueful as the water poured off his strong body. She had been half in love with him following his first letter to her, but the sight of him at the train station had left her utterly infatuated. He was beautiful, with his dark brown hair and long limbs. She hadn't followed her Uncle and Aunt to greet him as she had been sure that she would make an utter fool of herself, and so she had. Thankfully though, he seemed to be just as enamored with her as she was with him.

She shivered as she remembered his kiss. That delicious melding of lips, the warmth of his body against hers and the taste of his tongue still haunted her every waking and sleeping moment. But, from this morning that torment would be no more. By midday they would be man and wife, and she would be able to kiss him and touch him whenever she wished. She could not wait. She had never expected to fall so irrevocably in love with anyone, much less a man she knew so little of and yet she had. They had the rest of their lives to learn everything there was about one another.

"Are you ready?" Aunt Marian asked as she came into the chamber that Catherine had so kindly given over to her. "I have your dress."

"I am," she admitted as she took in the concoction of ivory silk and lace that her Aunt had labored over in the last week. "This is so beautiful," she said as she inspected the exquisite stitching and the tiny seed pearls on the bodice. "Thank you."

"It was my pleasure. Just be happier than your Uncle and I were, and your parents were my darling."

"I shall do my best, but it looks to me as though you and Uncle Frederick are more than making up for lost time," she teased. Aunt Marian blushed.

"We have purchased some land in Sun River; we will be building a house there as soon as Ardloe can do so. You will always be welcome."

"I know. Now, shall we get me into this dress and to the church?" Frederica held the gown up against herself and looked into the mirror. She had never looked happier. Her cheeks were flushed, and her eyes were bright. She felt beautiful for the first time in her life.

She walked down the stairs. Uncle Frederick had tears in his eyes. "Your Papa would have been so proud of you this day."

"I know, but are you? Am I making a wise choice? Everything is all so sudden," she said admitting her fears.

"He is a good man. He loves you. You will make it work – because that is who you are my darling."

"Then you had best take us to the church." She tucked her arm into his, and waited for Aunt Marian to join them.

Outside Tom waited on the dashboard of a smart open topped carriage bedecked in ribbons. "Well, my cousin is a lucky man," he said as they got inside.

The sunshine warmed Frederica's skin, though her hands stayed icily cold. She was sure it must be her nerves, but as they pulled up outside the church she suddenly felt calm. She knew she was doing the right thing. Inside, there was a man who made her heart sing, sent shivers of anticipation through her when she merely thought of him, and bolts of lightning when he took her in his arms and kissed her. There was simply no mistake to be made here, and when she glanced around at the faces of the family she would gain as Uncle Frederick escorted her down the aisle she knew that she had finally found happiness.

Aaron looked dashingly handsome in his suit, and wore a smile that warmed even her icy hands. When he took her hands in his she felt as if she was coming home, and she pronounced her vows proudly. He kissed her, as if nobody was looking, and she blushed when she remembered that they were still inside the church. It felt somehow blasphemous to be so focused on only him. They turned to face their new friends and family, and suddenly Aaron's smile faded. Frederica had never seen him angry, yet she was sure that was the emotion rushing through him as he took in a solitary figure at the back of the church. "Who is that?" she asked, feeling afraid.

"Someone I thought never to see," he admitted. "Stay with your Uncle and Aunt. Matthew and Tom will take care of you all. Go, now. Out through the vestry. Do not turn and look back, just go quickly. I have to know you are safe," he hissed at her.

He began to walk down the aisle towards the man, and Frederica went to follow him. But her way was blocked by Matthew. "Come, he will join us later," he said firmly.

"But whatever is happening?" she cried as he almost lifted her off her feet and dragged her away. "Why are you not staying to help him?"

"Because he always said that if the time came it was most important to him that you were safe."

"So, he told you something like this might happen, but not me? I am his wife!" she cried as Matthew finally set her down on her feet outside. Tom and Catherine followed with their baby, with Christopher and Emily not far behind. Uncle Frederick looked pale, and Aunt Marian furious as they joined them.

"I am to take you home," Matthew said to them all. "We need to stay together. There may be others watching. Do you have your rifle Tom?" he asked. Tom nodded.

"I have a pistol," Uncle Frederick said. "As does Marian. She is quite the shot."

"Why am I only learning this now?" Frederica said; everything she thought she knew was wrong, different. She didn't know what to think as she saw her Aunt pull a pistol from her reticule.

She didn't have time to think about any of it though, as they bundled into the carriage and raced out of town. But once they were at the farm, she began to wonder how even her Aunt and Uncle had been prepared for such an eventuality. How had they all kept this from her? Why had they kept it from her? She didn't understand what was happening, and she was more than scared for her husband. Frederica sat, and sobbed. She was wed to a man she barely knew, and she may be widowed just as suddenly as she had fallen in love with him. Was bad luck to follow her everywhere she went? It was not fair. How could this happen on her wedding day, of all days? She knew she was being selfish, should be standing up and fighting with everyone, but she felt so weak, so incapable of dealing with it all. What if he didn't survive? What if she never saw him alive again?

* * * * * *

Aaron walked right up to Quent Treyhorne and stared at him. He stared back. He had clearly been on the run for a long time, he stank of sweat – both his own and his horse's. His stubble had grown out enough to almost be a full beard. Aaron wondered when he had last slept in a bed. "So, finally," he said. Treyhorne grimaced.

"Finally. Nice place this. Shame to see it ripped apart, just because of the likes of you," Quent said dryly.

"You won't be harming anyone here. You came for me, so let's deal with this once and for all."

"Nah, I don't think so." Treyhorne spat on the floor, right by Aaron's foot. "I think I might stick around and get me a nice little wife. I believe there'll be a young widow in need of comforting right soon."

"Over my dead body."

"That was the plan!" He chuckled at his own wit. Aaron gritted his teeth. He had to keep this man away from his family, had to keep him talking so that Sheriff Partlin could get here and see he faced the justice he deserved.

"Well, you might just find I am not the easy target you wished for all these years."

"I know that, you've always been too wily for your own damn good," he said bitterly.

"You alone?" Aaron asked, trying to sound nonchalant.

"Think I am that much of a fool as to open up to you about where my men are?"

"Yes, actually," Aaron said and laughed. "I think if you had any of the gang left at all that at least one of them would be standing right by your side now, and that I would have heard gunfire as my friends and family left the church." A curious look crossed over the outlaw's face. Aaron wasn't sure if he was angry, or just confused. He had never been too bright, but what he lacked in wit, he had more than made up for in brutality. Aaron was surprised he didn't already have a bullet lodged in his chest. Treyhorne was big on shooting first and worrying about it later. "Why are you here Quent?"

"To get my revenge. You ruined my life."

"No, you ruined your own life, I just wrote about it."

"Smart, ya always thought you was so smart," he sneered.

"Smarter than you," Sheriff Partlin said as he entered the church, and his deputy slapped the manacles on to Treyhorne. "He at least thought to warn the authorities you might not be far behind him so's we could all be ready with a nice cozy cell for you."

"You coward," Treyhorne yelled as he was led away. "I'll get you, see if I don't!"

"You had your chance, could have done it at any time since you walked into my wedding – but you didn't. You won't get another one," Aaron called back.

He leant against the pew, as he gasped for breath. He had done everything he could to appear calm, but he knew how close he had come this time. If it weren't for Treyhorne's arrogance he could have been dead. But he knew that facing Treyhorne would be nothing compared to what he would face at home. Frederica was not the kind of woman to take kindly to having been kept in the dark. But it was better to face it now, and so he did his best to stop shaking, and went outside to find himself a horse.

Epilogue

He raced up to the farm, part of him glad that he would be able to tell them all that everything would be alright, but the other part petrified that he had finally found the woman he wanted with every part of his being, only to lose her because of his own stupidity. But, he had his reasons for keeping it from her, he just prayed she would understand. As he reached the screen door he could hear his brother taking charge. Matthew had always been good in a crisis.

"Are you alright?" Matthew asked Frederica tenderly. She almost choked on the sardonic laugh his question created in her. Aaron felt his heart almost break at the fear and worry he must have caused her. He saw the pain on her face through the door and wanted to run to her, but he wasn't ready. He didn't know what he could possibly say to make it up to her.

"Will someone, anyone tell me what is going on?" she said, feeling almost hysterical. Matthew sat down beside her and put his arm around her. He was warm and solid and Aaron knew firsthand that his big brother could be very calming. He could see her face soften a little as she grew less anxious.

"You know Aaron was a journalist?"

"Yes of course, I read some of his pieces. They were ever so good, but he truly did write about some terribly dangerous people."

"Yes he did, and most of them ended up either hung or behind bars where they belonged. But, there was one man, the head of a rather brutal organization, who evaded capture. He has followed Aaron for years. He is not a pleasant man, but we hoped he wouldn't trace Aaron here to Sun River. But, I suppose with both Tom and I here, it was bound to be a place he would locate eventually. We have been prepared for him to come for Aaron, we had to be."

"But he let us come here, let my Aunt and Uncle come here knowing he might have to face this monster?"

Aaron clenched his fists, gritted his teeth and walked through the door. It was not fair that others make excuses for him to his wife. He should be the one to soothe her fears, all their fears. As he walked into the room everybody gasped. "Oh my goodness, you're alive!" Tom cried clapping him on the back. Matthew simply stood up and walked towards him. He wrapped him in his arms silently.

"I think we should leave Aaron and Frederica alone," Catherine said sagely. Everybody nodded and made their way out of the room. Young Christpher stopped and flung his arms around his Uncle's leg.

"I am glad you are safe," he said, a tear rolling down his chubby cheek. Aaron wiped it away.

"I am glad you are safe too," Frederica said once they were alone in a quiet, icy voice. He fell to his knees before her, took her hands in his and pleaded with his eyes. He could only hope that what he said now would be enough to exonerate him in her eyes.

"I know I should have told you," he started slowly. "And I hate myself for that. I truly believed I was finally safe, that he wouldn't find me here and I didn't want to worry you. I was here for so long, and there was no sign of him. He has always caught my tail so quickly in the past."

"But, why didn't you tell me. You told everyone else, and it would seem even my Aunt and Uncle, why not tell me?"

"I do not know. I love you so very much, and I did not want to give you any reason to leave me. I guess I was scared that you wouldn't want to run the risk of being with a man who jumps every time a door bangs unexpectedly in the wind, or spooks every time I hear there is a stranger in town."

"I would have understood. If I had known I could have been prepared."

"If you had known you would have tried to fight him yourself!" Aaron observed wryly. She smiled weakly at his joke.

"You are probably right."

"Can you honestly say you would have left the church as you did today if you had known?"

"No, I cannot. But it still does not mean I should have been the last to know. I have spent every minute since thinking I must be a widow. I will not live that way Aaron," she said firmly.

"I do not expect you to. There is nobody else out there, as far as I know, who is after my blood. But, please I beg you to forgive me. I love you, cannot live without you."

"I am sure I can learn to," she said her smile finally broadening, her dimples revealing themselves in all their glory. He kissed them and then claimed her lips. "After all, if an unhappy marriage like my Uncle and Aunt's can be turned around in such a short time I am sure there is hope for us."

The End

✶ ✶ ✶ ✶ ✶

A Bride for Gideon
Book 9

Chapter One

"Get me Aaron Simmons. Now!" Gideon demanded. His clerk looked petrified; his eyes were wide and he shuffled his feet anxiously. "Damn it man, I am not a demon. Please stop acting as though I am. Just get my campaign adviser here, and quickly." The poor man continued to stand in front of him, wringing his hands. "Do you not understand English? Oh, forget it. I will find him myself." He barged past the young man and rushed along the corridor. He was beginning to wonder if there was anybody he could trust to actually get any work done He was surrounded by idiots.

"Aaron?" he yelled as he poked his head round each of the doors.

"Do calm yourself Gideon," the handsome ex-journalist said with a smile. He was always so infuriatingly chipper, and nothing ever seemed to worry him. But, Gideon was sure that this time he had a problem his bright-as-a-button campaign manager might not be able to solve for him.

"To start with, who is that fool you assigned to be my clerk?"

"Alfie Cahill. He is a wonder with a typewriter," Aaron

said. "He is a little nervous, seems to go into shock if you speak too loudly at him, but I have never known a more conscientious worker."

"You should have warned me," Gideon admonished him. "I think I have probably just scared him half to death in that case."

"He'll get over it. I warned him you might get a little heated on occasion. Now, what has gotten you worked up this time my friend?"

"This." He handed Aaron a newspaper. The headline was bold, and it made him cringe. **'Can you trust this man?'** The columnist had gone on to deliver a damning personal profile, most of which was untrue.

"I had hoped that we might not have to deal with something like this, here in Montana," Aaron admitted as he looked up to look Gideon straight in the eye. "Gardener is known for his overly critical portraits of political candidates. I thought he was working for the Globe in Boston, but I should have known he wouldn't let any governor's race escape his eye."

"But it isn't true!"

"It doesn't have to be. It is an opinion piece. He is commenting about his own personal bias. The problem is that people like him, and read his columns most avidly. His opinion has a lot of sway." Aaron's voice was calm, his demeanor gave nothing away. Gideon simply couldn't believe that this hadn't rattled him, but he was doing a very good job of hiding it.

"So what do I do? Why aren't you more worried about this?"

"For a number of reasons really. Firstly, because I believe that people here in Montana are unlikely to read the East Coast newspapers too often. Secondly of those that do, few will be impressed with this kind of posturing, and finally because there is a very simple thing we can do to get him to change his mind."

"How do you come to such conclusions?" Aaron said incredulously, raising an eyebrow quizzically. "No, I don't think I want to know, am sure it is best if I don't. But I am intrigued. What is the single thing I need to do? You know I will do anything!"

"Be careful who hears you saying something like that my friend," he said with a smile. "You need to get married."

"Married," Gideon spluttered, his knees felt as though they might give way. It certainly wasn't the response he had been expecting. Bribe a few newspaper men to write rebuttal pieces, ignore the comments, make a grand declaration maybe, but not marriage! "But, why?"

"Because, when you read between the lines of all his complaints against you in that piece of drivel, that is precisely what he is saying. He doesn't trust you because you aren't married and do not have the unquestioning support of a loving wife with the right connections. You are suspect because you stand out."

"I don't have time to court a woman, marry her and fight a gubernatorial campaign Aaron! And, I hate to say it but there aren't exactly a lot of women in Sun River for me to choose from, nor do I really wish to be wed."

"She doesn't have to be from Sun River. She can come

from anywhere in the country," Aaron said with a grin. "Do you dislike women, or just the idea of matrimony?"

"You are enjoying this aren't you? And of course I like women, you know that if anybody does!"

"It is definitely amusing. The idea that the most honest and hardworking candidate I have ever met, as well as being the most confirmed bachelor I know is going to have to wed in order to win is quite funny. But it is also frustrating that people cannot see past that and vote on the issues. But it is easily solved."

"It is? I cannot for the life of me see how."

"Do you know how I met my wife?"

"I do, but I am still not seeing how that might help me. I don't really have the time to find a wife by mail order."

"Well, we cheat a little," Aaron said cautiously. "You know Madelaine Butler and Tom's wife Catherine don't you? Both of them come from good families in Boston. I am sure they must know suitable young women who might agree to a marriage of expediency. It could speed things up a little if we can use their contacts to find a bride who wishes to make a change to their situation quickly."

"But I don't want to be married!" Gideon pouted, but then realizing how petulant he must sound he sighed. "I do want to be Governor though. But can we trust the ladies to be discreet? It cannot be made known to anyone that I am seeking a wife for political purposes only."

"That is the spirit. I think we can rely on both women to keep your secret, though there is little reason to tell them the entire truth. I was intending to merely suggest to them that you were looking for a wife, as so many of us locally have done. They are both honest women and they believe in you and your policies. They will need little persuading to try and find you a wife, I know that they have both expressed concerns about your bachelorhood! You never know, you might be as lucky as all of us were with our wives and actually fall in love with whoever we find!"

"I doubt it, but then again I seem to have little choice. I only ask that she be tolerably pretty and enjoy good music. I could not live with anyone who did not," he said glumly. "I hate matchmaking women, and all of your damn wives these days seem to think that a man alone must be unhappy. It isn't true. I like living alone." Aaron grinned and slapped him on the back.

"It isn't as bad as you think. I'll admit I never thought I would want to be settled and wed, but I find I am rather enjoying it."

Gideon made his way back to his office. Alfie seemed to have recovered, and was sitting at his desk in the outer room. "I am sorry for startling you," he said softly. "Please, I am not ever angry with you. It is just there is much to vex a man when he runs for office."

"Ttthank you Sir," Alfie said. "I shall try and remember that. I am very sorry, I just get so nervous at times. I do not know how to stop it."

"We all have something about us we would like to change Alfie. I would wish to control my temper more and will do my best to do so. But then there are the things others want us to change, they just aren't so easy, " he said feeling more than a little worried about what his future might hold. He agreed with Aaron, a wife would solve many of his problems – but if it were ever found out that it was a marriage of expediency it could be even more damning for his campaign than his bachelorhood.

The next few weeks brought a flurry of letters into the campaign office and a number of similar attacks in the press. It was surprising how many people had seen the original article, and disconcerting to realize just how many agreed with its basic premise that a good politician should have a good marriage. He had hoped that his status as a single man would not be an impediment to him, but it was becoming clearer with every day that passed and every attack on him personally that there were too many people who would not vote for him, despite his policies and his dedication, because of such a minor detail.

He had tried to reconcile himself to the marriage he knew he would have to make, but even when he looked at his friends and the joyful relationships they seemed to share he couldn't imagine himself wed. He liked women, probably more than was wise for a politician, but he did not truly wish to saddle himself with just one for the remainder of his days. But if Aaron could find him a woman who understood that the union was simply a measure required, then maybe it would be tolerable. Someone who understood the need to keep up appearances in public, but who would be content to do what she wished and allow him to do the same the rest of the time. But, he found himself wondering, was there truly such a woman? Every woman he had ever known became clingy, demanding – even when they claimed that they accepted he wanted nothing more from them than their company from time to time.

"In my hand, I have the answer to all your woes," Aaron said, sidling into the office with a single envelope in his hands.

"You do? You can convince the entire world that marriage is an institution that does not make a man a better politician?" he joked wryly.

"Sadly, no. But I do have this," he waved the envelope triumphantly. "I have not even had to ask the women to try and think of a friend of theirs, so nobody knows that this is a marriage for your career and not your heart – which is of course a very good thing. If only you and I are aware of that fact, then there is no risk of the press finding it out."

"So, how do you know that this is the solution to my situation, if you have asked no questions of anyone?"

"This is a friend of Madelaine's who wrote to her of her desire for adventure, and her envy that she had found such a suitable match here in Montana. They told me of her over supper a few weeks ago. I did not wish to say anything to you until Madelaine had written to her and asked her to write to you, in case she had merely been expressing romantic desires, rather than a genuine wish for change.

"The woman in question has a good family name – possibly the very best name you could wish for considering you are running for office! She is well connected on the East Coast, and across the country. Madelaine is sure that she would be more than content to make a marriage without knowing you too well. Women of her class are bred to expect that their Father will marry them off to the most suitable candidate, whatever their feelings being considered, and so she has low expectations of finding love in any union. Coming from the stock she does, I almost feel sorry for her, despite her wealth and position; she will have known her entire life that she was merely a pawn." Gideon took the envelopes and placed them on the leather blotter in front of him.

"You are sure this is the only option?" Gideon asked, hoping there may yet be an alternative to this cold and business like marriage, though he knew there was little else he could do with so little time.

"I am sure. But Madelaine also said that she is a good woman, with a wonderful sense of humor and that any man would be lucky to have her by his side. I have had her, and her family, checked out in every way possible and I believe that had we been doing this from choice that you could not find a better match."

"You are terribly thorough," Gideon marveled. It never ceased to amaze him how much detail and care Aaron took over everything. He truly couldn't have asked for a better man to be by his side. He had needed a lot of convincing too, had been determined that he was going to become a dairy farmer, but his herd had taken time to arrive, as his new bride's Uncle had made arrangements to have his own herd shipped from Boston. But the wait had been long, and so Aaron had finally agreed to assist Gideon to save himself from boredom. Now the cows were in Montana, and Aaron was still here, but Frederica and her Aunt and Uncle were more than capable of doing the work needed on the farm. It had been his gain, and he was more than thankful for it.

"That is why you employed me Gideon, for that very reason. Now read the letter, write to her. I will put matters in hand for her to be escorted to Great Falls as soon as is possible, where you will be seen courting her very publicly and then there will be a big Society wedding. We need to get as much publicity about your relationship as we can, so make it look like you find her wonderful even if you hate her."

"I never thought you would ever let me resort to subterfuge Aaron. Like me, I know you hoped we would win it on the issues."

"I can continue to hope that it will not end up being a sham marriage," Aaron said lightly, but Gideon could tell that it bothered him too. "Now, I have things to do and so do you."

Gideon stared at the letter for the longest time. He truly didn't know what to expect, but he couldn't help but think that this was the oddest experience he had ever had. It felt as though he was picking his wife from a store, and it left a rather unpleasant taste in his mouth. He squared his shoulders, and picked up his letter knife. The cool ivory handle felt slick in his hand. He adjusted his grip in order to slit it open, slicing through the thick parchment with the sharp blade. A sudden pang of anger surged through him as he thought of the compromise he was being forced to make, and he stabbed the knife into the mahogany desk, leaving it quivering where it had wedged into the surface. But it did no good, and so he read and did his best to hope this wouldn't end in disaster.

Dear Mr MacAlpine,

I have been asked by my friend Maddy to write to you as she believes we might suit. I had not originally thought of following her example and becoming a mail order bride, but must confess to having been more than jealous of her adventures in Montana. Her letters make it sound as if she has found paradise on earth. She speaks so highly of all her new friends, and especially of yourself. I understand that you are seeking to be elected as Governor of Montana, if you are able to live up to even half of your policies as she extols them, then you will be a formidable man indeed, and one much needed by the people of Montana. I admire your ambition, a man should have ambition – it is most becoming. I come from a political family myself, so understand the breed!

I am also told that you are a good man. I am sure that this is true, as Madelaine is hard to impress, and offers her affections only after due caution. This is a quality that is all too rare I find amongst my Father's peers, and I hope that you will remain so once in power. I begin to wonder if she has been trying to make a match between us for some time, as when I look back over her letters, they are quite often full of praise for you. I feel somewhat odd writing to you now, as if I am forcing myself upon you – but she has assured me that you wish to find a wife and that I am not just writing because she wishes to see everyone she loves as happy as she now sounds.

I was told you only had two stipulations, that your wife be tolerably pretty and that she like music. Well, I have included a small portrait photograph, taken by a rather talented young man here in Boston so you can decide the former for yourself. As to the latter, as all young ladies must, I have been schooled in the pianoforte and paint a little, but my passion is for singing. If I were not in Society I would have chosen to become an opera singer I think. So, I would like to think that I fulfill both your requirements adequately!

I understand that it is unlikely that we might be wed for love and passion – it would be difficult to find that on such a short acquaintance, and from a knowledge of one another only by letter. But I have never truly felt the need for them. I always expected to make a match to further my Papa's political needs at some point, though time is passing rapidly and he does not seem to be in any hurry to offer me up! I am involved in so many charitable organizations I have not had the time to consider that there might be an alternative for me. I would very much like to be able to continue to do the same, my charitable work, should you choose me to become your bride in Montana. I believe it would be prudent as the wife of a politician to be seen to be doing so too.

I must admit to getting a little tired of waiting for my life to start, and so am happy to be able to take this matter into my own hands at last. I believe that by being wed to yourself, I will finally be able to lead my own life. I think that even my fastidious Father would be able to agree that the Governor of Montana would make a most suitable son-in-law!

I look forward to your response, and hope you will consider me.

Yours Most Sincerely

Alberta Freemont

Freemont? He could have run down to his friend's office and kissed him. The daughter of Martin Freemont, adviser to the President's right hand man - and himself a past Governor of Massachusetts - might possibly be the ultimate in political matches. He could hardly believe his luck. She had admitted herself that she had always expected to make a marriage of alliance, he hoped that meant that she understood that he would never love her. She would know exactly how to behave – probably better than he himself did. She would be an asset that no man could attack.

Gideon tapped his fingers against the desk, and re-read her words. He was slightly surprised at Alberta's letter, but couldn't help a nagging worry that crossed his mind as he did. He found himself admiring a woman who clearly knew her own mind, and would obviously be no kind of a burden to him. He also detected a wry sense of humor in her, and he liked that. He liked that a lot. He picked up the photograph she had included. She was a handsome woman indeed, with high cheekbones and long curling hair. She was dressed in the height of fashion, and wore it well. She would undoubtedly help his campaign. Yes, Alberta Freemont was most definitely worth wedding, but what if she secretly hoped to find the love and affection her friend Madelaine had found with William?

Chapter Two

Mrs Lockheart yawned. Not a polite, hidden behind a gloved hand kind, but the wide-mouthed moaning kind. Alberta wanted to laugh, but knew she should not. She held back a chuckle as best she could, it turned into a snort. She often felt bored to tears herself at some of the charity functions she was condemned to attend, but it simply wasn't done to show one's displeasure so vividly. Poor Mrs Lockheart simply didn't know the rules, and this could well be the final insult to the Society matrons who had only reluctantly allowed her position as Christian Lockheart's wife sway them. Lockheart was one of the most powerful men in the country, was the right hand man of the President and his family wealth was almost legendary. But Mrs Lockheart had once been his housekeeper, and sadly had not been taught the things that this clucking gaggle of women deemed suitable.

The speech had been interminably long, the speaker unutterably dull. Alberta had wished she were able to show her own displeasure, but years of breeding had stayed her hand. She almost found herself wanting to cheer the poor woman who would now be ostracized she was sure. Well, she would not do so. She thought about the letter she had written to Mr MacAlpine and wondered if having a little personal sway with the wife of Christian Lockheart might be to her advantage one day. She had no clue of course as to whether he would wish to correspond with her, let alone marry her and rescue her from the tedium that made up her life, but as she looked at poor Mrs Lockheart's anxious blushes she knew that she would befriend her anyway. It was the right thing to do, and that mattered more than any advantage she may gain from it personally.

After the speech had finally ended, the women made their way into the courtyard of the hotel, where a buffet and refreshments had been laid out. The women were already beginning to cluster in their usual cliques, and Mrs Lockheart was being shunned by them all. She stood alone at the table by the punch bowl, sipping at the fruit concoction almost absent-mindedly. "Mrs Lockheart, how lovely to see you here. Politicians get such terribly short honeymoons. I presume your husband is back at our President's side already? But I must offer you my warmest congratulations upon your nuptials. My Father and Mother said the ceremony was quite beautiful," she said, loudly ensuring her voice carried to everyone present. It wouldn't hurt to shame some of these old biddies a little and remind them of exactly who it was they were being so mean to.

"Indeed, he is a busy man, and he is needed. Our country comes above a honeymoon do you not think?" Alberta nodded. "And thank you, it was a wonderful day. So many lovely people wishing us well. Please do thank your parents for the delightful crystal vase they gave to us as a gift. I use it every day for our hallway arrangements. Everybody remarks upon it." Alberta could sense her nervousness, her voice was thin and her hands were quivering, and yet she was still able to find just the right answers.

"They were honored to be invited. Father thinks your husband should be our next President. Says he is a man without fault."

"Well, I think so – but then many might say that I am biased." Mrs Lockheart giggled. Alberta's heart went out to her. She was just trying her best to fit in, to do right by her husband and yet she was being met with scorn at every turn. Well, not Alberta. She would take her under her wing and do what she could to get her accepted and even appreciated by this bunch of harpies.

"It is good that you are in love with your husband Mrs Lockheart."

"I know many people do not believe that, they seem to think that I only married him for his money. But I would have married him if he was penniless." The words were vehement, and Alberta did not doubt that she meant them. She hoped a few people around them might have heard too. "Please, do call me Sarah," she said. "It is so nice to have someone who is prepared to speak with me; I will have to make you my best friend."

Alberta spotted the winces on a few faces nearby, and was amazed at the courage of this young woman to have spoken her truth so simply. She had made light of the words, but her meaning was clear. It hurt her that she was on the outside, and that she found herself in a world she did not understand, without help and guidance or even a friendly face.

"I shall be more than honored," she said briskly. "Now, we shall have to go shopping. You are going to need to spend inordinate amounts of your husband's money in order to keep up with fashion. Why, my gloves are already terribly déclassé, and I only purchased them this morning." They laughed and Alberta could see the gratitude in Sarah's eyes.

"I should like that very much, have not had much time until recently to consider doing so. Much of my wardrobe is hopelessly unsuitable."

"I shall be delighted to change that for you. There is nothing I enjoy more than purchasing clothing, and our delightful new department stores make it so terribly easy now."

By the end of the rally Alberta was pleased to note that a few more women had gravitated towards them. A few had even complimented Sarah on her morning gown and neat hat. Alberta had smiled to herself with each little victory, and had been happy to share a wink or a raised eyebrow surreptitiously to show their amusement at the women's shallow vanity. When her carriage pulled up outside she turned to Sarah and kissed her warmly on both cheeks. "I shall see you tomorrow? Is eleven too early?"

"Alberta, you forget I was a housekeeper. To me eleven is

quite late!" A few faces looked stunned that she had so openly admitted her past occupation.

"I suppose it would be. But, will it suit?"

"It will. I look forward to it."

Alberta sat in the back of her comfortable barouche and thought about how difficult life could be for those not born into the ranks of the upper classes. Young ladies were encouraged to take up their causes, to champion the poor and the sick and even to help working women stand up for their rights. Yet when one of the very people they campaigned for, so vociferously, appeared in their midst, Society did not approve. Yet, they could not take Mr Lockheart to task for his infringement, and so they blamed his wife. It was simply not deemed to be possible that such women could genuinely love their husbands, they must only have married them to get their dirty hands on their money. Yet, it seemed to Alberta that she knew of few genuine love matches amongst her own class. Most had married for money, or to create links politically. Maybe that was why so many of these unhappy, unloved matrons so despised those wives who had been married despite these things and were truly loved and cherished by their husbands.

She had known that she would make an advantageous match since she was a girl. There had been no secret made of it in her home. Yet Papa still had not found her a husband. She was getting older, and she was beginning to wonder if he ever intended her to marry. But she longed to have children, and she knew that time was running out for her. She raised her hand to her hair and began to twirl the long golden strands around her fingers as she tried to think of why it could possibly be that she, as one of the most eligible heiresses on the East Coast, had not yet been found a suitable husband. She would have to ask her parents, but both of them were always so vague and so often tried to change the subject whenever she brought it up that she had simply stopped trying. And so, when her old friend, Madelaine, had written to her of her friend Gideon MacAlpine's intention to advertise for a bride, she had thought it to be the answer to her dilemma. If a marriage would not be arranged for her, then she would do it herself before it was too late. Everything seemed to have worked out wonderfully for Madelaine and William, they had even found a deep and abiding love. Maybe she might be so lucky too.

The carriage stopped outside an elegant mansion and her driver jumped down to open the door. A neat set of steps dropped down and he offered her his hand to assist her. She alighted gracefully and skipped inside the imposing building. "Chalmers, is Papa at home?" she asked as the butler swung the heavy oak door closed behind her. She took off her hat and gloves and passed them to a maid, who bustled out of sight with them.

"He is in his study Miss Alberta. There is a letter for you in your room. It was delivered just after you left for your rally. It is from Montana, I presume from Miss Madelaine, sorry Mrs Butler," she corrected herself. Alberta grinned, she still found it odd to think of lovely Maddy as married too, but it was definitely so. She didn't doubt it would be long before there was the pitter patter of tiny feet on the way too. "I know you always look forward to her letters Miss."

"Thank you, I shall read it later once I have seen Papa," Alberta said, dismissing the faithful old retainer with a warm smile.

She walked across the grand hallway and down the corridor towards the wood paneled study. The scent of her Papa assailed her nostrils as she opened the doors. It was a heady mixture of hair tonic, cologne and cigar smoke. It always made her feel safe and cosseted somehow. "Good afternoon my darling," Papa said as he looked up from his desk. "How were the dragons today?"

"Breathing just as much fire as usual," she said with a grin. "Poor Mrs Lockheart seems to be their current prey."

"Oh dear, that won't make Christian a happy man."

"I'm sure it won't, but I doubt she will ever mention it to him. She would not wish to trouble him I don't think."

"You may well be quite right. She is a sweet little thing, utterly besotted with the man. Have no idea why, he can be an intransigent devil!"

"You know you admire him, and his politics, so you are fooling nobody Papa," she chided him gently. He smiled at her indulgently.

"So, what did you wish to see me for?"

"An advance on my allowance, if I may? I offered to take Mrs Lockheart shopping, and it would look most peculiar if I do not purchase some new gowns and hats myself," she said batting her eyes at him and trying to look girlishly innocent. He laughed, seeing through her ploy quickly. He stood up and moved around the desk to kiss her on the cheek.

"Thank you my darling. Christian will be very grateful I am sure. Have the seamstress, or the department stores, of your choice send the bills to me, and here," he handed her some money from his pocket, "treat her to a nice lunch somewhere too." She hugged him.

"Thank you Papa."

"You are a good girl, have never been any trouble. I simply couldn't say no to you, especially when it is for such a good cause - now get away from me before I give you the world. I have work to do!"

She ran up the stairs and into her room. As Chalmers had promised there was a letter waiting for her on her bureau and she picked it up and flung herself down on the chaise in front of the fire to read it. The handwriting was unfamiliar, a male hand she was sure. She looked at the return address, it was from him. She sucked in her breath, and felt a flutter of excitement as she ripped the envelope open. She prayed he would be amenable to their meeting, to their being wed. She so wanted to start a family, to have a child of her own to love and care for.

Dear Miss Freemont,

I am delighted that you were open to the proposition I sent to you, via our mutual friend Mrs Madelaine Butler. I read your letter with much hope that between us we may indeed come to some kind of arrangement that will suit us both. William and Madelaine have both been most vocal on the subject of you, and both seem more than eager for us to find the kind of contentment that they have found. I must tell you now that Sun River seems to have had more than its fair share of 'mail order' romances; many of my friends have either placed or answered advertisements to achieve their happiness. I do hope that their luck will rub off on us!

I will not deny that your Father's political contacts would be of particular benefit to me, to have the ear of such a distinguished ex-Governor cannot harm my own gubernatorial campaign after all. But it was your pragmatism and straightforward manner of writing that made me think we truly might suit, and what I detected as a wry sense of humor too. I do not wish you to think that I would choose a wife simply because of the contacts and support that she might bring to my campaign!

I would have no objections to your wishing to pursue your singing further, should you choose to do so here. I know it would be frowned upon in Boston and New York, but Montana likes to do things a little differently. Women have, in some ways, much more freedom here to follow their own paths. I would certainly not wish to get in your way. However, I would need you to be circumspect, and obviously discreet about any views you may hold that do not agree with the policies I stand for. I would also need you to attend many key functions with me, especially in the early days of our marriage, should we decide that we suit.

I do appreciate that this may be hard to do, but I can assure you that I will more than make it worth your while once the campaign is done and I am elected. You will be free to ask me for anything you desire, and if it is in my power to grant it I shall do so.

I have enclosed a ticket to Great Falls. The sooner you can come here the better, though I must warn you that our every move will be scrutinized in the gossip columns, and we shall rarely have a moment alone. But the campaign will be over in time, and then a few weeks of work and then we can fade from sight a little. I know it sounds a terrible chore, and I know I am asking for much as I do not yet know you, nor do you know if you will even like me – but I can assure you wholeheartedly that I will do my best to ensure you have a good life, a happy life, with me.

Yours most truthfully

Gideon MacAlpine

Alberta sat up, and perched on the edge of her seat. His letter was surprisingly affectionate. He had not been rude, or demanding. Nor had he seemed arrogant. His confidence that he would be elected was actually quite attractive. She firmly believed that a man should believe he is going to win if he is to even stand for election. But he gave her neither false claims, nor platitudes and she respected that. He was prepared to admit that his life would be less than pleasant for some time, that she may not be high on his priorities until it was all done.

She had her doubts; no sensible woman would enter into such a situation without them she was sure. But he sounded genuine, as if he wished for a wife for all the normal reasons, someone to support him and care for him, someone for him to cherish and to honor. The letter was not gushingly romantic, but she felt sure that she could consign her fears that he was simply looking to wed to further his chances in the election to rest. He seemed to want to share in the kind of good fortune that his friends had found, and she did too. She looked at the ticket he had enclosed. Understandably he could not come to her at this time. Her train would leave Boston later in the week. She barely had even three days to get packed and ready to make the biggest change of her life. But she knew she was ready for it, and she knew exactly what she would ask of him when the campaign was done.

She sighed heavily. It was exciting, and daunting to think of her new life, as the wife of the Governor of Montana – should he, please God, be elected. There was much she would have to do before she left, not least telling her parents of her intentions. But, it also meant that she only had three days to transform Sarah and get her accepted into Society. It was a difficult ask but, like her soon to be husband, she had the confidence to do it. Sarah had all the raw materials. She was bright, funny, attractive – and most importantly she had a lot of money now. If she looked the part, and knew the rules, she would soon have them all eating out of her hand. Alberta would make sure of it.

Chapter Three

Gideon paced anxiously in his hotel suite. He didn't know if he was worried that she would be on the train, or that she might not come. He had never felt so nervous in all his days. He had far less concerns about whether or not he would be voted Governor or Montana than he did about meeting Miss Alberta Freemont. He needed her. He didn't want her, but he needed her and that was a situation he did not like the idea of. He despised feeling beholden to anyone, it made him feel weak and powerless. If Alberta agreed to marry him he would be in her debt. Her family name, her Father's connections could all hand him the election and he wanted the governorship terribly. But, he couldn't stop asking himself if he wished to win, and never know if people had voted for him because of who he was and the policies that he stood for rather than his wife's not inconsiderable attributes.

Aaron had wisely decided that their first meeting should happen in private. They did not want him to be seen greeting his future bride from the train, wanted no rumors to be spread that they had met in anything other than the most respectable manner. There was to be a ball, here in Great Falls this very evening, where they would officially meet and fall in love for the very first time. Gideon hated the need to stage every element of this, but there was little time and much to be achieved to negate the press coverage that had been ravaging his campaign. "Are you ready?" Aaron said popping his head around the door.

"No," Gideon joked. "I don't think I will ever be. But, thank you for everything you are doing for me."

"It is my job, but I really think this is going to work out perfectly. Madelaine and William will be meeting her about now. They will drive here to the hotel and get her settled into her room. We will have a private lunch in the suite here, where the two of you can meet surrounded by friends. Freddy is just getting dressed, and Emily, Matthew, Christopher and the baby have just arrived and will be here shortly to stop you fretting. You know how Chris loves to play with his Uncle Gideon." He did indeed, and he loved the young lad. He even found himself wishing that his friends had brought their talented donkey Claude with them, he would break any tension in moments with his circus antics.

"Gideon, you look more nervous than I was the day I collected Emily from the station," Matthew's booming voice said as he entered the suite of rooms. Christopher burst in front of him.

"Uncle Gideon, have you seen the carriages outside? This hotel must be full of lots of very important people," the lad said as he hurled himself into Gideon's arms for a cuddle.

"It is indeed," he said solemnly looking at the little boy's serious face. "And none of them are more important than you or your Papa."

"Mama is with Clara," Christopher confided. "She is too little, and is tired after the journey, but Mama will be here soon."

"I am sure she will be. Now, if you look over there in the corner I think you will find that there is a large box with your name on it. I am sorry I was away for your birthday." Christopher ran over to the large gift excitedly.

"May I Papa?" Matthew nodded.

"You don't have to, you know," he said to Gideon. "I know that you are fond of the lad, but..."

"I know I am not real family, but he is a good boy. Nothing could spoil him, not with you and Emily keeping his feet firmly on the ground."

"Thank you, I think! Well, you look positively petrified, and I see you have no nails left," Matthew said as he looked at the bitten tips of Gideon's fingers.

"I can't help thinking this is all going to go wrong somehow. I find myself more than a little concerned that the press will see right through such a ploy; that she will take one look at me and decide that I am a fool; or that we hate each other and cannot reconcile on any issue."

"That is why we are all here now. This way you can get accustomed to one another a little more slowly. It is going to be

a whirlwind romance, but this will at least help you find out if
there are any major clashes before you are ever seen in public."

"I am so glad Aaron told you about this, it is good to have
your counsel my friend."

"I have told nobody else, not even Emily. But it will all be
well. Madelaine says that Miss Freemont's father campaigns for
many of the issues you do yourself, it is likely she will share his
views. I think Aaron is right, we couldn't have found a more
perfect wife for you if we had searched every inch of the land."

"I do so hope you are right!" Gideon said emphatically.
So much was riding on this marriage. It had to happen, and
everything must go smoothly. But, they stopped speaking of it as
a column of waiters appeared, bringing a large round table into
the room, and sufficient chairs to seat them all. They moved the
furniture to accommodate it, and then laid it with immaculate
linen table cloths and gleaming silverware. Gideon watched
avidly, it helped to calm his mind as they paid such close
attention to the position of every item, the deft manner in which
they put a shine on the glasses and the dramatic flourish of the
napkins.

Aaron entered as the waiters departed. "She is in her
room freshening up. She and Maddy had a tearful reunion, and
she seems utterly impressed with William. Let's hope she finds
you as favorable," he joked.

"Don't, Aaron I am not sure I can take this. Maybe we
should just take our chances."

"I don't think so. I think you will be more than happy my
friend. That photograph did her no justice. She is quite

magnificent."

"She is?" Frederica said as she entered the room behind her new husband with Emily and baby Clara. "Do I need to be concerned that you will throw me over for her?"

"Not unless she comes with a healthy dairy herd," Aaron teased as he put his arm around his wife's waist and kissed her affectionately. Matthew moved to embrace his wife too, and cooed at his little daughter. Gideon felt an unexpected pang of envy at the closeness they shared. He hadn't ever felt that way about any of his friends as they had wed, but as he looked around him at the happiness these people shared, he began to wonder if being alone was such a good idea after all. He shook his head, trying to get rid of a feeling that just wouldn't die. He was not a man who needed anyone else, did not need a woman to make him feel whole. Yet, if that was true why did he long to have the connection with another human being that he saw all around him? Why did he find himself hoping that Alberta Freemont truly was the kind and generous person that Maddy assured him she was?

"How much longer do I have to wait?" he said, exasperated with himself and the ridiculous way his thoughts were headed.

"You don't," a smooth and elegant alto voice said. There was a hint of laughter, but also a tension in it too. Gideon looked up, and saw Alberta Freemont standing in the doorway. She was a perfect vision. Her long blonde hair had been stylishly curled, and hung down over one shoulder. A neat hat was pinned at a jaunty angle on her head, and her elegant gown was at the height of fashion. It clung to her curves, and flattered her tiny waist. But it was her face, with the lusciously full rose-red lips and the brightly intelligent blue eyes that held his gaze. "I didn't know if I should knock, but the door was open," she added with a smile.

"Wwww…welcome!" Gideon stuttered. "I am so terribly sorry. We thought you were freshening up?"

"I was, it doesn't take me long. I'm not one to primp and preen," she said smiling.

"That is good to know." Gideon could sense that his friend's were finding it funny that he was so tongue-tied, it simply never happened to him before. But, he had been caught unawares, and he hated to be at a disadvantage. "Shall we sit?" he said pulling out a chair for her. She sat and unpinned her hat, he took it and put it carefully on the bureau in the corner. He tried to take a couple of deep breaths. He had truly not thought that he would find his future wife so very attractive, her pure physical impact was having an effect on his body and mind that he had not anticipated. What had seemed to be such a good idea, to have this meeting amongst friends to ease the mood suddenly seemed the most foolish thing in the world. He wished that they were having this meeting alone, so nobody else but she were witness to his discomfort.

He indicated that everybody should sit. Madelaine snuck to his side as the others chose their seats. "She is lovely isn't she?" she whispered. He nodded, a lump unexpectedly had formed in his throat and he barely trusted himself with speech any longer. "She was so excited, couldn't wait to meet you." He took his seat at Alberta's side, and took a large gulp from the water glass that she had filled for him. He wished it had been wine; that might have given him the courage he felt he was lacking to deal with this insane moment.

"My Father tells me that you are by far the President's preferred candidate," Alberta confided quietly. "He was a little surprised, I think, when I announced that I was coming here to meet with you – but he said I could do much worse." Gideon knew she meant the words to reassure him, but just the sound of her voice seemed to make him feel even more nervous. His body was reacting in a strange way to her, his skin was prickling and he felt flushed.

"I am glad to have his approval," he admitted. It was true, but he longed to be able to say something more, but he seemed to have lost every word he had ever known.

"Now, Madelaine told me that you wish to extend the scope of the Homestead Act, "she said. "Do you not worry that it may attract too many of the wrong kind of people to Montana? People that think they can get everything for free?" He could see that she was not being judgmental, was truly curious. He couldn't help but find that attractive too. She asked sensible questions and there was a strong intellect within her, he was sure of it.

"All of us here have all benefitted from the old provisions, and I am sure every person here can attest that carving out a living from your acres is definitely not being given something for nothing," he said with a grin. Matthew, Aaron and William all nodded their agreement. "I hope it will attract even more adventurous, hard working men like those that have already come to Sun River. We have all this land, and much of it lies unused. We could be as wealthy as Massachusetts, or New York – more so if we can get the people here to build Montana and help it take its place amongst the wealthiest States in the Union." She nodded, and he liked that she didn't immediately speak, that she took her time to think about what he had said.

"Yes, of course that makes perfect sense. You have truly grand plans then?"

"I do. Montana is a big State, with a big landscape – it should have big ambitions too don't you think?"

"I do." She smiled at him and he felt his breath catch. Her entire face lit up, as if she had an electric light inside of her. Her eyes crinkled at the edges, and he found himself wanting to kiss her delightfully plump lips. This was not what he had expected at all, but he couldn't help but think that being so very attracted to this woman might make things more difficult. He could not afford to be distracted at this time, and Alberta Freemont was definitely a distraction. He simply could not afford to be attracted to his wife to be. This was to be a marriage of expediency, it could not ever be more than that. He needed his wife to support him, to appear in public as the perfect ambassador of his campaign. He did not want to find himself fascinated by her, could not permit himself to have feelings for her other than admiration. He would have to tell Aaron to send her back to Boston. He could not be seen in public mooning over her, even worse looking as he felt right now – as if he would ravish her if given the slightest encouragement.

The luncheon finally over his guests retreated to their

rooms. "So, what do you think of her?" Aaron asked him quietly, after blowing out the smoke from his fat cigar. Gideon swirled the brandy in his glass, watching the golden liquid slosh around as he wondered if his life would ever be simple again.

"She is witty, attractive," he said, trying to sound nonchalant. His all too visceral reactions to the woman would remain his secret.

"Attractive?" Aaron asked him, his eyes wide in surprise. "Good God man, are you blind? If I weren't already happily married, I would be fighting you for her. I simply do not understand why her father hasn't yet married her off. It certainly can't be for wont of offers!"

"She is attractive," Gideon asserted, doing his best to keep control of his words while his body still remembered the light touch of her hand on his arm as she had left and he could still make out the light scent of gardenias and jasmine lingering in his nostrils from her perfume.

"So, will she do?" Gideon sighed. It was the question he had tussled with from the moment she walked through that door. She was perfect in every way, but one. Most men would be more worried about that reason than any other when choosing a bride, and yet for him it seemed impossible that he should be so drawn to his wife. He did not want a slavish devotion, he needed a pragmatic union. His wife must understand that his work would take him away from the home for months at a time, and he must not dread the thought of leaving her. He could not afford to be enamored of his wife, it would make him weak and Alberta Freemont had everything in her power to make him adore her.

"There is no reason to reject her," he said reluctantly.

"But...?" Gideon asked perceptively. Gideon had no answer for him. "I see, you think you may end up liking her too much."

"It is a possibility."

"One can never like one's wife too much. The public will like you all the more if you seem to genuinely be in love with her. Trust me, as an ex-journalist I know that the gossip columns are the most popular in any edition. The public love a scandal, but they love a romance even more. Here, take the ring," he handed Gideon a small box. He opened it. A sparkling diamond nestled within, set into a simple gold band. It was exquisite, and he had no doubt that it would look even more so on Alberta's delicate hand. "Ask her at the ball tomorrow night. Let the newspapermen see that ring on her finger. We'll see your popularity soar."

Chapter Four

The maid had laid her gown out on the bed. Alberta had been delighted to find this beautiful blue silk in her shopping excursion with Sarah before she made her way here to Great Falls. It was the perfect shade, and set off the color of her eyes perfectly. She checked the seed pearls were all still in place, and her inspection complete she began to feel that she was almost ready to face the public at the ball. This single day was so important, much would be decided upon following her performance tonight, and she was determined not to let herself, or Gideon down.

She had been surprised to find that Gideon was so young. She did not know why, but she had expected him to be closer to her Father's age when he had run for Governor – yet he was only a year or so older than herself. He was handsome too, with a patrician look that she knew would serve him well. His well cut hair looked soft, and it fell over his forehead in an endearing way that made her long to push it back, to see the full glory of his sharp cheekbones and strong jaw. His green eyes were full of humor, and intensity. She could tell he would make a good politician for his people, would not allow himself to be bullied into accepting less than his convictions would allow. Few politicians seemed to have that quality anymore; it may not make him popular within government but would certainly make his constituents love him. He would be formidable, she was sure of it

Sitting so close by him at the intimate luncheon yesterday, she had been utterly distracted by his sheer physical presence. Though she hoped that he had not noticed just how deeply the very scent of him, warm citrus and spice, had impacted upon her. But she knew that this marriage was important to him. She would have to ensure that she did her best to keep her desire hidden from everyone, including her husband to be. Passionate love was not often an asset in politics. It would be her job to be seen as demure and supportive, the perfect wife and mother. To let anyone see the desire she had felt from the moment he had looked up at her would do him no favors.

As she gazed at her reflection in the looking glass, she admired her high cheekbones, and fiddled with her hair to ensure it fell perfectly. She picked up a brush and applied kohl carefully to her eyes to make them seem larger, and a tiny touch of rouge to her cheeks and lips. She hoped that Gideon would at least think her attractive, even though she was resigned to the thought that he may never love her. She was not sure if she would learn to love him either, but she had certainly felt a thrill of pure pleasure just being in his presence. But, she knew it was essential she not show it, that even he never know just how his lightest touch sent such thrills through every inch of her body. She shivered as she remembered how his strong thigh had brushed against hers under the dining table, and how his gentle kiss farewell, demurely on the cheek, had sent her into raptures of delight.

"Miss, are you ready?" her maid asked. She nodded and stood so that the young woman could lace her tightly into her corset. She clung to the bedpost, holding her breath as the laces were expertly tightened. "Can you still breathe?"

"Barely," she gasped.

"Then it's just tight enough," the maid said in a matter of fact tone.

"I think we can afford to permit me to breathe a little more easily," Alberta said as she began to feel a little lightheaded. "I do not need to impress too much, I am sure that my name and who my Papa happens to be are far more attractive traits to the attendees of this ball than my waistline ever needs to be."

"Miss, I am sure that is not true. There will be many important people there, and the press of course. Lovely young lady like you could make quite an impression, could maybe even find a handsome husband."

"Even more reason that I be able to breathe, it would be most impolitic if I were to have a feinting fit as I am introduced to someone who might wish to wed me, don't you think?" The maid grinned at her and reluctantly let out the stays a little. Alberta gasped for air, and rubbed at the skin where the corset had pinched tightly under her arms. "Thank you," she sighed. In moments she was dressed, and she made a few final adjustments to her hair and dabbed perfume at her throat, wrists and décolleté.

"You look lovely," the maid said approvingly. "I bet you'll have a wonderful time. I've always wanted to attend a grand ball. But, it isn't the place for the likes of me. But, I must admit all the politics is a bit beyond me, but that Mr MacAlpine is ever so handsome isn't he? And always seems so nice. If I could vote, I think I'd vote for him." Alberta smiled inwardly at the young woman's praise of the man she most hoped to impress tonight. She hadn't expected to feel too much for him, even though she had come here to meet with a view to matrimony. She had simply longed to be able to start her own family at long last, and it had been too good an opportunity to pass up on – one that just might offer her that chance. She had not believed in love at first sight, had scorned her friends who said that they had felt that way about men in the past - yet she had been smitten from the second she set eyes upon him.

She took out a single strand of rose pearls, and handed them to the maid. She lifted her hair carefully and the young woman fastened the clasp. The maid swiftly tidied the room and made her exit, Alberta was left alone. The silence was tangible. She looked at herself in the mirror and took a deep breath. She looked as beautiful as she had ever done, and she had her father's name on her side. There was no reason why this marriage should not happen and every reason why it should, and yet she found herself filled with nervous tension. Butterflies flew in a torrent in her belly, her fingers shook, and her shoulders felt tight.

A knock on her door broke the silence. She opened the door and Madelaine entered. She looked as beautiful as ever, in an elegant green silk gown. "I had to let the seams out. I have gained so much weight!" she chuckled.

"Could you be pregnant?" Alberta asked her curiously.

"It is possible, but I think it is because I am so content. We live a relatively simple life, William and I, but it is a good one. I no longer have to fret about whether my eyebrows are perfectly plucked, my hair set just right, or how tightly my corset must be laced. I eat what I like without fear for my figure and it is delightful."

"It sounds it," Alberta said enviously. "But I doubt that will be my lot."

"No, as the wife of a politician you would remain under close scrutiny I am afraid."

"I am sure I can stand the burden," Alberta said with a wry smile. She had been in the public eye her entire life because of her father, she knew no different way to live. She could not miss what she had never had.

"You like him don't you?" Maddy asked perceptively. She wondered if she should be honest with her dearest friend, her concerns seemed so strange.

"Yes I do," she said eventually, making up her mind that she needed to confide in somebody. "I did not expect to, but I find him utterly fascinating."

"I felt exactly the same way about William. Do not worry, it isn't a bad thing to be in love with your husband. In fact it can make it all so much more pleasant." Maddy grinned lasciviously.

"But your husband loves you back. I am no fool, I know that a man like Gideon is only marrying because it will do his campaign good – but I am not sure if I can agree to a marriage where there is no love returned. When I believed it would be a simple trade off for us both, he got a wife and I got a child, it was equal somehow. But, I do not think I could bear the thought of him choosing a mistress over me, or not being by his side every moment now."

"You have a difficult decision to make. I can only offer one piece of advice and that is this. Follow your heart and not your head for once my dear friend. You have done the right thing, in every situation your entire life. Why not, just this once, grab at something for yourself? He may have deeper feelings for you than you can ascertain, he may learn to love you in time – but even if he does not would you rather have a life with him, or without him?"

Maddy tucked her arm into Alberta's and they made their way downstairs to the grand ballroom. Her friend's words echoed in her ears as she was introduced to more of Madelaine's friends from Sun River, and to some of the more influential citizens of Great Falls and all around Montana that had made the trip tonight. Her years of education in deportment and manners served her well as she smiled and made small talk. Nobody would have known of the turmoil inside her as she eased her way around the room. It was not long before her dance card was full, and she had yet to even find Gideon in the crowds. She had kept the first dance before supper, and the one following it for him, she hoped that would please him. She could hardly wait to be in his arms, to have his tall, strong body pressed so closely against her own.

"Miss Freemont, I see you have been making an impression on all you meet," a deep and rich voice she would have recognized with her eyes closed said from behind her. She turned, smiling nervously. Gideon looked spectacular in his formal evening wear.

"Maddy, Emily and Frederica have done their best to introduce me to everyone they know," she replied, smiling nervously.

"You look stunning," he said simply as he took her hand. Even through her long gloves she could feel the heat of his skin. "I do hope I am not too late to claim a dance with you?"

"I have saved you two," she admitted honestly. She saw no reason to play coquettish games.

"Before and after supper I hope," he said politely.

"Of course."

"It will be my pleasure," he said as he gallantly kissed her hand. "I am sorry, but I must circulate amongst the guests. This is sadly not a pleasurable event for me, I must work for my supper!"

"Then I shall allow you to go and do what you must." He bowed, and then disappeared into the crowds. Alberta felt strangely bereft. But she was soon being whirled around the dance floor by a parade of lively young men.

She had barely stopped to catch her breath for over an hour when Gideon reappeared, tapping her then partner on the shoulder to announce his intention to cut in. "You seem to be the belle of the ball," he said smiling down at her. "I have found it hard to tear my eyes from you, thought I should have been busy talking to rich and powerful men who just might help me become Governor," he teased. She was flattered by the flirtatious tone, but she doubted that he had been distracted for even a single second. She was sure that Gideon MacAlpine was more than capable of focusing on what he wanted.

She did not know how to respond to him, his physical presence was overwhelming. To be held so closely to him, to be held in his strong, yet gentle, grip was tantalizing. She felt quite lightheaded, and was more than glad that she had insisted on loosening her corset. "Miss Freemont, you have gone quite pale," he said, his voice concerned, but she could barely make out his words. He suddenly seemed so far away and everything was muffled. "I think you have danced too much, and I prescribe fresh air," he added as he whisked her swiftly towards the open doorway, out onto the verandah.

He sat her down on the stone balustrade and knelt down at her side. "Take some deep breaths my dear," he said gently. She did as she was told and found her mind begin to clear and her strength return.

"I am so terribly sorry," she said feeling quite mortified. "I have never been the type to have a feinting fit before." He stroked her arm tenderly, a supportive gesture that sent shivers racing up and down her spine.

"It is quite alright. I think I should feel quite weak too after all that dancing. You are a wonderful dancer. I found myself wondering if you are as passionate about everything in your life as you seemed to be about your enjoyment of the music and the steps."

"I do love to dance, and to sing," she admitted. "I do seem to feel things deeply, I either love a thing, or despise it. Rarely do my feelings fall in between." He nodded thoughtfully, and she wondered if she had maybe said the wrong thing. It felt tantamount to admitting that she felt deeply for him, and she did not want him to feel in any way beholden to return those feelings.

"Miss Freemont, Alberta," he started awkwardly. "This wasn't quite what I had intended, but I find I do not want to wait, I cannot wait in fact. I need a wife. No, that sounds terrible, even though to some extent it is definitely true." He looked so confused, and so out of control that Alberta wanted to comfort him, but she also wanted to laugh at how tongue-tied he suddenly seemed. He was such a suave and poise man, to see him this way was quite a revelation. "I want a wife. I want a family, and I want you to be my wife."

She had to some extent expected the betrothal, but not the proposal. It was so endearing, that he seemed as nervous and anxious about everything as she herself felt. She cupped his face in her hand, and smiled at him. "Are you asking me to be your wife?" she clarified. He nodded.

"I am sorry, I am making a terrible hash of this. It sounds

like such a simple thing until you actually have to ask a girl to do it! But yes, I am asking if you will be my wife?"

"Well, that is why I came to Montana after all," she admitted, trying not to sound as if it was the thing she wanted more than any other. Just because he was fumbling over the proposal did not mean that he had feelings for her, it just meant that he was nervous about entering the state of matrimony.

"So that is a yes?" He looked up at her hopefully.

"Indeed, it is a yes." He leapt to his feet, and took her hand. His other delved into his pocket, and pulled out a ring. The diamond was flawless, and glistened in the moonlight. He slipped it onto her finger. Unable to stop herself she sighed.

They shared a look, one that confused her and left her feeling raw and exposed. But, she was sure she had seen the echoes of her own desire in his green eyes. But she didn't have time to think of it as he dipped his head and claimed her lips. His kiss was fierce, not the gentle and demure sealing of a bargain, but the passionate embrace of a man who wanted a woman. Alberta wound her arms around his neck and gave herself to him willingly, allowing him to pull her onto her feet and up against his body so that she could feel every inch of him. She had no awareness of anything but him and the exquisite sensations that he was creating in her body as he let his fingers trail over the revealing neckline of her gown. Her chest was heaving, and she gave a little moan as he kissed down her neck and left a trail of moist kisses across her décolletage. She forgot all sense of time and space, and lost herself in him, caressing the tendons at the back of his neck, allowing her hands to wander down and cup his pert derriere.

A gong sounded in the distance. Gideon looked up at her, his eyes bright. His face changed in an instant, from a man enraptured to one utterly ashamed. She wanted to tell him that it was alright, that she did not mind. They were now affianced after all. But she held her tongue and tried to contain her disappointment as he stepped away from her. She smoothed her dress, and tidied her hair, then took his arm most properly and allowed him to lead her in to supper. She clasped the kiss inside of her, burying the knowledge – for now at least – that at the very least he did find her attractive enough to lose himself in the moment. She prayed that it would be enough for her to know she was desired, even if she was never loved.

Chapter Five

The next few weeks flew by. Gideon found himself deluged with support for his campaign, and good wishes on his upcoming nuptials. Thankfully his work kept him from having to think about any of it, as he travelled up and down the State, giving talks and meeting as many voters as he could. He rested safely in the knowledge that Alberta was arranging a wedding suitable for a future governor, as it was looking more and more likely that the race was now his to lose. He had tried to convince Aaron that a small wedding, a quiet and private ceremony would be for the best but his wily campaign manager had other ideas. He was determined that the worlds should see the connections this wedding would bring to Montana, that the State would gain not just a trustworthy governor who truly cared about the people of his State, but one who had friends in the highest places who would help to deliver them more than anybody else could. Politically he knew it was the right decision, but he couldn't help feeling that it was the wrong one for him and for Alberta.

She seemed to be in her element, had made no complaints of him at all. He wasn't sure if that made him happy or not either. Every time he was with her he felt that it just wasn't long enough, and he wondered that she could be so calm about dealing with his many absences. She always greeted him with a smile, and they would enjoy a dinner in one of the States more fashionable restaurants, or would attend the theatre together and she was always turned out immaculately. He simply could not have asked for a better partner, and that was the role she played to the hilt. She was supportive and she understood his needs, and knew better than he did how to present himself whilst in the political arena. But he couldn't help feeling that there was something missing. Try as he might he hadn't been able to erase that passionate kiss, the evening of the ball, from his memory. A spark had come alive inside him that refused to die, one that demanded more of this union than he had ever wanted it to deliver.

"Are you ready for tomorrow?" Aaron asked him as he greeted his carriage outside the office. He had just come from a presentation in Billings, and felt weary beyond measure.

"As I will ever be," he admitted as they walked inside. In fact he could hardly wait to have Alberta be his wife, to be able to take her home and explore that passionate side of her he had only been lucky enough to glimpse so fleetingly.

"She has been a wonder," Aaron marveled. "I know few

women who could arrange the biggest Society wedding of the year, whilst also campaigning tirelessly for their husband to be."

"She is marvelous," Gideon admitted. She truly was too good to be true, and nothing ever seemed to daunt her or stop her in her tracks. He felt quite inadequate in comparison at times. But no matter what she was doing, whether she was up to her elbows in flour with a local group of women bakers, or singing as part of a choir, or standing beside him on the podium as he spoke of his plans he always found himself wanting her. She had become a thirst he had to quench, and he prayed that his undeniable desire for her would be slaked upon her possession.

"She is giving a speech to the women's suffrage movement this evening. It is on your calendar, but I hadn't thought you were going to attend as this past week has been so full of travel – you must be exhausted?" Aaron queried.

"I just wanted to see her in action. I have not seen her speak yet, though everyone tells me she is quite mesmerizing."

"Just don't cause any ruckus, and make sure you are both home and in bed early. You have a big day tomorrow!" Aaron chuckled and Gideon smiled weakly. He wanted to go to Alberta's meeting because he hadn't seen her in six days, and he simply couldn't wait another moment. He knew that he shouldn't, that he was making a fool of himself – but he kidded himself that an impromptu visit to see his fiancée would endear him to this group of strong-minded women. But he knew it was his own need to be with her that he was satisfying, it had nothing to do with his political aspirations.

He put away the papers and documents from his trip carefully, and then straightened his tie and brushed his hair before making his way down the Main Street towards Tom's Saloon. The meeting was held in his large back room, and as he made his way through he could see that it was full. Alberta stood at the podium, her long blonde hair pinned in an elegant chignon. She spoke emphatically and passionately, and just like the rest of her audience he found himself responding to her words. He was grateful that his competition for governor wasn't so fierce, she would have beaten him by a landslide! He hoped to catch her eye, to let her know how proud he was of her, but he wasn't sure if she even knew he was there.

"Well, it would seem we have an intruder in our midst ladies," she suddenly said with a gentle laugh. "My erstwhile fiancé is here, loitering at the back of the room." All eyes shifted from her to him, and he grinned, despite feeling thoroughly discomfited. "Please give him a round of applause, he believes as we do that women have much to offer, that we should have our say in politics as it affects our lives just as much as any mans!" He moved reluctantly to the dais to join her, but was heartened by the riotous applause that greeted him.

As he reached her side, she reached out and took his hand then leaned in and kissed him tenderly on the cheek. The crowd roared its approval. He turned to face them, knowing he was blushing. "My fiancée is too kind in her praise. I have been away all week and have missed her, could not wait another day to set eyes upon her. Please forgive me for my intrusion." He kissed her hand gallantly, bowed to the women in the audience and then made his way back out of the room. He didn't see Alberta's face flush with happiness, nor did he see the tear that welled in her eyes at his words.

He made his way to the bar, and accepted a glass of beer from Tom with a smile. He sat and chatted with his friend while he waited, wondering if he had said too much, or if he was being a fool to entertain the idea of marrying a woman for political reasons. But, he knew he no longer wanted this match because of the ties she came with. He wanted to marry Alberta Freemont because she made his pulse race, and his heart skip a beat every time he saw her. But, she was so aloof that he had no clue as to her true feelings for him. He couldn't help but wonder if he had been the biggest fool alive to think that he could find a woman who would stake no claim on his heart. But he did seem to have found one who had no desire to make her own claim on his.

With the meeting over, and the women dispersed back to their homes Alberta emerged, a look of triumph upon her beautiful face. "Would you like a drink?" he asked her, pulling out a chair so she could sit and join him.

"That would be lovely," she said.

"Tom, a claret sangarees for my lovely wife to be," he said happily. She was even more perfect than he had remembered, and he was content just to be with her again at last.

"How did your travels go?" she asked him, clearly genuinely interested.

"Very well. We have been sent so many cards and notes of congratulations for tomorrow. It seems that the entire State has fallen in love with you," he said happily. Her face fell a little, and it surprised him. Surely the popularity of their union was a good thing? "I know they are all waiting with baited breath to see your gown."

"Well, I hope they will all be happy when they do. It is quite beautiful. I shall hardly dare breathe in case I ruin a single stitch!" she joked, but her voice sounded strained.

"Are you quite well?"

"I am a little tired, it has been a busy time for us both."

"Well, we shall have a few days to rest and then I am afraid we will be busier than ever."

"But at least we are nearing the end, the campaign will be done and you will be Governor of Montana."

"I certainly hope so. But are you sure that all of this is what you want?" he asked her, he knew he could think of nothing better than to have her by his side, and for them to lead Montana into the new century together.

"It is," she said simply, but her eyes were cast down and he couldn't help but wonder if she truly meant it.

"I would drop out of the race right now if it would make you happy," he said impulsively. She looked up at him, her eyes wide.

"But..." she said, and then tailed off.

"Alberta, maybe I should have said this much earlier than this but I love you. I think I fell in love with you from the first, that very wonderful letter you wrote to me."

"You... you do?" she queried, he could see she was trying to hold back tears, but whether they were of joy or sadness he could not tell.

"I do. I never meant to. I cannot lie. I did not want to be wed. It was all Aaron's idea. There was this terrible article in the newspaper and the only solution seemed to be to take a wife. I wanted to find someone discreet, someone who would understand that marriage can be based upon respect rather than love, and that sometimes there is a need for pragmatism. I needed the contacts your family could bring to my campaign. When Madelaine told us you might consider being my bride it seemed that nothing could stop me. But, I was a confirmed bachelor. I did not believe in love – until I met you."

"You truly love me? Would truly give up the campaign if I asked it of you?"

"I would, gladly. As long as I have you by my side I would be happy. You do not have to love me back. I know you probably do not feel so deeply for me as I do you – but I would treat you so well, would do everything in my power to make you happy."

"Oh, but I do love you. I love you with all my heart. I was so very frightened that you did not love me, could never love me. I was resigned to a marriage of alliance, knew what I brought to your campaign. I wanted a child, someone I could love. But I found myself loving you too, even though I believed you would never love me." Gideon took her face in his palms and kissed her lips tenderly.

"Then it is as well that I do, and that you do," he said, his joy was indescribable. "But I meant it, I would give up politics if you wished it of me."

"There is no need for that. The State needs you, needs us

both," she asserted firmly. "Just think what we can achieve together, truly together!"

"So you have no misgivings about marrying me tomorrow?" Gideon asked, still hardly believing his ears.

"None whatsoever. Now I know you love me, I would follow you anywhere," she said as she pressed her lips to his and kissed him deeply.

Chapter Six

Alberta awoke early the next day. She could hardly believe that she was to wed the man she loved this very day. His confession in the Saloon last night had made all her dreams come true, and she knew she would never regret the decision she had taken to come here to Sun River. He was a good man, and he would make her happy, she was sure of that. She jumped out of her bed and ran to pull back the drapes. Warm sunlight flooded in and she stretched languidly as she gazed out along the quiet Main Street. Maggie and Ellen were fussing about their window display at the bakery, and a lone carter was trundling along, but otherwise the little town was quiet.

She turned and moved to the washstand. Pouring water from the ewer into the bowl, she contemplated what her life might bring and knew that she had nothing to fear now she knew she had Gideon's heart. She splashed her face, enjoying the cool water against her warm skin. A knock on the door made her jump, but she quickly grabbed at a cloth and wiped her face and went to open the door. Maddy stood outside her room. She looked happy, and in her arms was Alberta's wedding gown. "We finished it last night," she said shyly. "I hope you like it. We were up until the wee hours!"

"I am sure it will be perfect. I know few people with a better eye, and I know you could put many a seamstress to shame."

"I had a lot of help. Catherine and Myra especially. But Emily is a dab hand at sewing on seed pearls – it must have been all those years of making her costumes for the circus!"

"You are all wonderful, every one of you. I do not know that I would have had the courage to do something like this, to travel all this way to meet a stranger if I hadn't known how wonderfully it had turned out for you, and so many of the women here in Great Falls."

"We have all been rather lucky, I think there must be something in the water here in Sun River. Everybody seems to find love. It is all rather romantic, don't you think?"

"I do." They both giggled at Alberta's unintentional use of the traditional response to the vows she would be making later that day.

"I have the bath down by the fire, William has gone out to visit a sick widower and so we have the house to ourselves," Madelaine said. "Why don't you head down and you can have your breakfast in the bath."

"The very height of decadence!"

"Indeed. Your parents arrived safely on the train yesterday, stayed in Great Falls overnight and will be here an hour before we are due at the church."

"However do you know that?" Alberta asked.

"They sent word with Aaron. He met them at the station yesterday, and got them settled in to the hotel. They were surprised that the wedding was not to be held there, or in Billings."

"They would expect only the biggest and best," Alberta said. "I doubt they would understand why Gideon and I wished to be wed here, even before we acknowledged our feelings for one another. But, it is because this is our home, it is where we will bring up our children and so we wanted it to be the place where we were joined together."

"I think everyone here is glad that you did so. It has helped Sun River more than you know. People will flock here to see you emerge from the church you know, Gideon has never been more popular since you came."

"I just hope their affection for him will turn into votes in the election," Alberta said emphatically. She still worried that Gideon may regret his choice of bride if he lost the election, but she had to have faith that he meant the words he had spoken, the words that had made her heart sing with joy. He loved her, he didn't just wish to marry her because she was of benefit to his campaign, but because he cared for her as deeply as she did for him.

The water in the bath was warm, and Maddy had put in a handful of oatmeal to soothe and soften her skin, and rose petals to scent the water delicately. She brought Alberta a cup of chocolate, and some warm bread fresh from the oven, slathered with rich butter from Frederica's dairy and a conserve made from local berries. "Enjoy the calm. It doesn't remain this way," Maddy joked as she disappeared upstairs to get herself ready.

Alberta washed her hair, lathering up a lovely lavender scented soap and then sank back into the tub, submerging her head below the bubbles. She listened to the gentle slosh of the water and the dulled pings as her fingers tapped against the side of the tin bath. Everything seemed otherworldly under water, and she could almost imagine herself as a mermaid as she swirled her long hair in the water. But, delightful and soothing as the warm water was, she had to get ready and so she eased herself back to a sitting position and then pushed herself up. She grabbed at the bath sheet Maddy had left for her, and stepped out of the tub onto the rug, allowing the warmth of the fire to help her to dry off.

Alberta pulled a robe around her shoulder and sat beside the fire. When Madelaine came back downstairs she was toweling her hair as dry as she could. "Here, let me," she said as she took the towel from Alberta and continued to rub gently. Then she took a comb and began to ease it through the long lengths of golden blonde hair. She pulled a box of pins across the table so she could reach them, and started to section off the hair and expertly pin it into place. "Do you want flowers in your hair?" Alberta nodded. Maddy smiled and began to tuck fronds of delicate white and blue flowers into the plaits and coils.

She stood back, and admired her work. Alberta couldn't

help but grin at her friend's pride in her efforts. "Whoever would have thought that you would become the perfect ladies maid," Alberta teased her.

"I certainly never would, but it is rather fun. Like playing with dolls when I was a girl." She handed Alberta a looking glass.

"Oh my!" Alberta gasped. "I look...."

"Perfect," Madelaine said, a tear in her eye.

The rumble of carriage wheels outside the little house alerted them to the arrival of Alberta's Mama and Papa. Forgetting herself, she ran outside and flung herself into her father's arms, almost before he had gotten out of the comfortable barouche. "I am so glad that you are here," she cried.

"Alberta, get inside. You are in your undergarments!" Mama cried as she emerged from the carriage and took in the spectacle of her daughter in only a robe. Everybody laughed.

"But you do look lovely," Papa whispered as they went inside. "But I think a dress would be more traditional."

Alberta had expected to be full of nerves as the time approached to leave for the church, but she had the most delightful sense of confidence and calm as she was helped into her dress by Maddy and Mama. Both were near tears as they made her turn and show them every angle. "My darling girl, I have never been so proud of you," Mama said hugging her awkwardly.

The sun was warm on their skin as they made their way in the lovely open carriage to the church. There were people lining the streets, aching to get a view of Gideon and his bride. She waved at them, and was overwhelmed by their cheers of good luck and happiness. William was waiting for them outside the church. He helped his wife down from the carriage, and gave her a swift kiss before turning to assist Mama. "You are sure this is what you want?" Papa asked her quietly. "I must confess, I don't want you to be so far from me."

"Papa, I have longed to be wed and to have a family of my own for so long. You will like Gideon, I know it. He is honest and good."

"Not much of a politician then," Papa joked.

"He is like you in many ways," she said gently. "I am sorry we will be so far away, but you will always be welcome here and I am sure that Gideon's career will mean we will find ourselves on the East Coast often. I shall visit as much as I can."

"I never wanted to let you go, my darling. I have been selfish. Now I see how radiant, how happy you are just at the thought of this marriage I am sorry if I put my needs and wants ahead of yours for so long."

"I love you Papa," Alberta said as she kissed him on the cheek. "Now, shall we?" She held out her hand, he clasped it firmly and helped her to stand. William assisted her to disembark, and then hustled Mama and Maddy inside. Papa eased himself down from the carriage, and took her arm and they made their way slowly towards the man Alberta adored.

The inside of the church was cool, but the pews were full. Alberta recognized faces from the town, but also many of Gideon's supporters had come from all over the State. But, it was Sarah, and her husband Christian's faces that stood out amongst the crowds. She could hardly believe that her friend had come all this way, but the endorsement of her husband would do Gideon's campaign no end of good too.

But then she glanced down the aisle and saw Gideon standing there strong and tall, waiting for her to come to him and she forgot everything else but him. She fixed her gaze on his beautiful green eyes and moved gracefully towards him, her lavish ivory silk gown trailing behind her.

Papa placed her hand in Gideon's as they reached the altar, and removing her veil pressed a gentle kiss upon her forehead. "God bless you my darling," he whispered as he stood back. Usually such a stoic man, Alberta was sure that she had seen a film of tears, and as she glanced over at him quickly was not surprised to see him surreptitiously wiping them with his handkerchief.

"You are quite perfect," Gideon said as he looked down at her, his love for her clear for all to see.

The minister spoke, welcoming everyone to their wondrous union, but Alberta heard none of his words. She could not focus on anything but the handsome man standing by her side. When he began to speak his vows to her, she could hardly believe that he was saying them to her and when it was her turn she could barely get the words out as she felt so overwhelmed with emotion. The touch of his hand upon hers and the knowledge that he would be hers, to have and to hold forever, seemed too wonderful to be true.

"I now pronounce you man and wife," the Minister

finished triumphantly. Gideon dipped his head to hers and kissed her. It was a sweet and tender promise, and one she knew she would hold him to for the rest of their lives. It said everything a kiss should, that she was cherished and that she held his heart. She hoped he knew that she felt the same way, that she adored him and would care for him no matter what may come their way.

They emerged from the church, and Alberta was astounded by the wall of noise that hit them. The cheers were deafening as the crowds clamored to get a glimpse of the happy couple. Gideon leapt up into the carriage, and helped Alberta to follow him. He stood for a few moments, then offered calming gestures to the crowd. Eventually they hushed. "Our friends, welcome to Sun River," he began. "Thank you for making such efforts to come here and to celebrate with my wife and I on this very special day. Our families wished us to have a small and intimate wedding breakfast, but we knew that you would all wish to celebrate with us – and so please, eat, drink and be merry with us!" He flung up his arms, and much to Alberta and the crowd's surprise Maggie, Ellen and Alice emerged from the bakery their arms laden with goodies; Tom and Catherine from the Saloon emerged with crates full of drinks. There were tables laid out along the Main Street, and soon they were filled with food and beverages as a small band struck up with lively tunes for people to dance to.

It was not the wedding anyone would have expected of a politician and his Society bride, but it was perfect. Alberta took her husband's face in her palms and kissed him soundly. The crowd roared their approval. She giggled. "Thank you," she said. "I would never have thought of such a thing, but it is perfect, just perfect."

"Will you dance with me?" he said as a particularly vigorous jig began to parade past the carriage. She nodded and hitched up her skirts as he jumped down, then lifted her and whisked her into the fray. "I love you Mrs MacAlpine."

"I love you, darling Gideon," she replied breathlessly as they whirled past her Mama and Papa. "Come, join in!" she cried happily. Her Mama looked aghast, but Papa simply chortled and took his wife in his arms.

"Why ever not?" he said as he followed his daughter's lead.

Epilogue

Three Weeks Later:

Gideon stood on the dais, the entire ballroom applauding. Alberta thought she might burst with pride. He looked so handsome, yet so very humble as he received the news of his victory. She blew him a kiss as he scoured the crowd for her face. He pretended to catch it in his fist and clutched it to his heart as he beamed down at her. "Dear friends," he began. "I cannot tell you how happy I am to be standing here today, Governor Elect of Montana. All of you here know how hard I have worked to reach this position, the sacrifices I have made." Aaron and Alberta shared a conspiratorial wink and smiled thinking about the marriage of expedience that never came about. She fiddled with her wedding band, thinking how close she had come to a loveless union, and how glad she was that instead she had found passion and abiding adoration.

431

"But, without you, my friends and my supporters none of this would have been possible. I would like to thank everyone who contributed money and time to help me, but most importantly I would like to thank my friends from Sun River. What a motley collection of folk we all are, bound by ties of friendship and respect as we carve our way to making this majestic part of the world a prosperous and hospitable place. As I look out at the couples who have inspired me, your courage in reaching out, placing advertisements to secure your happiness gave me the strength to look for something I did not even know I wanted." Alberta looked at the loving glances her new friends gave one another, and the pride they all shared in their friend on the dais. It warmed her heart that she was a part of this wonderful community.

"Madelaine, where are you?" Maddy blushed as everybody turned to look at her. "There you are. Don't look so scared! I want to say thank you for your personal contribution – not to my campaign but to my life. If you had not introduced me to your delightful friend, Alberta, then I would not be standing here a happily married man. You have given me a gift beyond measure, one I will cherish until the day I die." Everybody clapped and hollered. Alberta felt tears well in her eyes, as her friend turned and hugged her tightly.

"Without Alberta by my side throughout this campaign I think I might have given up. Her unstinting love and support has kept me strong, and I know she will continue to be by my side, battling for all of you as we take Montana into the Twentieth Century and beyond. The future is bright, and I pray that you will continue to have faith in us that we will deliver what you need."

He stepped back from the podium and bowed gracefully. Alberta accepted the kisses and embraces of her new friends, as she made her way towards him. He had made his way down from the stage and was doing the same. She surreptitiously wiped her tears away, as she watched him lift up baby Clara and then kiss her on her tiny nose, as he ruffled Christopher's curly locks. But she could hold her emotions back no longer as she embraced Aaron, the man who had engineered everything for Gideon, and had been a true friend. Freddy came up beside her, and slipped an arm around her waist. "You must be so very proud."

"I am."

"And you are happy?"

"Over the moon."

"You've been wearing your corsets a little looser recently, or am I imagining things?" she asked with a sly wink.

"Don't say anything," Alberta gasped. "I didn't want to trouble him until the election was over!"

"I don't think it will trouble him in the slightest. Think it will make him the happiest man alive."

"I already am, nothing can make my life any more perfect," Gideon said as he overheard Frederica's last words. He hugged her, and then turned the full force of his smile on Alberta. Her knees went weak just at the sight of him. She didn't care that it wasn't right, or proper, she flung her arms around him and lavished his face and neck with kisses. "Maybe I should win elections every day," he teased as he wrapped his arms around her and kissed her as if nobody was looking.

"I am so very proud of you," she whispered. "You are going to be an excellent Governor."

"And an excellent father too," he said with a grin.

"You knew?" she exclaimed.

"Of course I knew. I have many faults, but even I can spot when my wife begins to get plumper and more delicious every day, despite eating like a sparrow and working every hour God sends!"

"Are you happy? It is all I have wanted for so long," she said, praying that he would understand. They had said that they would wait until he had been in office and she didn't want him to think she had broken her promise – not that there was much she could have done about it anyway.

"I am delighted my darling. You have made me the happiest man alive."

The End

Thank you for reading and supporting my book and I hope you enjoyed it.

Please will you do me a favor and leave a review so I'll know whether you liked it or not, it would be very much appreciated, thank you.

Other books by Karla

SUN RIVER BRIDES SERIES

A bride for Carlton #1
A bride for Mackenzie #2
A bride for Ethan #3
A bride for Thomas #4
A bride for Mathew #5

About Karla Gracey

Karla Gracey was born with a very creative imagination and a love for creating stories that will inspire and warm people's hearts. She has always been attracted to historical romance including mail order bride stories with strong willed women. Her characters are easy to relate to and you feel as if you know them personally. Whether you enjoy action, adventure, romance, mystery, suspense or drama- she makes sure there is something for everyone in her historical romance stories!

Made in the USA
Columbia, SC
22 January 2025

52238276R00267